# LADY ESTRID

## A Novel of Eleventh-Century Denmark

### M J Porter

# CONTENTS

Title Page

Copyright

Before you begin.                                    1

MAP                                                  3

DAUGHTER                                             4

Prologue                                             5

SISTER                                               7

Chapter 1                                            8

Chapter 2                                            19

Chapter 3                                            27

Chapter 4                                            35

Chapter 5                                            46

DUCHESS                                              72

Chapter 6                                            73

Chapter 7                                            85

Chapter 8                                            96

Chapter 9                                            107

Chapter 10                                           115

Chapter 11                                           129

Chapter 12                                           136

Chapter 13                                           141

AUNT                              147

Chapter 14                        148

Chapter 15                        160

Chapter 16                        173

Chapter 17                        183

Chapter 18                        202

Chapter 19                        217

Chapter 20                        227

Chapter 21                        235

Chapter 22                        245

Chapter 23                        250

Chapter 24                        257

Chapter 25                        270

QUEEN                             284

Chapter 26                        285

Epilogue                          289

Genealogical Tables               298

Historical Notes                  302

Cast of Characters                306

Meet the author                   310

# BEFORE YOU BEGIN.

## Note on names

Here goes,

There is a prevalence of people all sharing the same first name throughout this book. I have adopted variations to try and differentiate them, using the version most often found in the texts I consulted for that particular person.

Swein, Svein, Swegn.

Harold, Harald.

Oláfr, Olof, Olaf

Second names were taken, usually, from a father's first name, hence, Cnut Sweinsson or Úlfr Úlfrsson, Gytha Sweinsdottir or Estrid Sweinsdottir.

Sometimes, the mother's name was used. So, Beorn Estridsson.

## Note on the name of countries

Denmark, Norway and Sweden didn't exist as nation states in the eleventh century as they do now. Yet, for clarity, I have referred to Norway as Norway (the North Way), and Denmark as Denmark, but not Sweden. For Sweden I have adopted the term 'land of the Svear,' or Svearland. This is because areas of Sweden belonged to Denmark at this time period – most notably Skåne (in the south), and it would cause confusion to refer to the area as Sweden.

## The Thing

A public assembly of the free-men in Scandinavian countries at this time period.

# MAP

# DAUGHTER

# PROLOGUE

*Kiev, the land of the Rus, AD1012*

"*Dearest Mother, Lady Sigrid. Queen of Denmark.*"

"*This marriage doesn't agree with me. How could you agree to it? I trusted you more than any other to understand how difficult it would be to be forced to live amongst strangers. I relied on you to argue with my father about the necessity of the union.*"

"*And don't tell me I will one day be the queen of the Rus, as my father planned. Prince Ilja is not a strong man. I don't foresee him living long. Not at all. The poor man. He has barely been able to consummate our union. I hope I will not carry his child. It will be weak and feeble, and I will not tolerate such.*"

"*My children will be strong and powerful. One day, it is they who will be kings and queens. But these children will not be shared with Prince Ilja. I am sure of it.*"

"*And even if he were to survive, his brothers are a treasonous coven. None of them wishes the other to succeed at their expense. I foresee only bloodshed and paranoia when Ilja's father is dead.*"

"*Frida is my only friend and ally, reminding me of home. I hope to return to Denmark one day. I never imagined leaving her. I miss her. The kingdom of the Rus is not the same. Not at all.*"

"*Send me news of my father and brothers. I wish to know if my father has finally triumphed in England over King Æthelred. I should like to know that he didn't callously send me away without* so much as seeing me in person for no good reason, because he was absent, in England, as so often the case. If he fails in England again, I will never forgive him for his actions towards me."

"Your despairing daughter, Lady Estrid Sweinsdottir, from Kiev."

**"Dearest Mother, Lady Sigrid, Queen of Denmark."**

"Why have you not responded to my letter? Not that it matters now. Prince Ilja is dead. I hope it was not at the hands of one of his brothers. His father mourns but threatens to wed me to another of his many sons from his numerous wives. I'll not tolerate that."

"Make it known that I must be returned to Roskilde, along with dear Frida. There is no one to protect us here. Send my brother, Harald, or even my younger brother, Cnut, or even better, Jarl Eirikr, my oldest sister's husband. He's the sort of man that Prince Ilja's father will not ignore if my father is too preoccupied to assist his youngest child."

"I fear being trapped here for all of my life. Perhaps with a terrible husband, or maybe no husband at all. I can't bear it, mother, I simply can't and I won't. Send word immediately of your intentions, and ensure my father knows of my plight. Perhaps he could drag himself away from the promise of riches in England, and protect his youngest daughter. It would be pleasant to be more highly esteemed by him."

"Oh, Lady Mother, I beg you. Have me retrieved from here before winter. I'm already shivering in my bed at night, even with Frida there to warm the other side. This is intolerable. Assist me, I beg you, or I will write to my brother, King Olof Skotskonung of the Svear. I'm sure he'll be more open to helping me if only to offend my father, his step-father. Don't test me because I will involve my step-brother. I will not shy away from it. I will write to my father as well. My words will not be at all diplomatic."

"Your loving, if distraught daughter, Lady Estrid Sweinsdottir, from Kiev."

# SISTER

# CHAPTER 1

*Roskilde, Denmark*
**AD1013**

My brother sits on my father's chair at the front of the hall. I watch him through narrowed slits.

Harald has taken my father's place for more of my life than he hasn't. My father is a brave warrior, it's said, but little more to me than a stranger.

I've recently returned from the failure of my first marriage, in the land of the Rus.

I've not seen my father since before I left Denmark two years ago. It feels as though it was half a lifetime ago. But it wasn't.

It burns that I warned my father the union would be a disaster, only for him to dismiss my fears. I'll have to allow myself to let my anger sizzle out. There's no chance I can singe him with it. Not now.

Yet, my thoughts return to the letter I've only recently sent to him. The words were not skilfully chosen, but I was furious with him, and determine to remain so, no matter what.

*"My Lord Father, King Swein of Denmark and part of Norway."*

*"I write to inform you of the death of my husband. He was injured in a mock-battle, fell to the floor, and didn't wake again, although his death took a further sixteen days, and was unpleasant*

to behold. Why he was fighting, I'll never know. He was too weak, but then, his brothers goaded him on. Is it always the same with brothers? It infuriates me."

"I told you, father, that the marriage would not be successful. I have returned to Denmark, although without your intervention. Thankfully, my mother was unprepared to leave her only daughter amongst the Rus, even though she's unhappy with the outcome of the marriage. She's been cool and implacable towards me ever since my return."

"You would know this, but of course, you remain in England. I've been informed that you've not set foot in Denmark for nearly two years. I wish you well with your ambitions but would know what you plan for me next, and when you'll give up on your single-minded plan to claim England. Surely, after all this time, you must realise that the only possible outcome is defeat? I will say that to you, even if others will not."

"My husband's father attempted to marry me to one of his other sons, but of course, that goes against God's wishes, and I staunchly refused. I was forced to use your name as a threat against those ambitions, and when that didn't work, to petition my mother, and my brother, King Olof Skotskonung, who at least was in Old Uppsala and could have come to my rescue more quickly than you."

"Tell me father, why you didn't heed my warnings about the marriage? Are you so blinded by your ambitions, that you'll have no one gainsay you? I would truly like to know. I would. I find it impossible to understand your motivations and what drives you. Why can't you be content with Denmark? I would be."

"My brother, Harald has, at least, welcomed me home, if not with open arms, then with sympathy and understanding for the trauma of my marriage and a dead husband. I know I wouldn't have received the same from you. No doubt you blame me, even though it isn't my fault. It seems that one of your grandchildren will not claim the kingdom of Kiev when they're older. No doubt that upsets your careful plans but I won't apologise for that. It was in God's hands, not mine."

"When will you return to Denmark? I must speak to you im-

*mediately of the future. I find it impossible to express myself adequately using words, and of course, I have no assurance that you will even receive this letter while you linger in England. I imagine the place to be as inhospitable as the kingdom of the Rus, even though you assure everyone it's rich in wealth, and enjoys rolling green fields ripe with crops."*

*"Your dutiful, if aggrieved, daughter, Lady Estrid Sweinsdottir, from Roskilde."*

The dream of the night before has made me sluggish, slow to rise and fearful of leaving my bed. As the sizeable wooden hall in Roskilde, smoke billowing in the rafters above my head, begins to fill with men and women, I know I've lost my chance to speak in confidence with my older brother.

I eye Harald, all the same, from my place of near-concealment, close to the far end of the long room, filled with benches and long tables made of seasoned oak. Soon the tables will groan under the weight of ale and food prepared for the men and women invited to this gathering. For now, greenery adorns the length of the tables, herbs hanging from the blackened beams. They are there to drive away the lingering and pervading stench of ale and fat, vomit and piss, and all the other smells of too many bodies in too small a space, during the winter storms.

Outside, the day is already drawing in, the hint of darkness spreading quickly, tinting everything a thousand shades of brown. I hate this time of year—the dark times. My true-dreams stalk me more often, their hints and illusions, awkward to decipher, and impossible to ignore.

Yet, I'm pleased to be back in Roskilde. My grandfather first built this place, and then my father continued the work. He wished to establish his dynasty with an impressive testament to the House of Gorm. This settlement was a step away from the noble sites of our pagan forefathers, and to crown it, there's an elaborate church, constructed half of stone, and half of wood.

There's a royal estate, surrounded by a sturdy wall and ditch. Of course, as the name implies, it is well provided with springs, the water fresh and sweet. Nestled, as it is, on the edge of the fjord, it's well protected from the fierce seas further north. It boasts a fine quayside to encourage trade, and the agricultural settlement of Lejre is not far to the north.

Harald is still a youth, and although he tries to adopt my father's kingly-warrior stances, it's not quite the same thing. Not to my critical eye. And I'm always critical. So my women tell me as I slap hands away from my hair and dress when I'm tired of such messing and disgruntled with their ineffectual efforts.

If they did it correctly in the first place, it wouldn't be a problem.

I can only trust Frida to do everything as it should be done. But Frida can't be everything to me. She's my companion more than my servant. Her blood is almost as royal as mine.

I've stayed abed for too long, not wishing to rouse sufficiently from the unsettling dream and face the reality of what it's revealed to me. Only then, my women have fussed on and on, regardless of the time. Eventually, I've stamped my foot and stalked from the bed-chamber. I'm happy with my appearance. It's my dream that concerns me. And the contents mean it little matters how I look.

I continue to watch Harald as he speaks with those men he's deemed worthy of his attention today. He's trying to grow a blond beard on his long, thin face, but for now, it's more a smattering of fuzz. As men with full beards bend to speak with him, it's a shocking juxtaposition – the old and grizzled against the young, and as yet, untried.

He's my father's first-born son and has always been feted by those keen to win King Swein of Denmark's approval. It's made my brother a powerful man, especially in light of my father's frequent, and now permanent absences in England.

I watch as Jarl Úlfr converses with my brother, my lips slightly curdling as his sister simpers beside him. If I weren't so judgemental, I might think her beautiful, but I'm disparaging. I can see how her lips are just that little bit too thin, and her nose just that little bit too long, her chin weak, and her eyes more likely to be downcast than truly looking at the world around her.

And her clothes! Well, she's outfitted as though she's a queen already. Gytha is too much under the control of her two brothers. I shudder at the realisation of how alike we now both are.

I swallow heavily. I would sooner dismiss my dream, but it's not the first such reverie I've endured. I know the truth of it.

I gather my courage, resolved to speak to my brother regardless of those who vie to claim his attention. My footsteps are soft over the polished wooden floorboards as I leave my hiding place. I keep my eyes firmly ahead, focused on the raised dais on which Harald sits. My father built it to celebrate his kingship over the Danes. I don't wish anyone to distract me from the unpleasant task I've set myself.

My brother might be my father's substitute while he's in England, but I'm not without some influence. People try to catch my eye, but I pretend to ignore them all.

My brother relies on my sharp observations. My father disdained them all.

For once, the men and women summoned to dine with the king's son leave me alone, even Jarl Úlfr and Lady Gytha bending to take their leave at my approach. I'm almost grateful to them, but I won't allow that. Úlfr and Eilifr, his brother, have grown too influential in my absence. I intend to put a stop to it. My nephew, Hakon, offers me a brief grin before rushing to find his seat next to his mother, my much older half-sister. Hakon is the same age as I, give or take a year or two. We've been more like brother and sister than nephew and aunt. Jarl Eirik, his father, is with my father, in England. Or at least, he was. Now, I have no idea.

But, I'm forming the words in my mind that I need to say to Harald, just about to step onto the dais, my brother's eyes already welcoming me, when a heavy silence abruptly falls. Sentences are left hanging on everyone's tongues as something attracts the attention of all.

Frustrated, I turn, almost missing the raised lip of the wooden dais in my surprise. I'm forced to accept Lady Gytha's simpering help. I'd sooner not be in her debt, even for such a small thing as her hand to keep me from falling in front of those who would witness my stumble, but the act is instinctive.

A messenger has been admitted to the king's hall, his clothes showing hard-wear in the creases on the leather elbows of the byrnie worn beneath a thick fur cloak. The ooze of the quayside splatters his boots, and every single eye watches him—every single one. No one speaks; no one dare even breathe, not even me.

This man has come from England, in the height of a winter storm. He must bring news from King Swein.

I eye him, my mouth opening in surprise.

I thought my dream a true one. I believed it told me of events that only happened while I slept.

It seems I'm wrong, and that makes me even more unsettled than the news I wished to share with my brother.

More sedately, I stride to my brother's side, keen to hear the messenger speak, more relieved than I should be not to be the one to inform my brother of what I've seen while I slept.

My brother offers a tight smile, his fledgeling beard and moustache flickering in the candlelight, as I take my seat, and I reconsider. A warning would be a blessing. Perhaps I owe him the courtesy for his warm greeting, and refusal to blame me for the failure of the Rus marriage.

Only then the rider is before us, a broad grin on his long face. I'm forced to assess what I've seen and what this messenger knows. They can't possibly be the same thing. Can they? Unless of course, this is Harald's sworn man. But I don't believe he is. I don't recognise him at all—just another of the things that have changed in my absence.

"My Lord Harald," the messenger has a deep voice, his blonde beard and moustache flecked with the salt of the sea, as he quickly lowers his head and takes to his knee. I'm amazed anyone would risk the crossing from England in such challenging weather. Just crossing the short distance from Skåne was danger enough for me.

At this time of year, anyone in a ship runs the chance of encountering terrible storms and getting lost in the near-constant darkness. The winds have been ferocious, on land. Out at sea, I can't see any boat keeping its sail under control. The ship-men who brought this man to Roskilde have rowed the entire way, battling the swells and the currents of the hungry sea.

It must have taken days.

It must also have been deemed necessary to take such a risk.

"Siward," my brother's greeting is restrained because he's unaware of the nature of the man's message, even though it seems that Siward is well enough known to him, that he can recall his name. News from my father has always been a double-edged blade. Others might accord Harald honour because he's my father's son, but I think Harald prefers it when he at least has the illusion of ruling alone.

"Your father, King Swein of Denmark, the first of his name, has been proclaimed King of England," the voice is muffled but rings with excitement at the message he's been ordered to convey. Abruptly, I understand his keenness to voyage despite the terrible storms raging outside.

The air leaves my body in a soft sigh. This is not what I thought it would be.

My brother turns to me, his eyes blazing fiercely. He's already on his feet, Siward, bowed low over one knee, forced to remain there because my brother hasn't permitted him to rise yet. The scent of the sea reaches my nostrils, as I fight back nausea caused by the realisation that my true dreams haven't deserted me, far from it.

They didn't show me my father's triumph, but then, they've

never revealed the pleasant aspects of the future, only the sharpened edges, meant to wound, to make me wary, to make me doubt so much.

"Jarls and Ladies. My father is victorious. England belongs to him!" My brother's voice is rich with satisfaction, as he holds the focus of everyone in that room. He stands, his stance wide, his arms open to either side of him. I notice that my sister, Hakon's mother, is amongst the first to rise and add her approval to the news, an ambitious bitch. No doubt she already counts the wealth promised to her husband by my father for his involvement in the English endeavour. I've never known Lady Gytha Sweinsdottir to do anything without the prospect of reward.

They tell me she's much like her mother. I'm relieved that Lady Gunnhild has been absent from Denmark for so many years. Bad enough my own mother, let alone my father's first wife as well to attempt to rule my life.

Amongst the rest of the audience, my eyes flash to Jarl Úlfr and his brother and sister. Their faces show their dismay not to have been in England to take advantage of King Swein's largesse on finally accomplishing what he set out to do well over a decade ago. Their arrival in Roskilde, from their home on Orkney, has come too late. That pleases me.

Further back, I see those who've grown weary with my father's continued absence, grin with delight, the older men, those who've long hung up their swords and seaxs for a quieter life, the women whose sons and husbands have sacrificed their lives on the whim of a king.

King Swein's triumph is welcome. It will stop the complaints and moaning that my brother has been forced to fend off in his absence. The jarls left behind had hoped to find Harald easier to control than my father. Instead, they found someone unprepared to act without Swein's express approval, unhappy at being asked to act counter to his father, even though he craved the opportunity to do so.

To follow in my warrior father's footsteps will not be easy

for my brother.

"Wine and mead all around," my brother, never one for raucous behaviour, calls for drinks for the jarls and ladies as though he's been drinking hard all his life. It helps that the servants are waiting, with full jugs, to distribute drinks to those attending the feast.

Harald's joy can't be mistaken, and I swallow heavily around the sudden lump in my throat, as I eye the clothes he's wearing for the celebration. The blue of his tunic matches the blue of his cloak. It's a good choice. I picked the tunic for him to celebrate the anniversary of his day of birth, and the reason for my continued hesitation in imparting the knowledge that only I know about in this room.

But my dreams are never wrong.

This will not last.

Yet, I have no choice but to take the goblet of rich wine handed to me by the giddy servant, eyes bright with delight, face pink from the excess heat the twin hearths and press of bodies has built up within the hall. Then I must toast my father's ultimate success in England after so many years of heavy fighting, and join in with my brother's abundant laughter. I can't tell him now when he believes the news has been delivered on the anniversary of his birth day, as though by the intervention of our Lord God. I can't warn him of what will come in the next few weeks.

I watch carefully as my father's jarls toast to his health, speak of past fighting exploits with him, and dream of the vast wealth to be gained in England. Tovi and Osgot are particularly expansive, probably with good reason. No doubt they hope that with Swein's success their star will rise. I could almost pity them such ambitions, although rather their dreams than Jarl Úlfr's. I know that Tovi and Osgot desire only to be wealthy and respected; they don't hunger for the same as Úlfr.

Úlfr is not to be trusted. Not at all.

Harald is filled with expansive hopes of how he'll rule Denmark while our father rules England. With our father in England, there's no chance of my other brother, Cnut, returning to Denmark and upsetting Harald's careful rule.

My father will ensure both of his sons have more than enough land to govern. He doesn't plan on making the mistake his own father did, of hoarding everything to himself, only to be usurped by his son. I can almost see Harald's hopes for the future they're so clearly etched into his smile and slightly too high voice, his cheeks roughened by heat and excitement.

I look for Jarl Thorkell's son amongst the crowd. He's here as a sort of hostage to his father's loyal behaviour; only it hasn't been as faithful as my father demands, far from it. He's lucky that my father is in England, or he might not be quite so alive. He's also fortunate that he shares my brother's name – just another Harald to confuse everyone, but of course, he's Harald Thorkellsson, not Harald Sweinsson.

The smile on my stiff cheeks remains forced, and yet no one comments or questions my lack of enthusiasm, even though I feel my pretence is ineffectual. Well, all apart from Frida, who knows me far too well. But I keep her away with a stern look. I don't want her asking questions, I can't now answer. She should have asked me earlier when I failed to rise from my bed, but of course, surrounded as we were by too many of my attendants, it was impossible to hold a private conversation, and then I wished to share the news with my brother, not my ally.

The feast, which lasts long beyond the time it was supposed to, only ends when it's closer to dawn than sunset. The long, long hours of deep winter have been expended in eating and drinking far too much, of talking too loudly, and of espousing on a future that I know is never going to happen. The hearth remains stacked high, fiercely blazing throughout the raucous night, the servants rushing to tend to it. Still, despite such concerted efforts, I stay cold, my fingers claw-like as I bunch them into my fine maroon dress. I wish I'd chosen something much warmer, but opted not to, because from experience, such feasts, with so many people, are always far too warm when I wear my thick winter dresses.

I watch, always feeling apart, trying to hold back my tears.

My father, King Swein of Denmark, is dead. He's not King of England and King of Denmark, and king over parts of Norway, as these people regale. Not anymore

He's gone, and I'll never see him again.

My true dreams are never wrong.

All these years of absence from Denmark, have amounted to nothing more than the briefest spark of triumph. I hope the afterglow is enough to warm King Swein in the grave, wherever that might ultimately be.

# CHAPTER 2

## *AD1013*

I wait impatiently for confirmation of my true dream with the arrival of a new messenger from England. I curse the continued storms and try not to listen too carefully to the bragging of my Lady Gytha Sweinsdottir, as she lauds it over me and my other sisters, who haven't been blessed with such martial, and influential husbands, as she has.

I wish she'd return to Avaldsnes or Hove. They are, after all, her homes. But I know my hopes will never be realised. Lady Gytha never willingly steps foot in the territory her husband rules, and which her single son, Hakon, will rule in time.

No, Gytha much prefers Roskilde to her homes in Norway, citing the terrible weather during the winter in the more northerly country. But I know it has more to do with not wanting to miss anything happening in Denmark or England. My father's first wife took her time in providing the much longed for sons that King Swein needed to secure his dynasty for the next generation. Lady Gytha, their firstborn child, might well be losing her looks as she teeters on the edge of her fourth decade, makes up for it with her constant illusions to her husband and adult son.

I wish to grieve, but I can't, not while everyone still celebrates the king's successes in uniting England with Denmark. Where, they ask, eyes ablaze with ambition, will King Swein strike next? I don't miss the glances my way, which assure me that they believe my father will be angry that I've lost him his alliance with the Rus.

The women who serve me bear the brunt of my sorrow and frustration. I slap them more, refuse to obey their instructions and generally behave in a way I know does not befit my rank as the daughter of the king.

Only he isn't the king any more. Now, I'm the sister of the king.

Only Frida is alert to my problems, and only then because she knows me well. I don't inform her of the specifics. I don't wish to lose my most loyal friend and advisor by speaking of the king's death. Some would call it treason, even though I would only be speaking of something that has already happened.

The only comfort is in watching Jarl Úlfr and his brother being so ill-tempered at their perceived loss. Their sister is as demure as ever, in fact, possibly even more so, as I find her increasingly in my brother's company. It's only too easy to see what Úlfr has planned for his sister, and I refuse to even countenance it, especially in light of the information I know, but can't share.

I find myself observing Úlfr and Eilifr. The brothers are similar and yet very different. It's easy to see who leads and who simply follows. Úlfr has piercing brown eyes and is always alert to everything happening around him. Eilifr is far more placid. I imagine he would happily slink away to play *tafl* and drink with the king's huscarls, but his brother won't allow it.

The cold weather quickly turns to snow, and I shiver all the more, despite my thick clothes. When I travel to Ribe with my brother, on court business, I gaze at the heaving sea in the far distance, pleased to know we'll not be risking such a journey far away from land in our well-crewed war-ship. The wave caps in the distance, as we enter the fjords under the power of the oars, and not the sail, flash white, tossed and turned, end over end until they crash against the far distant kingdom of England. The thought makes me shudder, and Harald notices as we disembark in the small quayside on the western side of Jutland, the main peninsula of Denmark.

Ribe is not the thriving settlement it once was, and yet it's been deemed worthy of maintaining by my father.

"No one will be arriving from England anytime soon," I imagine he hopes it'll console me. Siward, when he travelled from England with news from my father, did not refer to my failed Rus marriage. Harald must think I fear my father's anger. But I'm keen to hear from England, and I try and hide my dismay at his words.

"When we next hear from father, it'll be to tell us of his coronation and triumph. King Æthelred, the weak old fool, has fled from England, no doubt to Normandy, the country of his wife's birth. I imagine Lady Emma might be regretting her marriage to the English king now. I know our father would have married her if she'd only agreed all those years ago."

"Her husband is still alive." I feel compelled to protect Lady Emma because the casual assumption in Harald's words stings me. Especially after my experiences of marriage in a strange land. To marry Lady Emma of Normandy, my father would have needed to cast aside my mother. I might not always appreciate her sharp tongue, but she's certainly deserving of the title of queen to King Swein.

"She can leave him," Harald's shrug is nonchalant, as though my words mean nothing.

"Is that all women are to you?" I shout the words, neck extended, eyes trying to sear him, just with that glance.

Harald shrugs once more, his surprise at my heated response showing in the circle of his fuzz-encrusted lips. It's not like me to be so angry, not with him.

"Of course not," his stuttering shows his unease at my question.

"You, sister, will remarry. Our father will find a suitable husband, and it'll be to the honour of our dynasty. He hasn't wed any of our sisters to men they couldn't admire."

I shake my head, tears forming unbidden. It hurts me to hear my brother speak of my father with such awe and assurance. It pains me to realise my brother doesn't see the truth of the marriages my sisters have endured, all apart from Lady Gytha. Or the one I was sent away to face. A cold land, and a colder marriage.

I consider Gunnhild, Santslave and Thrya. Their husbands are powerful men in Denmark. My father relies on them to support Harald as his absence has grown ever longer, England proving almost impossible to conquer, despite my father's belief that King Æthelred is no warrior.

But Harald's words bring me back to the present. I know my father is dead. My two brothers, not my father, will decide whatever happens to me in the future.

"What is it?" Harald's voice enchants, but I angrily wipe the tears from my eyes, stifling the burgeoning sob that threatens to burst, as white-capped waves do, when they crash against the craggy shoreline.

I sniff loudly.

"I miss our father," I explain, as close to the truth as possible, without sharing my secret. I wish I'd been able to speak to my brother before news of my father's successes in England had reached him. The last few weeks have been unbearable, and they're not yet at an end.

I feel his arm around my shoulders, and while I consider shrugging off his rare show of affection, I don't. It's pleasant to be comforted by him. It might not be for the reason I need it. But it almost is.

"Maybe he'll let you visit him in England," Harald mutters softly, his voice only just audible above the fierce wind. "Or perhaps he'll come to Denmark soon. There's business that needs his attention. Perhaps he'll find you an English husband."

"That would be good," I sniff, allowing myself to hope that Harald's fantasy could come true, despite my knowledge to the contrary.

I allow my vexed question about the role of women to go

without a real answer. Harald has not been as some of the other men in my father's court. He doesn't thrust himself on the female slaves and servants. Neither does he fawn over the daughters of other powerful men, the few not directly related to him. He's wise. My father will have a marriage in mind for him, as well.

Oh.

Now I shake my brother loose. His gentle words have made me forget too quickly. These pretty ideas will come to nothing.

"And what of Cnut?"

Harald's expansive face closes tightly. Cnut and Harald are not natural allies. They're brothers. They want the same prize, but they can't both have it. Denmark only needs one king.

"There's no need to worry about Cnut. Not for many years. He thinks to be like our father, conquering far distant lands, but he's not the warrior Swein is. Cnut, despite what he thinks, has much to learn."

I nod, but I hear the thread of fear in Harald's voice. He knows, as I do, that if Cnut were king, he'd spend more time in Denmark than he does at the moment. Cnut doesn't have the number of men who flock to support our father. Cnut doesn't have the reputations for killing other Norse warriors, even though his foster-father is Jarl Thorkell.

My father slew Olaf Tryggvason, the fabled King of Norway. My father exiled and then killed his father, Harald Bluetooth, to become king in his place, another man of legendary reputation. King Harald protected Denmark, built the forts at Trelleborg, Fyrkat, Aggersborg, Borrering, Nonnebakken and Rygge to house his warriors on mainland Denmark, and then added two more, in Skåne as well.

Cnut has killed no one of great renown, although there are rumours he was complicit in the murder of an archbishop in England. In itself, it's a terrible crime, only compounded by the fact he was once a hostage to the English king. Not even the years he's spent learning his craft from Jarl Thorkell, can entirely remove the stigma of his helplessness.

I doubt my father ever forgave Jarl Thorkell for forcing his son into such a dishonourable role. I imagine it accounts for Thorkell's son remaining little more than a hostage in Roskilde.

Perhaps I should be pleased that Harald will rule after my father, after all.

Perhaps Harald will let me help him. I could share with him the true dreams I endure, of the people whose deaths I see as they happen, unknown to those who are divided by the angry waves of the sea.

"Cnut is not well-known to the men and women of Denmark."

"No, he isn't, but the men of the Thing can be contrary. They will support the most charismatic ruler, the one who promises them the greatest rewards."

I know this, but the fact Harald repeats it to me shows his apprehension.

"If you were king of Denmark, who would you choose for my second husband?"

Harald laughs, surprised by my question. My silence assures him that this isn't a joke, not for me, even as the wind continues to howl around us.

"Who would you wish to marry?"

"Not a lord from Rus, or even a king from Rus," I state flatly. I found the Rus to be a cold, and hard people; my husband, even colder, and even more formidable. I'm glad the union was so short-lived, although I pity Ilja his death. No man deserves to have his time cut so short. But then, perhaps he would have been as cruel as his father.

"Must it be to a king?" Harald asks. "Or would you accept a lord."

"I wish to be a queen, just as my mother. I wish to rule, as my mother does."

My mother is Sigrid, called 'the haughty' by those who

know her personally, and those who only hear of her antics. They whisper the name in private and where they believe she'll not listen to them. Yet, she's only too aware of her fearsome reputation. I would almost say she acts in such a way as to grow it. She terrifies me when she's angered. She needs no weapon of hard-forged iron for her tongue is double-edged.

"So you would want a man like our father then?"

"I would not." Even I'm surprised by the outrage in my voice. "I want a man who spends time with his family. Not one who must win every kingdom for himself, and spends all of his time making war."

"For a man to be a king, he must be a warrior first. Men and women must fear him."

I sigh, the wind buffeting my long blond hair so that it whips into my face, almost blinding me, where it stings my blue eyes.

As I blink ferociously, an object in the far distance catches my eye, and I peer into the wind, eyes tearing with the force of it.

"Is that a ship?" I ask, pointing with a suddenly shaking hand out into the deeper waters that lie between Ribe and England's far away shores.

I'm sure I can see a ship far out to sea, battling against the waves and the wind, a speck of burnished brown in an otherwise grey day.

Harald turns, about to deny my remark, only to nod slowly, his hand held against his forehead to shield some of the fierce wind from his eyes.

"Bloody fools," he complains. "That ship should be on land, being caulked and made water-tight for the coming fighting season."

I know it should, and Harald's unease is heard in his string of complaints.

"They'll all meet their death," he continues, but already he's turning, keen to make his way back to the quayside we've only just left and to find out what's so important, now, that the lives of all men on board must be risked.

I want to follow my brother, along the gently winding path to the eerily quiet quayside. Nothing moves there other than the baying wind, and the carcasses of ships lying waiting for the better weather. But suddenly, I don't want to hear the truth of my dream. I want my father to still live.

Tears form in the corner of my eyes. I stamp my foot in agitation, unheeding of the looks that pass between the women instructed to keep me company, or amongst my father's warriors, the huscarls, who protect the royal children. Only Frida's gaze rests on the ship, and not on me. I consider whether she's guessed or not. I wouldn't be surprised.

I don't want my father to be dead.

But I know he is.

And this ship, when it arrives from England, will confirm it.

It'll no longer be my secret to keep unwillingly, and I'll be left to toss and turn on the heaving sea just like the ship. I can't foresee that my brothers will handle the coming changes well. And I'll be theirs to command. I don't want that. Not at all.

# CHAPTER 3

*AD1013*

**M**y sleep is disturbed, and when I wake, I'm twisted tightly around furs and pillows, and I'm drenched from head to toe in the stale odour of my body.

My chest heaves, and I reach for and then fumble the wooden beaker kept beside my bed in the event of such awakenings, the water spilling noisily onto the wooden floor. I tense, expecting Frida to rush to my side, as so often the case, but she doesn't. Perhaps she imbibed too much wine before sleeping. I wouldn't blame her. She rarely lets down her guard.

This true dream is different from my usual ones, the tendrils of it seeping into me, even as I shake my head, expecting it to dispel. I almost jump from my bed, pulling my abandoned cloak around my shoulders to fight the cold that seems to permeate everything, as though the coldest of nights.

A moment ago I was hotter than a flame-forged blade, but now an iciness has enveloped me, and I almost find it impossible to put weight on to my feet because they're so chilled as I swing from my bed.

I reach for my boots, slip them over my feet, fumbling in the small light from the brazier in the corner of the room. Only then do I turn and creep from my room, the creaking door overly loud in the depths of the night, when everyone sleeps apart from the huscarls on watch duty at the main door. I don't pity them such a cold night. I hope the brazier is piled high beside them, and that they wear thick cloaks, gloves and hats.

I tremble again, making my way silently to where I know a water jug will be waiting. In the main hall, the gloom is less, because of the embers from the massive hearth that smoulders at its centre. A few snores greet my steps but nothing else. With a shaking hand, I pour water into yet another wooden beaker and drink it desperately, hoping the water will root me firmly in my body, entirely extricating myself from the dream.

Only my eyes close involuntarily with the action of swallowing, and the scenes of my true dreams immediately reappear before my eyes. I'm gasping for breath as I seek a chair to steady myself, eyes fleeing open, hands outstretched, trying to banish the images that don't want to leave me.

What is this?

Why is this?

I crouch further into my cloak, facing the autumn-red embers as a way of holding on to the reality of the here and now. Only then do I allow the flickers of my dream to subsume me.

I need to see what's terrified me so much that my heart beats loudly enough that I believe they might even hear it across the sea, in Skåne.

I close my eyes, my legs and booted-feet extended toward the warmth of the fire, and then I focus on one of the images that I recall clearly.

Two bowed heads, one blond, and one auburn, and behind them, an array of others. My hands rest on those heads, and yet another blond-haired head tries to force their way between them, as they kneel before me. Behind the bent heads, eyes watch me, little more than hooded flickers of blinding white from the gloom, the only colour caused by the irises.

I don't know where I am, only that I'm the focus of attention.

I meet the first set of eyes, noting the green tinge in the

strange half-dusk, half-night light where the colours of the day are polluted by what seems to be tendrils of the hottest forge, blue and white at the centre.

But the eyes draw me in. I know those eyes.

And then another set joins those, the one pair green, the other brown. I would recognise those eyes anywhere; Cnut and Harald. Quickly, their gazes flicker to the three bowed heads before me, but my vision is filled with yet more eyes all fighting for my attention.

These I don't know. Not at all.

There are many of them. Gazes peer from the creeping shadows, all of them focused on me. I resent the scrutiny. I don't know all of these people. Yet I feel as though I should.

If only I could see more of them, determine who they are, and who the three dipped heads belong to as well, their faces hidden from me.

My heart thunders in my chest as I try and focus on only one set of eyes, try to recall what so frightened me that it chased me from my dreams, brought sweat to my forehead, urging me from my bed.

The first to willingly acquiesce to my scrutiny seems to shimmer as a sudden spark of light reveals more than just eyes. I have the impression of long hair, tightly braided, and a smile appears to play on tight lips, satisfaction emanating from the body.

I see the fall of rich fabric around a curvy body, reminding me of my plain figure, and I realise that those eyes focus on the one head trying to come between the two of whom I already bestow my benedictions.

I sense, rather than see, a desperate need in that look, a desire to accomplish a great deal, and also something else that surprises me so much it casts the figure back into the shadow, and I'm left swallowing the sour taste of envy.

The next eyes to truly focus on me, wash me with their superiority and rather than seeing their clothes or hair, I see only a vision of a sea teeming with warships, the cries of two embattled sides drowning out even the sound of my breathing.

I wrench my head away from the gaze, bile in my throat and my stomach rolling with more than the gait of a ship in a storm. The grey haze of the future swallows a sanctimonious smirk, and then another figure appears.

I know what this is. It's a vision of what will happen in the future only filled with too much for me to be able to decipher.

I've never dreamt of so much before.

But one of those first sets of eyes draws me back, seeming to clamour for my attention.

Harald. My beloved brother. He stands apart from the other seething mass of scrutiny, I realise now, and I hold his green-tinged eyes, trying to understand his place in all this. But although his mouth moves, the sound of his words is lost to me, and I hear nothing, nothing at all, although his concern is easy to decipher. His soundless words are short and sharp, his mouth moving furiously through them all, a vision of his balled hands adding to the feeling of intense unease.

And then his eyes shift toward Cnut, and abruptly I understand so much more.

Not that I'm given the time to let him know that. Far from it.

A new shape emerges, close to Cnut, and this is someone I've never met before, or at least, I have no recollection of having done so.

The image of laughter suddenly ripples through the air, more substantial than sound. Yet my brother welcomes this new visitor. It seems Cnut is unaware of the bleeding knife the man covers in his hand, or even his leering glance my way. And there is the suggestion that he's just one of many, the others all cowering behind him.

Whoever this person is, I must stay away from him, and caution Cnut to do the same. The warning is clear to see. I wish I could see more, know who this figure is.

But what of Harald? He's gone, no longer watching me.

A rattling sound in the darkness wrenches me back to the here and now. Sweat pools down my face, and then beneath my cloak, even though I shiver.

I peer into the gloaming, trying to determine if I'm in danger, or whether it's merely the footsteps of one of the servants come to revive the fire, or the huscarls changing positions as they guard the main door.

My gaze skims the room, seeking into the secret places, the shadowed corners where someone could hide if they needed to, but I see nothing, my eyes rimmed with the light of my dreams, making it difficult to see well.

I judder, wishing I could banish the feeling of being watched as well as the lingering fatigue of my strange dream.

A breath of air passes over my face. My eyes turn to the door, where a slim figure seems to creep through the night, even though the door has neither opened nor closed. Only, the figure is insubstantial, merely a wisp and nothing more, and when the woman looks at me, I see someone I think I recognise, but I'm not sure. Her hair is white, clumps of it missing from her head, and I know what this is, and my hands clench the arms of the chair, as though I can use them to hold on to reality.

I'm not awake. Not yet, despite what I thought.

In her wake, the wreath-like figure brings more wavering figures, all seeming to steal through the closed door.

She beckons to me, but I stay seated, wishing I could close my eyes but knowing that to do so would only bring back the other half of my dream.

What is this? Why tonight do so many visions torment me?

Behind her, the woman brings my father, and I can suddenly see the resemblance clearly, even though I never met the woman, dead before I was born. This then is my grandmother. Swein strides as though for war, a grimace on his familiar face. His beard covers his chin as always, although now it's shadowed with grey frost.

I can see where blood pools from a wound in his side, and his face, although resolved, shows the strain in the white and blue that marbles his skin and touches his lips and eyelids. I gasp. I don't want to see this. He's dead. I don't need to see the pain he was in before he took his last breathes.

And my grandmother brings more of the dead with her. I harbour a guess that the one man is my grandfather, his resemblance to my father too obvious not to remark on, although, again, I was born after his death. The great warrior, King Harald Bluetooth, killed by his son. He carries a wound as well, and the scent of rotting flesh suddenly envelopes me.

I blink, try and clear my sight, only for the eyes of my initial vision to seek me once more. I open my eyes wide, torn. Do I wish to see the dead or the living?

I swallow, rub my hands together, wishing daylight would break and the hall would fill with people, busy about their tasks. I need to be distracted from these strange hallucinations, and only the light will wholly banish the dead.

Marble hands seem to reach for my chin, and I move my head, keen not to feel the creeping flesh on me, and yet they seem to dig deep inside me. I turn aside, reach for my beaker of water, only to have my face turned aside.

My grandmother's mouth opens, but no words pour forth, and the scent of her is disgusting. I want to gag, but I can't, her hand holding me transfixed.

Where her eyes should be, there are bottomless pits, but I can't turn away. The blackness of nothing beckons to me, a promise that if I follow it, all of this will disappear.

But can I? This is undoubtedly a gift, isn't it, to step aside from my future?

Or is it a curse?

Still, the slack jaw of my grandmother tries to speak to me, but I swallow, yank my head away from her hand, trying not to hear the clatter of her dislodged finger bones falling to the floor, and I close my eyes once more.

No matter these warnings from the past, I need to see, and I need to know precisely what the future holds. I allow myself to sink back into the dream where a collection of eyes pierce me, all trying to tell me one thing, while others vie for my attention. I want to know. I need to know.

Yet, despite my brothers being there, both of them, I now see, it is to the women that my gaze turns, time and time again.

I wish I knew who the woman was, her reaching hands floating through the air, as though she means to gather as much as possible, the one bowed head most urgent of them all. I open my mouth, as though to shout a warning to my brothers, and the three heads before them, only for the woman to laugh at me, the hint of menace intensified as her hands scoop up more and more of my vision.

But she's not alone, another woman is there as well, and all I can detect is a huge belly, as though she holds a litter of puppies inside her, and not children at all. Her hand rubs the protruding bump, and more and more of the eyes flock to her, seemingly keen to be under her command. Amongst them is the man, with the sea teeming with warships, and another, who seems to go unwillingly. And yet another, who floats eagerly toward her.

My gaze slips downwards, and I shudder, for there are no longer three bowed heads, but rather, seven, with two others squirming between them. Who are they? What are they? I can't tell, although it seems clear to me that I'm supposed to know who they are.

And then I blink awake, Frida before me, her face pale with the lack of sleep, the worry in her eyes making me blink back tears.

Her arms are around me, rocking me gently. All of my dreams are banished, and there's only me, and Frida, and the light of day to oust both of my nightmares.

For all that, I wish I knew who the people who inhabited my dreams were. Without such knowledge, the horrors that I've endured are impossible to decipher.

All the same, I take stock of what I saw; the three bowed

heads, my two brothers, and eleven others as well, a woman, a man with warships and another with a bleeding knife. I hardly know who the images represent. But I vow there and then that I'll find them all. I'll protect my brothers.

Even if they won't thank me for it.

# CHAPTER 4

## AD 1013

My gaze slides between the two of them. They couldn't be more different if they tried. Harald, long and thin, his growing beard and moustache the only thing that saves him from looking like the boy he always appears to be, Cnut, with his burly physique, his hard hands, and his quick-moving eyes. Even at rest, Cnut is active. He's lived a life where betrayal has never been far, and I see that rather than accept it, he's merely alert to the potential.

I'm glad this meeting is happening in private. It wouldn't be right for the Danish nobility to witness such anger and discord between the two sons of King Swein, king of Denmark, and for the blink of an eyelid, king of England. I can only imagine what Jarl Úlfr and his brother would make of it. Bad enough seeing the delight in the eyes of Jarl Thorkell's son at the news that he's free from his captivity, ten times worse to see it on the faces of those who realise how much they can now gain, provided they choose the correct brother.

Harald holds a piece of parchment in his hands, whereas Cnut's hands are talon-shaped, tense, his shoulders hunched. I can almost smell the battle-field emanating from his clothes for all he's dressed in court clothes, his tunic so new that it almost makes my eyes smart from the solutions used to dye them such bright colours.

"Our father made it clear. I am to rule in Denmark. Alone. I have the support of the nobility. They know what my father planned. A kingdom for each of his sons." Despite Harald's thinness, there's iron coursing through his body. His words filled with resolve, his refusal to relinquish any part of his power in Denmark, evident in every aspect of his bearing.

"Our father didn't hold England long enough for me to assert my right to rule on his death. I'm king to my ship men and my father's noble warriors, including Jarls Thorkell and Eirikr, but I have nowhere to rule. Not at the moment. You must accord me a joint role with you. It's what our father would have wanted." Cnut doesn't beg, or whine, his words spoken with the assurance that his older brother will do precisely as he says, almost staggering. Cnut is the younger brother, and yet his time away from Denmark has assuredly made him a man.

I wish I could lay claim to such surety.

Cnut's time away from Denmark has also made him and Harald strangers.

"No, he wouldn't." The woman who speaks isn't my mother, but she's mother to Harald and Cnut, two boys who both believe they should be king of Denmark.

Cnut doesn't round on his mother, as I suspected he would, instead he sighs heavily, and only then turns to gaze at her.

I consider what he sees when he looks at his mother. The resemblance to his older sister is undeniable, and not in a good way. Their faces are implacable. They might both wear fine dresses and have hair that's intricately braided, but it's in the lines of their faces, the angle they hold their heads, and in the way they expect to be obeyed without questioning.

When Cnut speaks, his tone is remarkably calm, but I've seen the flicker of relief on Harald's face that another makes the assertion on his behalf. Harald might have found the stones to make the claim, but whether he can argue it remains to be seen.

"And how would you know our father's plans. You've been absent for many years. You had only Harald to thank for summoning you back to Denmark." Cnut is right to announce. As soon as the news of King Swein's death was well known, Harald summoned his mother back from her homeland, where she'd been sent when Swein took my mother as his new wife.

"I might not have been your father's wife anymore, but that doesn't mean I didn't know his intentions. What, did you think your father and I never spoke of the future in our long years together? I can assure you that we did. Two sons, no matter how late they arrived in his life, can be a burden for any father."

I eye the woman with interest. She was absent throughout my childhood, the place of king's wife, accorded to my mother instead. Lady Gunnhild has surprised me by being a woman who is not only beautiful but who retains that beauty. I would have expected a woman of near enough sixty years to have lost her appeal. But it seems not. I wonder why King Swein ended his marriage to her. Or perhaps he didn't. I suppose my mother would have put such a spin on it, even if it wasn't the truth.

Lady Gunnhild is tall and elegant, long hair, still mostly black, intricately plaited so that it falls well below her waist when she stands. Her eyes are brown, and quick, filled with intelligence, her hands, held demurely in front of her, clasped tightly together, slim and festooned with rings. They catch the light from the candles with each and every movement she makes, even the smallest.

She's certainly a woman to hold the eye of every man, woman and child in a room. I confess I feel a twinge of envy.

Her accent is light, for all that Danish is not her native tongue.

"Then, Lady Mother, explain my father's plans to me." Cnut's voice is still calm. I keep anticipating that he'll rage at my brother and his mother, call on his four other sisters to support him, only he doesn't. Cnut has learned valuable skills of diplomacy to go with his warrior prowess. He's more like my father than Harald, although my father's diplomacy was always rimmed with the threat of violence.

"Your father planned for Harald to have Denmark after him. It was always his intention. The first-born child should hold Denmark. The promise of England, or even Norway, with Jarls Eirikr and his brother, Svein, was to ensure his two sons didn't bring the country to civil war, as happened with your father and his father. You must win one of those other kingdoms for yourself."

Like Cnut, Lady Gunnhild speaks with surety. She expects her words to be heeded, accepted, and for the two brothers to go about their business. She anticipates no argument, and certainly not from her daughter. Lady Gytha flashes a look of fury toward her mother. I can see that she resents the implication that Cnut should have all of Norway, trampling over her husband's lands. Honestly, one moment she hates the land her husband rules, and the next, she looks about ready to wage war to keep hold of it.

It's best that my sisters' husbands are all absent from this family meeting.

And yet Cnut, for all his composure, shows a tremor of unease in his broad shoulders. Just the one.

"Lady Mother, how am I to win England with no means to fund my ship-men? I can't believe that our father would expect me to survive without the means to support myself."

"You must raid, as your father would have done, and make allies. Conquering England is not Denmark's burden to bear."

"But it was while my father lived?"

"Your father was the king of Denmark. You are not."

I almost gasp at the criticism in those words. There's no softness to Lady Gunnhild. My mother would have capitulated by now, forced the two brothers to an accord. It seems Lady Gunnhild doesn't intend to do the same.

Harald watches Cnut carefully from where he stands, beside a desk that holds parchments that require the attention of Denmark's king. While Harald might have been pleased by his mother's support for him, I can see that it makes him uneasy. Perhaps the illusion of the war between father and son has made him wary.

Certainly, Cnut can call on a vast fleet to aid him, and of course, his foster-father is Thorkell the Tall, lord of the Jomsvikings. They owe fealty to whoever can pay them. Harald has no such options available to him. He has his huscarls, and what remains of the Danish ship-army that didn't go to England with my father, but little else besides.

In effect, both of my brothers are as weak as the other. Both of them can only hold on to what they want with my father's combined resources. Only those holdings are to be split. My father has made them both weak. I can't imagine that was his intention, no matter what Lady Gunnhild implies.

"My father died as King of England, but their kings are elected. I didn't have the necessary support after only eight weeks of my father ruling there." Cnut makes his point eloquently, his gaze firmly on Lady Gunnhild. I can see that he means to argue his way out of this.

"It little matters. Your father is dead. He made his expectations well known in his will, written in his final days. He proclaimed your brother king of Denmark, and you, king of England."

Cnut nods. He doesn't deny that truth.

"It was imperative that my father made his wishes known. He assured me that my brother would support me. He swore me that Harald would know his duty, as my brother. The parchment is a legal document, intended for the people of Denmark, and to smooth my brother's transition to being king in actuality as opposed to merely filling my father's boots. It was not my father's intention that it would exempt Denmark from ensuring England was mine."

Still, Cnut maintains his cool façade. I am almost speechless. My memories of Cnut when we were younger, always ended with him furious and using his fists to achieve what he wanted. But then, we were both children then. Neither of us is that, now.

"We have only your declaration for that." Harald finally

speaks again. His words are weighted.

"Do you truly believe that my father intentionally left me a beggar? With men to feed and keep through the winter months? His men. Men who fought for his vision of a united England and Denmark? They've barely warmed their back-sides on an English seat before being thrust back into the turbulent sea, cast out from England, by ealdormen who suddenly see no reason to remain loyal."

"I don't know what our father planned, other than what's written, here," and Harald again waves the parchment. My father's will has been committed to thick parchment in flowing green ink. Even from here, I can decipher some of the well-rounded letters, recorded for perpetuity by an English monk. "I had not seen him for several years. He never spoke to me of the future, as it seems he did to our mother."

I can sense Cnut's growing frustration, and yet he remains cool-tongued.

"I can tell you what our father proposed. I could recall one of the many jarls and ealdormen who witnessed his death and have them tell you what he said. I will summon Jarl Eirikr, or Jarl Thorkell, or even Ealdorman Leofwine from England." The last name is cast into the air eagerly. We all know the story of the English lord and King Swein. It's the stuff of legends, and yet it means nothing, not here, and not now. And why would Cnut rely on this English man who has determined to support King Æthelred, rather than Cnut, in his quest for the kingdom of England?

"There's no need for that," Lady Gunnhild is quick to inter-ject. "I've spoken to the jarls who never left Denmark. They're eager to pledge themselves to Harald, in exchange for keeping the lands your father gifted to them." I sense, rather than see, my three sisters shifting at this revelation. It seems that their husbands are to play a large part in determining what happens now.

This seems to perplex Cnut. Even I was unaware of this de-velopment, despite keeping a careful eye on the small groups that have sprung up in recent weeks, intrigue their main concern. It's been evident that they discussed the future, but I didn't know anyone had made a final decision. Not yet.

"So, brother, what would you have me do?" Cnut seems to deflate with this news. I'm impressed he doesn't implore his sisters to speak to their husbands, but then, Cnut is not one to beg.

"Leave Denmark. Take your shipmen with you. Go to Borre or Skiringssal. Denmark is peaceful; for the time being, we do not need ships and men who expected to be paid with the spoils of England. See what you can cobble together in Borre. I'm sure the Northmen will be pleased to see you." This isn't true, none of it. My father lost his command over those places because he was obsessed with England, and Harald knows it, as do the rest of us.

Harald is casting my brother out. We all understand that as a heavy silence fills the space. Beyond the walls of the hall, I can hear men and women calling one to another. I can even hear the sea, not so distant, but far enough away that I can't usually detect it unless a storm rages against the coastline.

I can't help but think it's a brave stance for Harald to take. What if Cnut gathers the support of the ship-men? Their home is Denmark. They will be left with a choice, stay with their oath-sworn lord, or remain at home? What if Cnut leaves Denmark only to return with more warriors and claim it for himself? It wouldn't be the first such family squabble for my father's dynasty.

Harald places the parchment on the tabletop, the scrawled words visible to me, but not their actual intent. I've read the document. I know what it states for Harald and Cnut. They know their destiny. That it makes no mention of my future, infuriates me, and I'm not as skilled at Cnut at masking my true feelings. It seems my potential is for my brothers to determine, and I can't see that ending well. Not when they're already bickering over Denmark.

My sisters are all married. Their futures are assured, even if they have husbands they'd rather cast aside.

"The English have taken back King Æthelred. He has many sons who can rule after him." Cnut makes the assertion a final time, perhaps just to ensure Harald understands what is being agreed.

"And yet our father said England was to be yours, so I suggest you determine a way to win it back, and with it, your wife." Harald stabs Cnut with those words, and for the first time, I see a flicker of unhappiness on Cnut's face and triumph on Harald's.

I'm still not entirely sure why Cnut left his wife behind in England. I mean, I have a good idea, but even so, I'm speechless that my brother could abandon his pregnant wife quite so easily. After all, should she birth a son, then he'll have secured the next generation of my father's legacy through the male line. Gytha Sweinsdottir has a son already, but my nephew, Hakon, will rule after his father, in his Norwegian lands. Hakon has no claim to Denmark itself.

"Then you leave me with little option," and Cnut turns and leaves the small room, with a cursory sign of respect for his mother. His eyes sweep over me, but he gives no intention of his thoughts toward me. I can only hope that continues.

But it seems that Lady Gunnhild hasn't yet finished with Harald, and although her daughters make to rise, they all settle back into their seats, as she sweeps them with a firm look. Even I find myself sitting more alertly, and she's nothing to me. I owe her no honour. Until a few days ago, she was little more than a name.

"Do not squander this opportunity. Your father always knew you would be the one to remain in Denmark. He expected you to rule, and rule well in his absence, but in doing so, he made it impossible for you to gain the reputation as a warrior that your brother enjoys. There's no denying that Cnut undoubtedly deserves the acclaim he receives. I will not interfere to settle an argument again. You must make of your reign what you can."

And Lady Gunnhild sweeps from our presence, clicking her fingers to ensure her daughters follow her, as though they're her ducklings. I watch a myriad of emotions threaten to engulf Harald's demeanour. I think he's forgotten about me, but suddenly I feel his heated gaze on me.

"I'll not make you choose between Cnut and I. We are both your brothers, but while I'm king, and he has no kingdom, I'll dictate your future." His words shouldn't surprise me, and yet they do. I hunt for the trace of the kind brother I've known in the past, but he seems to be missing.

I swallow heavily.

"Lord Brother, I am yours to command." But the words burn, and more, they stink of a lie. I don't believe that Harald should order my life. More, I don't believe him capable of acting maliciously toward me. However, I don't think he has my best interests at heart either.

"You can go," his dismissal is kindly given, and I curtsey before leaving him, alone, in his office. My brother looks pensive but also resolved. I swallow, noting the long shadows behind him. I don't know if they're truly there, or if I add them to his bent head, so reminiscent of my true-dream, that's been so hard to banish, it finds me even when I'm awake.

Outside, in the great hall, I seek out Cnut amongst the mass of nobles and warriors. I can see where he crouches low, others leaning forwards to hear him speak. I notice Jarl Úlfr with a grimace, his sister perched close to the hearth, impossible to ignore with the way her hair shimmers in the reflection from the flames. I would go to her, eclipse her, but it's my mother who takes my attention.

She sits, at the opposite end of the table on the dais, to my step-mother, and I can see that neither woman is genuinely comfortable with the other. Lady Gunnhild thinks to command the king's hall, side-lining my mother, and yet the servants and the nobility, seek out my mother's attention. It's been this way ever since Lady Gunnhild arrived in Roskilde. I can't see that it will end well for either of them.

When men take their wives and then replace them with another, they do not consider what will happen after their deaths, or even to what will happen to the children from the different unions. No matter that the children share a father, there's always a perceived difference between them.

Lady Gunnhild gave King Swein two sons and four daughters; my mother gave Swein a daughter. That marks her as lesser, even though she had two sons with her first husband, and one of them rules as king of the Svear.

As Lady Sigrid's daughter, I'm treated differently to my brothers, and it's not just because I'm a woman.

"Lady Mother," I curtsey before her and then take a seat. I almost wish that I could sag into it, but there are too many eyes watching to take my leisure, Lady Gytha's being the ones that bother me the most. There are too many keen to know what has transpired between the two brothers. I won't be the one to tell them.

"I take it that went well," my mother speaks softly, keen not to have our conversation overheard by Lady Gunnhild, as she bends to talk to me, to all intents and purposes, checking for the dog who is her constant companion.

"Yes, Lady Gunnhild threw her support behind Harald. Cnut will have to leave Denmark."

"Where will he go?"

"He didn't share that information."

"And what of you?"

"Harald says as king he has control over my future."

"Well, it could be worse. It could be Cnut. A man who leaves his pregnant wife in a hostile country would have thought nothing of marrying you off to your detriment." Lady Sigrid speaks disdainfully, and I startle, realising that she meets the eyes of Lady Gunnhild with scorn as she voices her deepest thoughts.

I share my mother's opinion of Cnut's probable ambitions for me but feel compelled to stay silent. Not that I want to defend Cnut. I'm just not sure how I feel about either of my brothers at the moment. Everything feels unsettled, despite Harald being King of Denmark.

I can't help but fear for the future. Harald and Cnut have always shared such a good relationship in the past. It pains me to see them being driven apart by ambition and the hasty Will my father had written because he knew he was dying.

I would wish I'd been there, to stare into his eyes one final time, to determine what he truly meant and what his actual intentions were. I'm not sure they were the same thing.

I also wish he'd made some provision for his wives. I think they might just be more destructive than his sons. Lady Gunnhild means to reclaim all she lost when she was asked to leave Denmark. But my mother holds everything that Gunnhild wishes to claim. And my mother has been wife to not one, but two kings, and almost a third. She's beloved in Denmark, and Lady Gunnhild is not. The memory of Gunnhild's queenship has quickly faded, and been superseded by that of my mother's.

I wish I weren't alone with the two women. I could do with the support of my sisters, only, of course, they are the daughters of Lady Gunnhild, and for all they might not agree with everything Lady Gunnhild says, they'll not publicly criticise her.

I meet my mother's eyes. I'm sure she knows where my thoughts have taken me. But she smiles, her eyes alight with pleasure. It seems that she'll enjoy the continuing discord. She's never been one to stand aside from any argument. And I have no warnings of how the problems will resolve. None at all. It seems I must wait and see what happens. I don't honestly believe that pleases me.

# CHAPTER 5

*AD1014*

"There's a messenger here for Cnut," my mother's words reach me, even though I'm deep in thought.

"Cnut isn't here," I turn, and my mother shrugs an elegant shoulder, her fur cloak rippling with the movement, as though the animal still lived while showing her disdain for the cast-out brother. I stand and beckon the man closer. It's not the first time I've had to redirect messengers hunting out Cnut. It seems that everyone assumes he'll be in Roskilde, but of course, he isn't.

Cnut left with his fleet, and I have no idea where he's gone.

The messenger is salt-stained and stinks of the sea.

"A difficult crossing?" I ask, and he nods, his eyes trying to peer into the recesses of the shadowy hall.

"Lord Cnut is not in Denmark at this time. In all honesty, I'm unsure where he is. Can you relay the message to me?"

"It regards his wife." The man is evidently from England, his words clipped, for all I understand them. He's not Siward, the man who brought the news of my father's triumph, neither is he Olaf, the man who brought the news of my father's death. This then is someone entirely new, and I have my suspicions about who sent him.

I feel a stirring of unease, although my true dreams have shown me nothing of late, and so I feel perturbed but not for the reason the man might think.

"Is Lady Ælfgifu well? Is the child born?" My words are too sharp, but they seem to settle the man.

"A son, named Swein, for his grandfather. Lady Ælfgifu was keen that her husband knew of his safe arrival." I can see just how keen she was. Violent storms have raged for weeks now. I can't imagine that the journey has been without mishap. Yet the man has survived, and that speaks for the skilled shipmen he's employed to get him to Denmark.

I beckon the man closer, determined to take him into my confidence.

"I've heard rumours that he's in Norway, close to a place called Trondheim, but nothing has been confirmed to me."

The ghost of a smile touches the man's wind-reddened cheeks.

"Then I'll follow him further north. My thanks, My Lady." He hesitates, perhaps unsure of who I am.

"Lady Estrid, his youngest sister."

"Ah, of course." And he turns to move away, but I call him back.

"One moment, please." His steps falter, and I stand beside him, back facing my mother and Lady Gunnhild. I'm sure Lady Gunnhild will be thrilled to know she's a grandmother once more, but I might just keep the information for a while longer. I must let Harald know first. This affects him more than it does Lady Gunnhild.

"Will you inform Lord Cnut that all is well within Denmark. And, one more thing, how can I contact Lady Ælfgifu?"

The messenger pauses, as though considering the wisdom of informing me, but then he nods. After all, she is my brother's wife.

"Lady Ælfgifu is in Gainsborough. She waits for your brother there, as previously arranged."

"And events in England? Is King Æthelred fully restored, and much loved."

Again, I sense hesitation before the messenger replies.

"England requires a strong king," he states enigmatically, and then he's gone, and I think it won't be long until Cnut once more goes to war, provided he has the ship-men he needs. And the funds to pay them. England isn't safe, that's obvious.

I wish I knew more about King Æthelred's sons, but all I remember Cnut telling me is that some of them were his age, while others were merely small children. Certainly, Æthelred was blessed with sons, if not the wit to defeat my father and Jarl Thorkell. Not that I blame him for that. Both my father and Thorkell have a reputation because of their skills and relentlessness. It's a trait I find missing in Harald. I know that Cnut has it.

"What did you say to the messenger?" Of course, it's Lady Gunnhild who asks, sweeping close to me, now that the man is gone. I consider not responding, but realise it would be churlish, as the scent of her perfume surrounds me, almost making my eyes water.

"News from England. I must inform Harald."

"Why didn't you let the man speak to me?" Her tone is sharp, waspish, reminding me of why I don't feel the urge to take her into my confidence.

"You saw him. You should have spoken to him."

I hear the sharp hiss of annoyance, and note my mother's smirk of amusement, but I must find Harald. He, after all, is the king, not his mother, or my mother, no matter how much they might wish they ruled here.

If I were in their position, I wouldn't spend my time trying to see who could infuriate the other the most. They are women with influence, but at the moment, they squander it in useless, petty arguments. If I had their power at my fingertips, I would make much better use of it.

Striding away, I feel my shoulders relax away from the tense atmosphere. I'm not surprised my father chose to keep his two wives separate, and not just in different royal settlements, but in two entirely different countries.

I consider whether my mother might prefer to return to

the land of the Svear? There, she would be feted as the king's mother, here, she's merely the king's sister's mother. I can't see that the two are even comparable. Yet, she's been gone from Sweden for many years. She may fear to return knowing that she'd no longer be important in her own name, but only in King Olof's. I imagine that makes Denmark preferable, even with Lady Gunnhild in residence.

"Harald," I find him, as so often the case, sequestered with his holy men. There are few enough of them in Denmark, and it seems as though all of them assist my brother with the business of running the country. It's so different from my father's attitude, but then, my grandfather and his father had the more straightforward job of overpowering the nobility to claim the kingship. It was my father's role to continue ruling through military might. Such forcefulness is no longer required. My brother must rule the jarls, and they're a cantankerous bunch, as keen to bicker as my mother and step-mother.

They sharpen their words more often than they do swords and spears.

"News, from England," I speak before asked, determined to share the information before Harald chases me away, with his usual complaints of the pressures on his time.

Harald stills, and I appreciate that he anticipates the birth of Cnut's child. Perhaps we've both been waiting for the same news to arrive.

"A son, Swein." I offer, trying not to see the flurry of emotions on his long face. Harald has yet to take a wife. I know he wavers, unsure whether to marry a Danish noblewoman, or take a bride from Poland, or even from amongst the Rus. None of the options will prove favourable with everyone, and his mother is vocal about most of the possibilities.

"Then I'm an uncle once more." Harald manages the vestige of a smile, and I feel my lips quirk, more in sympathy for him than in joy for Cnut.

"And I'm an aunt as well." I curtsey, prepared to leave Harald to contemplate what this might mean for him, but he shocks me.

"Estrid, I would speak with you." I bob upright, my surprise seeming to rock Harald as his head wobbles backwards.

"Is it really so hard to speak with me these days?" Harald demands to know, his slim fingers indicating that he wishes to be left alone by his holy men, and while I hunt for diplomatic words, he chuckles.

"Come, sit. Let's talk as we used to, before our father's death."

I settle in the chair he indicates, before his vast work table, and I eye him.

It seems that for all his accession to the kingdom of Denmark was accomplished smoothly enough, that the responsibilities of ruling alone, are heavy. I see the strain of exhaustion in the furrow of his brow, and in the discarded tray of food to the side of him.

"You must take the time to look after yourself. Others can shoulder these responsibilities with you."

"Perhaps, sister, perhaps. But some would see it merely as an opportunity to exploit. My father warned me about most of the men and women who would serve me. It seems better to keep them distant, ensure the temptation isn't too much for them."

"Surely your mother?"

"She's the worst of them all. It pains me to say it, but it's the truth. She's been trying to forge her own circle of adherents. It's so brazen; it's laughable."

"And my mother?"

"She at least ensures my mother knows that we're all aware of what she's doing. You might find the bickering ceaseless and infuriating, but it's better this way. I believe I was too hasty in recalling her, for all she supports me." Harald's words surprise me.

"My sisters' husbands are all too caught up in their own petty squabbles, and I don't trust Jarl Úlfr and his brother and sister at all. What of you?"

"What of me?"

"You could assist me. You learn quickly. You could help me with church matters. I know they're close to your heart, and the archbishop of Bremen-Hamburg seems to delight in sending constant and continual letters to me. Often, they contain only the briefest snippet of information that I truly need to know."

"Really? I don't believe the archbishop would approve of my involvement." I try to deflect his request, even while my heart leaps at the thought of such trust being placed in me.

"In England, I'm told, the queen is responsible for the nunneries, and sometimes, the monasteries as well. I don't see why it should be any different in Denmark."

"But I'm not the queen."

"No, you're not, but you're my sister. Denmark has no queen, although I wouldn't tell your mother, or my mother, as such."

"Then I'll help you if you think it would assist you."

"Yes, yes," and Harald looks eager now, his eyes raking over the items on his work table, as though he can find something else that he doesn't need to keep careful control over.

"And there'll be other matters as well. Yes, let's see how much time you have to devote to such affairs. And," Harald pauses. "It will give my mother something else to complain about, and something else for yours to crow over her. That should keep the pair of them gainfully occupied."

I grin, pleased to see Harald's heavy brows unfurrow. I can help him with this, I know I can, but, and I don't tell him this, he'll need to marry, and no doubt, I need to marry again as well. But for now, it seems I have much to learn.

Of course, Lady Gunnhild takes the news of the birth of young Swein Cnutsson as though she's somehow been involved in the whole thing. I expect her to send gifts and messages to Lady Ælfgifu in Northampton, and when she does no such thing, I determine to do so.

**"Lady Ælfgifu,"** I'm unsure how to write to someone I've never met, and who Cnut only mentioned in passing. I consider whether she's beautiful or merely wealthy. Or was the match entirely political? I wouldn't be surprised to learn that it was. I've never known Cnut to be impetuous. I understand that Lady Ælfgifu's family hated King Æthelred. I believe that Æthelred murdered her father and blinded her brothers. I'm sure my brother would have found such a combination too heady to resist.

*"I send warm greetings on the birth of your son, and some small gifts that I hope will be suitable for you, and him."* And that's about all I want to say to the woman, but I know I must make more of an effort. I consider gifts. They might not be suitable for a child, but they are valuable, especially the golden cross. I will not have my nephew raised in poverty. Perhaps, young Swein Cnutsson will approve of the soft linens and the small wooden horse I've had one of the craftsmen make from dark wood.

*"I have sent the messenger to track down Cnut. Denmark is not currently his home, but I believe the messenger will find him further north. I hope that he'll soon return to England, and meet his firstborn child."*

And here I pause once more. What more can I say to Lady Ælfgifu? I could ask her to pray at my father's tomb, in Gainsborough, but I'm not entirely sure that's a reasonable request for a new mother. I could ask after King Æthelred, but I don't honestly believe that I'm that interested in events in England. It was my father's desire to conquer England, not mine.

I sigh.

*"If you are ever in need of assistance, please know that you will be welcome in Denmark."*

I'm not sure that's entirely true, but no matter what, Lady Ælfgifu is now a member of my family, and whether Harald or Cnut like it, that means that Denmark should be her home.

*"May God bless you and your son."*

*"Lady Estrid Sweinsdottir, sister to your husband."*

And then I find I have an entirely new conundrum. Who can

I send to England with such a message and such a gift? Who will take the risk? My eyes alight on Jarl Úlfr, but of course, I don't wish to honour him. And then I smile because Siward has appeared within the king's hall, and I know I can trust him with the burden.

I watch Harald from the corner of my eye. He's been waylaid by his mother, a litany of complaints on her tight lips, all of them far too audible, and the majority of them, regarding me and my new 'position,' as she keeps referring to it.

I can tell that Harald's temper is tested, and I wish I could help him, but I'm not the king, he is.

"Lady Mother," his voice oozes with charm. "I am your king; you must remember that I'm not a child to chastise. Not anymore. You wouldn't speak to Cnut in such a manner. I know that. So does the entire court."

"Your brother doesn't treat me with such scorn. He would have ensured I had a place by your side. He would consult me. I might seem old to you, but that also makes me wise, and you seem to be lacking such wisdom."

I'm grateful that she only speaks so openly here, away from the prying eyes of the court. There are few to witness her tirade other than myself, and the holy men who labour beside me. We're all busy, and she's disturbing us. I'm not even sure how she gained entry to Harald's inner sanctum. No doubt, she bribed one of the servants or forced one of the slaves to give her access. It's not the actions of a woman whose son is king, and indeed, a woman who supported her oldest son, against her youngest son. I try not to smirk as I hear her try to use the one brother against the other.

"My brother is not here, and never likely to be. Why don't you go to him, in England? He now holds half the kingdom." The hint of frustration in Harald's voice is only partly aimed at his mother.

Cnut is as demanding as Lady Gunnhild. What he'll ask for next, I hardly dare think. Still, it's good that Cnut now has his kingdom. King Æthelred is dead. The wars that have raged for so many years across England have been resolved, following a battle at a place called Assandun. Now, King Æthelred's son holds the southern lands, and Cnut, the northern. Surely my ambitious brother will be happy now?

"I'm not going to England," Lady Gunnhild almost screeches. "My place is here, at your side. Cnut thinks only of war and weapons, just like your father. I prefer the more civilised nature of Denmark."

I feel my eyebrows rise high into my hairline at such words. I'm not sure that Denmark is truly as civilised as she thinks. Denmark is surrounded by the sea, and by enemies who would claim the land for themselves. And within the great halls of Denmark, many would like to succeed at the expense of another. Harald once spoke of Denmark being peaceful, but much has changed since then.

"Then you'll accept the role I've given you, as my honoured mother. I have given you estates, and lands, not only here, but also on mainland Denmark. You're free to dispense such largesse as you see fit. Is that not enough for the king's mother?"

Now I cast my eyes hastily downwards, not wishing to witness the malice that slithers over Lady Gunnhild's face as she peers at me. I know only too well what she thinks of me. My mother assures me that Lady Gunnhild is merely jealous of my youth, and intelligence, and relationship with my brother, but I believe her hatred goes even deeper than that.

"I," and here her voice drops to a whisper, and although I can't hear the actual words, I can perceive the fury behind them. No doubt, she speaks of me, and probably of my mother.

"Lady Mother," Harald's voice is firm, although I daren't look at him. "That's enough for today. I suggest you think of what you just said to me, and then let me know if those words reflect your true thoughts. If they do, I'll make arrangements for you to return to your homeland. Perhaps you would be happier there."

The silence at the end of his statement, rings loudly, every single person in the room holding their breath.

"Well," and Lady Gunnhild seems unsure what else to say. "Well, indeed." And she marches away, her head held high, and her arms jangling with the replica silver arm-rings she insists on wearing, as though earned on the battlefield, and not in the bed-chamber.

The sound of industry fills the room until Harald slumps down on a stool beside me. His sigh sends parchments air-borne, and I reach out to grab them all, while he calmly gathers those that have fallen in his lap.

"She grows more wilful, not less." I hardly like to criticise his mother, but know he wouldn't take me into his confidence unless he meant me to speak freely.

"Can you not send her to Viborg or even Lund?"

"I would sooner it were England or even the land of the Svear, but no. It's better to have her where I can watch her. It's not as though she's subtle when she tries to undermine me. It's better if men and women see that she has no sway over my actions."

"Perhaps, but it doesn't make for an easy life, does it?"

"No, it doesn't. But she's my mother. I must show her some favour."

"Then, she needs to learn to show you the respect that you deserve."

Harald's grunt of annoyance is all the agreement that I get.

"I received word from England today. King Edmund is dead. Cnut is now king of all England and not just the north."

I gasp. "But, King Edmund was only a little older than Cnut. What happened to him?" I feel a stirring of dread. Has my brother murdered the man?

"A wound, taken at Assandun. It became infected with the wound-rot. There was no chance of his survival." I feel my lower lip tremble. To hear of such a young death unset-tles me, drives away all reassurance that I have many, many years ahead of me. Harald gazes at me intently, no doubt his thoughts running similarly to mine, as I try and determine whether any of this is related to my dream on that fateful night.

"But that is not all."

"Not all?" I can hardly think what else Cnut might have done in his time in England. It seems that he has merely to think of something and he accomplishes it. How different to when he and my father tried to conquer England.

"He has another son, this one named for me."

My eyes seek out my brother's, for all he tries to look away. Some might think him abashed at the compliment, but the slither of ice-cold dread down my back tells me something else.

"It's a family name," I try and deflect, but I think my brother sees my fear. And yet he doesn't ask me why I snatch my fingers from their place on the table, my arms immediately covered in goose-bumps.

"Two sons and I'm yet to father even one," Harald complains.

"Then, brother, I suggest you set your mother to the task of finding you a wife who can be a mother to your children. At least it might keep her occupied." Harald grunts, and stands, only to pause and look back at me.

"Sister, that might just be the best idea you've ever had." As he turns away, I bring my hands back in front of me. They shake, uncontrollably, and I know another part of my true dreams has been fulfilled. Perhaps these two sons were the ones I saw?

I only wish I knew whether these events boded ill for Harald, or not.

I eye the women before me with barely concealed interest. These women, it seems, are those that Lady Gunnhild thinks will make Harald a good wife. Not that they're all here, that would be unseemly. These are the Danish women, born into prosperous families, all eager to profit from allying so closely with the ruling family.

I wonder what my step-mother is thinking. Tying Harald to any of these families will be catastrophic. I had at least expected her to make a reasoned and sensible attempt to arrange a marriage for my brother.

Two of the women are little more than girls, far too young to wed, and no doubt, not even able to have children yet. Another is perhaps too old to become a mother again, although she has five children with her previous husband, ranging in age from older than Harald to little more than a few years old. That leaves three who might be suitable if only their families were not the very ones that my great-grandfather quashed when he claimed the kingship of all Denmark. And of course, there's Gytha, sister to Jarl Úlfr. Eilifr is in England, while Úlfr and Gytha remain in Denmark. Any fool can see what they're doing. Well, any fool other than Lady Gunnhild.

I watch Lady Gunnhild as she introduces my brother to the women, my mother beside me. In a low voice, my mother echoes my thoughts.

"Too young, too old, too frumpy, too delicate, too pointy," the last words make me gasp, and I turn to my mother, to see her eyes dancing with delight.

"What does that mean?"

"There's not enough meat on her bones to allow a man a comfortable night's enjoyment."

I chuckle, she's perhaps not wrong, but I feel a flicker of pity for the poor women. They shouldn't be subjected to such scrutiny. It's belittling and reminds me too forcefully of my first meeting with my first husband and his family. I wait for my mother to criticise Gytha, for all I don't know if she's aware of my feelings toward that particular family.

"And she's too beautiful and likely to cause too much trouble. And her brothers! Well, such ambitious men are not welcome in Denmark. They should both go to England."

It's not quite what I want to hear, but my mother is already speaking again.

"He'll not marry any of these women. He needs a bride

from overseas. Perhaps he should consider King Æthelred's widow. She's proved her fertility, and of course, she's half-Danish by birth. Your father wanted her, you know. I would not have been best pleased if I'd been cast aside for such a young woman."

My mother's suggestion, so flippantly spoken, stumps me. I try not to show the shock I feel as her words flare in my mind, bringing my vision to the fore, but my mother is perceptive.

"What?" she demands to know. "Do you think it's a suggestion worth pursuing?" her forehead wrinkles, as she considers the wisdom of what she's broached only in jest.

"Would it be a good match for Harald? I don't see why it couldn't be, but of course, in the past, Danish kings have chosen wives from the northern lands. Not that Normandy isn't filled with norsemen who think to call themselves by a more civilised name." Her voice ends in derision. The men of Normandy think to distance themselves from their true heritage, with a veneer of civility as they distance themselves from their Raider heritage. It is worth mocking.

"It might be a good suggestion," I waver, keen to distract her from my startled reaction. I reach for, and swig the cold water from my wine goblet, wishing I'd not thought to sit in such an easily overlooked position. I can't creep away from the scrutiny of all those men and women who've brought their daughters to be inspected by the king and his mother. Neither can I deny that my mother's words have unsettled me.

No, I concentrate on holding my goblet upright, on taking small sips, the enjoyment in my mother's criticisms, entirely gone, as my thoughts swirl back to my dream.

Lady Emma. She would perhaps be an ideal choice for my brother, but I also don't believe that's her fate. I've long pitied the woman I've never met. Married to an old man, forced to change her name because she had the same one as his dead wife, lie with him, birth his children, vie with his adult children, only for him to lose his kingdom to my father, only to gain it back, only to die and leave the domain to one of his much older sons from his first marriage, a son, I understand, who had no regard for his step-mother.

I don't know whether Lady Emma remains in England or not. Perhaps she's returned to her homeland of Normandy, taken her sons and daughter with her. I can't imagine that Cnut welcomes any man, or even boy, in England who would have a claim to the crown he's fought so hard to win, and not only once, but twice.

Before me, I watch Harald being as courteous as ever to the group of women but I already know he'll not choose any of them, even Gytha, who simpers before my brother. His smile for her is more because of her familiarity than because he means to marry her. Maybe it should be Lady Emma, he marries. I might broach the subject with him.

Although, would Harald welcome Lady Emma and her half-English children to Denmark? I'm sure he wouldn't wish to upset Cnut, and Cnut would see it as a further provocation. The last few years have been unsettled, but a sense of serenity has prevailed ever since Cnut claimed England for himself, at least in Denmark, if not in England.

Maybe I won't suggest it to Harald, after all. Perhaps, that way, my growing unease will cease. It seems that Lady Emma might be harmful to my family. Perhaps. I've never quite deciphered all of the warnings concerning the women I saw. Gytha I know to be wary of, but Lady Emma? I genuinely don't know.

"I expected Lady Gunnhild to show some sense," my mother has returned to her favoured pastime, of complaining about her second husband's first wife, dismissing my strained face, thankfully. "It doesn't take much intelligence to realise that these matches are all wrong for Harald. He needs a woman who can rule in his absence, as well as birth sons for him. These all look as though they might not know how to dress themselves, let alone anything more taxing. And Gytha will only ever be ruled by her brothers. That alone makes her unsuitable. It's a pity that none of the girls has the upbringing that you enjoyed."

I open my mouth to speak but then snap it shut again, my eyes caught by movement at the rear of the hall.

"I've been waiting for this," I stand, excusing myself, and making my way to the side of the messenger, Osgot's brother, who waits for my brother or me.

The man is tall, almost entirely bald, but trusted with much of the king's highly confidential matters.

"A letter, from England," he offers, and I nod, and reach out to take it, only the man hesitates.

"I'm supposed to hand it to Harald. Cnut was explicit."

"Then you'll have to wait. Harald is busy." I indicate the mass of bodies in the king's hall, and the messenger's face twists in frustration. He stinks and fails to suppress a yawn. I know he'd sooner be bathing and sleeping.

"You'll give him the letter?" he asks, hoping for assurance, and I give it willingly enough, although I have no intention of waiting to read the news from Cnut. I imagine it will be filled with the spectacle of his English coronation, and I'd sooner know its content before Harald so I can be prepared for his complaints of our brother's extravagance.

Harald relies on me more and more. I might have begun to assist him with letters to the archbishop, but now I pen much of his personal correspondence. It's not unusual for me to intercept messages from Cnut, or for me to write back to him. I know what to share and what to keep secret.

But for the sake of the messenger, I snap my response, as though offended. "Of course, I will. I'm his sister. It doesn't serve me to keep anything from King Harald."

"Very well," and I feel the thick parchment being placed into my hand, and immediately, I'm making my way to Harald's chamber, filled with the scribblings of the holy men, the saga of who Harald will marry forgotten about in the blink of an eye.

**"Dearest brother, King Harald of Denmark."** I read the opening line as soon as I unroll the parchment, and force my eyes lower, expecting to pick out the words, coronation, robes, crown, gold and silver, but that's not at all what Cnut has ordered his scribe to commit to the parchment.

I read quickly, almost tripping over the words, and with every one of them, I feel cool sweat forming on my brow, dripping down my back, and I appreciate then why my mother's words upset me so much when she mentioned Lady Emma, the widowed queen of England.

King Harald is not to have Lady Emma as his bride. Far from it. It seems that Cnut has beaten Harald to it. Cnut now has two wives, whereas Harald can't even find one. I can't see that Harald will enjoy this news. And even more, I find Cnut's request, added to the end of the letter, to be shocking. How dare he try and make Harald a party to such a scheme? And what has Cnut done with his first wife, Lady Ælfgifu, and two sons, Swein and Harald?

I think of my mother, and step-mother, locked in their battle to outdo one another, and I consider my father's children and the often-antagonistic relationship we share. Certainly, my older half-sisters disapprove of the trusted bond I share with Harald. What if Cnut has more sons with Lady Emma? What will happen to the two he already has? I can't see that they'll see each other as anything other than opponents. Does Cnut truly mean to drag England into another series of wars, where brothers vie for the same position? At least my father had mostly daughters. There is only so much damage that they can do to one another unless they involve their husbands.

Even more sweat beads down my neck, and beneath my dress. This is it. Here, is so much of what my vision once told me. I only wish I knew what it all meant.

"What is it?" I've not even noticed Harald coming into the room and sinking wearily into his chair, exhaustion making his movements laboured.

"From Cnut," I explain, suddenly aware that I have no way of softening the information I know.

"You should read it," and I place the parchment directly into Harald's hands. I don't wish to form the words. I'm sure Harald will understand as soon as he reads for himself.

I stay beside him, my gaze fixated on the wine goblet set to the side of him. The colour of the glass is warm, filled with the promise of heat, even though it's empty. I would pick it up and drink from it, even without knowing what it contained, it is that alluring. In the reflection of the glass, I see flames dancing, and know it tries to warn me of yet more danger. But I'd be a fool not to understand that, anyway.

Harald's silence alerts me to the fact he's read the letter.

"Does he truly expect me to agree to this?" His voice is filled with disgust, his lips downcast.

"I can't see that he wouldn't have written it if he didn't expect you to." I'm as furious as Harald by the presumption that Cnut takes in thinking he can ship such a problem away from England and expect Harald to deal with it.

"He says the boys and their mother are coming, anyway, and regardless of what I say."

"He does, yes."

"Why does he not murder them himself, if two small children, the only grandchildren of King Æthelred, worry him so much?"

"I don't know."

"Surely, he has enough men in his employ who would take his money, and ask no questions?"

"He must, yes." It's no secret that Cnut has surrounded himself with some men who will do whatever their king demands of them, whether it's morally correct to do so, or not. It seems in the game of kingdoms, there's always someone prepared to dirty their hands, and then to make their absolution to their God.

"So, why involve me in this?"

I shake my head. I have no idea. Of all the things that Cnut could have asked Harald to do for him, this is the most ridiculous, and most dangerous. If it's such a problem, he should control the problem himself, not impose it onto his older brother.

"I won't do it."

"Good."

Harald finally looks at me.

"Then you agree that this shouldn't be done?"

"Absolutely. They're babies. It's not their fault if they happen to be related to King Æthelred, and therefore considered æthelings." The English word is a strange one, but it means that the children are 'throne worthy' whether Cnut likes it or not.

"No one will rally around a baby. No one will want a child for a king, when England has endured so many years of war, and not stumbles to a peace."

"No, I know they won't."

"I'll write to Cnut and tell him that he must not send the children to me."

Only, suddenly I'm not sure I agree with Harald. Is there a chance here to do some good?

"No, no. Have him send the children. If we leave them in England, Cnut will ensure an accident befalls them. Bring the children to Denmark, and that way, we can ensure that they live."

Harald's eyes cloud at my words, as though about to disagree with me, but then he nods. Despite all my desires not to cause any friction between Harald and Cnut, I find that I will, to protect two innocent children, I've never even met. I surprise myself.

"Ask your mother."

"My mother?" I exclaim, surprised by his words.

"Yes. She'll know what to do. I'm sure of it." I'm not convinced that she will, but I'm pleased that Harald thinks to ask her. It shows that he respects her with something so important. It clearly shows how little he trusts his mother.

"I'll do as you say," I assure him, and I think our conversation over and done with, only for Harald to groan.

"Now he has two wives, and I don't even have one." And I chuckle in sympathy.

"I'd just been thinking the same. I'd just been thinking that Lady Emma would have made you an excellent wife."

"Not that it matters now."

"No, it doesn't. But, a wife from beyond Denmark will be better for you. Your mother hasn't provided you with good options."

"No, she hasn't. Not at all. What did your mother say of them?" I consider how truthful to be.

"She said they were too young, too old, and too pointy." I mimic my mother when I speak, and Harald chuckles, the lines bleeding away from his face, as he relaxes.

"She was right." He sighs, peering into the distance, his one hand rubbing his cheeks.

"And of course, Jarl Úlfr's sister is to be avoided at all costs." I'm pleased that Harald acknowledges that truth.

"I really wish I could send my mother to Cnut. I would much sooner he had to endure her than I."

"Then you should do it. Cnut has asked you to do something deeply unpleasant. I suggest you inflict the same on him."

But, we both know that Lady Gunnhild will not leave Denmark, not without a fight, and not without a great deal of unpleasantness. And, as Harald said, it's better to have her where she can be closely watched.

My mother is pensive as I whisper to her of Cnut's new demands later that evening. There's a skald performing for the pleasure of the king, and it's the perfect excuse to speak of matters that need to be kept secret.

But first I listen to the words of Thord Kolbeinsson, wishing they didn't honour my sister, but only her husband. The words are new to me, almost as though Cnut has sent his skald to Roskilde to ensure Harald knows of his great victories in England.

"*The brave warrior, who frequently gave swollen flesh to the raven, marked men with the print of the sword's edge. The bold Eirikr often diminished the host of the English and brought about their death."*

Thord is well skilled, his voice rising and falling, as he utters the words with just the right amount of emphasis, holding the attention of everyone within that room. Well, apart from my mother and I. We whisper beneath the skald's voice as he arrests the attention of everyone, even Harald.

"We'll send them to my son, King Olof, in the land of the Svear," she announces firmly. "I'll take them to him personally, and explain what needs to happen."

Her response surprises me, and she places a hand on my forearm.

"I've not seen my son for many years. I feel it's time to meet my grandchildren."

"Then I'll come with you," I offer, but she shakes her head.

"No, it'll be better for you and Harald if you're ignorant of all the details. That way, Cnut can never blame you for not entirely doing as he asks. I will travel, with a small entourage, to visit my son. If King Edmund of England's exiled wife and their two young children are part of that entourage, I'll be better able to explain it, or even, mask their true identities."

"What will King Olof do with them?"

It feels strange to speak of the half-brother I've never met. I have little idea of his personality, our painfully stilted letters shared, no more than once or twice a year, offering no indication of his true feelings. He doesn't even write them himself. And neither does Emund, my other half-brother, who assists Olof in ruling the disjointed kingdom of the Svear.

"I'll ask him to keep them safe, perhaps to gift them one of my properties. He'll not allow them to come to any harm." My mother's belief in her son is both reassuring and worrying. After all, she's not seen him since he first became king on the death of her first husband. That's nearly two decades ago now.

"Don't worry. Olof is a good man. An ambitious man, yes, but also inherently wise, as his father was. He'll not allow the woman and her children to come to any harm. And in my absence, you must support Harald, and take my place in defying Lady Gunnhild. The woman is really quite devious. She's even profited from those families who put forward a prospective bride for Harald. He's right not to choose any of them."

The knowledge should infuriate me, but nothing Lady Gunnhild does is overly surprising.

"Perhaps you could find Harald a wife in the land of the Svear," I offer, ending on a long sigh of sufferance. I'm unsure why Harald's marriage is such a problem to arrange, but it is.

"Potentially, but my prime focus will be on King Edmund's children and widow, and of course, on meeting my grandchildren."

"You have my thanks," I offer, taking her hand and squeezing gently, and she grunts softly, implying it's nothing. Still, I know she's taking a considerable risk, not only in leaving Denmark but in relying on her son, who must be almost a stranger to her after all this time.

"I'm pleased that Harald refuses to do as Cnut demands, even if a deception must be carried out. He's an honourable man, more admirable than his father. King Swein could carry a grudge, and it made him do despicable things." My mother's words speak of events I know nothing about, and yet what I do know of my father far from casts him as a hero of old. But I understand that my mother means to keep such from me. I appreciate her protectiveness, even if I'm old enough to know the truth. Perhaps there are some things that a daughter should never know about her father.

Yet, the arrival of the two father-less children and their mother is not quite the secret it should be. I think the deception has been kept, watching as my mother and her wards prepare to set sail for the land of the Svear.

The weather is glorious, the rippling expanse of sea that lies open between Roskilde and Skåne, gentle, but I groan as Lady Gunnhild makes her way to the quayside at Roskilde. I hope she comes to gloat, thinking that her petty ways have driven my mother away, but her eyes are keen.

"My Lady," I dip a curtsey, keen to draw her attention away from the men and women on the ship, and the presence of two such young children amongst them.

"Lady Estrid," her tone is brittle. "Why has your mother decided to leave, now of all times?" I would have thought she'd be pleased to see Lady Sigrid departing. It just shows how little I know.

"She's visiting her sons and grandchildren, in the land of the Svear," I state, still trying to stop Lady Gunnhild from seeing everything happening on the ship, by standing in front of her, making it look as natural as possible. Not that it's easy to do, not with a vessel of such size. I also don't think I'm succeeding, not as I notice Frida's shaking head. I wish she'd assist me, but Frida and Lady Gunnhild are firm enemies.

"She travels without her women?" Lady Gunnhild tries to see around me, and Frida smirks.

"No, but she's only taking a small entourage. After all, her son is king in the land of the Svear, and there's no need for her to take much with her. She has great wealth there, and will be honoured."

The reminder of who Olof is settles an unflattering line on Lady Gunnhild's exposed forehead. In the harsh summer sun, she seems aged beyond her years. It appears as though the shadows and candlelight of the king's hall, flatter her too much. I only hope that Cnut hasn't contacted his mother directly with his terrible commands. She'd be sure to enforce his instructions, no matter how unpalatable they were.

"I don't recognise everyone on board. They're not all members of her inner circle."

"No, no. I believe she's been prevailed upon to escort a noblewoman to her new husband in Skåne along the way. I don't know them all either." I shrug, as though it's nothing of importance.

It's a perfectly reasonable excuse, and yet Lady Gunnhild

opens her mouth to argue with me. Or at least she would, but King Harald abruptly arrives, and she bites back her question, at the sight of her son and all his kingly splendour.

"Is everything ready?" Harald calls to me. It seems he knows of his mother's interest, for all he doesn't directly look at her. "I have a small gift for the king of the Svear. After all, he is my brother, in a way." At least Harald has a better explanation for his presence than I do for the strangers amongst the others.

"Why would you send a gift?" And just like that, Lady Gunnhild is entirely distracted, and as she rounds on Harald, her back to the ship and the slim woman with her two children, I offer him a smile of thanks. He raises an eyebrow, as he threads his arm through his mother's, keen to draw her away. I can hear him murmuring to her, no doubt asking that they discuss it elsewhere.

For all the honour shown to her, Lady Gunnhild seems reluctant to walk away, and I wish the ship-men would hurry to disembark. The fewer questions, the better.

"King Harald is becoming devious," my mother's voice is filled with respect, as she appears behind me.

"Sometimes, there's no choice," I feel my lips turn down with the admission.

"Come, embrace me, and then we'll be gone. The children are beautiful. It would be a travesty to have them murdered, just because of who their father was. Their mother has already been widowed twice. I can't even imagine it, not at such a young age."

I didn't expect my mother to feel any sympathy for King Edmund of England's wife, but she can always surprise me.

"I will see you soon," my mother advises me, but before she turns to board the ship, waiting for her, she offers me one more sentence of advice.

"Be wary of Lady Gunnhild. She'll stir the pot when I'm absent, and some will listen too keenly because they're jealous of your growing influence with your brother."

There's no need for my mother to say more. I know those

who mean me ill, and what I'm learning is that it's not those who are blatant in their hatred that's the problem, but rather those who mask it behind their court façade.

As Lady Sigrid settles onto the ship, a heavy wooden casket is passed across, and I'm startled that it takes three men to carry it. My mother might be sure of her son's reaction to his involvement in this scheme, but it seems Harald is taking no chances.

That pleases me. Harald is quickly learning that the bonds of family might not always be enough. After all, allies can be chosen, but family can't.

"Lady Estrid," I eye Lady Gunnhild with trepidation. My mother was correct. My father's first wife has been no ally to me in her absence, none at all. And not only that, but she's grown close to Gytha Úlfrsdottir, sister of Jarl Úlfr. The simpering bitch might not have been chosen as Harald's wife, but that doesn't mean she doesn't press her claim in the absence of her two brothers. Úlfr has grown weary with Harald, and taken himself to England as well. It seems there are riches to be claimed at Cnut's court for just the right sort of man.

"Lady Gunnhild," I infuse my voice with the warmth of a glacier, taking some delight in watching her shiver even at just those two words.

"King Harald wishes to speak with you." My heart sinks at those words, but I don't allow my unease to show on my face. I should perhaps have guessed that my brother's recent distance was something to do with his bloody mother, and not because I'd offended him.

"Then I'll go to him," I assure her, only I catch sight of Gytha Úlfrsdottir just behind Lady Gunnhild, and I don't appreciate the smirk of triumph on her face. Not at all. I wish she'd gone to England.

I note, with disdain, the trinkets that she wears around her neck, and wrists, almost in imitation of Lady Gunnhild. For a moment, I consider where her mother is. She should be here, keeping a judicious eye on her daughter. Perhaps she's dead. I truly don't know, and I refuse to find out. I don't want anyone to think that I perceive Gytha as a threat, even though I believe she might be one, come to haunt me from my vision.

"My Lord King, brother," I bob a curtsey to Harald even though he doesn't lift his eyes from the parchments before him. The scratchings of quills over vellum normally soothes me, but not today, and not when I see that Harald has a letter from Cnut before him.

My heart sinks. What damage has Lady Gunnhild done to me now? Relations between the two brothers have grown cordial, no doubt because Cnut believes himself in debt to Harald for removing the problem of King Edmund's children.

"Ah, sister, come, sit, we need to talk."

I perch on the edge of the chair he offers me, almost gripping the handsome arms, carved into the image of a wolf on one side, and a raven on the other. I don't like this, not at all.

Harald finally looks at me, and I'm surprised to find myself looking at a man, not a youth. I'm unsure when this change came over him. Perhaps recently, or maybe not. I see him each and every day. It's not often that I truly see him, though.

I'm startled to find the green eyes from my vision looking at me, and a tremble of foreboding shimmies up my legs.

"Sister, you look well," Harald begins, a smile on his lips, his moustache dropping over them, and I think he'll continue the farce. But he doesn't.

"King Cnut of England," the formality only adds to my apprehension, "has arranged a fine marriage for you."

"King Cnut?"

I want to mock him, but I find it impossible to offer more than that, my jaw locked tightly together. No wonder Lady Gunnhild and Gytha Úlfrsdottir looked so pleased with themselves. I imagine that if Cnut has arranged my marriage, then it must be to an Englishman. Rage begins to burn inside me. Denmark is my home. I don't wish to leave it. Not again.

Harald clears his throat, his bright eyes seeming to beg me

for clemency from my fury.

"Yes, King Cnut," Harald confirms, and I almost think to forgive him, until he speaks again. "But I agree it's a fitting marriage for you. I can't make you a queen, but this marriage will make you a duchess."

"Duchess? There's no position of duke or duchess in England," I feel my forehead furrow, while Harald shakes his head.

"No, you're right, there is no position of duke or duchess in England," but suddenly I understand, and I'm on my feet, my hands on the wooden desk before me, before I even realise that I'm standing.

"How could you?" I hiss, my voice sounding as though it belongs to a tempest, and not to me at all.

"Sister," Harald cautions, his eyes suddenly wild, but I'm shaking my head.

"How bloody could you? All these things I do for you? How could you just forget it all? Who will assist you with all this?" and my hand sweeps the parchments before me, the pile of documents just waiting for my attention on my desk.

But I don't allow Harald time to answer.

"I know who's to blame. Your mother has always hated me. It didn't take her long to make her move when my mother travelled to the land of the Svear. I'll never forgive you for this, never." And with that, I storm from the room, heart pounding in time to the stomp of my boots over the wooden floorboards.

How could he? How could Harald do this to me?

I will never absolve him of this.

# DUCHESS

# CHAPTER 6

*Normandy AD1017*

T he eyes that greet mine are as cold as I feel.

"My Lord Richard," I curtsey deeply, despite the gust of frigid air that finds its way beneath my many skirts.

"My Lady Estrid," his voice is rimmed with the self-same ice, and I already know this marriage will not work. It was a foolish idea, and I'll tell Cnut that, when I see him once more, which I doubt will be long in the future. Not if I have my way.

Cnut sent his missive to Harald, his demand for what should become of me, and I curse Harald for agreeing to it. I thought I meant more to him than that, but evidently not.

My mother was right to warn me against those who were jealous of my close relationship with my brother. I'm sure it's their fault that Harald agreed to this ridiculous marriage alliance so quickly. We've not parted on good terms. I blame Harald. I'll not forgive him quickly. And I also blame his mother and my other sisters. They had no sympathy for me. After all, they said, almost mirroring one another's words, they have married for the good of our noble family, so I must do the same.

"Welcome to Normandy," Lord Richard's voice sparks, and I can see the grief that has lined his face and made him old before his time. He'll never be happy again, and this is an entirely political marriage.

As though to prove the point, my new husband is surrounded by a range of children who all look identical to him. The older boys stand proudly, eyeing me with the scrutiny and arrogance of youth. The oldest boy is not much younger than I am. It will cause problems if we marry, I already sense that.

The youngest child, a small girl perhaps no older than three or four, stands, red-eyed and weeping. It seems that she misses her mother. I would embrace her and reassure her that everything will be alright, but that's not my role here. Far from it.

Duke Richard wants the protection that this alliance affords him, from both Denmark and England. My two brothers wish to a more magnificent union than the one I had with my first husband. The land of the Rus seems a long way away, now that the focus is once more on England. My father's death, almost as soon as he won England, forced Cnut once more to war, and only now does he hold England again, as her king, and he has a new wife as well, so I must have a new husband. Such logic defies me, but it seems that my brothers believe it makes perfect sense. How I detest them both.

"I'm honoured to be here," I know the words expected of me, even if my heart is as chill as the wind.

"Come, we'll get inside," and Duke Richard marches to my side, offers me his arm, and I have no choice but to allow him to escort me, even though I suspect my reception will be colder than the journey here. Why I consider, my brother could not wait for the better weather, I have no idea? Why he couldn't wait for the woman I'm replacing to have had time to grow more than cold and rigid in her grave, I am also unsure? This is a hasty move, and it'll not bring any of those involved the outcome that they desire.

I walk the path, watching where I place my feet, the ground both hard from a frost, and flowing with water, where the selfsame frost melts under the hazy gaze of the sun.

I shiver, despite my best intentions not to, and the fact that Duke Richard, with his hold on me, doesn't even notice, tells me all I need to know about his preoccupations.

Behind me, those of my party I've been allowed to bring, trail back to the ship. They have wooden caskets and rolls of cloth to bring to my new home. I'm also envious that they're allowed to linger.

Not that I'm alone, but my brother's man, sent to ensure all is done as it should be, is no firm ally of mine, not yet. Siward, who was once merely a messenger to a king, knows his future ambitions rest on ensuring this alliance works. Equally, he realises that he's now permanently associated with a marriage that will not last the length of the coming winter.

I would feel sorry for him, but he tests my patience with his desire to please Cnut, and not me.

I take comfort from knowing that I at least have Frida for company. She could have stayed in Denmark. I'm conscious of her sacrifice.

I feel the curious eyes of those who've spilt from the settlement to view their duke's new wife. I walk with my chin high, my stance firm. I know how to look the part of a nobleman's wife.

I think of Harald, back in Denmark, and his determination that Cnut should have no part in ruling there. I consider Cnut, in England, with the trail of spilt blood that must follow him everywhere. He's taken missteps and countenanced deeds to ensure his position as King of England, many of them far outside the bounds of acceptable violence, even in a society in which men and women must always be armed. Perhaps, I'm better in Normandy, after all. I wish Harald luck with his mother and step-mother. He's welcome to their bickering and petty arguments.

I'm escorted into Duke Richard's hall, my eyes trying to take in as many details as possible. It seems that Duke Richard is a wealthy man, and not just in terms of children. And certainly, there are many waiting inside that hall to catch sight of me.

Here, Cnut has been particular in what I must do. He wants me to seek out the children of his second wife's first marriage.

He wants me to determine if they're a threat to his kingship in England, or if, unlike King Æthelred's children from his first marriage, they're content to accept the change in their circumstances and future. I try not to consider Cnut's intentions towards Æthelred's young grandchildren. My mother assures me they're well hidden in the land of the Svear, and that my half-brother is happy to have such an advantage over Cnut.

I would say that King Æthelred's younger children are too young to have such concerns about their future and England, but I know better. The children of kings and queens are only too aware of the positions they expect to inherit, in good time.

I scour the audience, even though the vast majority have their heads bowed, while I'm escorted to the front of the sturdy wooden hall, a flourish in Duke Richard's steps. It seems he's prepared to make much of this marriage, in public, if not in private. He hasn't spoken to me on the walk from the quayside. Not that I've spoken to him either.

Yet, amongst that vast audience, there are only a few that show me no respect, and I know that they must be Lady Emma's older children, Edward and Alfred, and of course, Godgifu, their sister. Once more, I realise that I am not alone in having two brothers who are responsible for my future.

There's an arrogance to the stance of Edward and Alfred, that assures me of their identity. The richness of their clothing further highlights that these young men, for that is what they are, know only too well who they are, who I am, and what my being here no doubt means for them.

I've not met my brother's second wife, or in fact, his first. Even in that glance, I try and determine Lady Emma's appearance. Both boys are pleasant on the eye if lacking the full height and weight of full-grown men. Whether they retain their fair features or not, will remain to be seen. Few grown men enjoy such light hair, unless they come from the far, far north, where the sun rarely sets during the summer season.

I incline my head to them, acknowledging their part in the

farce that is to come. None of us is where we want to be, and only one of us will be able to make the best of the next few weeks and months. I'm hardly inclined to try at all.

Godgifu looks at me from beneath thick eyelashes, and I want to harden my heart against her, fearful that my sympathy for her, will surface. I find it easy to detest Gytha, the sister of Jarl Úlfr and Eilifr. But there is none of her guile on Godgifu's face. I will have to watch myself around her.

"Rise," Duke Richard's voice cracks through the almost silent hall, and the moment is gone, Edward, Alfred and Godgifu, disappearing amongst the sea of other faces, all eyeing me with anything from contempt to mild interest.

I've stepped into a morass of ingrained conflicts. There will be men and women here who were close to the previous duchess. Their position will have faltered with her death, and now they'll look to see if I can offer them anything, or if they must tie themselves to the duke's sons and daughters.

"I present Lady Estrid of the House of Gorm, sister to King Harald of Denmark, and King Cnut of England. She'll be my new duchess." I'm unsure why Duke Richard feels the need to say as much. Surely, it's all been arranged, through both of my brothers, and Cnut's new wife? Only, as I glance at Duke Richard do I consider that he's as much against our union as I am. Perhaps this marriage will be even shorter than I dare hope.

*"Dearest brother, Cnut, King of England."* I know I'm too angry to write to my brother, and yet I determine to do so, all the same. I simply can't keep my fury contained.

*"I have been in Normandy for two weeks now, after a terrible voyage in which I was battered and bruised by the rough seas. As I remain unmarried, I can see no reason for the great rush. Surely, I could have remained in Roskilde until the season changed. Tell me, brother, why I've been put to such inconvenience. This situation displeases me. I am your sister, not a prized mare to be bartered to the highest bidder, whether he wants me or not."*

*"Your man, Siward, is unable to make any headway with Duke*

Richard either. How long am I to remain here, humiliated by the duke? Write to me immediately, or I will return to Roskilde, regardless of any treaty you might, or might not, hold with the duke."

"Your infuriated sister, Lady Estrid, daughter of King Swein of Denmark."

Only, the words don't banish my fury.

**"Dearest brother, Harald, King of Denmark."**

"Tell me, brother, why have you cast me aside? I believed I was your ally, your friend, your assistant in ruling Denmark. Why allow me such freedoms, and influence, if you were only to snatch it from me without so much as a thought for my opinions on the matter? Was it your mother? Did she make you send me to Normandy? I am yet to be married; you should know this. Two weeks in this place, and I've done little more than share one conversation with Duke Richard. I warn you; I'll not tolerate this situation for long. I will return to Roskilde, or perhaps I will go to Cnut, demand answers from him."

"Your much-aggrieved sister, Lady Estrid, daughter of King Swein of Denmark."

But I know I'll get no satisfaction from my brothers.
**"Dearest Mother, Lady Sigrid."**

"You were correct to warn me of the intentions of Lady Gunnhild. I've been sent to Normandy, to marry the brother of Lady Emma. I have warned both Harald and Cnut that it will not end well, but they've not listened to me."

"I could have done with your support on this, but appreciate that for you, remaining with King Olof was a far more pleasant prospect than returning to Denmark. I am bereft. I thought Harald my ally, but it seems not. I thought he didn't fear Cnut any longer, but in that, it seems I was also wrong."

"I don't foresee this marriage ever taking place. Duke Richard, with his shield-wall worth of children with his dead wife, is not my idea of a suitable husband. Lady Mother, I don't understand how you could endure such a position with King Swein, my father."

*"Write to me with news of the land of the Svear. I'm all but abandoned in Normandy."*

*"Your loving daughter, Lady Estrid Sweinsdottir."*

"My Lady?" I turn, unsurprised to see Edward, Alfred and Godgifu seeking me out. I'm walking in the grounds of the Duke's Hall. I've been in Normandy for too many weeks now, and I'm still far from married. Neither have I had any response from my three letters.

Perversely, I find I don't mind the slight anymore. Others might look at me with sympathy in their eyes, but I don't need it. I don't want to be a duchess. I have far loftier ambitions. I'm far angrier with my brothers for ignoring my letters than for the fact I remain unmarried. I will forgive my mother. It is not the weather for anyone to be travelling to the land of the Svear.

"Nephews, niece," I make the claim based on my brother's marriage to their mother, but all the same, they startle, and I feel forced to clarify. "I am not my brother."

This doesn't settle them, as I hoped, and yet they don't walk away from me either. From the looks that pass between the three of them, I believe this chance meeting has been planned.

There's a small bench that we could sit on, but it's too cold to linger, the bite of winter showing in the thin layers of ice that coat the water butts. I imagine our conversation will be quick, if held in secrecy.

It's Edward who speaks, the older of the three. I've heard rumours that he refuses to train with sword and shield and that even his Uncle thinks he'll not amount to a great deal. For all that, I've been watching him and listening carefully for any insight into his ambitions. I feel everyone is too harsh on both of the boys because that's all they are. There are kinder words for Godgifu, but then, she's only just becoming a woman, and she offers someone the prospect of a good marriage, if not the wealth to go with it.

The last few years of their lives can't have been easy for

them. Forced to flee to Normandy when my father won England for himself, only to return when their father reclaimed his kingdom. Then they were no doubt overlooked when their older half-brother Edmund was declared king, before being forced to flee again, when Cnut was named as king after Edmund's untimely death.

They must feel as though nothing is as they expected it to be when they were the honoured children of England's king. And of course, they've been abandoned by their mother. She's sent them to Normandy, to her brother, while she marries the very man who stands between her son and his kingdom.

"I wished to speak to you about your brother's intentions towards us. It's perhaps not court etiquette to waylay you in the garden like this, but all the same, you're the most likely to know."

Edward's lips quiver as he speaks and my sympathy ignites once more. I wouldn't like to have Cnut as an adversary. The fact that at the moment, I wouldn't want to have him as a friend either, is beside the point.

"I've not seen King Cnut since he left Denmark to seek his fortune in Norway before claiming England. I can offer you no insight into what he might want to do. Don't you hear from your Lady Mother?" It's Alfred's reaction that's the most telling, a look of swift fury covering his face, where the outline of a first beard settles both above and below his thin lips.

It seems that the sons are not allies of their mother's, or rather, that she's not their ally. I daren't even glance at Godgifu. What would I have done if my mother had abandoned me in such a way? Bad enough that Lady Sigrid went to the land of the Svear, what would I have done if she'd been almost entirely absent from my life?

"Our Lady Mother is busy with her new husband, and with governing her old kingdom." The stiffness of the words assures me that this is how the two young men, and woman, are forced to explain their mother's indifference toward them to any who asks. That they make no excuses for her doesn't surprise me.

"My brother is too busy as well to send me so much as a letter expressing his support for my intended marriage." And here, I note the shifting look that passes between the two boys and their sister and realise they know more than I do, even if Duke Richard seems unsure what to do with his niece and nephews. I don't ask further, I have all the confirmation that I need.

"What does your Uncle tell you, of events in England?"

"My Uncle is much concerned with Normandy."

Ah, so he shows no interest in England either. Does Duke Richard mean to support his nephews for the rest of their lives or is he merely waiting for a more opportune time to try and settle England's rule on one of his nephew's heads? I think it might be easier for the duke to do the former.

"Then it seems that we're all as uninformed as the other."

"Perhaps," Edward states, a thoughtful look forming in his bright eyes. The snap of the wind and the buckle of my cloak flies free, and I'm left reaching for the delinquent fabric, hoping to hold it tight against my body.

Alfred immediately rushes to catch my errant broach, while Edward steps closer, gripping the cloth and holding it tightly around my body. I appreciate the action, and even more when Edward speaks into my ear, our heights so similar, I realise then that he must still have some growing to do.

"There'll be no marriage. My Uncle has been offered another, and he's petulant and wishes to sever his ties to the House of Gorm. He doesn't wish to be dictated to by his sister."

With that, Alfred hands me my broach, and with shaking hands, I thread it through the thickness of the cloak, taking my time, keen to ensure against a repeat occurrence.

"My thanks," I offer, stepping away from the small huddle, a sudden worry that we might be observed, dismissed as soon as I've had it. What does it matter if Duke Richard sees me with his nephews and niece?

"I'll speak with my brother on your behalf when I next see

him. Which I imagine will be quite soon." Edward nods, his gaze holding mine for just a moment too long. Then I turn aside. I'm keen to leave Normandy as soon as possible. It seems I need to force the matter with my erstwhile intended husband.

"When will we marry?" I infuse my voice with the tone my mother has always used when she's determined to receive a response to her question, whether she likes it or not. Lady Sigrid is much better at it than Lady Gunnhild. I know that infuriates my father's first wife.

Duke Richard sits within a smaller room than his great hall, a small brazier warming the space. He's settled behind a solid-looking desk, a tidy pile of parchments, either awaiting his attention or already dealt with, pushed to one side. I've not been accorded admittance into the room before.

Although there's a wooden chair that I could perch within, I stay standing. The wind, so gentle in the garden moments ago, has risen to a fine howl, and I know there'll be a storm. I only hope it doesn't bring snow.

Duke Richard eyes me carefully, holding his head almost too straight. His hands grip a golden goblet, filled, I can smell, with warmed wine, and perhaps something else. His eyes are not as sharp as they should be, and I realise he's half on his way to being very drunk even at this time of the morning.

I refuse to break his gaze. I'll force him to this conversation because one of us must have the wherewithal to do so. Our situation is untenable.

"It's too soon for me to remarry. I still mourn my wife. She's barely been dead for six months."

"Then, that is what you should have told my brothers. I'm not going to wait for you to feel 'ready' to marry again. You can't take my brothers' coin, and spend it when you have no intention of marrying me."

He lurches to his feet, his eyes flickering uneasily from one side of the room to the other, although there's only the two of us in there.

"Who has told you that?" He begins to pace, a few steps one way and then a few the other, behind his desk. There's almost no room at all, and he looks ridiculous, his balance failing with every other step, forcing him to grip the back of his chair, and his desk, and even the wall.

"It's an open secret that you've received the offer of another marriage, more to your liking," I retort, hoping that no one has observed my meeting with his niece and nephews. I wouldn't want to imperil their future with their uncle.

"Don't be preposterous. I've made my pledge to your brothers, and my sister, that we'll marry."

"Then, we must marry, immediately, or I'll return to Denmark, or perhaps England. I would be intrigued to meet your sister."

"No. You'll not leave Normandy. We'll wed, in good time, and when I'm ready."

"No, I won't. Formally renounce your pledge before I do it for you."

With no further words, I stalk from his room, and into the main hall, the heat of the enormous hearth fire, causing sweat to break out on my brow. Hastily, I fumble with my cloak, but of course, I've now ensured that it's so tightly in place, that it refuses to come away as easily as it should.

Frida is suddenly beside me, her capable hands making quick work of the broach and taking the weight of it.

"What is it?" she whispers, her lips barely moving, as she faces me so that no one can see what we say to one another.

"He doesn't mean to marry me, as I suspected. We must make arrangements to leave here?"

Frida looks shocked at my announcement.

"Those are rumours, to be ignored."

"No, they're not. I've seen the truth, written in the parchments on his desk. It appears that Duke Richard is already contracted to another, and has the permission of his bishops and nobility to cast me aside. I'll not stay here."

From shock to ready acceptance, Frida nods, absorbing the news as though I told her little more than it was raining outside.

"Then we'll leave here, as you say. Your ship is still here. I'll have the men summoned, and we'll return to Denmark."

But I shake my head.

"No, I wish to go to England. I need to speak to my brother."

"As you wish," and I can see that Frida is already trying to calculate what I suspect, but she's too adept at keeping her own counsel to ask me outright.

"Arrange it for as soon as possible. Our departure might well be prevented. The men may be required to fight. Inform Siward."

"They'll do what needs to be done," Frida assures me, and only then do I step aside from her, walk to the dais and take my place there, where all eyes can watch me. Let them see that I would have made a fine duchess for them. Let them see that I'm not at all concerned at being spurned, as I have been. I knew this marriage would never work, and now I'm going to tell Cnut that, to his face, just as, a few years ago, I told my father, only this time I'm not going to be ignored.

# CHAPTER 7

## Winchester, England
### AD1017

"**W**hat are you doing here?" my brother's greeting is as welcoming as the deep cold that seems to have penetrated my very core. No matter what I've done on this journey, I've been unable to entice any warmth into my body. We escaped under a crisp sky, the moon showing the way, but that only made the crossing almost too cold to stand.

"Duke Richard has played you for a fool," I hiss, my pent-up rage and fury, finally spilling from me so that I find my patience evaporated. "He's contracted to another, and always was."

I enjoy the satisfaction of watching my brother absorb the information, his handsome face seeming to waver before me from one of fury directed at me to one of outrage at his perfidious brother by marriage. I barely have time to even focus on my brother, and his rich clothes, the mass of gold and silver jewellery he wears around his neck, along his arm and most prominently, on his long fingers.

"Who?"

"Poppa of Envermeu. No doubt her father is more palatable as an ally than his sister's husband and brother." I pitch my voice so that I speak with contempt. The failure of the marriage is far more agreeable for me than its success, and yet that doesn't matter. Not where politics and protocol are concerned.

"Damn the man," I can see that Cnut is incensed and yet he doesn't doubt my words, and that's both reassuring and infuriating.

"You suspected?" I demand to know, pulling at my gloves, pleased that Frida is there to assist me, somehow always warm, despite the cold weather. I've not even taken my cloak from my shoulders, and the cool night air seems to steam from me in the heat from the fire.

Outside, the puddles on the road are frozen, and icicles hang menacingly from the eaves of houses. It's almost as cold as Denmark, perhaps even as cold as traders insist it is to the far, far north. Iceland perches there, as a welcome beacon on the vast expanse of the rolling waves for those who hunt whales, seals, and even the less dangerous, cod.

Cnut nods, just once, a firm movement.

"Lady Emma made some comments. I thought it might be done in a fit of pique."

"Well, thank you for warning me." My cloak is finally free, and I turn my hands and face toward the fire. The heat is overwhelming, and still, I shiver.

"Warm wine," Cnut barks the instruction and almost immediately, a wooden beaker is placed in my hands, not an elaborate goblet of gold or silver, but just smooth clay; easier for me to cup in my hands that are a shade somewhere between blue and white.

I don't even sip. Not yet. That pleasure will come later.

The hall is strangely quiet, and I feel my forehead wrinkle. Where is everyone? Has my brother been betrayed? But no, I've heard nothing of dissent against my brother. For the time being, the English seem to accept him as their king. Not that the beginning of his kingship has been accomplished without bloodshed. I will not ask him about the men I suspect he's had some hand in murdering because of their divided loyalties.

"The weather has been bitter," Cnut states, as though that

explains everything, even though it doesn't.

Behind us, the door to the hall opens and then closes, a great gust making the merry flames in the hearth dance, enticing them to rise ever higher. I don't turn my gaze from my brother.

"What now?" I demand, but he shakes his head, and then a chair is behind me, and I settle in to it, a rich fur across my knees, and another around my shoulders. Cnut stays standing, as two of his servants' fuss around me.

"How did you even get here?" he demands to know, the thought suddenly occurring to him.

"My ship never left Normandy."

"And where is Siward?"

"At Sandwich. The crossing was rough, but I was determined to reach you before anyone else could. I would have sent a letter, but you seem unable to reply to one." My brother ignores the second part of my tirade.

"At least you didn't leave Siward in Normandy."

"I toyed with the idea but thought it unfairly cruel. After all, it wasn't his fault he was placed in such a position."

"Then I'll have the pleasure of speaking with him at some point in the future."

"Yes, you will. But what of Normandy?"

"I'm powerless to act against Duke Richard with any military might at this time. I'll employ more subtle means."

My eyes narrow at his words. I've had time to examine him. The strains of ruling seem to rest lightly on him, and yet there's something that I'm not used to seeing in him. I wouldn't call it hesitation. Perhaps it's wisdom, although I waver to make such a decision when I've only just arrived.

"You'll leave Edward, Alfred and Godgifu alone?" My voice is icier than the outside air when I speak.

"What do you know of them?" His reply is a bark of unease, as he meets my eyes with his own.

"I know that their mother has abandoned them, and their Uncle is indifferent, for the time being. The girl, of course, will make someone an excellent wife, in time."

"So, he has no plans to support them in reclaiming England for themselves?" Cnut is too eager for the answer.

"I hardly know that man's mind. He's shadowed with grief and must care for his brood of children. But, I sense no harm in Edward, Alfred or Godgifu, even if they are sensitive to their royal status."

"Ah, so you would plead for me to look the other way, pretend as though they don't exist and pose a threat to me?"

"I would suggest that if you give any credence to the fact that they threaten you, that they'll do just that. Ignoring them gives them no power, and will allow them to live their lives, unmolested by your agents." I don't mention the children of King Edmund. I imagine that Cnut has no idea that I even know of his request to Harald to have them quietly killed. I'm forced to be grateful to Harald, even though I'm furious with him for acquiescing to Cnut's demands that I travel to Normandy.

"Hah," my brother chuckles at my words, but the arch of his eyebrow, as he turns to gaze at me, forces me to believe that he appreciates my words.

"When did you become so wise?" he asks, his voice rich with teasing, and I would like nothing better than to wipe that smirk from his face. But I don't. I find it strangely relaxing to spar with him. All the angry words I wanted to fling at him, but now I'm just pleased that he does not doubt my word.

"My mother has taught me well."

"And how is your Lady Mother?" The question is not without challenge.

"She remains in the land of the Svear, with her sons, King Olof and Lord Emund."

The news seems to shock Cnut. It's about time he realised that my mother is a woman of considerable influence.

"Your mother is as difficult as ever." What I want to say is that I blame her for my journey to Normandy, just as much as Harald and Cnut, but somehow, I keep those words to myself, and Cnut lets the moment pass without further comment.

"And how was my brother when you last saw him?"

"As unexciting as ever," I eventually settle on, unsure how to respond. I won't cast aspersions on Harald's kingship, even if I'm still furious with him. I eagerly take a bowl of pottage from a bowing servant. The food smells far from terrible, and I eagerly spoon the warmth into my mouth.

"I would wish him ill, but at least we both now have our birthright." With that, Cnut finally settles beside the hearth. He doesn't speak to me, but instead gazes into the flames, as though seeking answers there.

While I eat, I study him. When I last saw him, he and Harald argued so fiercely that Cnut was forced to leave Denmark with his ship-men, and no means of supporting them. I know that they found and forged a settlement in Norway. I also know that he left his pregnant wife behind, in Gainsborough. But, I don't expect to see Lady Ælfgifu and her sons here. My brother has, like my father before him, found a second wife, while his first one still lives. That sits ill with me, as it did when I understood what my father had done.

I've never met my nephews. I should like to. Not that Lady Ælfgifu ever responded to my letter to her. I can only hope that it was received. I'll probably never meet her to find out, and I don't want to ask Cnut. He would accuse me of meddling.

And then a shape materialises before me, and I look upwards and realise, even in the shadows and flickering flames, that Edward, Alfred and Godgifu don't take after their mother after all.

Yet, I examine her all the same. Her features are sharp, no sense of softness to her, her eyes piercing, even in the dim lighting. I expected my brother to have a beautiful wife, but she is not, to my eyes at least, a beauty. Striking, yes, with her long blond hair, and rich adornings, I can see where Cnut gets the fashion from, but not a woman to arouse a man to desire.

"Cnut?" the voice is stringent, a demand, and I notice the curve of her belly and realise that she's already ensuring her position as the mother of the Danish king's heir. Cnut must find her in some small way appealing to have accomplished such a task. Was the child in her belly one of the bowed heads of my vision? I wish I knew, I truly did. It would help me understand what to do now.

"Emma?" Cnut only slowly rouses from his introspection. "Ah, Emma, yes, I would introduce you to Lady Estrid."

Her gaze cuts deeper than any blade, and her lips immediately purse as she recognises the name.

"What are you doing here?" It's hardly a welcome between sisters.

"I've escaped from your brother's court. He had no intention of marrying me. It seems he was already contracted to marry another." I voice the words in an echo of her tone. I need her to know that while she might be my brother's wife, I'm his sister.

"No, that's not right. My brother will abide by his oaths. Return to Normandy, seal the marriage." She might as well just add, 'you're not welcome here,' to her complaints.

"No, no, my sister will not beg a man to marry her. She's far more valuable than that. Your brother has made it clear that he doesn't wish to pursue a further alliance between my family and his own."

Lady Emma dresses in a loose-fitting dress, and yet it's easy to see how fine the fabric is, draped over her growing pregnancy. It's as though it's alive, as it slithers over her. I know her age, but if I didn't, I would think her younger. Certainly, she's young to have children as old as Edward, Alfred and Godgifu.

For all that, her face is tight with rage, and it makes her unappealing, even as she rubs her hand over her belly, as though to ensure Cnut realises she's to be the mother of his child.

"Return to Normandy," Lady Emma continues, her tone almost wheedling. "I'll send word with you, one of my loyal retainers will escort you. My brother will soon appreciate that he erred, and the marriage will take place and be consummated." As she speaks, Lady Emma runs her left hand over Cnut's back, as though to soothe a babe and once more, I consider just what has happened to my brother. I hope he's not about to be made a fool of by his new wife.

"My sister will do no such thing," Cnut's voice is firm, for all he reaches out and holds Emma's hand still over the bulge of her belly. "It will be necessary to find a different husband for Estrid, someone who appreciates the honour, as opposed to someone who either fears it or simply dismisses it as unimportant." Emma's eyes flash with vehemence, and yet she holds her tongue.

Maybe I only imagined who had the greater hold over the other.

I don't much like talk of another marriage.

"I would sooner return to Denmark," I interject, but Cnut is shaking his head, and the rest of my words remain unspoken.

"No, no, a husband for you can be found in England. It would be a waste to offer you to one of the few Danish jarls loyal to Harald."

I think to argue, but in my heart, I knew that by coming to England, I would place my future in Cnut's hands. I must be more furious with Harald than I'd realised. Not that many jarls in Denmark remain unmarried. My sisters got the best of the men, and I don't wish to be tied to one of the jarls sons. It would be beneath me.

"I saw your children," I say, instead of continuing to argue, perversely pleased to see Lady Emma startle at the announcement. Perhaps she didn't expect it, or maybe she's forgotten that she's birthed three children already.

"My brother will assist them in claiming land that's mine," Lady Emma states, the words staccato, a worry behind them that I can't interpret. "My father gifted me with several estates on his death, and my brother will honour my wishes when he's able."

I note that she doesn't ask how they fare. An unfeeling woman then. But Cnut is watching me, caution in his eyes, and I stop any further taunts from escaping my mouth. I can already tell that Lady Emma is as callous as Edward, Alfred, and Godgifu made me believe. She's all about ambition. I recognise it. Lady Gunnhild is the same.

A servant materialises from behind me, taking my bowl away, and bringing me a goblet of wine, rather than warm wine. I sip the fluid delicately, pottage and a hot drink, finally thawing me, the thick furs making my skin lose the cold, clammy feel of the sea, which has lingered because I've refused to wait before seeking out my brother in Winchester. I didn't enjoy the sea crossing in winter. I would advise against it to any who asked.

Cnut also takes wine, but Lady Emma is offered nothing. I think she'll linger, but abruptly, she turns to leave.

"It's a cold night," Lady Emma announces, the words reaching me even though her back is to me. "I'll be waiting for you," and the statement is strangely ominous, and yet Cnut makes no attempt to follow her, but instead sips his wine appreciatively.

"What of your sons?" I hiss, the words angry because I'm not sure that Lady Emma is the right wife for my brother, not at all, and I decry her lack of interest in her older children.

"They are well, in Northampton, with their mother, and her brothers. They'll come to no harm."

His lack of concern surprises me. They are his father's grandchildren, their claim to Denmark is as strong as his own. I would have expected him to care more. And more, I think he's wrong to be so passive about them. I might have gained his agreement that Lady Emma's children in Normandy will remain free from his concern, but I'm not at all convinced that Lady Emma will offer his older children the same protection.

"Sister," the tone of Lady Emma's voice almost has me scratching my arm in irritation. I've noticed that she oozes self-confidence when close to me. It infuriates because she doesn't do the same to any other. I consider that she fears me, or rather fears what I've perceived about her nature from the treatment of her older children. It gives me small comfort. I also take a slither of satisfaction in knowing that she believes her first husband's grandchildren are dead. That they don't means that one day, they might face the woman who was involved in their banishment. I should like to see that.

"Sister," I reply, the flicker of outrage in her eye assuring me that she doesn't appreciate the same being dealt to her. Will she chastise me? I doubt it, and yet I wouldn't be surprised if she did. I find her nature petty. Every new fact I uncover about my brother's wife, assures me that he chose unwisely.

"I would speak to you," Lady Emma quickly recovers, and I indicate that she should join me before the hearth. The weather is slowly starting to change, but outside, the rain pours as though without cease, and even here, in the royal hall at Winchester, I can hear the tell-tale sound of water pooling to the floor through some unseen hole in the roof.

"Wine?" I ask, but she shakes her head, hand cupping her belly. Her pregnancy proves her worth to my brother, and she's keen to allude to it continually.

"I've written to my brother in Normandy, and I've received word back from him that you were the one to refuse the match to him. He's willing to take you back. I suggest you arrange to leave as soon as possible, perhaps even as soon as when the rain stops."

I grin. I can't help it. Cnut has already informed me of this letter, and the potential for this conversation. But I know what I saw, and even now, Lady Emma is ignorant of the true nature of her brother. It surprises me. I've discovered that they were never close to one another and that he resented her banishment to Normandy when my father claimed the English kingdom for himself.

Why then, does she try and force the match? Does she fear my presence that much? I can't image why. I've done nothing to her, nothing at all, although it's evident that Cnut and I are often to be found in each other's company.

"I've also heard that your brother is already remarried. He plays you for a fool, and hopes to make a bigger fool of your husband."

It seems that Cnut hasn't informed his wife of this piece of information, and it reveals to me that Cnut is not quite as enamoured of his wife, as she is of him. Not that I can blame her. She was married to an older man, with almost ten children to his name, when she was little more than a child herself.

Cnut is an entirely different proposition. He's younger than her and a far more appealing man. No doubt it helps that her new husband is not locked in mourning for his first wife.

The flurry of emotions over Lady Emma's face is almost too enjoyable, and yet I've been at the court in Denmark for long enough. I know better than to make an open enemy, especially one who's a member of my extended family.

"I'm sorry, Lady Emma. Your brother is simply not the man you think he is. I believe you probably know that, in your heart. I'm pleased not to be married to him."

But my attempts at healing the gulf that threatens to open between us is a waste of my breath. Lady Emma's face is suddenly filled with loathing, and that surprises me once more. I thought, with all her court experience, that she'd have learned to mask her true feelings far better. Perhaps it's her pregnancy, or maybe it's the loss of her older children. I genuinely don't know.

"When I was in Normandy when my first husband lost his kingdom, Duke Richard was every inch the perfect brother. Any animosity between us that you think you perceive is entirely fictitious, my brother and I are united in ensuring the survival of our respective families."

I open my mouth to make some sound of acceptance, but it's too late. Lady Emma stands before me; her blue eyes seeming to pierce me.

"You would do well to remember that you're little more than the king's sister, and no good to him, at that, because your marriages amount to nothing."

She marches from my presence, and I'm abruptly aware that others have witnessed our conversation, amongst them bloody Jarl Úlfr and his brother. Úlfr smirks. I would wipe that smile from his face.

I would feel some sympathy for the misguided queen, but in her attitude towards me, I can only expect to encounter more difficulties.

I can tell that she's the sort to make my time in England uncomfortable. Perhaps, after all, I should have returned to Harald and Denmark. It would have been easier to forgive Harald than to endure the tediousness of another irate royal woman and a royal woman that I already suspect of doing my family more harm than good.

# CHAPTER 8

## *Winchester, AD1018*

I watch my brother carefully as I approach him. He stands beside the sturdy wicker fence, his gaze meant to be focused exclusively on the inhabitants of the field. But I know better. I know what he's about to say to me, and yet I'm going to make him say it all the same.

England is not important to me, and yet to Cnut, it's everything. He must fulfil my father's ambitions, no matter the cost to him. Or to me. Over the last few months, I've observed my brother vigilantly. I can see how ambitious he is and how single-minded his focus is. Without Denmark to claim as his own, he must make England and her unruly ealdormen accept his rule. The birth of his first child, a son, with Lady Emma, has begun the process, but there's much further to go. Harthacnut is no more than a promise for the future, and I'm unsure what that promise is.

"Sister, dearest," I dredge a smile from deep inside me and incline my head, coming to stand beside him. Cnut half-heartedly watches his horses as they frolic in the warm early summer sun, his eyes, as ever, picking out his horse, Blue, easily, as do mine. It's impossible not to note the king's horse. He's an arrogant bastard, just like his master.

It's been a long, cold winter. I hope it'll be an equally long summer, but I have my suspicions that it will start well enough and quickly fade away to nothing before plunging us back into a terrible winter. I merely hope that the crops will be harvested before the first of the winter storms arrive.

"My Lord King, brother," I use the familiar to take the sting from my tone. My brother winces all the same, and I confess, I enjoy his evident unease. Damn him.

"What do you think of England?" he asks me, and I almost laugh out loud, his thoughts so closely mirroring mine.

"I think it wasn't worth my father's life." I've still never forgiven King Swein for his death. I doubt I ever will.

A flicker of frustration is evident in the downward quirk of Cnut's lips.

"Do you not find the land beautiful and bounteous?"

I consider replying, and then merely sigh.

"What is it you want of me?" The tightening of his lips assures me that this isn't how Cnut wanted this conversation to progress. I take pride in unsettling him.

"You must marry again." There he's said it.

"And who must I marry, dear brother?"

"Jarl Úlfr."

"Jarl Úlfr?" The question is because he sounded less than sure for all he only spoke two words.

"Yes, Jarl Úlfr, you know him. You'll wed him. I would bind my jarls to me, like family."

"You think to emulate King Æthelred?"

Cold, blue eyes rake in my face, and I know my derision has worked. Cnut will have nothing good said about King Æthelred. He means only to blacken the name of the man who was king before him.

"You will do it?" Cnut asks, rather than responding to my jibe. I've tried not to be too critical of my brother as I've learned more and more about how he finally came to quell the English. It doesn't make for easy listening.

"Jarl Úlfr wouldn't be my first choice of a new husband, I confess. He's far too ambitious. I was pleased he left Denmark when he did. A pity you made him and his brother welcome in England. I would sooner he'd returned to Orkney and stayed there. I'm only pleased that Harald never married their sister."

Cnut stiffens at my criticism.

"Jarl Úlfr has been invaluable in assisting me in quelling the English. I've rewarded him with lands, close to the border with the Welsh kingdoms. His brother as well. That means that Orkney is closely bound to me." By rights, the jarl of Orkney should look to Denmark, not England. This is another petty way that Cnut thinks to claim dominance over Harald. It's tedious.

"What of the sister?" My brother has been plotting this for some time, that seems evident. It dismays me to realise just how successful Jarl Úlfr and his brother have been in winning Cnut's regard. It infuriates me to learn that my brother expects me to marry a man I've long derided for his excessive ambitions. If I marry him, Úlfr will think himself one step closer to what he desires.

"Lady Gytha Úlfrsdottir will bind another to me, in good time," Cnut admits, and there's no sense of apology in those words. Cnut does mean to emulate King Æthelred in making his jarls members of his family. I know it's only what my father did in Denmark, but even so, it makes me uneasy.

"Another who doesn't deserve one of your birth sisters?" I feel stung into complaining.

"Exactly." Cnut continues, without offering a further explanation, as though the fact I've worked that out myself shouldn't be a surprise.

I believe I know who he speaks of, and my lips curdle. I don't trust the man he wishes to join to him. Godwine is, again, not a suitable ally for my brother. Not that Cnut will heed my warnings. Godwine is just as ambitious as Jarl Úlfr. The two of them working together would worry me. But it seems, such thoughts are beyond Cnut.

I wish, not for the first time, that I could share my vision with Cnut, but he would deride it. Yet, over time, I've been able to identify more and more of the men and women who appeared in it. I believe that Godwine and Úlfr were there. I also think that one of the bowed heads was that of Harthac- nut. What it all means, I can't yet say, but I know that none of it is good.

Why, I consider, couldn't my brother just be happy with the allies he already had? Jarl Eirikr, married to my oldest sister, is a worthy man, as is Jarl Thorkell. Surely, my brother could have worked with the English ealdormen, as jarls are called, to control England? Why did he need to involve Eilifr, Úlfr and Hrani? Perhaps he should have executed or fallen out with fewer of the existing ealdormen.

Even now, I'm unsure why my brother executed the son of Ealdorman Leofwine. Leofwine is an honourable man. He would have ensured England stayed loyal to Cnut after the death of King Edmund.

I pull my fur-lined cloak tighter as the wind stirs the grow- ing grasses. England is cold. Not as cold as Denmark, and cer- tainly not as cold as the land of the Rus, but still, it's colder in early summer than I always imagined it would be when my father spoke of England's great wealth, both in silver, iron, salt, good crops and cattle.

"And when will I be married?" I say the word 'again' under my breath.

"Soon."

"And when will I be able to return to Denmark?" This con- cerns me more than my marriage. I think little of England, but Denmark is my home. I came to England through choice, but I'm already wearying of the place. I've long since forgiven Har- ald his involvement in the Normandy match, and I should like to see my mother again. It's been over a year now, and writing to her is simply not the same as seeing her, face to face.

Cnut's silence worries me, and I realise that, for the time being, he intends to keep me close to him, and far from Harald. Somehow, this surprises me, although it genuinely shouldn't.

"I will marry your Jarl Úlfr," I retort, chin raised, deter- mined to make the best of this that I can. I know I'm being used as one of the warriors in my brother's game of tafl. He thinks to surround himself with men and women who are tied to him through bonds of family, rather than oaths. I can't see that it will succeed, not in a kingdom riven by the conflicting interests of the English earls and the Danish jarls. It seems my brother is discovering that being a conqueror is not as easy as he thought it would be.

"And I thank you, sister."

"But, I wish to return to Denmark as soon as possible. It's my home. England can never be that."

Cnut's mouth opens, and I think he'll argue with me, but instead, his eyes flash, and I know that when he next speaks, it'll be a lie.

"You'll return to Denmark as soon as I can allow it."

They aren't the words I wish to hear, and yet I already know that I must make England my home for some time yet.

Jarl Úlfr is not the sort of man I would have chosen to marry. Aside from his ambitions, there's also the problem of his reputation. He's a violent man, a warrior of great renown, and with this union, he thinks to draw ever closer to what it is he wishes he could achieve, the title of king before his name.

It will never happen. It can never happen. Not that my vision has warned me of Jarl Úlfr, rather my experience of seeing him in Roskilde, with his sister and brother, have influenced my opinion.

"My Lady Estrid," his voice is gravelly and well oiled. I try not to grimace as I offer him my hand. My personal opinion matters little when I've given my consent to the match, but if I did have a choice, I'd never marry a man such as Jarl Úlfr. Úlfr is not worthy of me. But then, no man ever can be. Not unless I choose him myself, and that's never going to be allowed to happen.

"My Lord Úlfr," I convey only coldness with my reply, and yet he grins all the same. Perhaps I'll try a different tactic with him, after all.

"So, we're to be married?" his voice is edged with excitement. To marry the king's sister is a high honour that hasn't been offered to the vast majority of Cnut's loyal warriors. It doesn't seem to cross Úlfr's mind that Jarl Eirikr has one of my older half-sister's for a wife, or that Jarl Thorkell is both already married, and Cnut's foster-father.

"Yes, the king has decreed it," I state, trying to determine how to best approach my new husband. "I assume you'll be more amenable to me than the previous consorts chosen for me?" Úlfr startles at my words.

"I assure you, My Lady, I'm a man worthy of you. I have a son already, Asbjorn, to prove my ability to father children, although his mother no longer lives. Your brother thinks I would make a suitable match."

"What my brother thinks, and what I believe, are not identical. I have different needs to Cnut's." I hold Úlfr's triumphant eyes, and he tries to maintain the look, but the relief is evident when a loud crash resounds through the hall, allowing him to break the gaze. There's a distinction between a man who can lead in battle, and one who can simply lead. My brother is already learning that valuable lesson. I doubt Úlfr will take the time.

"We'll live in Gloucester." Jarl Úlfr speaks as though such information should excite me.

"No, we'll live at the king's court. He'll make rooms available for us, or perhaps even a house in Winchester." I've no intention of disappearing into the English countryside, allowing Cnut to forget my desire to return to Denmark. I've heard rumours of what befell King Æthelred's daughters when they were wed to the king's loyal ealdormen. I'll not be falling into obscurity as they did.

"Perhaps," Úlfr capitulates, attempting a smile, his gaze still scouring the room.

"I'll speak with my brother," I stand abruptly. I see no reason to continue the conversation. We'll be married the following day. Then there'll be time for us to speak further. Only Úlfr reaches out, his hand almost encircling my narrow wrist. I try to shake him free, but his grip is tight, and many people are watching us, Lady Emma, most prominent of all, the hint of a smirk on her face. Just like Lady Gunnhild in Denmark, Lady Emma allows her triumph to show far too easily.

"You'll be my wife, and under my command," Jarl Úlfr growls. I bend to his ear, as though to kiss him, and instead speak.

"You'll be my husband, and I'll have the right to leave you, should you prove unsuitable to me. Remember that, Jarl Úlfr." And I straighten, pull my skirt down, now that his grip has relaxed, and stalk from his side, head held high. I see now why my brother needs me. Cnut thinks he needs Jarl Úlfr and his brother and I must keep Úlfr in check. Perhaps the marriage isn't quite as unpromising as I thought it would be. It will bring me great pleasure to frustrate Jarl Úlfr in everything he wishes to achieve.

As I stand beside Úlfr, while the bishop presides over our union, my thoughts are slow and sluggish, my responses coming more through familiarity than anything else.

Last night my true dreams returned to haunt me, those same eyes and faces from before, some more familiar to me now than then, and I know that once more, fate will play its part in my future and that my brother, King Harald, is dead. I've allowed Frida to bring me drinks to fortify me, and her fingers to pinch my pale cheeks, all in the hope of covering what I know.

I have, because I had no choice, shared my knowledge with her. In the past, such an announcement might have worried her, but no more.

"We'll mourn ourselves, tomorrow when the ceremony is over, and you and your husband are bound," her voice, while sympathetic was also etched with authority. She knows as I do that, my true dreams can't prevent what must happen today.

"Your brother will need you even more now. He must claim

Denmark as well as England. Harald left no son, and your father's inheritance must be secured." Her words, as unfeeling as they sounded at the time, have stiffened my resolve.

Cnut will have to rely on me. Perhaps, after this ceremony is concluded, and news of Harald's death reaches him, he'll allow me to return to Denmark, and I'll see my mother once more.

It will feel strange and hollow without Harald to greet me at Roskilde. He was so young, so very young, and I don't know why he's dead, only that he is, and the naming of Cnut's second-born son has taken on even greater significance.

"Sister," my brother swiftly takes me from Jarl Úlfr's arm once we're returned to his hall at Winchester. Outside, the sun is shining, a gentle breeze carrying the promise of new growth and new life, and it's a terrible juxtaposition to the knowledge I have.

"What ails you," Cnut asks under his breath, and I shake my head, the words of denial already on my lips.

"A bad night's sleep, strange dreams and portents," I think to still my brother's questions, but it seems he's not about to allow that.

"Portents of Jarl Úlfr?" Cnut asks, and in those words, he cements his need of me.

"It's impossible to decipher my dreams, dear brother. They merely disgruntled me on the eve of my new marriage."

Cnut lapses into silence, his arm firm on mine, as he guides me to the front of the hall. A fine feast is waiting to be consumed, a celebration of a royal marriage, Lady Emma giving way because it's my marriage, although I can see her down-turned face.

"Watch your husband," Cnut whispers to me, in the act of gifting me a magnificent tiara that settles around my brow, the weight of it, forcing my hair flat. "Watch him, and tell me if you suspect anything amiss." It's hardly the words I wished to hear before opening my legs and sharing my bed with the man, but at least it assures me that I have Cnut's full support and trust. I can only hope that he feels the same about me when he learns of Harald's death.

Cnut comes to me, his eyes filled with sorrow, reminding me of when Harald learned of the death of our father. Then, I needed to pretend that I didn't know, even though I did. Today, I must do the same. I've been grieving, in my way, but it's been difficult with a husband keen to prove his virility. Not that our time together is unpleasant. If I didn't mistrust his over-eagerness to prove his loyalty to my brother, I might think it a fine match indeed, even if only in the bed-chamber. I can't deny that Jarl Úlfr has surprised me. Perhaps an ambitious man isn't quite as terrible as I thought it would be. I can hardly believe I think it, but I do.

"Sister," my brother's voice is ragged. Somehow, he's arrived when I'm praying for Harald's soul in the Old Minster at Winchester. Fortunately, I'm already morose, with Frida at my side, my husband, thankfully, on the hunt. He'll have to slack his bloodlust that way, for the next few days.

"Brother, what is it?" Frida watches me closely from beside Cnut, as I stand, my face showing my worry. The slight incline of her chin, assures me that I've pitched my voice to show my concern.

"Ah, it wounds me, but I must inform you that poor Harald is with our father." Hearing the words spoken aloud sends a tremor down my spine, as Cnut grips my lifeless hands. I'm cold, despite the mild weather outside.

"Harald? How, how did it happen?"

"A wound that festered. My mother has sent word, along with a demand that I make my way to Denmark immediately. She states that I have an heir to rule in my name, in my absence." His tone reflects his frustration at Lady Gunnhild's uncompromising attitude.

"Then you must go. And I'll come with you."

"No," Cnut's firm refusal surprises me.

"Harald was my brother too. I would be there to pay my respects for his soul. He was too young," my voice catches, and a single tear falls down my cheek. Cnut tracks it rather than meeting my eyes.

"I know, but for now, you must pray for him here, and hold England for me. I can't allow it to fall back into the hands of Æthelred's relatives." He speaks of Lady Emma's sons; I know he does. I open my mouth to speak but close it abruptly. I've no idea if Edward and Alfred now have the support of their Uncle. Perhaps there's an army just waiting for an opportunity to strike and restore England to its long-running House of Wessex as soon as Cnut is absent. Perhaps, Lady Emma is even aware of such plans.

Certainly, I know that a son of King Æthelred caused an uprising only last year. Perhaps my brother is right to be wary of Lady Emma's older children.

Cnut, finally convinced of his hold on England, has reduced the size of his ship-fleet to only forty ships, and their attendant men.

For all that, he appears uncertain about leaving England.

"Your mother will ensure Denmark stays loyal to you. My mother will do the same; in fact, she'll do it more effectively than Lady Gunnhild, I assure you."

"Yes, they will, and yes, I know I can rely on Lady Sigrid. All the same, Denmark needs to see their new king. It's been too many years since I was last there."

"I'll assist your wife, and the ealdormen and jarls who remain in England."

"I know you will," Cnut's complete faith in my skills almost makes up for the fact that I must stay behind. Harald trusted me as well before he sent me to Normandy, and I realised that trust didn't quite mean what I thought it did.

"When will you leave?" Only now does he look unsure.

"As soon as I can," he announces, his eyes already flickering to the door, as though he can go, just like that.

"But not immediately?"

"No, not immediately."

"Then you can pray with me," I inform him, already bending

my knees once more. Beneath me, the bones of some of the previous kings of England, rest in perpetual peace. How lucky they are, to all be in one place. It's not the same for my family, although my father has been returned to Roskilde, from Gainsborough, to lie in the family crypt.

I hear Cnut settle beside me, his rough voice mumbling his prayers, but my thoughts are far from Harald. If all I have seen so far has come to pass, then so too must the rest of my true dream. It seems to foretell children, and war, bloodshed and loss. And at the heart of it, is some sort of betrayal. I'm not yet sure who the traitorous bastard will be.

There are several possibilities, but I'm convinced that my husband will be the worst of them all. A shame really, for he's proved to be the sort of man to thrill me, and yet I can't allow myself to love him. I'll not suffer a broken heart because my affection is given too freely. I'll not be like Lady Emma. I can already tell that she adores my brother, even as she fights for her son to be known as the king's true heir, rather than his older sons with Lady Ælfgifu, who are banished from Wessex.

I think Lady Emma is foolish to worry so much. With Harald's death, there will be England and Denmark to rule, in good time. Provided that Cnut can hold both of them. And of course, her son can't fend for himself, not yet.

When my brother stands, his prayers at an end, I stay where I am. I haven't yet finished allowing my thoughts to run free, trying to determine the future. I have hints and illusions, but nothing is sure.

I must stay alert, and do all I can to assist Cnut and his dreams. It's what Harald would have wanted and my father. Still, I wish I'd not left Denmark with my argument with Harald unresolved. I know we've since healed the wounds, but even so, to realise that I'll never see him again, makes me question my previous anger.

I ache for Denmark. I truly do.

# CHAPTER 9

## AD1020

"Where is your brother?" the outrage in her voice surprises me. I suppress a sigh, cradle my sleeping son close to me, and turn to meet her gaze.

"He's in Denmark," I say the words slowly, trying to keep the frustration from showing. Lady Emma has grown more and more distressed with my brother's continued absence, as her waistline has expanded. Cnut has been absent from England for as long as it's taken Lady Emma to reach her current state of full-pregnancy. The intervening months have not been kind on any of us.

"I know he's in Denmark," Lady Emma delicately settles herself on a chair to the side of me, her cheeks blowing. I know what it's like to be so pregnant that it's impossible to be comfortable, and yet I still feel no sympathy for her.

"He'll return when affairs in Denmark settle." I try and reassure, even though I don't want to. This is not a new discussion. It's tedious, and as it's beyond my ability to know, it exasperates me, and yet Lady Emma can't seem to stop repeating it.

"Have you seen the letter he sent to the English? He knows that there are problems here." It seems she's in one of her persistent moods today.

Of course, I've seen the letter, but I don't want to discuss

Cnut's words. I have them memorised.

*"If anyone, ecclesiastic or layman, Dane or Englishman, is presumptuous as to defy God's law and my royal authority or the secular law, and he will not make amends and desist according to the direction of my bishops, I then pray, and also command Earl Thorkell, if he can, to cause the evil-doer to do right."*

*"If he cannot, then it is my will that with the power of us both, he shall destroy him in the land, or drive him out of the land, whether he be high or low rank."*

Only Lady Emma has returned to her complaints, leaving me no time to mule over the words, or to consider why Earl Thorkell was named regent, when I'm here, and so too his wife. I'm forced to presume that Cnut knew that while England was settled, after his invasion, there was still the genuine possibility of insurrection. Why else leave a military commander as regent of a supposedly 'peaceful' kingdom when he returned to Denmark? I've not yet forgiven my brother, the oversight.

"He must return for the birth of his child."

"How is he to know when the child will arrive? Are your children usually early, late or on time? Does he even know that you are with child?" Somehow, I dredge the required questions to my lips. If I ask enough questions, she'll content herself with replying, regardless of whether I'm listening or not.

Only, Lady Emma does none of those things, and I startle to full wakefulness as her silence continues.

"What is it?" I demand to know.

"There are rumours regarding the other woman."

I almost say, 'what woman' but stop myself, I know who she means, but I'm surprised that Lady Emma speaks to me of something so personal to her.

"What rumours?"

"That he means to reunite with her. That he intends to have both of us as his wife at the same time. It's against God's wishes." Emma's outrage pitches her voice too high, and I hear the rustle of bored people turning to stare at the king's wife and his sister, no doubt trying to decide what excites Lady Emma so much.

"You're the king's wife," I seek to reassure. In all my two years in England, I'm yet to meet Lady Ælfgifu or my two nephews. I'll not risk bringing her to Winchester, and neither will I risk travelling from Winchester. Perhaps, one day, her sons will visit me in Denmark. But, I have written to Lady Ælfgifu during my time in England, and again sent her gifts for my nephews. I've received no formal response. It seems the woman is as arrogant as my mother.

Svein startles in my arms, and I shush him, running my fingers over his soft cheeks, marvelling that I made the child before me. Already, I move to distance him from his father, even as Jarl Úlfr grows in prowess. He's been summoned to Denmark, along with so many others of Cnut's followers. I wished to go, but Jarl Úlfr was able to use my recent childbirth as an excuse to keep me in England. While Úlfr is gone, I hope my brother is ensuring he stays loyal.

Úlfr might please me in bed, but his ambition runs rampant. My brother sees it, even if few others do.

Harthacnut toddles on chunky legs toward his mother, only for Frida to distract him with a small wooden toy. I think it's supposed to be some sort of cow or even a pig, but I can't honestly tell despite the excellent craftsmanship of the highly burnished toy.

Frida gabbles away to Harthacnut in Danish, and for once, Lady Emma makes no complaint that she doesn't speak to him in English. It alerts me, more than her words, to just how distressed she is.

"My brother has not the time to rekindle any relationship with Lady Ælfgifu," even just hearing her name aloud, makes Lady Emma twitch. I don't believe the two women have ever met. I'm not surprised. Lady Ælfgifu has her loyal supporters in northern England. Lady Emma is firmly a woman of the southern court.

"Then why would there be rumours that she's travelled to Denmark with her sons."

"I hear no such rumours."

"That's because you'll not hear anything about your brother that you don't choose to hear." Her tone is rich with contempt, and her words infuriate me. I feel stung into replying.

"On the contrary, I determine to be alert to every rumour about him. He's my brother and my king. I'm twice-loyal to him."

Lady Emma refuses to meet my eyes, turning instead to beckon a servant close.

"Bring me wine and some sweet delicacies." Her voice is reasoned when she speaks to the servant, unlike when she confides in me.

"Your brother uses me ill."

"It's not his fault that King Harald died so young, and he's the only other son of King Swein to hold a claim to Denmark."

"Surely, his mother can rule for him in Denmark?" In all honesty, I entirely agree with her, but Cnut will not be convinced that anyone can govern better than he can. Nor will his mother. I receive long and detailed letters from my mother. They would be laughable if it weren't all so bloody serious.

"Denmark needs a firm warrior to rule her."

"And England doesn't. There are reports of unrest on the extremities. The kingdoms who border England are aware that Cnut has been gone for so long. They sense an easy victory."

"And yet, there have been no reports, as yet, of any stirrings on the borders." I've taken the time to check, with Earl Thorkell, if there are problems brewing. He assures me that there aren't. Not that Lady Emma will be convinced of that. If I were crueller, I'd say that Lady Emma doesn't appreciate peace. She's so used to war that without it, she must seek out aggravations.

"It's early in the season. The enemy may be waiting for better weather."

"Yes, or you might be susceptible to the stories that you hear. Trust Cnut. He'll not want to lose England or Denmark."

"His ambitions are too great." Lady Emma speaks with finality in her voice.

I chuckle then, I can't help it, even as I know it will infuriate Lady Emma further.

"You once had a weak man as your husband; now you have a far more ambitious one. Tell me, would you rather worry that your son will have no kingdom to rule when he's older, just as for your older sons?"

The words, meant only to prove a point, send a shiver of dread down my spine, and I consider that I've inadvertently stumbled on something my vision has shown me, but whose meaning has eluded me until now.

"No, no, of course not," but her voice has lost its stringent tones, and I realise that somehow, Lady Emma has lost sight of what's truly at stake.

Only then, she rallies.

"Just because you prefer a distant husband, doesn't mean that all women do."

I shrug. I can't deny Lady Emma's words. I wish she were less observant, but it can't be helped.

"Jarl Úlfr was not my choice of husband. I would have wanted a man who was less ... ruthless, as well. Úlfr's aspirations are ill-founded. He has no right to rule in England, or Denmark. He should think of serving my brother, and not of trying to out-do him."

Lady Emma's eyes narrow at my words, and I almost wish I'd said this, at the beginning. It appears that alerting her to the threat so close to Cnut has made her forget her whining complaints.

"My brother does well to keep Jarl Úlfr close to him, or me. It would not do to have him claiming too much power for himself."

"Perhaps not," Lady Emma muses, her expression pensive. "Your brother took great risks to conquer England."

"He did yes, and along the way, some of his choices of allies and alliances have been questionable."

"Yes, they have." Lady Emma admits, and I hide a smirk, as I fuss with Svein's fur covering. She doesn't realise that I mean to include her in that. Cnut could have held England with his first wife, of that I'm sure. Lady Ælfgifu's powerful family would have been more than enough to drive all prospects of rebellion from the minds of the English ealdormen and their subjects. And then Lady Emma would have been far from England, returned to her brother, and reunited with her three older children.

She would have lacked the military might to try and win back England on behalf of her sons, and Cnut would have had a woman to support him who was less inclined to fret and more likely to provide him with strong and healthy children. Not that Lady Emma's children are weak, but, well, my personal opinion seems to matter little, but Cnut could have done much better for himself if he'd thought more before he acted. I won't allow that he was desperate for peace. I will allow that he found an easy solution to a difficult problem.

If I'd been with Cnut, I would have done things differently. But I was not. That can never be changed. Not now.

"What is it?" my voice is laced with exhaustion as Frida calls my name.

"A messenger, from the king, in Denmark."

Her words bring me to full wakefulness with a gasp; my thoughts already flickering to my absent husband. Surely not yet?

"Can it not wait?" but I'm already pulling the fur coverings away from my body, while Frida, by the light of a single flame, waits to assist me into one of my cloaks. In front of my bed, soft shoes wait for my naked feet. Once more, I'm grateful to Frida's forethought, as a servant waits to light my path to the king's hall at Winchester.

In silence, I make my way to the hall; cloak pulled tightly

around me; for all, it's not cold. The chill that strikes at me comes from somewhere other than the warm wind spiralling around my feet as doors open and close elsewhere in the king's hall.

Frida follows at my heels, and I can almost hear her thinking and trying to determine why the message was so important that I needed to be woken in the middle of the night.

"My Lady," the messenger has been given food and ale by a sleepy-looking servant, but he's not at all tired, I can tell just from those two words, offered just that little bit too loudly. Those sleeping in huddles close to the hearth, stir, but quickly settle to sleep once more. I recognise Siward, the unfortunate man sent to Normandy with me. I'm pleased to see that Cnut has forgiven him for the failure that wasn't at all his fault.

"Come, sit with me here," I beckon him away from the hearth, and toward a selection of stalls arranged in a tight circle. No doubt someone was playing tafl or plotting before they retired for the night.

"Tell me," I instruct, as soon as I'm settled. The slither of a grin forms on the man's face.

"The king is well, as is your husband. The king sends word that you're to return to Roskilde as soon as possible."

"What, what has happened?" I demand to know.

"Nothing, My Lady. The king is keen to return to England, and wishes Jarl Úlfr to rule in his stead, in Denmark, with you at his side."

"Ah, I see. That's excellent." I'm pleased Cnut has finally acquiesced to my wishes. I have had enough of England and her difficult men and women, and I include Lady Emma in that.

"Ships are waiting for you, at Sandwich. The journey can be accomplished quickly."

"Yes, yes. I'll need a day at most, and then I can be ready."

Siward nods.

"That's what I thought."

"Does the king say anything else?"

"Only that you hurry. King Cnut is keen to return to England."

"I'm sure he is," I offer, although why, I'm unsure, even if it suits me.

"I'll escort you. I have a force of twelve warriors with me. They tend to the horses."

"Why have you arrived so late?"

"Some problems on the road, nothing to worry about, but it delayed us, and I was determined to reach you today."

"Then you have my thanks, now, arrange food and ale for your men, and then sleep. I have much to think about." And with that, I dismiss the man and turn to Frida. I can see her teeth gleaming at the news that our time in England has come to an end. I confess I'm just as relieved that I'll be free from Lady Emma and her fractious worrying.

# CHAPTER 10

## AD 1020, Roskilde

I step foot onto the quayside with delight. The crossing has been calm, and I'm relieved to be home finally.

I didn't expect any form of welcoming party, and yet somehow, my mother, and Cnut himself are waiting for my son and me. Only my husband is missing, and that pleases me more than it should.

"Sister," Cnut envelops me in his arms, and I return the embrace. It gives us the opportunity we need.

"Your wife misses you," I inform him.

"Your husband doesn't miss you," I would chuckle at such a brutal statement, but my mother is before me, her hands beckoning for her grandson to be brought for her inspection.

"And hello to you, Lady Mother," I find myself complaining, stepping back from Cnut, but remaining close to him.

Here, on this busy quayside, clear of some of the fishing vessels and merchant ships, but by no means all of them, stand a large percentage of my brother's noble family. It's good to be seen as such a cohesive force by the men and women busy about their business.

"He's a beautiful child," my mother finally admits, forcing Frida to release her hold on my squirming son. "He has the look of your father about him." The statement makes me chuckle.

"How can you even tell? His cheeks are plump, and his legs and belly as well. I don't believe my father ever suffered from such excesses."

But my mother is not to be distracted.

"It's the eyes. Your son has your father's eyes." I might have accepted that without question, only she continues. "And his noble chin," and that makes me laugh, and Cnut joins in, Frida as well. Svein, wide awake, startles at the sound, and then reaches out to grab my mother's golden necklace, with his fat little fist. He pulls and pulls, his mouth open as though to chew on it, and Frida is there, to smoothly replace the necklace with a more suitable wooden toy that he can gnaw on without the risk of choking.

"He's strong, as well," my mother continues, and I walk to her and place a kiss on her lined face. Her hair has turned white while I've been away in Normandy and England, but she's still beautiful. I only hope I retain my good looks when I have as many years to my name. I'm pleased that Denmark will be my home for her final few years.

She accepts my kiss and then turns aside.

"Come on, little man, I'll show you Roskilde, and the people will see their little prince." For a moment, I think my mother has said too much of her ambitions, but Cnut merely rolls his eyes at the words, good-natured because my mother had no son with Swein, only a daughter, and a daughter can't rule in Denmark.

'Not yet,' I think to myself, but now is not the time for such thoughts.

"The adults will go and seek food and drink, and talk politics," Cnut calls to my mother, but she's not listening, her attention entirely focused on Svein, Frida and two of my servants, rushing to keep pace with her. I'm pleased to see four of my brother's warriors accompanying the royal party, even if at a discrete distance, Siward amongst them.

"Right, come on then sister, let us discuss what the other needs to know, and then I can set about preparing to return to

England."

I link my arm through Cnut's, breathing deeply of home, and trying not to choke on the waft of fish guts that overlays everything. I hope never to leave Denmark again. I hope that Cnut will never ask me to do so, but of course, I'll do so, if I must.

"Earl Thorkell is tested while you're absent from England. There's talk of rebellion from one of the English earls, and the name Eadwig has been mentioned." I think this the most pertinent news for my brother, but he waves his hand, his eyes bright.

"I'm aware of all that. I'll deal with the problem as soon as I return. The damn fools." Cnut's tone is far from angry.

"Denmark is peaceful, although her enemies are everywhere."

"Why have you allowed Earl Thorkell to rule in England, but not in Denmark?" This has been worrying me ever since I left Winchester. After all, Thorkell is just as tied to Cnut through extended family as Jarl Úlfr.

"I would sooner have Thorkell close to me. With Jarl Úlfr, I can rely on you and your mother to keep him loyal. It's not the same with Thorkell. He's already showed himself to be wily and disloyal if the need arises."

Cnut doesn't object to my question. Indeed, he seems to have been expecting it.

"And how is my son?"

"Your son is well. Your wife is ripe with child. She frets you'll miss the birth."

Now Cnut does startle, turning to gaze at me.

"She didn't mention a new child."

"Well, it's yours, there's no question of that." I retort. "She's been a trial. I'm always relieved when Jarl Thorkell distracts her with matters of state."

"You're not fond of my wife?"

"I find little to like about her, but you know that."

"She fulfilled an important role when I was newly king of all

England."

"And that role is now accomplished?" I ask, curious as to whether Cnut might take another wife, now that Lady Emma has performed her allotted tasks.

"I'll keep her," Cnut announces, chuckling when I tut with irritation.

"You could do better," I child him.

"I could yes, but none of us has married through choice. I think we should all suffer the same."

"Speaking of suffering," and Jarl Úlfr is before me. I've not seen him for just under a year. In that glance, I feel a stirring of desire. I should like another son. Perhaps I'll even find the wherewithal to make one.

"Lady Estrid, wife," Úlfr stands on seeing me, his place on the dais in my brother's hall, broadcasting to all that the king much favours him.

"Husband," I dip a small curtsey, nothing more. After all, I'm the royal sister; he's not the royal brother.

"Where is Svein?" Úlfr's eyes glance behind me, and I suppress another sigh of irritation.

"My mother has stolen him," I assure, while Cnut leads me to a chair, and ensures I have everything I need.

"Then he's well," Úlfr's tongue slicks between his pink lips, the image of a frog catching flies, flickering in my mind.

"He is well. My mother announces that he has the look of his grandfather, King Swein."

This pleases my husband, and his chest seems to pump up even more.

"She made no mention of any resemblance to you," Cnut quickly deflates him, a gleam in his eye. Does my brother have a full understanding of Úlfr and his ambitions? I hope so. Cnut makes a brave decision in allowing Úlfr to hold Denmark for him. I know there's little choice, now that Harald is dead, but even so, even Thorkell might have been the better option, no matter Cnut's concerns regarding his loyalty.

Úlfr opens his mouth to speak, and then thinks better of it.

"To Denmark," Cnut says, raising his silver goblet high, the red of the heady wine, glinting in the light of the open doorway.

"To Denmark," I touch my goblet to his, and we both wait for Úlfr to do the same. His eyes flicker from mine to Cnut's, and I think, just maybe, that he understands that having his wife returned to him is not a boon of his king, but rather a means of keeping him under control.

The damn fool, how can he not have realised.

Drinking deeply, I savour the rich wine, feeling my body relax in the familiar hall that I've known all my life. Cnut is welcome to England. I'm content to be home, away from Lady Emma and England. For the first time in three years, I feel settled.

Cnut leaves four days later, his ships ready to escort him back to Sandwich, Lady Emma and England. I watch him from the quayside, knowing that I'll see him again soon. Gytha Úlfrsdottir accompanies him, and that pleases me, even though it accords Úlfr more honour than I'd like. She's welcome to her marriage with Earl Godwine. And England, even if I felt a flutter of worry at such a development.

"Right," Úlfr is determined at my side. "I have things to be doing," he does not explain, and I watch with narrowed eyes, as he forces a path through the people of Roskilde come to witness their king leaving Denmark. He's hardly regal as they're almost shoved aside.

"You'll need to watch him," my mother's soft words are spoken directly to my ear.

"Why do you think I'm here?" I ask her, and she nods, perhaps worried that I was too enamoured of my husband to understand his true nature.

"Get yourself with child again," she further offers, Svein once more in her arms. She has barely left his side since our arrival, and Úlfr has already been complaining about her.

"I have every intention of doing just that," I assure her, "but tell me all the things that Cnut and Úlfr believe I don't need to know."

My mother links her arm through mine, Svein held tightly in the other. She's lost none of her strength with the years. Svein is a hefty weight, and yet she doesn't even breathe heavily as she holds the chubby child close.

"Your half-brother rules well in Sweden, but of course, he's ambitious, especially since the marriage of his daughter to King Olaf of Norway. They may all be related to you, but both kings have their view firmly settled on Denmark. If your brother hadn't arrived when he did, I believe Denmark might have been invaded. As it is, King Olof has willingly secreted away the royal children, on my instructions, and I believe the deceit makes him feel superior to Cnut."

I nod, pleased that my mother has lost none of her political astuteness.

"There are those within Denmark who would sooner have a Swedish or Norwegian king than a man obsessed with England. Your brother needs you here, because you represent continuity from your father, and the promise of the future, because of your son, named for Swein."

I've deciphered this for myself.

"And what of the jarls?"

"Ah, they're sometimes loyal and sometimes not. The Danes are still too new to the idea of kingship to truly embrace it, no matter what your father and brothers might have thought."

"Tell me, how is Lady Gunnhild?" My mother's lips purse at the mention of her.

"She's no better and no worse. Cnut exerted a firm hand against her. She has what she needs, but no more, and no less." That pleases me.

"And how are my sisters?"

My mother's face curdles at the mention of my older sisters. Gytha is content while Eirikr's in England, and she has her son, Hakon, to herself. Your other sisters do well enough with their husbands. I pity them, in all honesty. Tell me, is Cnut's wife as beautiful as they say?"

"Ah, mother, don't listen to such gossip from the warriors," I rebuke her, but then lean in closer.

"She might well be beautiful, but she's besotted with my brother, and that's not right. He doesn't share the same feelings, I'm sure of it. I find her to be quite annoying and not a little bitchy. She was most unhappy when her brother refused to marry me. She wanted me to go back to Normandy and beg him to fulfil his promise."

"The House of Gorm does not beg," my mother speaks firmly.

"I know, I had no intention of marrying him. Even Jarl Úlfr makes a better husband than he would have done."

My mother pulls on my arm, and I'm forced to stop and meet her surprised expression.

"Truly, Jarl Úlfr is better than Duke Richard?"

"Most assuredly," I affirm, and her soft grunt of surprise brings a grin to my face. I've missed my mother. She might have been rigid and uncompromising when I returned from the land of the Rus, but I've missed her while I've been absent in England.

"Lady Estrid," my husband's voice is soft and insistent, for all I fling my arm above my face and turn aside from him.

"Estrid," Úlfr complains, his rank breath on my face as he leans over me.

"What?" I huff, wishing that he wouldn't seek our bed when he's drunk himself into a stupor, only it's not night, but daylight, and I'm immediately far more alert.

"What is it?" I demand to know.

"Jarl Thorkell."

"Thorkell is in England." I want to sleep. Beorn, my second son, is a restless child, and I feel as though I've only just closed my eyes.

"No, he isn't."

I sit upright, almost knocking my forehead against Úlfr's chin.

"Where is he then?"

"Fyrkat."

"Why is he in Fyrkat?"

"He's claimed the fortress. He sends words of his intentions to hold it."

"Why would Cnut have sent Jarl Thorkell to Fyrkat and not told us?" Outside, the wind moans fiercely, and somewhere, a door or gate bangs in the wind. Why can't people close such things after them?

Úlfr settles on the bed beside me, his weight forcing me toward him, even though I'd rather keep my distance.

"I'm not sure that Cnut has done any such thing?"

"What?"

"The messenger was coy about Thorkell's actions. I read treason and betrayal in his denial to be more honest with me."

"Where is this man? I would speak to him?"

"Yes, yes, come, he's in the hall. I've given him food and ale, but I think he probably deserves cold iron around his wrists."

Úlfr holds my cloak, while I quickly dress, and with my boots and cloak firmly in place, I allow him to lead me to the king's hall, well, really my hall, but I don't say that aloud. It's one thing for me to believe I rule here, it's quite another to act and speak as though I do. I've long appreciated that.

The hearth is piled high with logs, despite the late hour, and I shiver into the welcome warmth and appreciate that the flames also allow me to catch sight of the messenger before he can see me.

From the side, I see that he's suffered from a broken nose, perhaps more than once and that a slicing scar extends down his left cheek. The man is a warrior. Maybe he'll simply tell me all I want to know because he's unskilled in diplomacy.

"My Lord," the man is instantly on his feet when Úlfr comes to a stop in front of him. It's evident that he didn't expect to see Úlfr again. And then he sees me as well, and his eyes narrow, and then he stands, bowing his head

"My Lady."

"Who are you?" I demand to know.

"My name is Regna."

"Thorkell's nephew," my quick recollection has Úlfr gasping in surprise, and a wan smile playing across Regna's cheeks.

"Yes, My Lady."

"Tell me everything."

"Yes, everything. What has happened between Cnut and Thorkell?"

"With all respect, My Lady, I suggest you come to Fyrkat, speak with Thorkell yourself."

"Is it really so bad between them?"

"Yes," a simple reply.

"I'll set out in the morning. You'll accompany me. Did you come alone?"

"No, others are sleeping elsewhere."

"I suspected as much. Ensure they know our plans."

And with that, I turn aside, ensuring Úlfr follows me. We've barely taken three steps when he hisses at me.

"You can't go. It's my responsibility."

"You may escort me, and Svein, if you must, but this is something that I must do."

"I forbid it," Úlfr's voice is laced with fury.

"You couldn't forbid me anything, husband," I stop so abruptly, that Úlfr has taken another four steps before he even realises.

"I am Cnut's regent in Denmark," his face is all shadows and angles, his anger evident to see.

"And I'm his sister, and my sons are his nephews, and Jarl Thorkell understands what that means, even if you don't."

Úlfr's jaw hangs open in shock.

"And what does that make me?"

"You're my husband, Úlfr. Don't think that means more than it does."

Within sight of Fyrkat, I beckon Regna to my side. The sea crossing has been relatively mild, the ships hugging the coastlines, before making a quick rush across the more open expanses. I've enjoyed the feel of the wind in my hair. Perhaps I should have been a Viking leader myself, leading my men and women to far distant lands.

"When we arrive, go and inform Jarl Thorkell of the arrival of Lady Estrid, and her son, Svein, her husband as well."

I sense, rather than see, Úlfr glare at me when I list him the least of the three of us. Svein has endured travelling well. I expected him to sleep and plague Frida and I with demands for stories and games, but instead, he's watched everything that we've passed with wide eyes, drinking in all the new experiences. It seems that he's a natural sailor.

Even Úlfr has taken Svein along the ship, deigning to explain things that have excited him. Beorn has remained in Roskilde, under the care of my mother. She'll allow nothing to happen to my youngest son, who's still far too young to be embroiled in politics.

While we disembark, Regna rushes to the main fort. It's visible before us, the wooden stakes rising high in the air, the ditch and rampart making the place appear menacing. Yet, I know it's in desperate need of repair, having been all but abandoned since long before my father's death. Regna returns only a short time later, alone, other than for a familiar figure.

"Hand me Svein," and Svein settles in my arms. My mother was right; for all I teased her presumptuous statement, my son does look like his grandfather. He shares the same forehead and chin, if without the birthmark that scarred my father.

"What of me?" Úlfr demands.

"You must escort us, but hold your tongue," my voice is severe. I've been replaying different conversations in my head whenever I've had a moment to myself. I'm unsure of the severity of the rift between Cnut and Thorkell. I'm uncertain if I can bring it to an end before it becomes more serious, well, more severe than banishment from England, for this is what I've determined has happened.

Thorkell looks old and worn in the early morning light, the rush of the river suddenly loud behind me, for all his famous height hasn't diminished.

"My Lady." His voice is rich with respect, even though I can sense, rather than see, the mass of men and women who support him, trying to watch from all available viewpoints from inside Fyrkat itself.

"Jarl Thorkell," my voice is both edged with the wind from the glaciers, and relief at finding him still here. Thorkell could have gone anywhere, claimed any part of Denmark for himself, even taken himself back to his home at Jomsburg, and I doubt many would have argued too forcefully with him. My brother has no idea of the man's loyalty, always too keen to question him because of his one-time support of King Æthelred of England.

Some would say that it was Jarl Thorkell's fault that my father invaded England, keen to conquer her, to prevent Thorkell from gaining even more from his alliance with King Æthelred. I don't believe that my father feared Thorkell that greatly, but perhaps he did. Certainly, Thorkell is the epitome of a Viking warrior.

"I didn't expect to find you here," I offer, no hint of criticism in my voice.

"I didn't expect to be here," Thorkell confirms, standing close enough that we no longer need to shout. There's a look of faint surprise on his face as his gaze takes in both Svein and Úlfr, just behind me. I imagine that Regna has informed him of the number of warriors who escort us, as Thorkell doesn't even seem to notice them.

"Is that young Svein?"

"Yes, my firstborn. Svein, this is Jarl Thorkell, he's your uncle."

I can't see Svein's face, but I can imagine it as he looks at the man before him. It's impossible not to be overawed by

Thorkell's height. He towers over all men, no matter how tall they might think themselves to be. I can see Thorkell's face, though, and I appreciate that my tactic is working. Thorkell is remembering who his king is. And before Cnut, the man he first pledged himself to, my father.

"Tell me, do you hold only Fyrkat or have you taken control of the other forts as well?"

A flicker of surprise on Thorkell's face, and I know I'm right to suspect him.

"Do you plan on using Danes to attack Denmark?" It's this that concerns me. I won't allow my brother's argument with his foster-father to pitch Denmark into such a war. What point in countrymen killing countrymen when there are Norwegians and the Svear content to do the job for them?

"My plans are rather dependent on what Cnut does." Defiance rings in the older man's voice, and yet I sense something else as well.

"Tell me. I'm not Cnut. I'll not judge as hastily as he does."

Thorkell's stance stills, his eyes far away, and I almost anticipate his words even before he speaks them.

"Earl Godwine is to blame."

I'm no fan of Godwine, but he's now married to my husband's sister, and I feel Úlfr tense at my side. I imagine the fool knows more about this than he's told me. I refused to ask him on the journey here. I'll not allow Úlfr to think he's privy to facts that I am not.

"To blame for what?"

"Spreading lies about my intentions to claim England for myself, about me recruiting Danish warriors to fight the English, and to reward them with English land."

"How could Earl Godwine have managed such a thing? My brother would have needed to see proof."

Again, Thorkell's eyes flicker toward Úlfr, and I stifle my frustration.

"Come, Thorkell, we'll converse more privately."

I stride away from Úlfr, each step reverberating with frustration at the petty feuds which distract the men who serve my brother. Perhaps, like Lady Emma, they're all so used to war that peace sits uneasily with them, and they must bring about combat, no matter what.

Svein remains with me, and his weight in my arms, give me the courage that I need to hear a truth that I already suspect.

"Tell me," I demand once more when I'm sure we're far enough away not to be overheard.

"Earl Godwine is a manipulative bastard and a clever one at that. He's interpreted my actions to the king so that they appear hostile when they never were."

"What defence did you offer to the king?"

"I saw little point in offering any." The bewilderment is too easy to hear in Thorkell's voice. He's been loyal for so long, apart from when he did support the English king, that he can't understand Cnut's championing of another. The fact it's Godwine, an English man, must burn even more.

"So, did he banish you?"

"Yes, he did."

"And now you're in Denmark, to do what?"

Thorkell considers his reply, his gaze settled on Svein, and refusing to meet my eye.

"To cause the king some problems."

"So not to uncover the truth, then?"

"Your brother has no interest in the truth."

I want to argue with Thorkell, but I don't. The man is entitled to his opinion, and there's something about his tone that's making me reconsider the words he's using.

"You didn't need to come here. There's no need for you to be any more involved in this than you already are."

I open my mouth to deny his words and then snap it shut once more.

"My brother's kingdom means everything to me. I wouldn't want it to fall into enemy hands."

"I'm sure you wouldn't," and I don't miss that his eyes settle not on Svein, but instead on Úlfr, and suddenly everything makes sense to me.

Úlfr is furious as we return to Roskilde.

"Why did you insist on travelling all that way?" his voice is almost a shriek, and I feel the gaze of everyone on that ship watching us. I would silence him, but he's not a child.

"I needed to see for myself, and now I have, and I know that there's no choice but to inform Cnut that Thorkell has further betrayed him."

"It didn't look as though you said a cross word to him."

"What you saw and what you think you saw are two entirely different things." I don't wish to argue with Úlfr. Certainly, I don't want to arouse his suspicions about my suspicions.

"So, is Thorkell about to apologise to the king, and hand back Fyrkat?"

"I don't foresee that, no."

"Then I must call the Danish warbands together, and prepare to attack him."

I nod. "I imagine you do, yes. But perhaps wait until the winter has passed. I don't envisage Thorkell doing more, not now he has a base to call his own."

"I don't think Cnut would approve of that," Úlfr complains.

"Cnut is in England. The seas are too rough for a crossing, and Thorkell holds Fyrkat. I think we can wait out the winter."

While Úlfr continues to complain, I've stopped listening to him, my focus on the water being carved up by the prow of the ship, sending spray high in the air.

Something is going on, something that I'm not aware of, and I don't like it. Not at all. And as I've just said to Úlfr, the weather is on the turn, and it's impossible to demand answers from Cnut, in England. Thorkell was correct; I shouldn't have gone to Fyrkat. Now I have all winter to worry that the problem might well be much closer to me than I would like.

# CHAPTER 11

## *AD 1023*

"Have you seen Úlfr?" I ask the question of my mother.

Lady Sigrid looks at me in surprise from her place beside the gently flaming hearth.

"You don't know that he's taken the ships and left Roskilde?" Her voice thrums with concern.

The news almost makes me shudder with fury.

"No, I didn't know. Damn the bastard." I stamp my foot, the sound rousing my mother's interest more than my words.

"What's going on?" Her question has been long in coming. I'm amazed she's not asked before. The winter has been long and filled with uncertainties. I've done my best to keep my husband close, even if I was uncomfortable allowing him to touch me. I have my children. To have more than two would cause problems in the future. I need only look at what happened between my brothers to know that.

"I wish I knew enough to say, but I suspect him of treason against Cnut."

"Úlfr? Does Cnut have any loyal followers anymore?" She speaks with dismay because she believes Jarl Thorkell is also his enemy. I'm not so sure.

I should have realised that as soon as the weather improved, Úlfr would escape my scrutiny. Admittedly, I'm also disappointed in myself for not managing to keep my misgivings from being discovered. Maybe Úlfr isn't quite as stupid as I believed.

I consider rushing to the quayside, just to be sure that he's truly gone, but I know it will be useless. And even if he remains, how can I detain him? What excuse can I have for insisting that he stay where I can see him? He is Cnut's regent, not I, even if everyone else knows the truth of that.

Only then my mother is standing before me, my sons playing quietly together under the watchful eye of Frida.

"What is this?"

"Thorkell believe it's Úlfr who's the threat to Cnut. I intended to keep him close to me until Cnut could arrive from England." All these months of keeping my silence, and now the truth rushes from me as though it's not a secret anymore.

A flurry of emotions sweeps over my mother's face, and I realise that the winter has been hard on her, perhaps too hard, the cold creeping into her old bones and forcing her to sit huddled under piles of furs, as close to the hearth as possible.

Her adversary, Lady Gunnhild, has also been ill all winter. I've been remarkably free from her complaints. Still, I hope she lives to enjoy the warmth of the sun on her face one more time.

"If he's no longer loyal, but others are unaware, he can call on the support of my son to support him, perhaps to even help him claim Denmark as his own, in the name of your sons. Or he could ask the king of Norway for assistance. There's no love lost between Cnut and Olof, and Olof thinks even less of him since the matter of the royal children." My mother speaks of her son as though he's no relation to her. I admire such cool-headedness.

All the same, I know this. That's why I wanted Úlfr where I could watch him closely.

"Damn the man," is all I offer, before turning to my sons. I suspected my husband would one day be a traitor. It isn't a surprise to me, but I'm disappointed in the inevitability of it all. But, I have my sons, and that's all that truly matters. A son can always rise above the treason of his father. I need only to remember my father's successes to know the truth of those words.

"Cnut is here," I don't expect to hear the words, not here, in Jelling. While my husband continues to evade me, I've come to Jelling, the heart of the House of Gorm, to at least show my loyalty to Cnut.

"Here?" I fail to keep the surprised squeak from my voice, as Frida nods, quickly.

"Yes, with a large force of warriors."

"I didn't even know he was in Denmark," I mutter to myself, already preparing to see my brother in the flesh. I'm thrilled he's here, able to take command of whatever is happening with Úlfr, Thorkell and Anund Jakob of the land of the Svear. My half-brother, Olof Skotskonung, is dead, his son ruling in his stead. The sorrow of losing her son, and first-born child, has driven my mother to her knees in prayer. But, at least Cnut is here in Denmark. I didn't expect him to act so decisively.

"They say he's been to Hedeby, but that Úlfr evaded them there."

"Úlfr seems to evade everyone," I complain, critically eyeing my attire to ensure it's suitable to meet the king, and his warriors. I've been hunting for my husband, trusted warriors visiting the most likely sites, but each and every time, Úlfr has moved on before them. I would not have thought Denmark was so large, but there are so many places to hide, and Úlfr, never one to be shy, has no compunction in making his presence felt in even the most loyal of settlements.

"Jarl Thorkell is with him."

"Then they're reconciled," that knowledge brings me some satisfaction. I would sooner have Thorkell beside my brother, than Úlfr. Just the thought of being in the same room as Úlfr chills me. I don't know how I've coped with it for the last year.

"Will you ride out and meet him?"

"Yes, but keep the boys here. They can meet their Uncle when all is settled."

I hasten to leave the hall, hoping that Frida has commanded the servants to prepare food and wine for my brother. I could curse him for not informing of his intentions, but then, perhaps he fears I'm disloyal, like my husband. But no, my brother knows me too well. I dismiss my worries as quickly as they've filtered through my mind.

Cnut expects Úlfr to be here, not me. That's why he comes armed and ready for battle. All will be well, once we see each other and he appreciates that I'm doing my damnedest to find my treasonous husband.

"Sister."

"Brother." The fire has burned low, the room filled with the sounds of men and women sleeping.

"You appreciate your husband will no longer be welcome in Denmark."

I nod, and then grunt because he's not looking at me, but rather down at his hands.

"I understand that." I don't need to tell him that I've always known my marriage would be a short-run thing. "Neither will I marry again." I feel it best to say this before he can suggest it.

"As you will," Cnut acquiesces far too quickly, and my eyes narrow.

"That was too easy?"

"It was, yes," and he grins as he looks at me, the worry removed from his handsome face by the shadows leaking from the wooden hall.

"Why was it so easy?"

"I have a further request to ask of you."

"Will the demands of my family never be at an end?" I ask, my tone far friendlier than the words imply.

"I think you know they won't." Cnut agrees but then falls strangely silent. I wait. He will speak when he's found either the courage or the correct words. I think his hesitation is probably a combination of the two.

"I've asked Jarl Thorkell to remain in Denmark." So, I'm to be replaced. I think. Or maybe not.

"And Harthacnut will also live in Denmark." Now I understand his hesitation to voice his vision of the future.

"Away from his mother?" I feel my eyes round at such a provocative decision. "Does Lady Emma even know?"

"I believe all will be arranged when I return to England, yes. Harthacnut will come to Denmark, and one of Thorkell's sons will accompany me to England. We'll exchange sons, and become foster-fathers to each other's children. It will bind us even more tightly together." For the time being, I don't consider whether such an agreement smacks of trust or not.

"Harthacnut is no more than four. Even you were older than that when our father trusted you to Thorkell's care." As much as I never appreciated Lady Emma, I feel I should speak in her defence.

"I'm aware of that, but still, I need Harthacnut in Denmark, if only to prevent your husband from trying to attack. He'll not move against a child."

I consider that. I'm not at all convinced that Jarl Úlfr has such restraint.

"You'll care for my son, alongside Thorkell. My nephews will become his friends and allies."

"A pretty story you tell yourself," I comment, lips downcast. "Surely, Harthacnut will see them as competitors for the kingdom."

"Why would he do that?" the bite of my brother's words surprises me.

I fix him with my gaze, angered beyond measure by the accusation he flings at me.

"He'll think that because that's what he'll see, and what he'll be told by those who wish to gain a hold over him. Tell me, brother dear, didn't you think the same of Harald? If he hadn't died, can you promise me that you wouldn't have invaded Denmark once you were secure in England."

His hesitation in replying is all I need to know I'm correct to worry.

Cnut shrugs a shoulder, as though to dismiss my words. Only the main doors open with a crash, and a warrior bellows to the sleeping men.

"We're under attack."

"Bloody Úlfr," Cnut complains, already on his feet, calling his men to him. I watch him. If I wasn't a noblewoman, I could have joined him in defending my country. But no, I must sit and wait, and hope that my damn husband is dead by the end of it all.

"Success?" I've been waiting patiently for news. Outside the sky has turned from the half-grey of daybreak to bright sunlight. I've not been fretting, but rather impatient for the result.

It's not Cnut who comes before me, but rather another man, one I almost recognise, but not quite. He's clearly from England. Perhaps I met him in Winchester, but it seems so many years ago now, that it's impossible to recall every person I met.

"The king has asked you to attend him." His tone is difficult to interpret because it's rich with respect owed to my position as the king's sister.

I feel my forehead furrow, as my heart beats a little faster. My husband must be dead; there can be no other reason for Cnut to want me to leave the hall.

Outside, the people of Jelling have formed up, keen to see their king protecting them. They're so confident of the king's success that the women remain unarmed without so much as an eating knife to hand. I would chastise them, but it fills me with pride to see how they respond to my brother. Certainly, Úlfr was never as popular.

I'm allowed through the gates that surround the settlement, the stench of the sea and the tang of blood and iron, almost making me wretch. I can see where Cnut stands, waiting for me, and I hurry, picking up my dress so that it doesn't drag through the mass of cooling bodies. Without even knowing it, I'm searching for men that served my husband, but I don't see any, none at all.

"What is it?" I ask of Cnut when I'm beside him.

My brother dresses for war, and blood marks his nose, although it isn't his. He seems uninjured, even from just a brief examination.

"This was not the work of Úlfr." The news isn't what I want to hear.

"Then who would dare attack Denmark?" Cnut's mouth settles in a grimace, and then he looks at me.

"It seems that King Anund Jakob has decided he has some claim to Denmark."

"What?"

This I didn't expect to hear, and neither did Cnut.

"My mother will take the news poorly."

"Then you can inform her," Cnut states, his gaze fixed on some object in the distance. "He's raided the home of the Jomsvikings and thought to take Denmark as well. Whether he did so to aid Úlfr or not, I don't know."

"It seems, brother, that your decision to bring Harthacnut to Denmark, might not be too presumptuous, after all."

"I quite agree." His words are not the reassurance they should be.

# CHAPTER 12

## AD 1023

"*Dearest Sister, Lady Estrid Sweinsdottir.*"

"*Why will you not take your husband back? If your brother, the king, can accept that Úlfr was as much a victim of King Anund Jakob and his attempts to unsettle Cnut, then why can't you? You are too cruel, far too cruel.*"

"*Why should my brother be denied access to his youngest children because of your nephew's heinous attack on Jelling? The boys need a father. I know only too well how much a father influences his sons. I warn you, Lady Estrid, that I will have no problem contacting Cnut about this, demanding that he force you to return the children to the care of your husband.*"

"*I beg you, sister dearest, to reconsider your actions toward your husband. He has been proven to be loyal and honourable.*"

"*If you do not do as I command, I will order my husband to speak to Cnut, and he is high in Cnut's favour. He will prevail, and you will not.*"

"*I beg you.*"

"*Your loving sister, Lady Gytha Úlfrsdottir of Wessex.*"

I confess, her letter makes me laugh, and I pass it to Frida, with raised eyebrows, keen for her to enjoy my amusement. She does, and yet I sense her hesitation.

"What, you can't believe that Lady Gytha and her husband

are more influential with my brother than I am?"

"She calls him Cnut. No king, no lord, just Cnut." I still at the implication in Frida's words.

"That means nothing," but I sense an edge to my voice.

"Do you call him Cnut, when you speak with him? Or do you call him 'lord?'"

We both know the answer to that.

"He wouldn't dare?" But suddenly I'm unsure, and I think of my bastard husband and my two small sons.

"I will seek shelter with my nephew if I believe Cnut will act against me."

"But you said you would never leave Denmark again."

"I will if my children are threatened."

"And will you reply to Lady Gytha?"

"No, I will not." But my veins run cold just at the thought of the influence she claims with my brother. It can't be true? Surely not?

**"Dearest Sister, Lady Estrid Sweinsdottir."**

*"I am disappointed by your continued silence. I have written to you almost weekly now for many months. What do you hope to achieve with such stubbornness?"*

*"You should know that Earl Eilifr means to petition the king on his brother's behalf alongside myself and my husband. I am sure that in no time at all, Cnut will take the necessary action against you."*

*"You have no allies and no one to support you in England. Hiding away in Denmark will do you no good, either. You forget that Cnut is almost more English than the English now. I pity you for your foolish behaviour. I will tell you it was all your own fault when Svein and Beorn are taken from you by Cnut and restored to their father, and you are left entirely alone."*

*"I will have no sympathy for you then, and I'll be deaf to your complaints."*

*"Really, sister, reconsider, and do it quickly."*

*"Your sister, Lady Gytha Úlfrsdottir of Wessex."*

"Bitch." I fling the letter to one side, watching with some enjoyment as the rolled parchment slowly closes. I wish it could be so easy to forget the words written, with anger, on the parchment. Would my brother act against me? I wish I knew. He is too distant from me, and I have begun to doubt that he would support me over his jarl.

"What does she say now?" Frida lifts her head from her sewing as she speaks.

"More of the same, threats and counter-threats."

"And they worry you?" She's too perceptive.

"Perhaps."

"Then you know what you need to do?"

I do, yes, and still, I hesitate.

### *"Lady Estrid, dearest aunt."*

*"I write to inform you that my sister, Ingegerd, has successfully birthed her first son with her husband, Yaroslav of the Rus. I know you didn't enjoy your sojourn in the land of the Rus, but Ingegerd is blessed with a far more successful husband than you were. Not that I write to offend you, but rather to inform you of how our family grows. Already she has two daughters, and now a son. She is greatly blessed. Please inform my grandmother. I know she'll be pleased."*

*"I hear worrying rumours that King Cnut blames me for the attack on Jelling. I will not deny any involvement, but I will say that he should be wary of who he trusts, as should you. I will name no one, but I'm sure you can decipher it for yourself."*

*"Remember, you will always be welcome in Old Uppsala should your brother, or other family members, threaten you."*

*"Write to your niece in Norway. I know she feels isolated in Avaldsnes. The weather is bitter, and the wind never ceases."*

*"Your loving nephew, King Anund Jakob of the Svear."*

### *"Lady Astrid, dearest niece."*

*"Please excuse me for not writing as frequently as I should have done. Your brother chastises me, and he's right to do so."*

*"Send me news of how your daughter fares. My sons both grow*

so quickly, I can hardly keep them adequately clothed. I feel as though all I do is sew and then sew some more. It's an impossible task. For all that, I am blessed that my sons are hale and healthy."

"Anund Jakob informed me of the safe arrival of your sister's first-born son. Your grandmother was overjoyed. I am sure she would write herself, but she is always embroiled in some deep intrigue with my sons. You would laugh if you could see her, on her hands and knees, playing on the floor, pretending to be a horse, or even, on occasion, a cow. Certainly, I do."

"Your loving aunt, Lady Estrid Sweinsdottir."

**"Lady Estrid Sweinsdottir, dearest aunt."**

"While I thank you for your correspondence, I would ask you not to write to me again. It makes my husband suspicious, and I'm sure that you can certainly appreciate it's not a pleasant situation."

"My sister is certainly fecund. I feel as though she births children as frequently as Lady Gytha, wife of Earl Godwine. I would be wary of those two. I hear worrying rumours, brought to me by the ship-men who insist on being received by the king. The stench is too much for me, and yet I persevere for the sake of my husband."

"I did enjoy hearing of my regal grandmother crawling around on the floor with your sons. It's a great pity that there is so much distrust and unease amongst our extended family. It would be pleasant to visit with you, but of course, it wouldn't be possible."

"With the death of Jarl Eirikr, I am aware that your half-sister, Lady Gytha Sweinsdottir, may have lost some of her possessions. I would have sent them on to her, but the messenger she sent to me was so rude, I'm not prepared to, not anymore. Tell her that I will ignore all of her entreaties to have her possessions restored to her now. She should have been less abusive and employed some tact, but then, her father was the same. King Swein was not a pleasant man when he was defeated."

"And now, I would remind you not to write to me for the foreseeable future. King Olafr is mistrustful, even as he seeks an alliance with my brother."

"Your loving niece, Lady Astrid Olofsdottir, Queen of Norway."

"Hum." Frida again catches my eye.

"What this time?"

"Something that Cnut should know about." I waver, and she grimaces.

"Will it aid you if you tell him?"

"Perhaps. It will certainly not aid me if I keep the information to myself."

"Then I suggest you write to your brother, or send Siward, or do both."

**"Dearest brother, King Cnut of Denmark, England and Skåne."**

*"I will not be rebuked by you. I have made it clear that my husband isn't to be trusted. If you decide to have faith in him, there's no reason why I should do the same."*

*"But, I write of another matter. My niece, Lady Astrid of Norway, informs me that her husband is seeking an alliance with King Anund Jakob now that Earl Eilifr is dead. It was a parting comment in a letter of a family nature, and yet it would be wrong of me not to inform you. I fear the possibility of Kings Olafr and Anund Jakob making war on Denmark while you're in England."*

*"Lady Astrid also informed me that our sister, the widow of Jarl Eilifr, has been despoiled of her possessions. It appears as though King Olafr is keen to move against you."*

*"I will notify you if I hear more, but my nephew made no mention of it, and Lady Astrid has asked me not to write to her again, because it makes her husband suspicious."*

*"I would ask after your children and your wife, but as I know you don't indulge in writing to me of such matters, I will merely inform you that my sons are well, as is my mother. I will not allow Jarl Úlfr, their father, to have any contact with them. I know my father would have approved of my firm stance. There is no room for traitors in the House of Gorm."*

*"Your loving sister, Lady Estrid Sweinsdottir."*

# CHAPTER 13

*Roskilde, AD1025*

"**I** was right," Cnut's words could be about anything, and I'm at a loss as to what to say.

"Your husband is a treasonous bastard." I know my husband still lives, but I appreciate that it won't be for much longer. That probably shouldn't please me, but it does.

And Cnut's not telling me anything I didn't already know. Still, I hold my tongue. Cnut and his ship-men have returned from a great ship battle at Helgeå, and now they are at Roskilde and Cnut intends to cast off those who turned traitor against him, my husband amongst them.

I always suspected the invasion on Jelling by King Anund Jakob was with my husband's support, and probably that of his brother's as well. But Cnut was prepared to offer him the benefit of the doubt. I imagine he now wishes that he hadn't. Indeed, the last three years haven't been pleasant.

"What will you do now?"

Harthacnut came to Denmark, three years ago, on Cnut's wishes, and under the care of Jarl Thorkell, but since then, events have been too dangerous for him to remain. He returned to England last year, much to the joy of Lady Emma, and now with the death of Thorkell and the betrayal of Úlfr, I imagine he'll have to come back to Denmark.

Cnut insists that the threat from King Oláfr and Anund

Jakob is gone. He might well be correct. After all, Cnut's ship-army might be depleted, but Cnut's fleet in the Øresund traps the vast majority of the Norwegians, and unable to return to Norway in their ships. They face a long trek home, over inhospitable terrain, or attacking the very allies they've just fought and died for, in order to gather food to survive the coming winter. It's a cruel way to kill warriors, but I can't help but admire my brother for his fierce resolve in commanding such.

He's not even going to remain in Denmark to ensure the enemy are overwhelmed. No, Cnut plans to travel to Rome to witness the coronation of the new Holy Roman Emperor. He's confident, and assured, at least about Denmark.

"I have decisions to make," Cnut offers, slumping to a seat in front of me. He might be the victor, but it seems to weigh on him.

I would call for wine and ale, but there's already plenty on the table, and Cnut reaches for none of it.

"You look tired," I comment when it seems he'll say nothing further.

"I am tired, of people who don't share my vision of a northern empire or people who would rather dwell on their own petty wants and needs." I assume he must speak of England because there's no one left in Denmark to deny him. Not the foolish bishop, who marched from the borders with the Germanic states to reclaim what he felt was taken from him, meeting his death in that way, or the Danish nobles who thought that King Oláfr of Norway or King Anund Jacob would offer them more than their true king.

"Tell me of events in England?"

"Lady Emma rules in my name, with the aid of Earl Godwine and the archbishops."

I feel my face pull down at the mention of Earl Godwine. "I believe they're all as rotten as one another," I state, dismayed to realise that Godwine is so influential.

"Earl Godwine is ambitious, yes, I would never deny that."

"He's too ambitious," I retort, thinking him too like my errant husband.

"He's done nothing to make me suspect him." It seems Cnut is at least prepared to explain his current stance to me. That thrills me.

Without either my mother, or Lady Gunnhild, both dying in the last few years, I'm Cnut's figurehead in Denmark. I stand for the dynasty of the House of Gorm, my two small sons, just as much standards as I am. I've earned the respect of the nobility who remained dedicated to my brother's kingship by being fiercely loyal to Cnut and his vision of the future, and by distancing myself from Jarl Úlfr for the last few years.

"He might now," I postulate. "With Jarl Úlfr," how it pains me to speak his name aloud, "destined to die, there's no saying what his brother and sister will do to gain restitution for that death."

Cnut frowns at my words. Has he truly failed to realise this? I would hope not. Whether the three of them liked one another much doesn't matter. It's the honour of the thing.

"If I can't rely on Earl Godwine while I'm absent, then who would you have me appoint as regent."

"What of your older sons, and their mother?"

Cnut chuckles at my words. Not the reaction I was anticipating.

"Do you mean to make Lady Emma despise you even more than she already does?"

"I mean to do no such thing, but young Harthacnut can't be in two places at once, and he has no need to be. And what of your daughter? Surely Gunnhild could also assist you. I know the children are young. Still, they're a better choice than some barely-related earl who thinks to enrich himself and his ever-growing family, even while one of his brother's by marriage is destined to be executed, and the other one has gone into hiding."

"I," Cnut opens his mouth to dismiss my suggestion, but then he closes it again, and grunts.

"It might not be a terrible idea," he offers instead. Already,

I imagine his mind has turned to Rome and what he hopes to find there.

"Hah," I crow. "You need to remember that my loyalty is untainted by any need to profit at your expense. I've married the men you instructed. I've done whatever you asked of me, with no thought for what I desired."

"I don't doubt you," Cnut admits. "But Denmark needs a strong leader, and so does England, and I can't be in two places at once."

"You should have considered that then before you claimed Denmark as well as England."

"It was hardly my intention to hold both kingdoms at the same time. My father wanted me to win England. He believed Harald should have Denmark. I believe you attended the meeting where that was decided, and that you had sight of that damn will."

"But Harald has been dead for years. Surely by now, you could have organised a better alternative than relying on men who don't deserve your trust." Not, I consider that Jarl Thorkell was truly ever a traitor. I can tell that Cnut feels his death keenly. For no other reason, was Úlfr allowed to gather a ship-army to support his king against Denmark's enemies. If Jarl Thorkell yet lived, there would have been no need. But then, if a combined force of warriors hadn't murdered jarl Thorkell, some Danish, many not, all under kings Oláfr of Norway and Anund Jakob of the Svear, there would have been no battle of Helgeå.

"Sister, you test me," Cnut grumbles.

In all honesty, I don't know where to direct my fury. If my mother still lived, she would have flayed her grandson and granddaughter for encouraging such disunity. I don't believe I have the status to do so myself, and yet, I've tried all the same. All summer long, I've sent stringent letters to them both, demanding they desist. I've been roundly ignored, and now it won't be they who are threatened, but rather the warriors beguiled into following their respective kings.

144

But equally, I'm furious with Cnut and Úlfr as well. I don't understand why Cnut thought to trust a man he already suspected of acting in concert with Anund Jakob.

"Denmark is safe, and secure, under your guidance. I know that. But, with Harthacnut returned to Denmark, he can begin to prepare for when he rules it himself. He's older now, and it'll be his kingdom to rule when he's gained all of the skills he needs."

"And so why can't the same happen in England? Or better yet, why not bring Swein or Harald to Denmark. It would keep Lady Emma happy, and then I might actually meet my older nephews."

"No," Cnut's response is simple and final.

I sigh unhappily.

"Jarl Hakon will rule in Norway when I return from Rome. He is, after all, the hereditary jarl of Hlaðir, now that his father is dead. He'll rule there, in my name. But, I must travel to Rome before I can install him in Hlaðir. There's not the required time to ensure all is done now."

"I concede that," I confirm, although it still doesn't explain Cnut's resistance to allowing his older sons to rule.

"Good, then this conversation is at an end, for now. I apologise, sister, for binding you to a man such as Jarl Úlfr. I'd thought to control him, but he was unmanageable."

"Yes, he was." I never wish to speak of Úlfr again, but first, well first, I must face the traitor. I will cast eyes on him one final time before his execution.

I gaze at his still face, almost wishing I could feel something other than this cold disdain. But I've always known how it would end, even before it began. There might have been some enjoyment at points in my marriage, but it doesn't compensate enough for what I've been forced to endure.

His features are well known to me, and I imagine, in years to come, they might be etched into our sons, or rather my sons. From this day forth, they'll not be known as his sons. I've made that clear to Cnut. I'll make it clear to everyone who attempts to speak of their father. For Úlfr is nothing. He's merely the process by which I gained my children.

But there will be no more. Not now.

From today, I'll be my own woman. I'll make my decisions alone. And I'll be more than a woman to open their legs for a man to gain my family what they think it needs.

My husband, who lies marbled and flaccid before me, is the last man I'll ever allow into my bed-chamber.

I haven't brought my sons to witness their dead father. I may not care for the man before me, but I adore my sons, and it's not fitting for them to carry the memory of his treason as their final recollection. Bad enough that in years to come, men and women will taunt them for what befell him.

I will not. I'll not speak of Jarl Úlfr after today. No child needs to know that their parent was a failure, lacking in morality and riddled with treason that ran like a poison inside him, leaking and staining all that he touched. Other than his sons.

I close my eyes, bow my head low, but it's not in prayer. My prayers have been answered. The words of the prayer that I've almost tripped over in my haste to have this done need never touch my lips again. I'm cleansed of Úlfr's poison and sickness.

It's about time.

# AUNT

# CHAPTER 14

## *AD 1026*

"*L ady Estrid.*" I read the missive before me. It's long, trailing almost to the floor, and filled with the small, cramped writing of one of the Winchester scribes. I don't expect Lady Emma to write her own letters to me, but I do expect them to be legible.

"*Greetings, Dear sister.*" I smirk at the attempt to be pleasant. It never lasts longer than a single line.

"*I demand to know how my son fares under your guidance. He's always been a boisterous child. Assure me that he has clothes that fit him, and which befit his rank as the king's son. I would know that he eats well, but not too much.*"

The letter will go on and on, the little details that are denied her by such a distance, and I'm surprised she shows such care. I have no recollection of her doing the same for Alfred, Edward and Goda when I lived in England. I seem to recall even mentioning them to her received an unpleasant response.

But no, I'm too harsh, and I should be kinder. My sons haven't been taken from me. In fact, Cnut allows me to control their destinies as I see fit, provided it's always to the honour of our family name.

Instead, I scan the letter, hoping for news of Cnut, England, and Earl Godwine. I only just stop myself from growling as I even think his name. I don't trust the man. I'm sure he was in-

148

volved in my husband's betrayal, even if I have no proof and Cnut dismisses my concerns without even considering them.

*"I would like to send Harthacnut a gift for his birth day. It will be a new horse, sired by his father's prized stallion, Blue. Ensure there's room for the animal in the royal stables. He must be treated well and kept from the extremes of the terrible Danish weather."*

I roll my eyes. Lady Emma is both tedious and detailed, in her anxiety to be seen as a loving mother. I can't even remember the last time that Harthacnut mentioned his mother. Certainly, I know he doesn't send messages to her, despite the many she sends to him. She would do well to direct her frustration at Harthacnut, and not me.

*"I would also welcome news of my husband, the king. Please advise how he fares in Denmark. England is not as peaceful as it could be without him."*

This startles me. Why would Lady Emma presume that Cnut was in Denmark? I understood it was common knowledge that Cnut planned to travel to Rome for the coronation. But perhaps, she believes he's cancelled his plans to ensure the safety of Denmark. That makes some sense. But, damn my brother, he could have at least informed his wife of his intentions to continue with his long-planned journey.

"Bring me parchment," I ask Frida. She nods, holding her tongue, interpreting my tone correctly. It's always the same when Lady Emma writes to me. No matter what the contents of the letter are, I end up feeling exasperated by her.

**"Dearest sister, Lady Emma, Queen of England."**

*"Good wishes from Denmark. I write to assure you that Harthacnut thrives. He's growing into a fine young man, and has playfellows to keep him occupied when he's not attending to his lessons."*

I sigh, consider what else I should say. I'm forced to write to Lady Emma at least once each week. It becomes mundane when there's nothing to report, but that Harthacnut is well.

*"I assure you that your son is always adequately clothed as befits his position. If you are not content with my assurance, then send one of your women to see for themselves."* I should perhaps not say that, but her constant questioning makes me believe she doesn't trust me to care for her son.

*"The nobility of Denmark accepts your son as their rightful future king. Even at such a young age, he's able to charm and delight them."* I don't mention that it's only on rare occasions, interspersed with much longer-lasting acts of stubbornness and arrogance. I hope that when Cnut next visits Denmark, he'll take his son to task. Certainly, I've had no success in curbing that side of his nature since he was returned to my care.

Harthacnut is tall for his age and strong with it. He shows no fear of anyone, even the warriors who consent to allow him to train with him. They're often the ones with bruises, and I have reports that it's not because they allow him to win.

*"Cnut is not in Denmark. He's travelled to Rome, as expected before the problems with King Oláfr Haraldsson and King Anund Jakob. I have no news of when he means to return, although he does mean to return to Denmark. I can assure you of that."*

Those words mask many more that I could say, and I'm impressed by my ability to hide so much of my frustration with Lady Emma.

*"I send this message with one of my most loyal men, Siward. He'll tell you all you need to know about Harthacnut."* There, I take pity on her. She'll only be content when she can pick and prod at the man. Not that Siward will approve of my sending of him. Poor man. I've ill-used him, but I'm sure that Cnut will reward him well, one day in the future.

I hold the parchment open, allowing the ink to dry, and then pull another piece toward me.

I need to write to my nephew in Sweden, even if he doesn't heed my words.

**"King Anund Jakob, warm greetings from your aunt, in Den-**

*mark."* Again, I pause, but then decide to be blunt with him.

*"King Cnut will not tolerate any further incursions in Skåne. I believe you're lucky to have escaped with the slight losses that you suffered. I fear that Oláfr Haraldsson was not so lucky. There has been more than enough blood shed in recent years. You have no claim to Skåne, and my Lady Mother, your grandmother, would caution you to the same, if she yet lived."*

Ideally, I want to tell my arrogant nephew that he has ambitions far above his skills, but he'll not heed any of my warnings if I do so. I've never met a king who enjoyed having his abilities questioned.

*"Be assured that my brother will not countenance losing any of his far-flung possessions. Also, be advised that his ambitions are far from quenched."* I refrain from informing him of exactly what my brother has planned, but I would be remiss if I gave no warning at all. There's still time for Anund Jakob to adopt a more conciliatory approach.

*"My sons are well, an honour to their grandmother. In time, I believe they'll be great warriors."* I confess, there's a threat there. Anund Jakob must begin to realise that Denmark's ambitions will not end with Cnut's death, whenever that might occur.

But I push the letter aside, eyeing the straggling lines with vexation. The words are not the ones I wish to say. Perhaps, just as with Lady Emma, I should send someone who's able to speak confidentially to my nephew, to determine his true intentions. They could make it clear that he risks his life, and the lives of his loyal men and women, if he persists in harassing my brother.

Once more, I feel perturbed that my father set such a potential future in motion when he married the Swedish king's widowed wife, and mother of his heir. Did Swein not see what might happen, or was he truly so arrogant that he believed he would rule Denmark, England and Sweden long before he met his death? I wish I knew.

Certainly, it's those concerns that bedevil me, not whether Harthacnut has enough clothes, or where his damn horse will be housed to avoid the worst of the terrible winter weather. That almost makes me laugh out loud. Lady Emma might well have had a Danish mother, but she's certainly never been to Roskilde. What does she know of winters here? My experience in England is that there is little or no difference.

I allow my thoughts to linger on Cnut. He should be here. He should be the one with these worries. Not me. He's too much like my father.

I reach for another piece of parchment.

**"Dearest niece."** My words are for Astrid, married to Oláfr Haraldsson, king of Norway, and of course, the reason why my niece and nephew are so content to conspire against Denmark.

"*I hear worrying news of events in Norway. Have the men who took part in the battle of Helgeå even returned yet? Has your husband? If he has, you must appeal to him for peace. I will write to your brother as well to tell him to stop stirring up trouble. I do not believe that either kingdom will be able to resist Cnut, and I understand that the nobility in Norway are keen for Cnut to rule there. They've had enough of your husband and his ambitions which upset them, and also extend beyond Norway's border. I trust your daughter is well.*"

"*Your loving aunt, Lady Estrid, daughter of King Swein of Denmark and sister of King Cnut, King of Denmark, England and Skåne.*"

I don't imagine that my niece or nephew will approve of my meddling, but my mother would, and I will take up her mantle. I must.

**"Dearest Aunt."** I hold the parchment away from me, making use of the bright light outside to decipher the flowing words. I suppress my envy that she has such a fine hand. I wish I could lay claim to the same.

"*My daughter is in good health. Thank you for asking after her. I would, of course, wish she were a son, but it seems that's not to be. I trust your two sons are growing well. I do not envy you, two* sons. I have only to think of the problems between Harald and Cnut to appreciate that more than one son is going to be problematic. I'm relieved that my father and his brother managed to work so well together before my father's death. I never heard them argue. Not once."

Her assertion brings a bark of disbelief. My mother could recite many occasions when Olof and Emund argued. But I read on.

"It must be tedious to have people constantly remind the boys that their father was a traitor, executed for his crimes. I hope they grow to be more trustworthy than their father."

"I will give you no news of my husband, other than to say that he will be prepared for any response from King Cnut. I can assure you that my brother thinks the same. You are the king's sister, not the king himself."

"Is it true that he has gone to Rome, even with my husband and brother prepared to take up arms against him? His arrogance astounds me. Does he not know that there are still four hundred ships prepared to attack Skåne or Roskilde, just waiting for favourable weather?"

I realise then that my niece is unaware of the true extent of what's befallen her husband and her brother. I consider when she last heard from them? It might even have been before the battle itself took place. I would pity her, but her next words force me to pity her for an entirely different reason than pure ignorance of the current state of the war between her husband, brother, and my brother.

"I should inform you that King Oláfr has a son now, whelped on an English woman, my servant, but now raised higher in my husband's court. I don't like the change, but accept that my husband requires a son, and I could not provide one. The child is fair. Do not pity me. Next time you write to me, please send a less inquisitive individual to deliver it. I have only just managed to secure his departure from Trondheim."

"Your loving niece, Lady Astrid, queen of Norway."

I might not like the contents of the letter, but I'm pleased to hear my mother echoed in my niece's tone. It reassures me that even if her husband has taken up with a mere slave, she's prepared to ensure her future.

I turn to the messenger, Halfdan. He meets my gaze evenly, his heavy eyebrows shadowing alert looking auburn eyes.

"What did you do?" I demand to know, and his tense posture relaxes, and he grins.

"Nothing that you didn't command, My Lady. I can inform you that King Oláfr lacks support in Norway. The nobility would welcome a return of the Jarl of Hlaðir, even if he were ultimately accountable to your brother."

This news pleases me.

"Then you have my thanks for your endeavours."

I dismiss him and muse over the contents of the letter. I'm not sure I'm entirely happy about the news of the birth of a son for King Oláfr. Being the father of a son can make men worry too much about ensuring the future.

*"Dearest Aunt."* I move the candle closer to the parchment. The ink is of poor quality, and the words difficult to decipher. Surely my nephew has access to better ink than this? After all, he is the king.

*"I hope you and your sons are well. I'll not ask after your nephew. I hear enough. I also understand that King Cnut is far from Denmark and England. I don't understand his concern with Rome when his kingdom is so exposed. A child is no true ruler, no matter how skilled he is with a sword and shield, and no matter how respected his aunt might be."*

I startle, almost dropping the letter. Who is there in my court who sends such reports to Anund Jacob? I would know and have them cast out. I will have to ask Frida. She knows everything there is to know about the men and women who make their home at my expense.

*"You well know that King Oláfr and I won the day at the Battle*

of Helgeå. Many Danes and Englishmen died in the battle. I would caution King Cnut to be less keen to shed more blood. Please leave an offering at my grandmother's gravesite. I've sent a jewel to grace it. She should have been interred with my grandfather in Old Uppsala."

"Your loving nephew, Anund Jakob, king of the Svear."

I might find it difficult to read the words, but the jewel is bright enough to see even if I were in England and the gem in Roskilde.

Could my nephew have made a more provocative act? I hardly think it's possible.

### "Dearest Sister, Lady Estrid Sweinsdottir."

"I again write to ask after my son. I've heard nothing from him. I assume you keep him from his learning and so he's unable to write himself. But, surely some scribes could record his words to me? Ensure this is done, and soon. I grow impatient with no news from him. The man you sent, Siward, could hardly answer my questions. Has he even met my son?"

I look at Siward as I read that part of the letter. He's offered nothing other than the new note. I appreciate his diplomacy.

"I've heard from my husband. His message to me was delayed by many months due to poor travel conditions. Do not fear that I was unaware of his movements." I roll my eyes. Lady Emma can never just admit that she was ignorant of my brother's actions. She will not allow herself even to believe that he slights her.

"My daughter, Gunnhild, is a delightful child. It's a pity that you were not blessed with a daughter, but only sons. I remember you in my prayers. It is truly a curse to have a husband who betrays your own family. What did Harthacnut think of his new horse? I am keen to know."

"Your infuriated sister, Lady Emma, queen of England."

"Harthacnut," the boy sits beside me as I reach the end of the letter. He looks at me with the arrogant tilt of his eyebrow that he's adopted of late. He's not learned such a look from my sons.

"Lady Estrid?" his voice is just about respectful.

"Have you written to your Lady Mother?" His pause is enough to inform me that he hasn't.

"Then you can do it now. I will summon the scribe."

"I can't, Lady Estrid. I must attend to my lessons." He's already standing, preparing to move away, Beorn and Svein encouraging him with their eyes and hands. For some reason, they're all great friends at the moment. I know it will not last. They often bicker and argue, and I'm sure it won't be too long before fists follow the hurtful, if childish words, they fling at one another.

"Then inform Brother Cuthbert that you're to write to your mother as part of one of your lessons. Be sure to thank her for that damn horse."

Harthacnut offers me a jaunty bow, and then races from the hall. I watch the three children go, and wish I could rely on them to remain such close friends and allies, but they're cousins and brothers. The odds are stacked against them. Just look at the rest of my family.

### *"Lady Estrid. Dearest Sister."*

*"Greetings from Rome. I write to inform you that I'm delayed for longer than I might have thought. Rome is a wondrous city, with fine riches to behold. I've sent word to Lady Emma, and you're to ensure the people of Denmark know of my whereabouts, and that when I return, it will be to continue the endeavour begun against Norway and the land of the Svear. I thank you for your good efforts with my son and my kingdom. You have my complete trust while I'm gone."*

I sigh, waving the parchment to stir some sort of breeze in the oppressive heat. My brother's continued delay has left me feeling ineffectual. I can do little but fend off increasingly irate letters from Lady Emma, while King Oláfr and King Anund Jakob remain contained, but with the threat of menace ever-present. At some point, they'll gather their forces once more. Of that, I'm sure.

My only consolation is that Earl Godwine is in England with his wife, Lady Gytha Úlfrsdottir. Lady Emma is welcome in trying to contain the ambitious English man and his wife. I'm unsure of where Eilifr is. I hope he never dares show his face in England or Denmark again, but I wouldn't be surprised if he did. It seems that having a traitor for a brother is no impediment.

What, I think, is it with my family? None of them is content with what they have? Again, I curse my father and feeling contrite, take myself to the family mausoleum to pray for the souls of my father and brother. It feels as though it's been many, many years since I last saw my father, and yet the problems he created, continue to influence my life.

"Sister," I know my gaze is cold, but Cnut hardly seems to notice.

"I've made a great marriage for my daughter." His grin is almost infectious, and yet I hold tight to my frustration at his long absence. He didn't need to make a marriage for his daughter. He needed to be here, in Denmark, finishing what he began.

Cnut's hair is long but tidy, his clothes unsuitable for the cold climate. Silks might well be comfortable in the heat of the southern kingdoms, but not here, with the pinch of winter in the air. The vivid colour is almost too bright. He seems to pulse brighter than the sun.

"Who will the poor girl wed?" I find myself asking because I know it's what he wants me to do.

"She's not poor," Cnut, surprisingly, has picked up on my use of words. "She'll wed the Holy Roman Emperor's son. She'll have a life of ruling, and will be revered by all who know her." I have no knowledge of the girl to know what her personality is, or even if she'll appreciate her marriage. I know she's a child. I also know that Lady Emma might not appreciate Cnut's matchmaking.

"I only hope she has the years to grow into her position."

And here Cnut's good cheer dims, just a little. I sigh. I imagine I know what Cnut has done and for a heartbeat, I feel some sympathy for Lady Emma. She's no ally of mine. I find her tedious, but she'll have lost all of her children thanks to her husband. I can't imagine she will welcome the development.

"Gunnhild will travel to her new family within the next year. They have a different culture and language, and she must learn all about it before she rules."

I shake my head. If he were my husband, I would be disappointed in him. As my brother, I can be a little kinder. But only a little.

"Ah sister, you should have seen Rome, and the Holy Father, and even Emperor Conrad. He's a fine man, an honourable man." I close my eyes, seek a thread of calm to stop me from debasing Cnut of all these illusions he has about the man. I would say, 'he is just a man.' I would say, 'the Pope is just a man.' I would even say that Rome was built by men and women and the labours of slaves. But I know that Cnut will not hear it.

"Our cathedral in Roskilde is magnificent, but still, it must be enriched. I must honour my God and my people further."

Cnut sips sparingly from the beaker before him, refusing wine, and preferring water. I doubt that will last long, but maybe he'll surprise me.

"Tell me of events in Denmark." He seems belatedly to have remembered that he's the king of Denmark, and not just a visitor.

"Denmark is peaceful, and your son well-beloved." Cnut startles, and again, I could slap my brother around the face for forgetting his child, as well as everything else.

"Where is he? I should like to see him."

I turn to Frida, and she nods.

"He's been summoned." I decline to tell Cnut what his son has been doing.

"Oláfr Haraldsson and Anund Jakob require your attention."

"Why? What have the bastards done now?"

"They seem determined to make war on you."

"And you have done nothing about it?"

My breath hisses through tight lips, and Cnut is already lifting his hands in apology, so that I allow the criticism to pass, almost unnoticed.

"I've been busy arguing with my nephew. He's disinclined to respond to my messages, but I persevere. I've also been in contact with my niece. Her husband has a son, although the boy is not hers."

Cnut grunts at the disclosure.

"I assured you I would deal with Norway on my return. Surely, nothing has happened in the intervening period?"

"I know what you said." I allow the sentence to hang.

Cnut nods, his good cheer hasn't deserted him, although I can see that he's more pensive now, no doubt reminded of his ambitions.

"I'll return to England, see my wife, and bring my daughter to Denmark. You should meet her before she leaves for the Holy Roman Empire."

I open my mouth to voice a complaint, only Harthacnut has arrived, and Cnut has eyes only for him. I wish Harthacnut had chosen a less provocative stance to adopt, but he feels just as abandoned as I did. I leave my brother and my nephew to become reacquainted. It's going to be only the first of many awkward encounters for my brother.

# CHAPTER 15

*AD 1028*

I watch the ships as they stream away. I know what my
brother has planned, and for a moment, I know pity for
my niece. Cnut can be relentless and remorseless when he's
so inclined. I don't expect my niece to have a husband when
this fresh attack on Norway is completed.

She should have heeded my caution.

"My Lady," Frida calls for me, and I turn, note the messenger
beside her. I sigh. It's not Siward's fault, but this can only be another complaint from Lady Emma about her husband, son, or
her daughter's new status. Cnut should be answering her letters, not I.

I take the parchment from his hand and turn to read it, my
brother's ships just within sight in front of me as they stream
towards Skåne before turning northwards.

**"Dearest Sister, Lady Estrid Sweinsdottir, written at Winches-
ter, England."**

*"I have not heard from you. Has my daughter arrived in Den-
mark? How long will she stay there? Who is to escort her to the Holy
Roman Empire, and how is my son? He has yet to write to me, even
though I have asked you, repeatedly, to ensure he does so. I see this
as a failure on your part. I have demanded that my brother speaks
to you about the situation. How can you be so cruel when you're a
mother? Does it run in your family?"*

*"I find Earl Godwine no better, and no doubt, Earl Eilifr is in league with Godwine, now that he's stolen his way back into England. What is it that the three of you plan? I know you're in league with them, despite your assurance that you despise Earl Godwine and his wife. I assure you, the kingdom of England will not fall into the hands of any of your children, no matter what you might think."*

I turn aside from her words, trying not to take insult from the fact she thinks I might ally with Earl Godwine and Eilifr. I fix Siward with a firm glance. He arches an eyebrow at me, and I feel a moment of pity for him. Lady Emma can't be an easy woman, especially when she knows he's my man, and likely to profit greatly from being so highly trusted by me.

"What is this of Earl Godwine?"

"He's a tricky man," he announces. "King Cnut is blind to his faults. Godwine has so many children now, I find it impossible to keep count. There are many sons, and at least one daughter. Cnut might not see the ambition, but it's evident to everyone else."

"I will write to Lady Gytha," I announce, trying not to grimace as I speak. "Perhaps she might even reply."

I turn aside from the quayside, dismiss my brother from my thoughts.

He'll be back, in good time. I can't see other than it will be a great victory for him. Certainly, my nephew, Jarl Hakon, is keen to reclaim his birthright as the jarl of Hlaðir, although much of that might just be that he's eager to get away from his mother. I know Hakon will rule well.

*"Dearest sister, Lady Gytha Úlfrsdottir. I write from Roskilde."* Just writing those words makes me shudder. I would sooner claim no family connection to her. There's a reason I don't often contact Lady Gytha.

*"I wish to congratulate you on your growing family. The king informs me that you are a mother once more. I can hardly keep*

count of all of your children. *The king couldn't remember, was it another son? Do write and tell me the names of your children. Your nephews are well, and much beloved of young Harthacnut.*" I smirk as I write that. I might be slightly exaggerating. They all tolerate one another. Surely that's enough, especially when it's impossible for her sons to have day to day interactions with the future king.

There's much that I should like to know, and yet I can't just ask.

I would like to know about the king's other sons, and about how people genuinely perceive the queen, but I'm not going to ask my despised sister by marriage about that. I try and consider another tact, some way that I might force her to give away more than she might intend.

"*I have news that your estates in Lejre are ill-managed. I would suggest you appoint someone new to oversee them, or perhaps send Lord Godwine on your behalf. I should not like them to fall to wrack and ruin, not when you have so many sons who might one day need the income. The king has sailed for Norway with Jarl Hakon. Pray for his success.*"

I add my mark to the rolled parchment. It might seem petty, but I can't deny that penning such words gave me a great deal of pleasure.

**"Dearest Aunt, Lady Estrid, written from Old Uppsala."**
I unroll the parchment carefully. I wouldn't be surprised to find something unpleasant concealed within, especially as the messenger who's brought it to me, is not one of mine, and I don't much like the expression on his heavily-bearded face.

"Why has your brother claimed Norway as his own? Why has he driven my sister, your niece, to seek shelter in her home country? Surely your brother, with his hold on Skåne, has more than enough land to command? Queen Astrid is bereft. Your brother has deprived her daughter of the only home she's ever known."

"*I warn you, dearest Aunt, that such provocative action will be met with retaliation. Inform your brother that he has made a new enemy with his actions."*

*"Your loving nephew, King Anund Jakob of the Svear."*

I tut as I reach the end of the hastily scribbled letter. Did I not warn my nephew? And my niece? Did they truly think that Cnut would allow them to continue unchecked? I tried to tell them what my brother had planned.

I hadn't believed either of them was such fools.

"I'll send a reply in a day or two," I inform Frida. "Have the messenger housed somewhere he can cause no problems." She turns aside, leading the man away, and instructing one of my trusted servants to see to the man and observe him.

I turn to watch my sons and nephew. They're engaged in heated rounds of *tafl*, the winner playing the loser and so on until I'm quite dizzy as to whose turn it is, and why there's so much arguing.

The young, Lady Gunnhild has been welcomed into the heart of Emperor Conrad's family. I'm sure I'll never see her again. I only wish her more luck with the husband chosen for her than I ever enjoyed.

"My Lady."

"Another?" I exclaim, taking the parchment from Frida. I anticipate the letter coming from my niece, Astrid, and I quirk an eyebrow when I recognise Lady Gytha's sigil of a wolf devouring its prey, instead.

"You've certainly taken your time," I mutter. It's been months since I wrote to Lady Gytha. It doesn't take a letter that long to travel from Denmark to England and then back again. I had thought that she might simply ignore it, but it seems not.

**"Dearest Sister, Lady Edith, written from my estates in Wessex."**
I can hear her conceited voice behind those words, and I feel a shiver down my spine, as though she stands beside me.

*"Thank you for your kind wishes on the birth of my third son,*

*and fourth child. As you can't recall their names, I will list them for you in order of birth. Sweyn, Harold, Edith and Tostig."*

Such names. They're almost more Danish than the names my sons have. I don't miss that Edith shares my name. Damn the bitch.

*"I'm dismayed to hear of problems on my family's estate. I had understood that Eilifr was in regular contact with the reeve. I'll make immediate enquiries, or rather, Earl Godwine will, on my behalf, for I'm with child once more. It's good that my husband will have many sons to bequeath his vast wealth and estates to, in England."*

I growl. Bloody bitch.

*"I pray for King Cnut each and every day. I believe he'll have a great victory, although I do worry for your niece. Perhaps she will be well. Poor woman. I have only just been informed that her husband has sired a son on an English slave woman and that he means to accept him as his heir. How humiliating for her. I'm pleased to hear that the king's youngest son is well. His older sons are, I believe, well-mannered and every bit as like their father as you could imagine. One day, perhaps, Harthacnut will be pleased to have half-brothers, even if Lady Emma refuses to acknowledge they are the king's sons. I am keen for news of Gunnhild. Is she settled in her new home?"*

*"Your loving sister, Lady Gytha Úlfrsdottir."*

I cast the letter to one side, standing abruptly before stalking outside.

Lady Gytha is right to gloat as she does, but it sits ill with me. Perhaps, I should contact Lady Ælfgifu? It would be strange, after all these years, to resume the attempt to communicate with her, but I'm sure that she'll be brutally honest about my brother's accomplishments in England. And, I am the boys' aunt, after all.

**"Dearest sister, Lady Estrid Sweinsdottir, written from Northampton, England."**

"How delightful to receive your unexpected letter. Perhaps it was to be expected. My husband said you were always fiercely loyal to him."

Lady Ælfgifu's letter is in my hand, and I'm sure I only wrote to her a handful of days ago. It seems she's keen to speak her mind to me, finally. I've lost count of the number of times I've written to her before. Still, I admire her for refusing to acknowledge that Cnut is no longer her husband. Her resolve reminds me of Lady Gunnhild's refusal to admit that my mother had replaced her.

Not for those two, the problems of a husband executed for treason, and one they'd sooner forget.

"It pleases me to hear that your sons are well. It's unfortunate that they have never met their cousins. Maybe one day, it will be possible, but for now, I must remain in England, caring for my blind brother. I can't leave him to fend for himself. The bastard King Æthelred exerted great revenge on my family, by blinding both of my brothers and killing my father. I'll never forget that, and I wait, every day, to hear that all of his sons are now dead. I'm overjoyed that his descendants will never claim the kingdom of England for themselves."

"My husband is remiss to spend so much time away from England. Earl Godwine is power-hungry and much-loved by the queen, who lets him rule almost entirely without reference to the other great earls. She, who has been deprived of all her children, has little to fill her time but listening to those who tell her what she desires to hear. Advise my husband, when you next see him, that his sons would benefit from some involvement from their father. Such fine sons as he's fathered do not take kindly to his abandonment of them. They should have riches to their names, and kingdoms to rule."

"Your loving sister, Lady Ælfgifu, wife to King Cnut of England, Denmark, Skåne and Hlaðir."

A tight smile touches my cheeks as I place the letter down. Lady Ælfgifu is only too aware of Cnut's accomplishments. I should have approached Lady Ælfgifu first. I hardly care for England and her criticisms of my brother, even if I do share them, but I'm mindful of Earl Godwine. He's the worst of all of Cnut's nobility, either in Denmark or in England. Earl Godwine has the experience of the deceits of his father, and brother by marriage, and he'll know not to make the same obvious mistakes. While he maintains such a facade, my brother will only think good of him.

I can only hope that my brother will not be foolish enough to reward Earl Godwine again when Norway is finally secure and in the hands of Jarl Hakon.

"Brother."

"Sister." The summer is nearly at an end, but Cnut has finally returned, glowing with pleasure.

"A great success, sister. A great success."

"I'm aware," I state flatly. Cnut's alert enough to notice my less than excitable tone.

"My niece?" I ask him coldly.

"It's her husband who's been cast out." There's no outrage in his voice because I criticise.

"So, she would have been welcome to remain in Norway?" But Cnut is already shaking his head. I thought as much. Cnut seems determined to ignore my complaints, but I have more yet.

"King Anund Jakob is much incensed by the arrival of Lady Astrid, and her daughter."

Cnut grins now, his pleasure making him appear years younger.

"Well, not all brothers and sisters can be expected to get on as well as we do. They have been apart for many years. I imagine that she finds much to condemn in the way that he rules. After all, when she left him, their father still lived."

Eyebrow high, I consider how to respond. But, he does me an honour. We might not agree with each other, but we do attempt to respect one another. For a fleeting moment, I consider what he must say about me to those he keeps in his confidence. Immediately my thoughts turn to Lady Emma and Lady Gytha. What does he tell them about me?

"Norway belongs to our family once more. It should never have been lost to King Oláfr, but that's an argument that no longer matters. I hold Skåne, and Norway, and of course, Denmark. Our father would have been proud of my accomplishments." Cnut speaks with satisfaction. Has he, finally, accomplished all that he wanted?

I notice that he doesn't say England, but I've always suspected that my brother's feelings towards England are different than towards the rest of his kingdoms. I'm unsure why. I hope never to set foot in the place again.

"So, you'll be going to England?" I demand of him, but he doses eyes half-closed, and I think he hasn't heard me.

"Soon, yes. Soon."

I nod. I'll miss my brother, but it'll put a stop to his wife's constant complaints, and hopefully, he'll learn of Earl Godwine's pretensions in his absence, and deal with him, once and for all. The entire Úlfrsson family needs to be cast aside, not just my husband. Until that happens, I don't believe that Cnut will be safe, even if he believes he is.

There's something about Earl Godwine and his wife, and her one remaining brother, that worries me. I would wish that my husband's son was where I could keep an eye on him, as well, but no doubt, he's with his aunt or his uncle, and that just means another potential source of trouble for my brother.

"Let us talk about the future."

Cnut pulls a chair closer to the table, where I play tafl with my oldest son. Svein is yet to learn the intricacies of the game. He plays only to attack. There's no subtlety to his actions, but I must persevere all the same. One day he may need to have learned the lessons of both being the hunter, and the hunted, and tafl is a bloodless way to do so.

I watch Cnut as he quickly appraises the table, an arch of his eyebrow, showing that he can already calculate that my son will lose. I shake my head, an attempt to prevent him from interfering. Harthacnut might not make the same mistakes as Svein, but Svein can learn. Harthacnut is as arrogant as my brother, and yet I can't help but love my nephew. I'm still unsure if my brother shares the same sentiment with regards to him.

Cnut is dressed fittingly for his new position as emperor, which I realise is what's driven him to accomplish all that he has. He retains his warrior's build, and the resemblance to our father is impossible to deny. The rich fabric of his tunic clings to his body, showing his physique. I imagine his little regarded wife thrills to see him when he visits her bed-chamber if indeed, he still does. Perhaps instead she's jealous of any who look at him and earns his attention. I'm not sure that she does, not anymore, not that I know. I've not been in England for many years. I'm thankful to be excused from the monotony.

Cnut sits and sips delicately from an intricate glass, the image of a snake about to strike twisting around the thin stem.

In the corner of the hall, the skald, Ottar the Black, is reciting his newest composition to a rapt audience. I'm surprised that my brother seems oblivious to the high praise.

"Destroyer of the chariot of the sea, you were no great age when you pushed off your ships. Never, younger than you, did prince set out to take his part in war. Chief, you made ready your armoured ships and were daring beyond measure. In your rage, Cnut, you mustered the red shields at sea."

I turn to the board, a slight smirk on my face. I consider my next move, while I wait for Cnut to inform me of his. The pieces on the board are expertly carved of whalebone. My 'attackers' have been dipped in ink, to stain them a darker shade, and then small details have been picked out on the faces and the tiny shields they carry. I'm not the king in this game, but rather the stalker, the one who wishes to remove all of the king's allies and leave him unprotected and surrounded.

The king figure, his face etched only in a dark ink against the whiteness of the bone, reminds me of my brother. I note how my son has allowed all but a few of the pieces to leave his side. He leaves his king exposed while his minions try to forge the correct path to freedom for him. That's not my brother's way. My brother would be there, at the forefront, unheeding of the danger, holding his sword, shield and spear. Cnut has never been one to stand aside from a battle.

Likewise, if I were the defender, I would not have left my king sitting, surrounded by his warriors. I would have moved him out from such a prominent position of weakness. Soon, he'll be trapped, with nowhere to go.

Perhaps my brother and I are more alike than I care to admit. That brings a smirk to my face.

I hope Cnut sees the same in me. Harald certainly did, but then Harald and I spent much more time together than Cnut, and I ever did. I've forgiven him for sending me to Normandy. It's impossible to stay angry with him when I know I'll never see him again. I miss him. I won't deny that. Each birthday, each anniversary of his death, the ache dims, but only a little.

I make my move, the piece coming closer to blocking any possible advance from my son, keeping the king trapped at the centre of the board.

"You've done well in my absence." I'm surprised by my brother's compliment. Of course, I have. Denmark is my home, and in time, Harthacnut will be my king. I've endeavoured to ensure he's happy and well-tended to in Denmark. I might not be his mother, but I hope I'm a better figure-head for him to model himself on. Lady Emma is unlike my mother in so many ways. My mother was a hard woman, and she knew her worth. Lady Emma is needy and seems to have forgotten hers.

"Now that Norway is secure, King Oláfr banished, and King Anund Jakob quelled from any further action against me, I'll return to England, and you'll continue to assist my son in ruling. Even when he's old enough to rule alone, you will stand at his side. Your sons will be his most loyal followers."

Since Cnut returned from his journey to Rome, he's started to adopt new mannerisms and to speak more slowly, as though he needs to consider each and every word. I would laugh at the change, and at the pretension it masks, but I don't wish to infuriate my brother or to have him think that I mock him.

In making his alliance with Emperor Conrad, in ensuring that the new Holy Roman Emperor was someone sympathetic to Denmark and her ruling family, Cnut has achieved vastly more than my father and grandfather ever managed. Whereas he once tried to arrange a union with the duke of Normandy, I know that his daughter, and my own, if I'd had any, will achieve a much higher price. Cnut is a warrior who's fought and won great victories, and now he turns to diplomacy to keep hold of his position.

Svein's clumsy move on the wooden board, sending two of his pieces scattering, breaks the suddenly tense atmosphere that's formed. I don't know why Cnut's brief words should have had such an impact on me, but it seems I'm not alone. Cnut shakes, as though a dog sloughing off water, and then looks to the board.

"You'll need to learn some more tact," he tells Svein, and I allow a tight smile to cross my face. Svein is all bold moves and mistakes. Not for him the sly manoeuvrings of his younger brother, or even his cousin.

'Tact?" Svein's face scrunches in thought, mouthing the word. "What's tact?" he asks his uncle and his king. Cnut considers his expression serious.

"Tact is when you mask your actions, when you take more than one move in order to achieve the ultimate goal, where you even appear to go backwards, before moving forwards. See, I would not move your king piece in the way that you do. I would allow his warriors to go first, to forge a path that he can follow, all the while protecting him from the enemy."

"But there aren't enough pieces on the board to do that." Svein's voice is high with outrage.

"Then, you must learn to use the ones you have differently."

Still, Svein doesn't understand, and his face is creased in thought, his mouth hanging slack, but I don't believe the lesson is directed at my son anymore. Now I think Cnut aims his words at me.

So, he means to use me differently, and as I demanded. I'm pleased. Only my brother is looking at my son, a hunger on his face. My brother has four children, what more does he need?

Does he wish he had the number of children our father had?

He already has more sons than our father, and even with just the one brother, they rarely saw eye to eye. If Harald hadn't died, I think the two would have warred against each other. What does he expect his three sons, from two mothers to do?

"Surely," Svein's high voice interrupts my musings, "it would be better to have peace then, not war?"

"That's not the game," I say quickly. My son's thoughts are counter to what they should be. I'll not have my brother think he's a coward. "The king's followers must always be prepared to die for him. Someone will always attack the king. Come, make your move."

Svein wants to say more, argue with me, I can tell, but I turn my attention to the board in encouragement, and quickly, he's once more engrossed, his upper teeth biting his bottom lip. I lift my head, glare at my brother, but his eyes are turned away, not even looking at my son anymore. Something has stolen his attention, and I sigh. Just for a moment, it was my brother and me, and Svein, but no one else. Just for a moment.

"My Lord King," a servant bows low, whispers something into my brother's ear, and he's up, on his feet and striding from the door. I watch him go, his steps strident, his call to action firm and immediate, and he doesn't even look back. I doubt he ever does. I wish I had his confidence and innate belief in my ability. But he's misguided in his confidence, and I'm not.

Still, this is how I wish to remember my brother. Even if this is not how I want to remember our friendship. He needs to be better to me, but he's too restless, too taken up with matters of state in Norway, and Skåne and in bloody England. England will be his death. I know it. And I know that it will not be the sort of death he aspires to, and I know that it will come far too soon.

For a moment, a tear clouds my vision, and I almost feel my shoulders shake with suppressed sorrow.

"Your move," Svein's high voice recalls me to what I'm supposed to be doing, grounds me in the actions of today. I don't know how the passage of time moves in my dreams, only that it does. I hope my brother has time yet. I genuinely do.

# CHAPTER 16

## *AD 1030*

The woman before me is beautiful, despite the ravages of age. I've never met Lady Ælfgifu before, or her tall son, standing at her side, but I can see the shadow of Cnut in his stance. I can also see why Cnut chose to marry her. As young as he was back then, I can see that her beauty would have trapped him, even though she's a few years older than him.

"Lady Estrid. It's good to put a face to the name and the handwriting finally."

Lady Ælfgifu speaks Danish effortlessly, and I hardly have the heart to tell her that it would be acceptable to speak English, even here, in Denmark. There are so many English men and women in Denmark now, sent here to enforce English conformity on the nobility and lower classes, that it's rare to hear Danish spoken in the king's hall in Roskilde.

"It's a pity it's under such circumstances, but yes, I'm pleased to meet both of you. Swein," I turn to her son. He glowers at me from beneath heavy eyebrows. He seems tinged a little green. Perhaps he's not enjoyed the sea crossing. "I would introduce you to my sons, Svein and Beorn, and of course, your brother, Harthacnut."

I know that Cnut's children have never met before. How it has become my place to facilitate such a meeting, I'm unsure —just another of my brother's presumptions.

The two look at each other, the one still very much a child, the other a man. It's impossible to deny the resemblance between them or the barely concealed animosity.

"Well met," Swein mumbles, while Lady Ælfgifu eyes Harthacnut with open dislike. I say a silent prayer that Swein and Lady Ælfgifu will not long remain under my roof. I could see a murder being committed all too easily. I don't believe Cnut's dynasty will survive another such act. My father's involvement in his father's untimely death is still openly condemned by those too deep in their cups to hold their tongues.

Swein is doing his best to stand like a warrior, and I wish he didn't look so comical. My brother must be desperate if he's prepared to trust the rule of Norway to his oldest son, but of course, following the sad death of Jarl Hakon at sea, my brother is indeed desperate to send someone who will hold Norway for him. He didn't go to all the trouble of forcing King Oláfr to flee, only to allow Norway to fall back into his hands.

And of course, I've been the one to argue that his older sons should be given more responsibility. Perhaps I shouldn't have been so vocal.

My sons watch their older cousin with mild interest, and Swein is the first to break the prolonged silence.

"Would you like to see my horse, and my shield and sword?" Swein is keen to show anyone these gifts from his uncle. At nearly twelve, Swein is eager to be a warrior and to train with the huscarls, even if he's too slight to do more than train with a wooden sword and shield.

I think his cousin will refuse, but then Swein's shoulders relax, and he nods, checking with his mother that he has her permission.

My sons' voices are high with excitement as they lead Swein away. Harthacnut lingers, and I think he won't go, only then he does. If I correctly interpret the look on his face, he's already decided that Swein is more likely to fall prey to one of his nasty schemes, than Lady Ælfgifu.

"Sit," I invite Lady Ælfgifu, lapsing into English, in the hope that she'll do the same. There is a selection of wines and foods for her to choose from, but her gaze lingers after her son.

"He'll be fine. Everyone knows to watch the royal children. News will have quickly spread of his arrival."

Lady Ælfgifu nods, but still doesn't sit, and I offer a quick prayer that Harthacnut hasn't pre-planned something to humiliate his older half-brother. I make myself busy, pouring wine and settling down. I can't imagine how strange this feels for her. She's been all but ignored for the last decade. Now Cnut entrusts one of his newly conquered domains to her keeping.

"Where is your other son, Harald?"

"Earl Leofric has become his foster-father. I'm a childhood friend of Lady Godgifu, his wife."

"Ah," I know of Earl Leofric. I find I approve of the arrangement. It seems my brother has still been forced to keep his two families separate in England. He would have done better to have brought Lady Ælfgifu to Denmark many years ago. It's far more acceptable for a man to have two wives, as his father did, in Denmark. Marriages have always been more fluid, and not the purview of the church, as they are in England. The overarching archbishop of Hamburg-Bremen might have tried to chastise the king, but no one would have taken it seriously.

"He'll be cared for well."

"He will, yes, but he should have his own kingdom to rule, just as Swein and Harthacnut have. My husband is remiss in overlooking him. He pampers to that woman, and it's beyond the time that Harald was able to travel south of the Thames without fearing for his life." Her voice is filled with outrage.

"I didn't know that Lady Emma had threatened him."

A slight cloud descends over Lady Ælfgifu's features, as she finally settles beside me, as though she too expected there to be some sort of trap awaiting her if she let down her guard.

"Well, that's what I heard. I've not allowed my sons to take any chances. She's a spiteful woman."

"She brought Cnut a kingdom, and he's been paying ever since."

I think my words will please, but instead, her eyes narrow coldly.

"My marriage brought Cnut a kingdom. He simply failed to act quickly enough to bring the matter to an end. He has only himself to blame."

I almost gasp in surprise at the criticism. Luckily, Lady Ælfgifu is busy with her wine and doesn't see my expression. Why I consider, is Cnut sending someone so openly critical of him to Norway? I advised Cnut to send his son. I didn't expect him to send Lady Ælfgifu as well. Surely, he has enough Danish jarls who could have travelled with Swein? Why not Hrani, or one of my sisters' husbands, or even Siward. Siward has become far too skilled to remain in his role as my messenger.

"Tell me of Harthacnut?" Lady Ælfgifu quickly changes the subject. I can see what she's thinking, but I allow it, all the same.

"A headstrong youth."

"So, not inclined to listen to the advice of others, then?"

"Sometimes. Harthacnut is young. He'll learn. All boys must learn, eventually, especially if they are to rule."

She wants me to criticise Harthacnut, and while I might do so to Frida, I have no intention of sharing those thoughts with Lady Ælfgifu. I'll not have her telling anyone who'll listen that Harthacnut is a disappointment. I had not expected to feel such fierce maternal instinct towards the boy.

"My sons are the same. Tell me of Swein and Harald? Are they headstrong, as well? Just as their father was at the same age?"

Once more, my question doesn't seem to please Lady Ælfgifu, and her lips purse with annoyance, as though the wine is too tart.

"They're warriors, both of them. I'm assured that they're both skilful."

She doesn't quite answer my question, and I'm too used to such evasiveness not to realise what probably lies behind it. It seems that all of Cnut's sons are a failure. For now.

"You've never visited Norway?" Lady Ælfgifu's voice wobbles a little as she speaks. I appreciate then that her conversation is stilted through nerves, and not arrogance, although she uses the one to mask the other.

"No, I have not. My niece was queen there."

"Is it true that King Oláfr's heir is the son of an English slave?" Lady Ælfgifu's eyes gleam as she speaks.

"It's true, but my niece is the boy's foster-mother. He's been welcomed into their family. Or at least, he was. He's little more than a babe in arms."

"So, storing problems for later years, then. And what of King Anund Jakob?"

I can see what she's trying to do, but no one has yet managed to discomfort me with constant reminders of how interconnected my family is with the politics and wars of the region, of how my brother fights with my nephew and niece.

"A firm king. It's unfortunate that he and my brother are locked together in warring for the same territories, but that's the way of it, and must be accepted. I don't believe that my niece and nephew will cause any problems, not for the foreseeable future. They're lost many warriors, and the nobility of Norway is keen to be ruled by Cnut, not King Oláfr."

"My husband says you keep in contact with them?" The accusation openly made, it seems that Lady Ælfgifu has no tact. None at all. And if she's been kept away from the English court, how could she have ever gained any experience? The Norwegians are easily offended, and, if the past is anything to go by, they'll switch allegiances easily if their king displeases them, despite their keenness at the moment.

I believe that if Jarl Hakon had lived, Cnut would have had no problems in Norway. But sadly, my oldest nephew was lost when his ship sank. It could still prove to be a disaster for Cnut. I must hope that Swein has inherited some of his father's skills.

"I do, yes. They're my family. I also keep up a correspondence with Lady Emma and Lady Gytha, my sister by marriage."

Lady Ælfgifu doesn't seem to like the reminder than I'm as bound to those two women, as I am to her.

"I suppose we have no choice in who our brothers and sisters marry." And if I hadn't thought she criticised me before, now I know that she does. I'd thought to build an alliance with Lady Ælfgifu. I'd thought to right the wrongs my brother inflicted upon her and her sons by casting them aside and taking Lady Emma as his wife. I don't believe I'm so minded now I've met her.

I read the letter in disbelief, almost turning it over to see if somehow the real message is scrawled on the other side of it.

"Well," I speak sharply, and Frida looks up from her sewing, a question on her face.

"It seems that Lady Ælfgifu is filled with complaints, even with a kingdom to rule for my brother."

"What does she say?"

"She complains about the state of her home, about the lack of fine glassware and good wine, about the cold wind, the freezing rain, the smell of the sea, and just about everything."

"What does she expect you to do about it?" Frida's forehead furrows as she speaks.

"She demands I send her my best glass goblets, the ones she drank from when she was here, the ones with the curling snakes. She asks for warm fabric for clothes, and spices from the southern lands to mask the smell of the sea and the damp. I'm quite determined to send her none of the things she asks for, and certainly, she'll not have my wine goblets. She should have taken such things with her."

"And what of the Norwegians?"

"Nothing, it's a letter filled with criticisms of Norway and nothing more."

Frida sucks her lower lip as she concentrates on her sewing.

"I hope she's less critical to the men and women she now rules over."

"I can't see it," I admit, throwing the letter down, where it slowly curls up, hiding the litany of demands and spiteful words. "I wonder whether Lady Ælfgifu writes in the same vein to Cnut?"

"What of her son?"

"Not a word."

"Then, let's just assume that everything is progressing well then," Frida offers, and I turn to her, an eyebrow high at the mocking tone in her voice. She grins and then laughs, and even though I know I should be concerned, laughter burbles from my mouth. My brother and the women in his life. Will he never learn?

"What's happened now?" I demand of the messenger before me. I can see that he has a parchment in his hands for me to read, but he's bruised and battered, a slice to his face starting to knit together. It speaks to me of recent violence.

"A battle, My Lady. A victory, but a battle all the same."

"With whom?" but I imagine I already know.

"King Oláfr Haraldsson is dead." The man advises me as he hands me the letter from Lady Ælfgifu. "The damn fool thought he'd be welcomed back to Norway. The lesser nobility soon showed that he wasn't. They marched out to meet him, and he was cut down in the heat of the battle."

"And what of the king's son?"

"King Swein Cnutsson is well. He was not involved in the battle."

I nod, dismissing him to seek food and ale, keen to see what Lady Ælfgifu has written to me. I don't want him to know that it thrills me to hear Swein named king in Norway. I have been concerned, but perhaps I did not need to be, not if the nobility have risen against the only genuine opposition to Cnut and Swein.

*"Dearest sister, Lady Estrid Sweinsdottir."*

*"A great victory for my son's supporters against the exiled king,*

179

*Oláfr. He's dead. A happy day. My son is a firm ruler, made in the same cast as his father. The people of Norway rejoice, as do I. Not one but four celebratory masses have been held, and all now acknowledge Swein as king. I'm sure my husband will be pleased. Norway is rightfully Swein's, as it was once his grandfather's."*

*"Why have you not sent me the glass goblets I demanded? Do so immediately."*

*"Your loving sister, wife of King Cnut of England, Denmark, and Skåne, and mother to King Swein of Norway."*

A sigh escapes my lips for the second to last line of the letter. Until then, I'd almost thought Lady Ælfgifu capable of adjusting to her changed circumstances. But it seems not.

"She still demands my goblets."

"She's not to have them," Frida is firm in her reply.

"No, she's not. But perhaps, I could arrange for something similar to be sent to her."

"Are you growing more amenable to her? I never thought to see the day."

"I'm tired of her ultimatums."

"If you allow the Danish nobles to hear that, their demands from you will only double, or triple. It's not like you to be frustrated by such a small matter."

Frida's words startle me. But, she's right.

"It seems I was wrong about Lady Ælfgifu and her son."

"I don't see how you can say that, not yet. It doesn't appear to me that Swein was responsible for King Oláfr's death. Did he even play any part in it other than to summon men to fight in the name of his father?" Frida has cast her eyes over the letter. I always allow her to read them. If I didn't, who else would understand my frustrations?

"You make a good point. Then no, I'll not send Lady Ælfgifu copies. They're mine. But I must write to my niece. She'll be bereft."

**"Lady Astrid, dearest niece."**

*"I write to offer my sincere condolences on the loss of your hus-*

band. I'll not labour the point that I warned you and your brother of what would happen if King Oláfr and he continued to antagonise. It's done. It can't be undone, but I know what it is to lose a husband, even in changed circumstances to your own. Keep your daughter safe. She'll bring you great comfort. I would advise against a hasty remarriage. One husband is more than enough."

"What was Oláfr thinking in attacking in the way that he did? Why did he not have a larger force? Why did he make himself so vulnerable? Was he betrayed or merely desperate? But no, I said I would not pour salt into the wound. Decisions can often be rash when seen in the light of the eventual outcome, but at the time they might well feel right. There is too much luck, and too little skill, involved in such altercations. I will say prayers for your husband's soul. Remain with your brother, in the land of the Svear. It will be for the best."

"Your loving aunt, Lady Estrid Sweinsdottir, sister to King Cnut of Denmark."

I lift my hand from the parchment, and place it to one side, hoping the ink will dry without running, and spoiling my hand. I confess I'm pleased with how well I form the letters.

Then I pull another parchment toward me.

*"Dearest brother, King Cnut of Denmark, England, Norway and Skåne."*

*"I'm sure you must be aware of the triumph in Norway. Lady Ælfgifu assures me that Swein has been proclaimed king there, just as our own father was, all those years ago. It doesn't bring me the joy it might once have done. I know how contrary the Norwegians can be. Perhaps you should send someone with more political insight and battle skill. I worry about Swein's future. I'm sure my niece and nephew will be keen to see King Swein replaced as soon as possible. Does he have the military support that he needs? Perhaps Jarl Thorkell's son could support Swein in Denmark? He has inherited much of his father's battle glory."*

"Your son is well. He grows arrogant, though, despite my

best efforts to drive the trait from him. He doesn't have your natural skill for speaking with the nobility. I'm trying to educate him, as well as my sons. Why are our children so lacking in basic skills? It displeases me. They must learn to be more tactical."

I reread the words, seeing that I've made no mention of Lady Emma or England, and certainly not Earl Godwine, although I hear reports of his continuing hold over my brother, and Lady Gytha churns out children at an almost yearly rate. Damn the woman. Damn the man.

Perhaps Cnut is not quite as able as I always believe him to be. The realisation is unpleasant.

# CHAPTER 17

## AD 1030

"*Dearest Aunt, Lady Estrid Sweinsdottir.*"

"*Your letter to my sister was not formed well. She's bereft, and your words were as cold and callous as the wind which blows from the glaciers. I would have expected more compassion. Your husband was executed for treason, while King Oláfr was, reports say, skewered valiantly fighting for his kingdom. I believe it is you who suffered the greatest ignominy.*"

"*I've taken it upon myself to raise my sister's foster-son. I'm sure that in time he'll reclaim his lost kingdom. Yes, he is but a babe, but powerful men and women will flock to his cause, and I'll be extravagant with my support.*"

"*I send another token for my grandmother's gravesite. Please do me the honour of ensuring it's placed there.*"

"*Your loving nephew, King Anund Jakob of the land of the Svear.*"

I find myself screwing the parchment tightly in my hand, only to reconsider, and fold it flat once more. My nephew speaks with the arrogance of a king, and perversely, that pleases me. My mother, for whom he sends a weighty piece of silver, worked into a decorative cross, christened with three warmly coloured rubies, would be pleased that her blood flows so strongly in her grandchildren.

I consider sending an immediate response, but no. My nephew might please me, but there's no need to tell him such.

But I do reach for my ink and a fresh sheet of parchment.

**"Dearest brother, King Cnut of Denmark, England, Norway and Skåne."**

*"I have word from my nephew, King Anund Jakob of the land of the Svear, that he plans on raising the son of King Oláfr. He says that powerful men and women will support the child to reclaim Norway. I would suggest you reconsider your current arrangements there. I hear worrying rumours that Lady Ælfgifu infuriates the nobility who wished you to be their king. I can't rule two of your kingdoms for you while you stay safely ensconced in England."*

*"Your sister, Lady Estrid Sweinsdottir, from Roskilde."*

I appreciate that my tone is far from diplomatic. But, I recognise the threat in Anund Jakob's letter too clearly to ignore it.

**"Dearest sister, Lady Estrid."**

Months have passed since I wrote to my brother. I'm both infuriated and pleased to finally hear from him. No end of other diplomatic letters have been sent from England to Denmark, but none of them addressed directly to me.

*"Do not think to tell me how to rule my empire. Remember who it is that forged it."* His opening sentence is not the reassurance that I would have liked, although I expected to be reprimanded.

*"My son rules well in Norway, with the aid of his mother, and others loyal to me. This child you speak of is no cause for concern. I'm sure that your nephew and niece will soon tire of the boy who has no blood tie to them."*

*"However, I would ask you to make enquiries as to how my daughter is enjoying her new position. Her mother worries about her, and it would ease her concern to know that she was well. Please arrange for someone to visit Gunnhild as soon as possible."*

*"Your loving brother, King Cnut of Denmark, England, Norway and Skåne."*

I scowl at his signature. Such reliance on his titles reveals more to me than he might realise. I might address him as such, but he is not one for falling back on his titles.

But I can't deny his request to find out how Gunnhild fares. While he might say it's because Lady Emma worries about her, I interpret it to mean that he does as well. It's more care than my father ever showed to me when he sent me to my first marriage with the Rus, and all but abandoned me there.

I consider who I could send to the court of the Holy Roman Emperor. I pity the girl. They've forced her to change her name to Cunigunda. I know her mother has no sympathy for the change, forced to give up her birth name of Ælfgifu to become Emma because Æthelred's first wife had been similarly named.

It'll need to be someone diplomatic, and with the sort of name that the Germans can pronounce. I wish my sons were older. I'm sure they would have been acceptable, but as of yet, they're not yet skilled enough to represent their uncle, and of course, their mother.

No, it'll need to be someone else. Maybe the bishop? Certainly, he would be welcome there. I muse on the matter, but really, I'm just trying not to consider what might be happening in Norway, and also in Sweden. I've heard nothing from Astrid or Anund Jakob since I wrote to Cnut. The silence is almost more worrying than all-out attack.

I can only foresee problems.

I wish my brother could as well.

**"Dearest Aunt, Lady Estrid Sweinsdottir."** I hold the letter carefully, trying not to inhale too deeply of the strange scent that envelops it. Bishop Othinkar assures me that it was like it when he received it. What strange spices do they force my poor niece to wear? I can only think of her with pity. And then I read her letter.

*"Thank you for sending Bishop Othinkar to reassure my beloved mother and father that I'm well under the care of Emperor Conrad. I assure you that although I still sometimes forget to respond to my new name, I'm quickly becoming used to it. The court here is magnificent, and I'm taught with the royal children, and can already speak the native tongue, as well as English and Danish."*

*"I understand that my brother, Harthacnut, rules Denmark well. My father must be pleased. As to Norway, I'm unsure who he has sent to rule there, but I have no other brothers. Inform my father it's unseemly, and unacceptable for a Christian king to claim more than one wife."*

*"Your loving niece, Cinigunda, bride in waiting to Henry, son of Emperor Conrad."*

Perhaps she pities me. I laugh, the sound forced from beneath clenched teeth. My niece is right to worry about events in Norway.

I lay the letter aside and turn to the man before me. He's been waiting patiently for my questions. I find there are almost too many to put in any reasonable order.

"Tell me again. Everything."

He bows his head, but as he begins to speak, Harthacnut appears, and I wish he weren't here to listen to the litany of complaints.

"There's a growing group of people who are unhappy with the rule of Swein *Ælfgifusson*, as they've taken to calling him. He's too young and has none of the skills of his father. His mother is no help at all. She's managed to alienate many people with her attitude and demand for more and more influence and power. Lady Ælfgifu is not much loved. Perhaps, without her, King Swein *Cnutsson* would be tolerated more."

He pauses, and I appreciate the distinction he's placing on the end of Swein's name. As Cnut's son, he's honoured. As his mother's son, he's not. I sense that Harthacnut is listening very carefully to everything I'm being told. Harthacnut's unhappiness that his half-brother rules in Norway, with the aid of his mother, is known by all. I can only imagine the letters of complaint he's sent to his father.

I think Harthacnut's even begun to write to his mother, knowing that in her, he has a willing accomplice to gnaw at his father's ear. I'm waiting for the day that Harthacnut announces he's old enough to rule alone and without my assistance in Denmark, even though he's much younger than his half-brother, Swein. Harthacnut's arrogance assures me that it will be sooner, rather than later, and I don't believe that Cnut will chastise his headstrong son.

"It's believed that the men who united to drive King Oláfr from Norway are considering the same to Lady Ælfgifu, and by association, King Swein *Ælfgifusson*. Einarr Thambarkelfir is furious. There are also rumours, and I give a great deal of credence to them, that the child, Magnus, has a growing power base in Old Uppsala. More and more people are flocking there, even perhaps this Einarr, buoyed by the knowledge that King Anund Jakob also supports the movement. There's little loyalty to the House of Gorm."

I appreciate the no-nonsense tone Styr employs as I nod at the words. I've warned Cnut, and indeed, I continue to do so, despite Cnut's refusal to heed the cautions.

The problems in Norway are caused by Cnut's demand for excessive taxes and outrage over the law code he's trying to enforce on the free-spirited people of Norway. It might well have worked in England when Cnut first became king there, but he was in England. He's not in Norway, and people will blame his figure-head, his son, or his mother, for all the ills that they feel Cnut's rule has brought them. The people of Norway have rarely been loyal to any single man, not since Olaf Tryggvason ruled over them.

"Who would they have as king, if not Swein?" Harthacnut has settled himself beside me, as he often does when I conduct royal business in the room that Harald first used when he ruled Denmark from Roskilde. As much as I'd sooner Harthacnut was busy elsewhere, he also needs to know what's happening in his father's vast empire. I would wish my sons showed as much interest, but they don't. Svein is more interested in learning to fight, while Beorn is too often found in his cousin's company, much to Svein's annoyance.

Styr looks at me, as though asking for permission, and I nod, hoping Harthacnut doesn't notice the action. He's difficult enough without realising that no one accords him the same respect that I receive. He doesn't see himself as a child, but rather, as the king, answerable only to his father, and certainly not to his aunt, irrespective of the fact that it's his father who accorded me the position.

"I believe they would accept a minority of King Oláfr's child, with Lady Astrid in a supporting role, rather than King Swein Ælfgifusson. Either that or King Cnut needs to go to Norway himself. The cult of the dead king continues to grow. The poor harvests are not helping either. People's memories are short. They remember King Oláfr as a benevolent man who brought Christianity to Norway, and with it, a period of excess and bounty."

"Do you believe the opponents of King Cnut will pursue the matter, even if it means war?"

"Sadly, yes. There's a great deal of unease and unhappiness. If I might speak openly, King Cnut doesn't have the support he thinks he does, not without Jarl Hakon. A pity Hakon died without a son to hold the position of jarl after him. Even that would have been acceptable." What goes unsaid, is that even my sister would have been more acceptable as ruler in place of her son. But Gytha hasn't recovered from the death of her son. She bides now in the nunnery in Roskilde, donning the habit of a nun, for all she's never taken her vows.

I find that for the first time in my life, I don't fear her, but rather ache for her pain. No mother should die before their child. It's against the natural order of things.

When Styr bows his way out of my presence, Harthacnut speaks.

"My father is squandering his achievements by remaining in

England and relying on *that woman* to rule Norway for him."

"I don't believe it's all Lady Ælfgifu's fault." I make a point of saying her name, taking only a small amount of delight in watching my nephew's dismay travel across his face. I know what it's like to hate, but equally, I see the power that refusing to face that hatred can allow the object to have over you. "It's more your father's fault, for remaining in England. He's been there for some time now. It's time he made a return to Denmark and Norway."

This seems to appease Harthacnut, and yet I'm far from convinced it's such an easy thing to accomplish. My brother enjoys living in England, and I don't foresee him returning.

*"Dearest brother, King Cnut, of Denmark, England, Norway and Skåne."* I find myself unsure of how to begin. I need to rebuke him, but as he's already proven, he doesn't take kindly when I do so.

*"I have news of your daughter, who enjoys her new position. She isn't yet married. This bodes well for her future. It seems her new family do not wish to task her with a woman's role when she's no more than a child. As to your other children, Harthacnut continues to learn his future role. I'm sure he will do you, and his mother, proud."* Even in that, I gloss over my worries for Harthacnut, in my desire to ensure Cnut appreciates the problems brewing in Norway.

*"I have reports from Norway, but I am sure you don't wish to hear them. I will merely inform you that the cult of St Oláfr, yes if you believe it, they have decreed him a saint, grows stronger and stronger. Bishop Grimkell, who was once so closely allied with King Oláfr, is one of the fiercest proponents of the new cult. I understand that Lady Ælfgifu has been forced to give it her blessing or face an uprising."*

*"The harvest has again been poor this year, the weather making it impossible to grow enough to feed the entire populace. You might think of sending supplies to Norway. I can assure you that Denmark has not escaped the weather either. It's been miserably wet,*

and I'm already strictly enforcing rationing on our food supplies. It will be necessary to slaughter more animals than normal because we simply won't have the feed to keep them alive during the long winter."

I stop then, unsure what else to say, aware that I've rambled rather than made the point clear that problems are brewing in Norway. Hopefully, my brother will understand my intent.

"*Your dearest sister, Lady Estrid Sweinsdottir, from Roskilde.*"

But perhaps not.

**"Dearest sister, Lady Estrid."**

"*I'm pleased with the news of Harthacnut and Cunigunda but would ask you to stop complaining of Norway. My son keeps me fully appraised of the situation there. The cult of King Oláfr must be tolerated. It's similar in England. Here, there's a cult to St Edward, the brother of King Æthelred of England. It's widely believed that his step-mother killed Edward to ensure her son became king. They even say that King Æthelred was doomed to fail because of the despicable deed. King Æthelred's sister is also the object of a following. Saint Edith was a woman most worthy of worshipping for her pious nature.*"

"*The crops in England has been affected by some damp weather. I'm informed that there's still ample for the coming dark season.*"

"*Earl Godwine has become a father once more, another son. He's often to be found at court. I must make war on the king of Scots, but I'm sure it'll not be a long, drawn-out attack. The Scots are not as powerful as they believe themselves to be.*"

"*I'm keen for you to pray at my father's tomb for me. Ensure the family mausoleum at Roskilde is well endowed, as he would have wanted, and as I've arranged.*"

"*Your loving brother, King Cnut of Denmark, England, Norway and Skåne, from Winchester.*"

I sigh and cast the letter to one side. I can't see that it's my responsibility to be any more helpful than I have been. I consider then just what Lady Ælfgifu is telling Cnut? I imagine she masks the problems; perhaps she's not even aware of them. That wouldn't surprise me.

"What does my father write?" Harthacnut has been waiting patiently to ask his question, and I dredge a smile from somewhere for him. He's a handsome child. I can see much of my father and older brother in his face. Not so much, his father, though.

"He's going to war against the king of the Scots."

Harthacnut's face turns slack as he considers those words.

"There's no king of the Scots in Norway."

"No, it's one of the kingdoms that shares a border with England." I don't need to see the swift look of fury that touches Harthacnut's face, and yet I appreciate it all the same. I'm pleased I'm not the only one to be frustrated with my brother.

*"Dearest sister."* I don't really wish to write to Lady Gytha Úlfrsdottir, but I'm keen for news of my brother, and Cnut hasn't written for many months now.

*"I send warm congratulations on the birth of your newest child. Your husband certainly keeps you busy."* I couldn't imagine being forced to endure pregnancy after pregnancy as Gytha does. Does Godwine not appreciate the risks she takes with each child? Just because all other births have occurred without difficulties, it doesn't mean that it will always be that way. The pair of them are certainly building a huge dynasty to challenge Cnut's much smaller one.

If I didn't have my two sons, and Cnut didn't have his three sons, I would fear the ambitions of Earl Godwine and his wife, even more. I consider asking after my husband's first child, Asbjorn, but I don't. Whatever he's up to, he's no child of mine.

*"Harthacnut is growing fast, as are my sons. They're all firm allies, and are rarely seen apart."* I certainly can't tell her the truth. That Harthacnut has made Beorn his close ally while forgetting all about Svein. I know that it pains Svein, not that he would ever say as much. Harthacnut is a devious soul. He's split the brothers apart, because he's already realised that if

they work together, they can accomplish more than he can, alone.

Svein, perhaps taking the words of his uncle to heart, or spurned to action because of Harthacnut, has become less headstrong, and more thoughtful. His brother's defection wounds him, I can tell, but I can't force them all to be friends. I can merely ensure that they don't hurt each other with blunt weapons and that Svein doesn't do himself irreparable harm in the eyes of Harthacnut.

*"I hope your children are such good allies to one another. It will make the future much easier."*

I sigh, my words falling flat even as I write them. I want to know about Cnut and Lady Emma, but how can I ask, without asking? I don't want Lady Gytha to know that Cnut ignores me. It would only give her something to spread around the court, if she's ever actually at court.

I also want to know about Earl Godwine, but of course, Gytha will not say anything against her husband. But, perhaps she might brag a little. I nibble my lip, take a deep breath, and then continue with my lies.

*"Your brother would be proud of his sons, had he lived. Svein and Beorn often ask about him. They're keen to meet the rest of their family, and I would not stop them from doing so. The years since Úlfr's death have taken the sting from his betrayal. There would be much that I would change if I had the time all over again."*

My hand shakes a little as I sign the letter. I thought the words were lies, but perhaps there's some truth in them. I would have to be a harder woman than I am not to admit that he was still, on occasion, a good man, even if those occasions were so rare that I can remember every single one of them.

*"From your loving sister, Lady Estrid Sweinsdottir, from Roskilde, Denmark."*

***"Lady Estrid Sweinsdottir."*** I receive a reply from Lady Gytha far more quickly than I expect.

*"Dearest Sister. It pleases me to hear you speak of Úlfr. I mourn*

him, as I'm sure you do. It was badly done by Úlfr to place himself in such a position as to earn Cnut's wrath. Eilifr is making some overtures toward the king, hopeful of being allowed to return to England, and of course, Asbjorn is a member of my family, and I care for him as though he were my child. Perhaps he might come to Denmark, and visit his half-brothers. I'm sure it would please their father to know they weren't strangers."

"King Cnut enjoyed a great triumph against the Scots, and of course, Godwine played a pivotal role in the action. The king rewards him with great riches and his greater confidence. Godwine and Lady Emma are close allies, and she sends many gifts for my children. Perhaps you might consider visiting England. It's been many years since you were last here. You would be amazed at the changes in Winchester. Your brother is a benevolent king to the English."

"If you could take the time to have someone visit my estates and ensure they're now being run as they should be, I would be most grateful. I know Godwine sent an Englishman to rule there, but Godwine is so often with the king, I'm unsure of the outcome, and I confess, it slips my mind with all my other parenting responsibilities."

"Your loving sister, Lady Gytha Úlfrsdottir, wife to Earl Godwine, from her estates in Wessex."

Now I understand why Lady Gytha was so keen to reply. Her words infuriate me. Earl Godwine shouldn't be so high in Cnut's estimations, and certainly, Asbjorn is not welcome in Denmark. Perhaps I shouldn't have written after all! I knew my lies would return to haunt me.

I consider calling for parchment and ink, but I know it will do me no good. Instead, perhaps a different tact is required.

"Siward," the man bows before me. He's done me many great favours in his time serving me, and I know that Cnut holds him in high regard. Siward has survived, even when many others haven't.

"My Lady Estrid," his words rumble with assurance and respect.

"I must ask you to travel to England for me, to the king. I really must know why King Cnut lingers in England, all but abandoning his other possessions, but of course, you must not say that to the king. He doesn't take kindly to my interference, and yet, interfere I must."

Siward nods slowly, considering the task I set before him.

"You can rely on me, Lady Estrid. I will find out all I can."

"Then you have my thanks, and while you're in England, perhaps you could also find out exactly what Swein and Lady Ælfgifu tell my brother of events in Norway. I have a suspicion that they're not entirely honest with him, or rather, that they tell him only the good and not the bad."

Not even a flicker of unease crosses Siward's face at my less than easy assignment. But, that is why I gave it to him, and not one of my other messengers. Siward is as reliable as they come. He's served me well since we travelled to Normandy together. I must also assume that he's become more accustomed to travelling by sea.

"I'll travel as soon as possible, and return as quickly as I can," Siward assures me, as he turns to leave the king's hall. I watch him go, wishing I didn't have to be so apparent with my actions, but Cnut continues to ignore me, and Lady Gytha has worried me more than I care to admit.

I can feel storm clouds brewing, but what they are, I'm not yet sure.

"My Lady," the voice is rough, and I gaze at Frida in concern, noting her pale face, pulling myself away from the piles of parchments before me. While Harthacnut, Svein and Beorn are off somewhere, I'm busy about the governance of the kingdom. I would wish one of them showed some interest in the tedium, but of course, they don't.

"What is it?" Frida knows I don't like to be disturbed when I'm embroiled.

"It's Harthacnut. Quick, he's unwell."

A shard of ice enters my heart, and I'm discarding my quill

and inkpot, unheeding of the mess I leave behind, as the ink tumbles over.

"Tell me," I demand breathlessly, as we flee through the doors, all left open by Frida in her haste, and out toward the stables, and the area where the king's huscarls train, my nephew and sons included in that number.

"He lies shaking. Perhaps a fall and a bang on his head, I'm unsure. I've sent for the herbwoman."

My heart beats ever faster, my ears filled with the sound of it, and I'm running. What will my brother think of me if his son and heir is injured? What will Lady Emma say to me? But more importantly, how will I ever forgive myself?

There's a small crowd, and I push my way through, to be met by the terrified eyes of Svein, whereas Beorn is on the ground, next to Harthacnut, attempting to help hold him steady, even as Harthacnut's legs shake and hit the floor.

"What?" I ask, but I expect no response, going to take Beorn's place while the commander of the huscarls takes Harthacnut's head. Our eyes meet over the youth's shaking body, and my fear is mirrored on his bearded face.

"Get everyone to leave," I command, the words a bark of instruction that I'm unused to giving. Frida leaps to drive people away, but so many are struck by what's happening, that I know it's almost impossible.

"What shall we do?" I ask, wishing that I knew more about such matters. "What happened?" I ask, not allowing the time for an answer.

"He fell," Svein admits, his words almost too quiet to hear, filled with fear. "He just fell to the floor."

"Where is the herbwoman?" I demand to know, my voice almost a shriek, but she's suddenly next to me, her eyes focused exclusively on Harthacnut. His legs are slowly stilling, and so too is the shaking of his head.

"We must get him inside," the woman's voice is light, but filled with composure. It seems that she's not concerned by who she treats, even if Harthacnut is her future king.

"Quickly, inside, and away from this place. Harthacnut needs to be somewhere quiet and dark. He'll recover. It will pass." Her words soothe me as nothing else could.

The commander of the huscarls quickly instructs four of his men to lift Harthacnut, and I trail behind, Frida and the herb-woman striding away in front.

"Come on," I urge Svein, Beorn already rushing away with Harthacnut, but Svein shakes his head. I see something in his stance that I both don't like, and also understand.

"Come to the hall," I urge him, unsurprised when I don't hear his footsteps behind me.

Inside, the servants are waiting, mouths open in shock, as they watch Harthacnut being carried so carefully by men bristling with sweat and stinking just as much.

Frida has at least kept her wits.

"Hot water," she calls over her shoulder. "Hot water, and warm wine, and clean blankets."

Immediately, people rush to do her bidding, and I feel sur-plus to requirements, but grateful all the same.

"Beorn," my youngest son turns to glance at me, and in his sorrowful eyes, I see all kinds of hurt.

"Come, sit with me. We must leave the herbwoman to her work. Frida will stay with Harthacnut."

My son reluctantly comes to me, taking a seat to the side. While I try and pour wine to steady myself, my hand shakes so much, that Beorn takes both the glass and the jug from me, splashing fluid into the goblet, before handing it to me.

"Tell me," I demand of him when I've taken four steadying gulps.

"It's just as Svein said. He fell and started to shake."

"He hadn't been hit, or been complaining of feeling unwell beforehand?"

"No, nothing. We weren't even training. We hadn't even started. We were watching the huscarls, waiting for our turn, joking around a bit, about who was good and who wasn't. We were, we were having fun." Beorn speaks remarkably clearly.

"He'll be alright, Lady Mother. I'm sure of it." I wish I shared Beorn's surety.

Time seems to pass slowly. While the commander and his men troop from Harthacnut's chamber, Frida doesn't. The servants are busy taking everything she asks of them, a steady stream that's reassuring because at least it seems that something can be done to help Harthacnut.

Beorn settles to wait, his hands in his lap, but I find myself unable to rest, and stride, time and time again, from my chair to the outside door, and then back again.

There are few people indoors on such a day. In the height of summer, even the most determined of royal supporters, are forced to see to their properties, in Jutland and Skåne. I'm grateful that it is almost exclusively the king's servants and huscarls who've witnessed Harthacnut's weakness.

I can't help but think the worst, and more, of how I will ever explain to my brother and Lady Emma if their son were to die, while under my care. It would be even more treasonous than my husband's actions against Cnut.

Equally, I can't help worrying about Harthacnut. He's so young, so very young. Yes, he has all the arrogance of his father and my father, but he has so many years before him.

But at the heart of all of my worries, are the fact that I've had no true dream to warn me of what might happen. I think back to that night, all those years ago, when I was forewarned of future events with the knowledge that my brother's dynasty would be imperilled. I didn't think it would come so soon. I thought I had more time. My sons are yet young.

Eventually, Frida comes to me.

"My Lady," the formality alerts me that all is not as it should be.

"Harthacnut is fine. He's sleeping naturally now."

"Thank goodness," I exclaim, but she doesn't seem to share my relief.

"Tell me," I demand, my hand claw-like on her thin forearm. Frida looks at me and then glances to Beorn, and only when she's sure that he sleeps does she bend and whisper in my ear.

"The herbwoman says this might just be the first of many. It more often than not is. She says, it will be possible to manage it for some time to come, but she also advised that the condition will become more and more serious." I can hardly breathe.

"She also says that they will shorten his life. It will depend on the frequency."

"But that is if they occur more frequently?" The sympathy in Frida's eyes almost drives me to strike her, as she nods, understanding that I grasp for only the positive news.

"She can't say. It will be a matter of waiting."

I swallow, my throat almost too tight, tears threatening to spill from my eyes.

"Then I will pray that it never happens again."

"And what of Cnut and Lady Emma. You must inform them."

I nod. I know this, and yet the temptation not to is great.

"I will. I will. But can I see him?"

"Of course, come."

Carefully, I stand and walk with Frida. I'm aware of people watching me, of the concerned looks, and I try and stand taller, push my shoulders back, and even find a tight smile from somewhere. They need to know that all is well even if it isn't.

My workplace is a mess when I return to it, the parchments scattered far and wide, although one of the scribes has thought to clear up the spilt ink and replace the damaged quill. My hand hovers over the items, trying to recall what it was that I was doing before everything changed. I can hardly think of what was important and what wasn't.

For now, I need only concentrate on writing to my brother.

I would wish that Siward was still in Roskilde. It would have been easier to send him to speak directly to Cnut, but he's still in England, his prolonged silence and absence warning me that I'm not going to like his report when I finally receive it.

How, I think, should I even begin such a letter?

I wasn't in Denmark when Harald died. Is it possible that he suffered from the same affliction? It was a tragedy, nothing more, or so I've thought all this time. But, perhaps Cnut does know the truth.

*"Dearest brother."* I know they will be the most straightforward words in the entire letter, as I don't even name him as my king.

*"I write to inform you that your son, Harthacnut, has been taken ill, but that he recovers, even as I pen these words."* At least, I hope that's right. When I visited Harthacnut, he lay still, silent, pale, barely breathing, while Bodil, the herbwoman, tended to him, forcing water through his tight lips, and generally administering to him.

She's a young woman, but well-versed in the needs and requirements of my court. I personally recruited her to tend to the childhood illnesses that befell my sons and nephew, and she's never let me down, never. I know that others find her youth off-putting, but they're the fools who think that only women who are old and shrivelled by a life-time of living, should know how to cure ailments. Much better to have a herbwoman young enough to be able to hunt for her cures in the rugged countryside, and to travel far and wide, should the need arise.

Bodil didn't even turn to look at me, and yet I felt reassured just to watch her confident movements.

*"Once he's fully recovered, I'll have him write to you himself. But for now, the herbwoman tends to him."*

I should mention the shaking, but I feel reluctant too, hopeful that it will be a one-off event. Certainly, I'll be praying that it is.

I sign my letter, aware it says very little to reassure my brother, but I feel too shaken to say more, and I won't be caught in offering platitudes. Perhaps it might even encourage him to return to Denmark and to see for himself.

**"Tell me more of Harthacnut's condition."** I don't get so much as a dearest sister. Harthacnut has made a full recovery, having spent little more than a handful of days lying under the ministrations of Bodil. "I haven't yet informed Lady Emma. She'll panic, and scold me, but I must know more. I've sent Siward to determine how he fares for myself, but know that Siward is to become a member of my court in England. This will be the last time you can make use of him. I believe it's time he was well rewarded for his long-lasting loyalty to our family."

I look at Siward, and he raises an eyebrow, as though in apology.

"Go, see for yourself. Harthacnut is outside, with the huscarls."

"I've already seen him, and spoken to him," Siward informs me with no trace of an apology.

"Tell me, what has my brother promised you? A rich estate in the southern lands, or something else?"

Siward has the good grace to look abashed.

"He wishes me to command the northern lands for him, now that the Scots have been tamed."

"You'll become an earl?"

"Yes, My Lady."

"Then the king is truly pleased with you, and I'll miss your presence at my court."

"As to your original instructions to me, I can confirm that Swein and Lady Ælfgifu do send glowing reports to King Cnut, but that he isn't so blind as to believe everything they say. But, that said, the king has no intention of leaving England, not any time soon."

"I'm surprised he allowed you to say as much to me," I know my words are sharp.

"The king asked me to ensure Harthacnut was well, and to speak plainly with you."

I find myself laughing at Siward's well-spoken words.

"Then you've done what you needed to do. I wish you luck in England. Be wary of Earl Godwine."

"Of course, My Lady. And I can assure you that I'm not blind to Earl Godwine's plans."

"I'm sure you're not," I confirm, realising that I'll miss his steadying presence, and suddenly appreciating that my dear brother has had precisely the same thought. No doubt, he wishes Siward to counter Godwine's influence. My brother has few enough earls to assist him, and of them all, Godwine is the most powerful. Perhaps, I shouldn't be as angry with the pair of them as I am for depriving me of a man I've come to rely on, even if I once derided him for sea-sicknesses.

# CHAPTER 18

*AD 1034*

"Lady Estrid," I startle to hear Harthacnut speak to me so formally.

"Yes, Lord Harthacnut," he's suddenly grown tall, and a soft fuzz of hair sits above his lip. He's sixteen years old, and every day, he hungers for more and more power at his fingertips, but I withhold it. For now.

"Have you been informed of events in Norway." Harthacnut holds a parchment in his hands, as though the information has come from it, but it hasn't. I should have cautioned my messengers and their loose tongues, but it's only right that Harthacnut knows of events elsewhere in his father's empire.

"What has happened now?"

I'm aware of why Harthacnut has chosen to call me by my title. It seems he wishes to complain about his half-brother, and Lady Ælfgifu once more.

"The nobility are conspiring against my father's representative. Is it not time we intervened?"

I admire Harthacnut at that moment. He might be keen for military glory similar to that his father enjoyed when a similar age, but Harthacnut has listened to, and correctly interpreted the complex information that's being received from Norway on an almost daily basis. It's a pity that his illness wasn't a one-off occurrence. Harthacnut should have

202

had a bright future, as his father's heir, but I don't believe my nephew will outlive his father. The thought dismays me. I would hold tight to this time with him if only I could stop the seasons from turning.

It's not how it should be.

But, Harthacnut is determined to make a lasting impression anyway. I admire him for that.

"It's not for me to intervene, as you say. The king has made it clear that he doesn't heed my warnings."

"But they're not just your warnings. How can the king so blatantly ignore what's happening?' Harthacnut's words mirror my frustrations.

"Does the king even care about his northern territories? Or for him, is there nothing but England and the money that can be extracted from Norway, Denmark and Skåne?" Harthacnut's fury is easy to hear, and I do not attempt to justify what's happening.

"The king will only realise when it's too late," I offer softly. I've forced myself to accept that. It's not been easy, not at all. It's as though Cnut thinks nothing of putting his son's life in such danger because that's what he's doing.

"That can't be right," Harthacnut complains, his cheeks turning pink with strain.

"I know that. I've done all that I can. I have cautioned the king's representative, but it has no impact, none at all." Usually, I would not insist on adopting Harthacnut's term for his half-brother, but it feels as though I speak to an adult, and it's reassuring to know he thinks as I do, without infuriating him further.

"What do you hear from King Anund Jakob?"

"Here," and I pull a parchment from the pile before me. "Read for yourself."

Harthacnut's eyebrow raises at the statement, but he takes the offered letter all the same.

*"Dearest Aunt, Lady Estrid, greetings from Uppsala."*

*"I'm sure that your sons must almost be men by now. How quickly the years pass. Young Magnus, my sister's foster-son, and heir to King Oláfr's kingdom is a delightful child, aware of his position, and with many valued supporters flocking to his cause. I am sure that my sister will soon be restored to her possessions in Norway. I will miss her, but it's only right that she and her daughter return to their home."*

*"I hear reports that Harthacnut is a fine man, much like his grandfather. I'm sure that must please you. A pity your sons have a less illustrious father, but, if they're ever in need of family support, I'll eagerly provide it for them. I'm not a man to turn family aside when they're in great need, no matter who their father might have been."*

*"Once more, I provide a token for my grandmother's tomb. It would have been better had she been buried in Old Uppsala. Then, I could have visited her as often as I wished."*

*"Your loving nephew, King Anund Jakob, king of the Svear."*

Harthacnut's eyes seem to grow huge as he reads, and I anticipate his response with a quick blink.

"King Anund Jakob clearly states his intentions here. How can the king not heed your warnings?"

"My nephew and niece have always been the same. They're so blatant in their refusal to accept the king's control of Norway and Skåne that it's become almost routine. Every word they say is filled with spite. They want the king to threaten them. If he does that, it gives them what they want, the opportunity to attack."

"That might well be the case, but the nobility of Norway is unhappy with the king's taxes, they don't wish to be subjugated, as the English are. And Lady Astrid and King Anund Jakob are eager to assist them."

"That's true; I won't deny that. The king is remiss to ignore matters in Norway, although he's probably right to believe that King Anund Jakob is all hot air and piss, for now."

Harthacnut looks far from happy, his forehead furrowed,

his mouth opening and closing, although no words pour forth.

"I will write to my Lady Mother," Harthacnut eventually announces.

"I'm sure she'd be pleased to hear how you fare."

"That will not be the point of my letter," Harthacnut barks.

"Then I wish you luck and would ask you to ensure your mother knows that I had no part in your writing. She'll blame me for everything."

But my gaze fastens on empty air, for Harthacnut has stalked to one of the scribe's desk, taken parchment and ink, and the air is filled with his angry scratchings.

*"Lady Estrid Sweinsdottir, Dear Sister."*

*"I write to you although there is little time. My son and I are forced to flee for our lives. The nobility, and the peasantry, have revolted against us. Our lives have been threatened if we do not leave immediately. I believe them when they say they will execute us."*

*"King Cnut has been too harsh with his demands on a country already ravaged by war and then further wrecked by poor harvests. I intend to travel to England, directly to my husband, but you must be aware that King Anund Jakob is involved, and he may attempt a simultaneous attack on Skåne, or even on Roskilde itself. I could not, in good conscience, leave without sharing my worries for you. Thank God you didn't send me those goblets I wanted because they would now be forever beyond my reach."*

*"Your desperate sister, Lady Ælfgifu, wife of King Cnut of England, Denmark and Skåne."*

I scan the letter, my lips settling into a thin line of disappointment. This is my nephew's fault, in Sweden, and my niece's, but overall, it's Cnut's failure to respond to the growing threat that has brought about this terrible state of affairs.

I've grown weary of demanding action from him, and the only comfort I can take is that Harthacnut has had even less success in involving Lady Emma.

It's as though both Cnut and his second wife, are oblivious

to affairs away from England. I would curse them both, but it would be a waste of good air, and entirely pointless.

"Here," I thrust the parchment into Harthacnut's waiting hands. Eagerly, his eyes scan the words, even though they're from a woman he's never acknowledged as his father's first wife, and I'm unsurprised when he flings it to the ground, disgust etched into every line of his face.

He's been afflicted once more, but his recovery has been swift and Bodil reassuring. I can see no trace of his illness upon him now. He looks vigorous and healthy, and while his friendship with Beorn is sincere, he and Svein grow ever further apart. I think that Svein might perhaps have my gift of true sight. Certainly, I think he fears Harthacnut, recognising that his illness might well be mortal.

I pity all three of the young men.

"So she's given up, just like that?" I might have guessed that Harthacnut would see this as Lady Ælfgifu's fault, and not his father's. He's been openly critical of his father, but now it seems he has someone new to blame.

"She's been threatened, and so has her son. Without the king's support, there's little choice. She's not a warrior."

"No, but *he* should be a warrior." I eye Harthacnut. He paces before me, I can see how much the spectre of his older half-brother haunts him. I know some pity for him, but then I harden my heart. Yes, I've kept Asbjorn away from his half-brothers, but none of them could lay claim to a kingdom between them. But Cnut, well, Cnut had the tools at his disposal, and he's failed to make good use of them.

"With what band of huscarls? I don't believe the king sent more than a dozen. They couldn't have kept the rampant nobility at bay. No. This is the king's fault, not theirs."

Harthacnut's eyes blaze fiercely at my statement, but surprisingly, he doesn't try and counter my argument. I'm impressed by his ability to think beyond his initial hatred.

"Let us simply hope that the king appears, soon, with his shipmen. Until then, I'll ensure the huscarls and ship-men in

Roskilde are on alert and ask that someone travel to Skåne, to forewarn them as well."

"A good suggestion. I will have messengers sent to the forts. They're not as well garrisoned as they might once have been, but the men are still Denmark's best warriors."

Harthacnut barely acknowledges my words as he strides from my presence, Beorn at his side, talking urgently to his cousin. Only in his wake does Svein make an appearance.

I try to ignore the heated look he directs at Beorn's back. The brothers grow further apart, not closer.

"What's pissed him off?"

"Lady Ælfgifu and Swein have been forced to flee Norway because the nobility has risen against the king's strict law codes and taxes. It was inevitable." I'm surprised by the fatigue in my voice.

"I imagine that Harthacnut wishes only the best for his older brother, in the future."

A tight smirk touches my lips, but nothing more. I would caution Svein about his words, but I can't make Svein think as I do. He must learn, and as painful as that is to witness, I'm confident that he will, unlike his uncle.

"Lady Mother, I come to bid you farewell, for a few months. I need to be far from Denmark."

"What do you mean? You can't leave Denmark." His words startle me from my reverie.

"Of course, I can. I can't stay here, watching my brother grow ever closer to my cousin. I need to live a little for myself. I'll not be gone long, and it's not really for you to grant permission or not. I merely come to bid farewell to you, in the hope, you'll offer me your blessings."

I glance at my first-born child, suddenly seeing him for the adult he's becoming, and not the child I still believe him to be. At close to seventeen, I should no longer coddle him.

"I," I confess, I have no idea what to say to my wayward older son. Perhaps he would benefit from being away from his cousin, and perhaps, even from me.

"You are too young," I offer, but I expect his laughing response.

"I'm much older than our king was when he first left to raid with Jarl Thorkell."

"But Jarl Thorkell was his foster-father."

"Yes, he was, and I'll merely travel with my allies, but still, I will be almost as safe."

I eye him, noting the challenge in his eyes, the slight mocking tilt of his chin. If Svein means to test me, then he's doing so, but equally, I'll test him as well.

"Then you may go. I'll expect you to return before winter. Travel safely." It gives me only the smallest amount of pleasure to see Svein almost judder as I speak. He wants this, and yet it terrifies him as well. Wherever he means to go, he will have to live by his wits, and not with the protection that being my son gives him in Denmark.

"My thanks," and Svein bows from my presence, no doubt leaving before he can beg me to reconsider.

He'd better return in one piece. I'll not forgive any who injures him.

"My Lady?"

"What?" My eyes are exhausted from reading all the reports sent to me about taxes, and law codes, and the state of the church. The archbishop of Hamburg-Bremen still takes great delight in sending pedantic and detailed letters for my attention. It's been years now, and still, every one contains some sort of slight. I can well understand why Cnut was so pleased to visit Rome, meet the Pope, and make his views felt on the way that the papacy regards Denmark. I only wish the fruits of that particular conversation had lasted longer.

"There's a ship, here. Lady Ælfgifu and Lord Swein."

"In Roskilde? She said she was going to England."

"Well, she hasn't." Frida's voice is filled with an ominous tone, and I feel my gaze drawn to her face.

"What is it?"

"The son, he's mortally wounded."

"What?" And suddenly, I'm on my feet, indicating that she should take me to them.

I have no time for further questions, as I run to the quayside. It reminds me too closely of when Harthacnut was first ill. I would shudder with the fear that envelops me, but I won't allow it. Frida has had the wherewithal to order servants and four members of the huscarls to escort me. I don't believe I need them, but Swein might well.

I can hardly believe what Frida has said to me.

The child, how old can he be? But then, of course, he's older than my children, and Harthacnut. He went to Norway as a man.

The quayside is thronged with people, and yet the huscarls quickly forge a path through them, and then I'm beside the ship, peering inside, looking for Lady Ælfgifu.

I don't expect to see the quivering woman whose fear-rimmed eyes meet mine.

"Come, come, get Lord Swein, bring him to the king's hall. Lady Ælfgifu, I'll help you to your feet." Only Frida is already there, kindly taking the arm of my brother's beleaguered wife, and with the aid of a servant bringing her to the gangplank, and escorting her to land.

I want to ask what's happened, but it's too easy to see, for Lord Swein is not the only injured man. Bloody bandages can be glimpsed on arms, and legs, and even around heads.

"They chased you, from Norway?" I can't quite believe it. Were they really hated so much?

"Yes, My Lady, they did." The man who speaks has a dirty bandage around his hand, but I can see one of his fingers is missing.

"Are you in command here?"

"I wasn't, not at the beginning of the journey, but now I am, yes. My name is Harekr."

"Then you have my deepest thanks for bringing Lady Ælfgifu and my nephew to me."

I don't miss the look of surprise on the man's face as I name Lord Swein, my nephew. My brother really should have made it much clearer that Swein was his son if even one of his huscarls is surprised by my claiming him. Perhaps then this might never have happened.

"I wouldn't thank me yet, My Lady. Lord Swein's wounds are severe. I'm not confident that he'll survive."

The news horrifies me, and yet I nod, as though I'm told every day to expect the worse.

"Then you have done your best, and you still have my thanks. It's not always in our power to save everyone."

The movement of the huscarls unbalances the ship, and I stagger, but Harekr grabs me and I steady, the scent of the sea enveloping me.

"Thank you," I offer once more, keen to be back on the quayside. But I wait. Lady Ælfgifu is being led away, but the four huscarls are struggling to move Lord Swein.

"You must bring your wounded to the king's estate. I'll ensure they're cared for by my herbwoman."

"Thank you, My Lady, but see, there's already someone tending to the more minor injuries. It's Lord Swein who needs the most help."

I notice then that an older man, with a woman beside him, is bending to speak to the injured ship-men. The woman passes items from a satchel that she carries whenever asked for them.

"Very well, but if they're unable to help, come to the king's estate. I'll expect you anyway. You must be compensated for your pains, and for the men who've been lost. I'll not have women and children going hungry when their men have lost their lives protecting the king's son and wife."

"As you will," but the man is already off, speaking to his men.

"Wait," and I turn, shocked to be spoken to in such a way.

"You should take this. The Lady was very adamant that she bring it with her." He hands me a heavy sack, stained by the sea, and probably with other less pleasant things as well, and I take it, trying not to wince.

"What does it contain?"

"I've no idea. But she wanted it. Everything else, we threw overboard in an attempt to outrun the enemy, but this she kept, close."

"I'll take it," I confirm, stepping gingerly back onto the quayside. The water is a soft gurgle beneath my feet, and it's not that which unhinges me, but rather the threat of the bloody ship-men. This can surely only be a portent of what's to come. The fact it makes me think of my son, and his ambitions, only serves to make me feel even more nauseous.

A handful of servants have remained behind, waiting for me, and I gratefully hand the sack to one of the more trustworthy women.

"Please ensure Lady Ælfgifu receives this," I ask, and she nods, already lagging, as I rush back through the busy streets, keen to see how Lord Swein fares. Lord Swein is not the child of Cnut's that I foresaw dying young, far from it, and my worries thrum with every step I take that I might well have misinterpreted my vision all those years ago.

"Why is he here?" Of course, Harthacnut has heard the news, and he intercepts my journey back to the king's hall.

"He's wounded. He needs assistance."

"Not from anyone in Roskilde," Harthacnut shouts, surprising me with the intensity that reverberates through his voice. "*He* is not welcome here, and neither is *she*."

"You aren't yet king here Harthacnut, and your father would be dismayed to hear you'd rather your brother succumbed to his injuries than helped him."

"What?"

"He's mortally wounded. It's unknown if he'll survive."

"Good," Harthacnut spits, stalking away from me, Beorn looking uneasy behind him. I dredge a smile for him. I adore Beorn, even if I do wish he hadn't chosen Harthacnut over his brother.

"Go, go. Stay with Harthacnut. I don't want him anywhere near his brother."

Beorn accepts the instructions easily enough. He might be Harthacnut's greatest ally, but for the time being, he still obeys my orders for him. I can't imagine that it will always be this way. Soon, Harthacnut will demand a more significant pledge from Beorn, and I believe Beorn will have no choice but to give it.

"Tell me." Frida is before me, her eyes flashing with ire, her hands bloodied and wrapped in linen as she tries to wipe the stains away.

"There's little hope. The wounds are infected, and he's delirious."

My heart bleeds for Lady Ælfgifu. I can't imagine being in her position.

"Lady Ælfgifu needs careful handling. She's determined that her son will live. She won't leave his side, and criticises everything that Bodil does, as though she knows better."

"I'll bring her away," I offer, already standing, but Frida shakes her head.

"No, no. There's so little time left; it would be cruel." The words are spoken with so much compassion, they bring tears to my eyes, and I feel my lower lip trembling. Such weakness is rare, and I wish I could stand firm and filled with resolve, but I can't. This is her son. This is my nephew.

"I am sorry."

"Then do what must be done. I will pray," and Frida surprises me by reaching her arms around me and offering a tight embrace.

"This is not your fault. Any of it."

She knows me far too well, and tears continue to fall as I summon three of my women, and have them escort me to the church.

There, I fall to my knees, unheeding of the hardness of the

floor, or the chill breeze that swirls around the vast building, finding the words of prayer easy to find, and far more heartfelt than even when my mother died.

Lord Swein is little more than a child to me.

I mourned for my nephew when he was lost at sea, but he'd lived to become a man. I grieved for my half-brother in the land of the Svear when his life was lost. But he had lived as a king, and left behind him a son and two daughters. Lord Swein has had no time to accomplish any of those tasks. He's like my brother, Harald. He's just as young, and in time, people will forget who he was, and what he did.

Grief tears at me, and I weep so hard, that one of my women plucks up the courage to ask me if I'm well. I try and find some humour, aware that never before have I felt such as this, or acted in such a way, but it's all too raw.

I'll have to write to my brother, I'll have to tell him of what's happened, and more, I will have to write to my nephew and my niece, informing them of how they hunted a young man to his death. I don't believe I will ever think of them in the same way again.

How could they? How could his father?

It's too, too cruel, and when Frida comes to me, when the candles have burned low, and the sound of yawning from my escorts, has become gentle snores, I know that Lord Swein is dead and that I must now deal with Lady Ælfgifu.

I find her, sitting beside Lord Swein's body, her hands tightly clasped together, the left almost a claw over the right.

"Look at him," I can only just decipher her croaked words. "Look at how peacefully he sleeps. I've never known him so still."

I kneel before her, take her cold hands in mine, trying not to see my brother lying on that bed, face pale and drained, the fuzz of a moustache, really little more than that.

It could be Harald before me. It could also be Cnut.

"I'm so sorry, sister dearest." Lady Ælfgifu doesn't even startle as I use such an affectionate term. She nods, as though the words are adequate, even though I know they're not.

"He'll be buried in Roskilde."

"He will, yes. With his ancestors."

"His ancestors? If it happens to be one of the rare days that my husband acknowledges his son, then yes, he'll be buried with his ancestors. If not, he'll be buried with strangers."

I hardly know what to say. Certainly, I can't deny her words.

"He was such a brave boy," Lady Ælfgifu softly sobs. "Such a brave boy." And now I notice her dress and the blood that seems to have seeped into so much of it. Lady Ælfgifu has held her son close, been forced to listen to his soft whimpers. His fatal wound, a sliced belly, gives the most terrible of deaths. I feel tears glisten in the corner of my eyes.

"You've been a valiant woman," I choke, but Lady Ælfgifu's eyes are far away, and yet she still speaks.

"His father will be proud of him, so proud of all he accomplished." As her head lolls to one side, I appreciate that Bodil has given her something to take the edge from her pain, and I'm relieved. My heart breaks for her, but still, I can't have a traumatised woman running riot through my hall.

I stand, turn to glance at Lord Swein once more, more to assure myself that it's not Cnut or Harald that lies there, but the resemblance is too great. It could be any of the boys, Harthacnut, Beorn, Svein, perhaps even Harald, Lord Swein's brother who remained in England.

What has my brother's ambition brought him?

Was it worth it, in the end?

That night my dreams are riven with shadows, reminiscent of that long-ago dream that has dominated so much of my life, and when I wake, gasping for air, as though I'm drowning, I know that there's more tragedy to come.

I hardly dare think what it is, my brother, my son, my nephew, perhaps also my niece and nephew in Sweden, or my nephew in England, or even my niece in the Holy Roman Empire.

What I don't expect is a letter from my brother.

"I must write a letter to my brother, before you leave," I advise the messenger who's replaced Siward, no doubt eager for the same advancement, even before opening the letter.

"I am instructed to wait," the man assures me, and there's something in his voice that acts as a warning.

**_"Dearest Sister, Lady Estrid, from Winchester."_**

_"I'm writing to advise you that I will soon be dead, perhaps I already am. Whether I am or not, I must make it clear to you that Harthacnut is to rule in Denmark after my death. Lord Swein is to hold Norway, with the aid of his mother. Skåne will be Harthacnut's as well. Although affairs in England are more complex, I expect that Harthacnut will also claim England, with your sons ruling in his name when he's absent."_

_"You'll continue to assist my son and nephews. I know I can rely on you. I would wish this wasn't to be my final few months, but I have felt the shadow of death for some time. Know that I have always respected and admired you, and that when I'm gone, I know you'll ensure the future of my dynasty."_

_"Your ever-loving brother, Cnut, King of Denmark, England, Norway and Skåne."_

The letter drops from my hand, the cry on my lips only just stopped.

I grasp my hands, one in the other, so reminiscent of Lady Ælfgifu last night that I almost bark with laughter.

My brother, dead, or nearly so. Of course, I've always suspected it, but what should I do now? Lord Swein is dead, Norway already lost, Lady Ælfgifu, an unwelcome guest at my court. Can I genuinely send such dire tidings to my brother, when he already fears his own death?

Only I know that I must. There's no choice.

With a heavy heart, I settle at my desk, find my quill, and dipping it in ink, begin to pen words that will only bring my brother further grief, but I can't lie to him. There's too much at stake, and he must reconsider his plans for the future that he'll not live to see.

# CHAPTER 19

*AD1035*

"Why is that woman still here?" Harthacnut has no compassion for Lady Ælfgifu.

"She's grieving," I hiss at him, wishing Harthacnut would learn not to have such discussions with me before the entire court. Why did he not come to me moments ago in my workroom, before I settled here?

"She must leave. I'll not have her here. My Lady Mother would disapprove."

I don't believe Harthacnut has even thought of his mother for months, if not years.

"She'll leave shortly."

"No, she'll leave tomorrow. She's lingered here for ten days since his death. I demand that she departs immediately."

I didn't need to share the contents of my letter with Harthacnut. For once, Cnut had remembered his sons and written to Harthacnut. I believe there was also a letter for Lord Swein, but it will have been lost, along with Norway. Unless of course, someone else receives it and learns the news. It will only further undermine Cnut's attempt to rule Norway if Einarr and Lady Astrid know of his impending death. But I don't find it in me to care.

"I'll speak with her," I state firmly. "You're not to meddle." I want to scold him for being so unfeeling, but I don't wish to upset Harthacnut either.

"I don't call it meddling," he replies hotly.

"Well, I do. I'll ensure Lady Ælfgifu leaves Roskilde. You're not to approach her."

I've been orchestrating the last few days carefully so that Lady Ælfgifu and Harthacnut need never meet. I don't wish her to glance at the youth who looks so like her son. It would pain her. Equally, I don't want Harthacnut to direct any of his ingrained furies, learned at his mother's knee, onto the grieving woman.

Lord Swein has been buried beside the grandfather and uncle he never met, and there's little to cause Lady Ælfgifu to linger in Denmark, and yet she does, all the same. I've not yet spoken with her of Cnut's illness. I hardly know what to say, and I'm dismayed that events have once more played out to ensure I'm the one responsible for informing Lady Ælfgifu of such terrible information.

"Then ensure it's done, Lady Estrid or I'll have her bundled away in the middle of the night, and that's if I'm feeling kind."

I bite down on my sharp words to Harthacnut. He's grieving, and I've noticed the slight tremor to his lips. I hope he's not about to suffer from his affliction once more.

I seek out Lady Ælfgifu, surprised to find her talking with Beorn. Beorn knows not to speak of the king's coming death, and his relief is impossible to miss as I seek to interrupt their conversation.

"Come, Lady Ælfgifu, I would speak with you." Beorn bows as she turns surprised eyes my way, but before she can resume her conversation with him, Beorn has scampered away.

"A sensible young man," Lady Ælfgifu offers, and I dredge a curve for my lips at her attempt to compliment me.

"He is yes, but close to Harthacnut. His brother has gone away, to find wars to fight, and to gain a reputation. I would have preferred to have him here with me. You must miss Harald?"

"Of course I do, but I could not bring both of my sons. My

husband wouldn't allow it."

"He can be wise, on occasion, but I must speak with you about him."

"Why? He's my husband, not yours."

"Come, let's walk this way."

I take a path away from the hubbub of the training huscarls, and away, towards where fields are neatly laid out before me. The crops are growing well, and the weather has been better this year than for the last four. We'll eat well come the colder season.

"What do you wish to say to me?" The confrontational words almost drive my tact away, but I persist.

"I've received a letter from my brother. He's also written to Harthacnut."

"Why would the contents of a personal letter involve me?"

"Your husband, my brother, he writes to inform me that he's dying. He doesn't expect to live beyond the end of this year."

I'd expected sorrow on Lady Ælfgifu's face. I'd even expected her to sob, perhaps beat her chest. I certainly didn't anticipate the swiftly descending fury that seems to turn her face grey.

"So now he thinks to die! He sends his son to his death, and now he'll no doubt leave Harald with no land, and no power. I'll not have it. I'll not endure it. I must leave Roskilde. Find me a ship. I must leave immediately."

Lady Ælfgifu stalks from me without saying anything further, and I watch her go, and I confess, my mouth hangs open in shock.

If only my brother hadn't married Lady Emma. Lady Ælfgifu would have made a far more impressive queen.

*"Dearest Aunt, Lady Estrid."* I almost don't want to read the letter from my nephew in Svearland, not while I know Cnut is dying, and there's nothing I can do to stop rivals usurping the position vacated by Lord Swein's untimely death.

*"I am doing the honourable thing in writing to you to advise that I fully support the claim of Magnus, acknowledged son of King Oláfr Haraldsson, to the kingdom of Norway. My sister also supports the claim. Even now, Magnus is being returned to Norway, and, as young as he is, he'll be proclaimed king, by the auspices of the nobility, led by Einarr Thambarkelfir."*

*"Your brother would have done well to have placed Einarr in control of Norway, rather than his son, after the unfortunate death of Jarl Hakon. Perhaps then, the nobility wouldn't have revolted. But, Cnut's loss is Magnus' gain. Ensure your brother is aware that any attempt to recapture Norway will be met with fierce resolve. The Norwegians will no longer be subject to the Danish king, and I will join any fray."*

*"Your loving nephew, King Anund Jakob of the Svear."*

I could weep as I read the letter. As much as it pains me to admit it, I have no love for Norway. I'm almost pleased that the kingdom has been lost. Cnut's sons will have to rule his vast dominions, and much sooner than any of us would have liked. They'll not be up to the task, and I'm fearful that as soon as my nephew is aware, he'll be quick to take advantage of my family's current frailty.

I know Anund Jakob wants Skåne added to his dominions. I must hope that Harthacnut can protect it.

**"Lady Mother, from your loving son, Svein Estridsson."**

I sigh at my son's scrawled writing. He really should have spent more time seeing to his letters when he was younger. But, I'm overjoyed to hear from him finally.

*"I've been engaged in several battles, but I'm currently fighting for Anund Jakob. He informs me of the loss of Norway. It must pain my Uncle. King Anund Jakob and I have agreed that I'll not join the forces in Norway. Instead, I'm engaged in altercations elsewhere. I hope this meets with your approval, and that you'll inform my Uncle that I've not turned against him. I don't miss Denmark. I'm enjoying the freedom of being absent from Roskilde."*

His words bring me only so much comfort. I don't wish to think of Svein fighting the Rus or the Wends. They're brutal warriors, all of them. But, I can't deny that even in such a brief scrawl, I can hear that my son is happier than he's been for many years. That pleases me, even as I wait for news of Cnut's death.

**"Lady Estrid Sweinsdottir. Dearest aunt."**

Once more, the letter smells of strange spices, but I open it all the same, keen to hear from Lady Cunigunda. I'm hopeful that Cnut has told her of his impending death. Only, it seems not.

*"I write to inform you of my marriage to Lord Henry. It was conducted with a great deal of pomp and ceremony at Nijmegen. It's a pity you could not be there to witness it for yourself, but I hear of problems in Denmark, so I'm unsurprised."*

*"My mother would have been proud to see me so well adorned with gold, silver and priceless silks. It's a day I will never forget. My husband pleases me. I hope he always will. Of course, there's no assurance that he will."*

*"Inform my brother of my marriage. He never writes to me, so I must assume he forgets he even has a sister. But then, it's been many years since we were together. I think we could both be forgiven for being all but strangers to one another."*

*"Your loving niece, Lady Cunigunda."*

The news pleases me. I'd been worried that Cnut might well die before the union could be formalised. There has, after all, been rumours that the emperor might prefer a different bride for his son and heir, that he resented the necessity of allying with King Cnut.

But all the waiting is tedious. I wait for news from Norway, news from the land of the Svear, and most worryingly, news from England. There's too much at stake. Far too much.

"Why has your nephew provided ships and ship-men to Norway?"

I eye Harthacnut critically, as he paces in front of me, his face red with fury.

"I informed you that my nephew planned to support King Oláfr's son. You've seen the letters."

"Yes, yes I have, but there's a world of difference in supporting him, and in attacking Denmark."

"What?" I'm on my feet at the news. The bastard. How dare he pretend to do me a family favour in keeping me informed of his involvement, and then take it to such an extreme?

"Yes, I have reports here of an attack on Aggersborg. I'll not tolerate it. I've already summoned my ship-men and huscarls."

"Do they hold Aggersborg, or have they merely attacked it?"

"Attacked it, stolen anything of value, and now they harry the coastline. They might even come to Roskilde, or perhaps Skåne. Why did you not tell me?"

"I knew nothing of this. I suspected an attack on Skåne, but not on the Danish mainland. Never that."

"Well, now I must go to war, to stop the presumptuous attack. Write to your nephew, inform him that he'll face the might of Denmark."

"Must you go with the ship-army?"

I know, as soon as I've voiced the words that I shouldn't have spoken them, and yet, I won't regret them.

"Of course, I must. I'll protect my father's kingdom." His pause should have alerted me to what was coming next, and yet it shakes me all the same. "Beorn will accompany me. Don't even try and prevent it." Harthacnut's eyes are cold and heartless. I consider, for a moment, that he knows of Svein's current whereabouts, but if he does, he makes no mention of it.

"I'll direct the effort from here, ensure the coastal settlements are aware of a possible attack, and that they must protect themselves."

"Good. It's about time you did something useful rather than sitting here with ink-stained fingers, sending and responding to letters that harm my father's empire." His words are harsh, and they bite deep, more than anything because I've never been allowed to do more. Does he not realise that I would have preferred to make war on Denmark's enemies? Does he not realise that the marriage alliances I've been forced to endure have been all the battling I've been allowed to do. I've bled for my family, just not in the same way that a man would.

I watch him leave me, refusing to move from my seat. I feel shaken. I can't deny it. It seems that everything is happening all at once. I suspect that my niece and nephew must be aware of Cnut's impending death, why else would they suddenly be so bold in their actions? Maybe the letter Cnut sent to Lord Swein in Norway was intercepted, as I suspected.

And in Harthacnut's actions, I can only detect his fear, which he's directed at me.

He has much to accomplish, and he's without the allies that his father once had, not that even with the mighty jarls of Thorkell and Eirikr, it was all that easy.

"Tell me," Jarl Gorm, my sister's husband, is flustered, his face bruised, and with a weeping wound on his neck. I would tell him, but I need to know how Harthacnut fares first.

"Some indecisive sea battles." His voice is rusty, as though he's not used it for some time.

"How many ships fight in the name of King Magnus?" I'm aware that the child has been declared king and undergone his coronation. I can't quite believe how desperate the Norwegians are that they'll take a child rather than a fully-grown man as their king.

"More than we have."

"How many more?"

"Too many more." The news isn't what I wish to hear.

"Lord Harthacnut is well?"

"Yes, he fights with great skill. If the numbers weren't so stacked against him, he would have enjoyed a great victory."

"When will he return to Roskilde?"

"Only when he's content that the Norwegians have given up."

"And when will that be?"

Jarl Gorm's shrug tells me all I need to know.

"I'll not expect him anytime soon then."

"That would be wise."

I've sent letters to Cnut, but I'm sure his thoughts are elsewhere. I'm not expecting to hear from him anytime soon, but I would welcome the support of Lady Emma. After all, Harthacnut is her son. She can only want him to inherit as much of his father's empire as possible.

I pray for the winter storms to arrive quickly and drive the enemy away from Denmark's shores. If not, I genuinely fear that my niece, Lady Astrid, and nephew, King Anund Jakob, might well lay claim to Denmark. I wouldn't be surprised. Not at all. It would, after all, be the ultimate revenge.

**"Dearest sister, Lady Estrid Sweinsdottir."** I dread the letter, penned not by Lady Emma, but by one of her scribes. I fear I can predict its contents.

*"I write to inform you of the death of my husband on 12th November at Shaftesbury. He's been interred in the Old Minster, Winchester. I will miss him, but I will continue to rule, in the name of my son, Harthacnut, who is now king of England, as soon as he comes here to claim it. I implore you to encourage Harthacnut to make the journey shortly. Nothing must delay him in Denmark. I fear that there are others with pretensions to rule the kingdom. Some persist in supporting the other claimant. Assure Harthacnut that Earl Godwine is his greatest supporter."*

*"I have taken command of the king's treasury in Winchester. I will hold it for Harthacnut. Send him, no matter the weather. He must be here as soon as possible."*

*"Your loving sister, Lady Emma, Queen Dowager of England."*

Tears sheet down my cheeks, and my hand trembles as it holds the letter. I can hardly believe the callousness of Lady Emma's words. Does she not even mourn her husband?

And how can I send Harthacnut away from Denmark when it's under attack?

I'm unsurprised when Harthacnut strides into the chamber. His face is white, fury evident in the harsh angle of his jaw.

"My Lady Mother must continue to hold England for me. It's mine. My father decreed it in his will, but I can't go to England. Not at this time, not when Norway threatens Denmark."

I agree with Harthacnut. I'm sure that Lady Emma must have the easiest task. She must speak of Lord Swein's brother, Harald, and Harald can't enjoy the support that Harthacnut does. I need only see how poorly Lord Swein fared in Norway to appreciate that Cnut, has made others doubt their parentage, by not openly acknowledging his oldest son.

"She's merely exaggerating, I'm sure of it," I try and soothe.

"Then we're agreed that I must remain in Denmark. Come the better weather, the forces loyal to the usurper Magnus will resume their attacks. I must lead the ship-men. Beorn will assist me, as will Jarl Gorm and the rest of the Danish jarls."

"You must inform your mother of your decision, send word of your intentions to return to England as soon as possible."

"I will, and you'll also mirror my message. If needs be, I'll send Beorn to England, as my deputy. I can do nothing further, not at this time."

"And your father's death?"

The shudder that runs down his face assures me that Harthacnut is not as unaffected by it as he appears. Perhaps he feels the loss more than his mother, and Harthacnut last saw his father many years ago.

"We'll inform everyone of it, and have a Mass said for his soul in the family church. Then, you'll organise my coronation. I'll be king of Denmark in name as well as deeds."

"I'll ensure it's all done."

"But first, we must pray for my father. He's been taken too soon."

Harthacnut's words remind me of why all this is necessary,

and my heart sinks. My brother is dead, and what a mess he's left for me. It seems he never learned the lessons of his father's multiple marriages. I would curse him if only I didn't feel his loss so keenly.

# CHAPTER 20

## AD 1035

"*Lady Estrid Sweinsdottir. Dearest Sister.*" I almost wish I'd not made the effort to open the letter. I already know what it's going to say. Or at least, I imagine that I do.

"*I told you to dispatch my son to me. He's needed in England. Denmark will have to wait until all is settled in England. I still hold the king's treasury in Winchester, but the other one has been promoted to the kingship by Earl Leofric and the men and women north of the River Thames. I'm fearful that he'll come to Winchester and take the treasury as well, and then there'll be nothing left for Harthacnut.*"

"*I am bereft. Earl Godwine is my fervent supporter, and I'm grateful to him, but something must be done. Send Harthacnut to England. Immediately. I can't be held responsible for what will happen if he persists in staying away. Harthacnut needs to know that Archbishop Æthelnoth of Canterbury supports Harthacnut's kingship, as do many others. Harthacnut has the support, but he must be in England to fully receive it. Your sister, Lady Emma, Queen Dowager of England, from Winchester.*"

"What does she say?' Beorn asks the question. For once, he's with me in Roskilde and not with Harthacnut, ensuring the Norwegians gain no foothold in Denmark.

"She says that Cnut's other son has been declared king north of the Thames." I can't keep the amazement from my voice. When Lady Ælfgifu left Denmark, after Lord Swein's death, I never anticipated that her ambitions extended to her remaining son claiming England for himself. Once more, I find I admire her far more than Lady Emma.

"What other son?" Beorn's voice shows no concern, and I understand his confusion.

"Lord Swein's brother. Lady Ælfgifu's younger son," I explain when Beorn still looks confused.

"But my uncle's Will made it explicit that Harthacnut was to have England."

"Yes, yes, it did, but Lady Emma makes it clear that the earls support Harald. She mentions Earl Leofric by name."

The name causes Beorn to still, and I'm impressed that it means something to him. It shows that Beorn pays more attention than I've ever suspected.

"The son of Ealdorman Leofwine? The man who was my grandfather's, King Swein, enemy before he became a firm ally."

"The very man."

"The man who was loyal to Swein once he became king of England."

"Yes, the self-same man."

"But he was one of Cnut's most devoted earls. It makes no sense."

"I know." I can't fault my son's reasoning. Earl Leofric's decision to support Harald Cnutsson as king is more than strange, and it makes me think that perhaps there's more to Harald's appointment than first appears.

"We must tell Harthacnut."

"But he'll be furious, and he can't leave Denmark, not at the moment. King Magnus' supporters grow almost daily. They threaten to overpower Denmark."

"I know, but it doesn't matter. We can't keep him ignorant of this. It must be Harthacnut's decision as to what he does."

My son sighs, the weight of the knowledge seeming to make

it hard for him to think.

"I'll tell him," I assure Beorn, but he shakes his head.

"No, no. I'll do it. You must remain here, ensure Denmark stays united against the threat while Harthacnut fights it."

"Then you must tell the king that I'll do nothing until he advises me, but he must let Lady Emma know that he'll be detained for some time yet. He must send his mother and Earl Godwine instructions as to what he wants to happen. If not, I fear they'll lose heart and capitulate to Harald's rule as well."

I don't like to think of Lady Emma as a traitor to her own son, but it seems that she might well become one. And Earl Godwine? Well, I can only imagine how much he must fear the thought of Cnut's other son becoming king. I can't imagine that he's been an ally of Lady Ælfgifu, not when he's so close to Lady Emma.

Ah, how have events become so muddled?

*"Lady Estrid Sweinsdottir. Dearest sister."*

*"My son has not yet returned to England, and I've not heard from him, or from you. I've had no choice, but to allow the other one to take control of the treasury in Winchester. I'm desperate for my son to return. Inform him that even Earl Godwine has sworn his oath to the new king. I have no allies, none at all. What am I to do? His father's legacy lies in tatters."*

*"I would turn to my brother for support, but, news has reached me of his death in the Holy Lands. Normandy is as troubled as England, and unless I come to Denmark, I fear for my safety. Inform my son that he must come to England. He needs to bring his ship-army with him. Tell him to hurry or risk losing all, forever."*

*"Tell him that I will not have that woman take my place as queen dowager of England."*

*"Your loving sister, Lady Emma, Queen Dowager of England."*

I read the words and dread engulfs me. It seems to me that Lady Emma is despairing, but so too is Harthacnut. His instructions were that I was not to write to Lady Emma. He doesn't want his mother to know how long he might have to remain in Denmark. But now, well, now I feel the edge of her desperation, and I fear something terrible will happen if Harthacnut doesn't offer some sort of reassurance, but of course, Harthacnut is not in Roskilde. He still travels with his ship-army, and I've no idea where they are, only that with my niece's support, the men and women behind King Magnus go from strength to strength. I fear they can scent the ultimate victory over Denmark, and if that happens, Harthacnut will be left with no kingdom to rule, either in Denmark or in England.

**"Lord Harthacnut, Dearest Nephew."**

*"I must inform you of the worrying news from England. I would never ask you to choose between Denmark and England, but your mother is unable to do more for you. I advise you to try and forge a peace with King Magnus. If not, I believe you'll never hold England, as your father decreed, and that Harald will be declared king over all of England."*

*"I'll do what I can. I'll write to my nephew, Anund Jakob, in Old Uppsala. Perhaps he'll urge some caution on the Norwegians. Your mother is fearful that Lady Ælfgifu will supplant her, but I don't know how realistic those fears truly are. Respond to this letter as soon as possible to inform me of your intentions. I will support you whatever you decide."*

*Your dearest aunt, Lady Estrid Sweinsdottir, from Roskilde."*

**"Lady Estrid, dearest aunt."**

*"My mother has always assured me that the English were loyal to me. Why then must I rush to England? Why can't she hold the kingdom for me? Has she lied to me all this time?"*

*"I'm infuriated by her constant worries. Send her word of how embattled I am. Tell her to do what she must, no matter what it is. I will come to England, as soon as King Magnus and I have made peace because I fear I can never beat him, not when his forces are so superior to mine. I can't see that peace will be long in coming, but I*

fear what I will have to give up to earn such a peace."

"Tell her to inform Earl Godwine that if he doesn't remain loyal, he'll lose his Danish possessions. I'll have no compunction in removing them from his control. I'm not to be denied my birthright. Your loving nephew and king of Denmark and England, Harthacnut."

### "Lady Estrid Sweinsdottir. Dearest aunt."

"I'm doing this out of the goodness of my heart. King Magnus, my husband's son, is on the brink of adding Denmark to his dominion. I've already spoken out to ensure that you'll not be harmed. You're my aunt, and as such, you deserve resources to keep you in the position you're accustomed. Once you've sworn loyalty to your new king, I'm sure you'll be allowed to live freely in Roskilde, if under careful watch."

"King Magnus won't harm a member of his extended family. I know that Svein is fighting on behalf of my brother, King Anund Jakob, and therefore safe. But I understand that Beorn is a close ally of Harthacnut. He needs to distance himself, or I won't be able to protect him, as I can you. I leave it to you as to how you bring this about. Know that my daughter is well. She will take holy orders shortly, I'm sure of it. Your loving niece, Queen Dowager Astrid Olofsdottir of Norway, written at Avaldsnes."

But I have no time to absorb the information before another letter is pressed into my hand.

### "Lady Estrid Sweinsdottir, dearest sister."

"It is hopeless, and I fear being expelled from England entirely. In an effort to fortify my position, I sent for my beloved older sons, Edward and Alfred, knowing that they would be able to hold England for their brother, Harthacnut."

"I can hardly tell you the outcome, but you must know that Earl Godwine has been his most ruthless and that my son, Lord Alfred, is lost to me. Edward, I understand has returned to Normandy, but Alfred has been captured and given into the hands of Harald, now declared king of all England. I can do no more for Harthacnut. I *will be eternally sorrowful that he didn't heed my warnings. Do not write to me in England. I fear I will not be there."*

*"Your beleaguered sister, Lady Emma, Queen Dowager of England."*

"Tell me?" I ask of Æthelwine, and he grunts, perhaps not wanting to voice what he knows.

"Lady Emma's loyalty to Harthacnut has been tested. She invited her older sons, Edward and Alfred, back to England. I believe she made the decision alone. Certainly, when Earl Godwine was informed, he took immediate steps to prevent the invasion, which came from the lands he's earl over. The two, Lord Godwine and Lady Emma, are no longer allies, and I hear rumours that Lord Alfred has been blinded at the hands of Lord Godwine, and is close to death."

I close my eyes and think of the young man I met all those years ago. The thought of what might have befallen him sickens me. I can't believe that they were so desperate to return to England that they did so because of their mother. Surely, after all this time, they must hate her for what she did to them? Lady Goda is married, or rather was married, but her husband died at the same time as Duke Richard of Normandy. Has she cast her support behind Alfred and Edward? How else would they have been able to afford warriors to assist them?

"Continue." I try to keep all feeling from my voice, but it's an effort.

"King Harald has the support of everyone, even Earl Godwine, although the archbishop of Canterbury refused to conduct his coronation. Harald is king over all of England, but I believe his most loyal supporter, Earl Leofric, is involved in hunting down Lord Alfred. There's a rift between them because of what happened, and yet the earl is still loyal, although he doesn't strictly follow the king's orders."

I almost smirk at the news. Earl Leofric is a wily man, and I know he's had his loyalty to my brother tested, and yet, I suspect that even in these actions, he's still the most loyal of all.

I've met him more than once. I admire him, just as much as I do Lady Ælfgifu.

"And what of Edward?"

"Edward has returned to Normandy. He's safe, but Lady Emma will not be welcome there, not now. It's been a complete disaster for her. I understand the brothers were close. I can't imagine that Edward will find it to forgive her for such an atrocity."

"Then where will she go?"

I don't want her in Denmark. I really don't. Harthacnut will take it poorly if his mother loses him his kingdom, and then expects to be treated royally in Denmark.

"I believe she may go to Flanders, to the court of Baldwin."

"Then she knows she's failed all of her sons?"

"I believe she's only too aware."

"You have my thanks," Æthelwine inclines his head, but then meets my eye.

"I would prefer to remain in Denmark, from now on. I'll serve Harthacnut and you better here if it pleases you."

"I'll miss you and your knowledge of England. But I understand the request. You have my thanks." He bows and walks from my presence. I watch him go. Is his decision to remain in Denmark just another indication of how poorly the Danes are considered in England? Only then do I stand.

I can't remain indoors a moment longer. I need to be outside, to know that the simple day to day tasks continue even while all around me, my brother's dream of a northern empire to rival that under the command of the Holy Roman Emperor falls to pieces.

It was always too much, and yet, somehow, and despite all I knew to the contrary, I thought he would succeed. It seems preposterous to think it will not even outlive him by two years.

Without being aware of where I go, I find myself at the great church in Roskilde, where my ancestors are buried. My mother and father amongst them. Not together, but in the same place, alongside my brother, my traitorous husband, even if his grave is hidden away, where none can find it unless they know where it lies.

But it's to my father's elaborate grave that I stumble, the memories I have of him, merging with those of Harald and Cnut. All three of them, gone far too soon, with varying degrees of a successful legacy left behind. And I know, oh how I know, that fate hasn't yet finished with my family.

I settle on my knees, hands clasped in prayer, determined to exhort my God for something other than what I fear, but the words die on my lips, as I gaze at the glittering golden cross, the rich red ruby and the image of my father that's carved into the stone below which he lies.

My father had dreams of Denmark; my brother had visions of an empire, what will my son dream of, when he becomes king? I can only hope that he aspires to less, to ruling, as opposed to conquering. That way, I hope, he'll get to live out all of his allotted days, unlike the other men in my family.

# CHAPTER 21

## AD 1040

"Your son?" Harthacnut is before me, all puffed up and filled with ire. I run my eyes along him, taking in the face that is both so like my brother's, and so very different. In the gleam of his blue eyes, I see Lady Emma.

I'm sorting through the linen and fabric available to me, turning my nose up at pieces that will not suit me, while holding others firm against my breast. Frida watches me with a hint of a smile on her lips. She knows me far too well. The arrival of my nephew forces her to dip her head, assume the expected position of subordinate to the king of Denmark, but I imagine the smile still plays around her lips.

I don't usually allow myself to be distracted by such mundane tasks, but I find myself unable to write to my family anymore. My niece in Norway, my nephew in the land of the Svear, my two sisters by marriage, one abandoned in England, the other in Flanders. They all weary me far too much.

"Your cousin?" I offer, placing the fabric on the long table and lifting my eyes to meet his. They flash with ire, and I genuinely wish I knew what Svein had done now. But it doesn't matter, my role here is to defend him, regardless, whether he's fathered another bastard or taken service with another of his extended family, to the detriment of Harthacnut's ambitions, it little matters. Harthacnut has driven Svein from Denmark and my side.

"He's been captured, by the Archbishop of Hamburg-Bremen for pillaging in the Elbe-Wesser."

I gasp at the news, my heart suddenly beating too fast, my mind running through all the scenarios I've imagined for my son. They don't include him being killed in captivity. Or do they? The bloody archbishop has never been my ally.

"It's inconvenient for me. I need Svein here. I sent word that he needed to return. I must travel to England immediately. This peace has cost me dear, and I need to move quickly, while my ship-men are still keen to satisfy their blood-lust."

Ah, it seems my nephew is not concerned for my son, but rather aggrieved.

"It's taken me three years to reach an accord with bloody Magnus of Norway's advisors, and now that all is nearly ready, Svein has managed to get himself locked up by the righteous archbishop."

"What does the archbishop want in return for Svein's release?"

I'd not truly realised that my nephew meant to leave so much power in my son's hands. It surprises me more than it should. The thought warms me towards my headstrong nephew while making me anxious for Svein. He's been absent from Denmark for the three years that Harthacnut speaks of, and yet, Svein is the ideal person to rule in his stead, especially as Harthacnut means to take Beorn with him, of that I knew. I admit I expected to be left to rule in Harthacnut's name, but whether it's in my name, or Svein's, I don't much mind.

There will be further bloodshed in England, but I know that Beorn thirsts for it just as much as Harthacnut does. Both young men have heads filled with the stories of King Swein and King Cnut, and of the many they killed to make England theirs.

"He demands nothing. Not at the moment. I only know by chance that Svein is even a prisoner, but it's inopportune. When the winter storms come to an end, I want to be on my way to England. I must win back my kingdom from King Harald. It was never meant to be his kingdom."

My nephew flings himself into one of the wooden-backed chairs that lines the table. I turn to truly look at him. Harthacnut is not my brother. I'm reminded of that time and time again, and he's certainly not the master of Denmark's enemies that Cnut once was, and yet, I almost wish him success. In England. It's beyond the time that Svein had the opportunity to prove his skills.

"I'll send word to the archbishop and make reparation for whatever it is that Svein has done. I can travel there, now, if it would suit you."

"No. No, it would not suit me. I need you here as well."

The hint of petulance in Harthacnut's voice is off-putting when I've just been comparing him to my brother, but I ignore it in light of the promise of more control for my son and me.

"Send Beorn. He'll speak well to the archbishop."

"What, and have both of my cousins far from me? I don't think that will work either. They are my heirs until I have my own child."

His voice is filled with firm resolve. Since the death of his sister, Lady Gunnhild, from the plague, following the birth of her only child, a daughter, Harthacnut has begun to take careful count of his family members. There are few enough of them left now that he trusts.

"Then you must send someone else, or instead, send a messenger with such wealth in gold and silver that Archbishop Adalbrand will not reject your requests."

I refuse to offer more options for Harthacnut to dismiss. He can complicate matters, or he can just act. In all honesty, I'm surprised that he's even thought to consult me. In the last few years, he's come to rely on me less and less.

"You're right, Aunt. I'll do as you suggest," and without pausing to add more, or even tell me which option he's decided to take, Harthacnut is standing and striding from the hall. I watch him go. With a soft sigh, I return to my task, while

Frida pours me wine and hands it to me.

"This is the opportunity your son needs," she whispers. "Svein, if he can keep his cock to himself, can begin to build the web of alliances that he'll need."

My oldest son has rarely sent messengers to me in recent years. But what he has sent are his children, born outside the bonds of marriage. Knud Magnus and Harald are little more than babes in arms, and with their mothers both in attendance in Roskilde, I can enjoy my grandsons, if not my errant son.

I don't need to agree with Frida; we both know that she speaks the truth.

"What of Beorn?" Frida adds.

I sometimes find it difficult to consider my second son. It's not that he's without ambition, far from it, in fact, but he's not the warrior that Svein is trying to become. Beorn is an ally of Harthacnut. His future, I believe, lies in England.

"Beorn will go to England, with the king. He'll make his life there." The words don't cut as much as I thought they might.

I try not to consider the problems of Harthacnut's peace accord with King Magnus. I can only think myself out of one problem at a time.

Harthacnut will leave Denmark, and so will Beorn, but Svein will return and fill the space filled by their absence. Then, he can become more a father to his two sons, and, begin to build on the future I've long envisioned for him, that of king of Denmark.

I watch Beorn with the critical eye of a mother, and also the love of one. It's a heady combination. He looks too much like his father in the wrong light, that has always been the problem, although I hope he might still mature beyond the arrogant tilt of the chin and the combative look in his brown eyes. When he grins, he's entirely my son, and a member of the House of Gorm, my father etched into his features. But he's not known for smiling. The last few years have been filled with the threat of invasion from King Magnus. It's left an indelible mark on Beorn.

He's dressed in fine clothes, his tunic so richly embellished with the emblem of the House of Gorm, that I think it must be uncomfortable to walk in. I imagine he's forced to wear an undershirt as well, or risk having the stitching raise welts all along his upper body. He doesn't wear imperial purple, but the blue he so often chooses is really not so very different. I'm always surprised that Harthacnut allows it. But he's so fond of my youngest son. It's they who should have been brothers, not Svein and Beorn.

In Beorn, Harthacnut doesn't see a potential rival but only an ally. And one who keeps the secret of his continued ill-health, just as I do, and Bodil, and the young man she's trained to care for Harthacnut, Frode. Having him in constant attendance on the king raises few eyebrows. He's not as well-known as Bodil for having the skill of healing.

"Lady Mother," he kisses my cheek before sprawling in the chair beside me. He has come to take his leave of me before joining the ship-army to travel with Harthacnut to England. I'm suddenly unsure of how I should feel. I doubt I'll see him again, not in this lifetime, but I don't believe that it's sorrow that makes me want to savour this moment.

"I see my brother has finally returned." Were two brothers ever so different? But no, I know of many other brothers who didn't appreciate one another, I need only look to my nephews to see it. Of course, in that situation, they had different mothers, and that's always a means to drive a wedge between two siblings who should esteem one another. I know that only too well.

"Yes, Svein has returned, and is grateful to Harthacnut for ensuring his release from the clutches of the Archbishop.'

"He would have been wiser to stay there. He'll only be tempted by more women and the promise of war booty from whoever makes the offer. I don't believe he'll linger in Denmark, not when you'll be ruling in Harthacnut's name." That's not quite what Harthacnut has said to me, but perhaps he's eager to ensure his ally travels with him. I don't believe that Harthacnut wishes to go to England with no family, other than his mother.

They've made some attempt at reconciliation, although I know it's stilted and Harthacnut only includes her in his plans because she knows England better than he does.

"I know your brother's shortcomings well enough. I wished to speak of you, not of him."

The quirk in Beorn's eyebrows makes me aware that he's surprised by this. Did he genuinely think I esteemed his brother more than him? I had thought not, but now I'm unsure.

"You're highly favoured by your cousin. It's to be hoped he gifts you great tracts of land and allows you to advise him in running England."

"Hum," it seems that Beorn is not convinced, although by what part, I'm unsure. Does he not see a life for himself in England? Does he mean to return to Denmark? Or is it merely that he realises Harthacnut could succumb to his illness at any time.

"I know little of England. I was born in Denmark. I have yet to be convinced of its advantages when compared to Denmark. What is it like? What do you recall about it?"

"England is much like Denmark; only the king there must rule with the aid of his earls."

"But what of the houses, and the palaces, and the landscape?"

"It's green and lush in the summer until the heat bakes the soil. In the winter it's cold and miserable, little different to the northern countries. It's rich in resources. I forget all of them, but there's iron, salt, lime, lead, copper, and silver, as you might expect. There's a fine wine from the southern regions. There's good honey to sweeten the mead. London is a vibrant centre for trade, but it's only the largest of the trading places. You can get fine spices, delicate herbs, anything you want if you can afford it."

"You sound as though you spent your entire time visiting markets and appraising England's worth." Beorn chuckles. It's better that he thinks that, than the truth, that I spent all my time in Winchester wishing to return to Roskilde.

"My father wanted England for her wealth, not her charms. Cnut was the same. You would do well to remind Harthacnut that England is to be exploited, not adored."

The joy slides from Beorn's lips as I speak, and I regret the harshness. My time in England was not pleasant. I would sooner forget it.

"And what of the royal court?"

My mind immediately flickers to Lady Emma, but I try to deflect my son.

"I'm sure I know a few of the men and women who inhabit the space. Of the earls, I knew Lord Leofric well. Of course, your father's brother resides in England, and you'll remember Siward, now earl of Northumbria. He once served me well."

"And what of Harthacnut's mother?"

I would sooner not speak of her, but it seems my son needs to know.

"She's a woman to be wary around. She's out of favour with Harthacnut. I would advise you to stay away from her and to make other allies."

"What with Earl Godwine and his sons?"

"No, not with Earl Godwine and his sons. Your other uncle is about as trustworthy as a fox. You'll need to step carefully with both him, Uncle Eilifr, and Lady Emma. Harthacnut will no doubt be doing the same. He must make his own decisions, and rely only on men who are loyal to him. And at the moment, I don't know who that might be, outside the party of Danes he'll take with him."

"Can't he even rely on Earl Leofric? I thought he was loyal to my father."

"Perhaps. He's an honourable man, as his father was before him. He would never not aid you. He would never not aid

Harthacnut, but his loyalty is to King Harald at the moment. I don't know why. I suspect the involvement of Cnut, despite everything, said and believed to the contrary. Step carefully and warily. The English court is filled with those keen to take advantage of even the smallest of weaknesses in others."

"You speak as though Harthacnut will win his war." Beorn grins as he speaks, but his eyes don't leave my face. Does he dare to talk about the impasse with King Magnus? Does he dare me to criticise Harthacnut even though I was the one who told him to do whatever it took if he wished to secure England?

"I'm sure that the two brothers will learn to rule together. There doesn't need to be a real war. That was their father's wish."

"No," and now Beorn leans forward, his head resting on his upturned hands as his elbows rest on the table. "It was Cnut's wish that Harthacnut rule, not Harald. It's only because of King Magnus that Harald has been able to claim the kingdom for himself."

I pause, consider how best to respond. It seems to me that Beorn desperately tries to unravel what's happened in England, but that he still doesn't understand all of the nuances at play.

"There are two kingdoms, and there are two brothers. What is it that you truly think Cnut had in mind?"

The confusion on Beorn's face almost makes me smile.

'Be wiser, my son," I caution him. "Don't accept what one person believes as the truth. Nothing is rarely so simple."

His eyes dim, just a little. Perhaps he considers the wisdom of his actions in leaving Denmark, where he has his place as a member of the House of Gorm, and replacing it with England, where he's potentially walking into a messy altercation that could rival the drawn-out process when Cnut claimed the kingdom. Nothing is assured.

"Don't let Harthacnut hear you speaking in such a way."

"Harthacnut wouldn't hear my words even if he did. Harthacnut believes what he wants to believe, and nothing else."

"Are you so very different?" The perceptive comments bring a smile to my face, as my son challenges me with words he think will wound, but don't.

"No, not at all. But I will temper what I believe with what I know. Harthacnut has yet to learn that necessity."

"Yet you send Harthacnut away with your blessing?"

"I do, yes. He's made the peace accord with King Magnus. Denmark is safe from attack."

Again Beorn surprises me with a narrowing of his eyes, yet he holds his tongue. I think that my son is learning some much needed political astuteness. There's power in knowing and not sharing. I've long known the truth of that.

"Will you care for my estates when I'm in England. I've assigned men to oversee the day to day business, but I want you to know interference will be appreciated if deemed necessary."

"I'll do what must be done, yes."

"And what about in England? Will my father's estates still be mine to claim?"

"I doubt it. He was a traitor. I'm sure that your uncle or even Earl Leofric will have long since claimed them. You'll need to wait for your cousins to reward you."

This doesn't seem to be what Beorn wishes to hear, and yet I won't retract my words.

"I've been gone from England for far longer than I ever lived there. Yes, you have powerful Uncles, and two cousins who would be her king, but no one there even knows who you are. Step carefully, my son." And with that, I meet his keen eyes, willing him to heed my words, unsure whether he will or not. Has he learned the lessons that Cnut failed to heed? I can only hope so.

As I should, I watch the fleet take their leave from Roskilde. There are over sixty ships, all of them Danish. I took my leave of Harthacnut with some sorrow. I'll not see him again. I'm sure of it.

Yet, as soon as the ships are out of sight, turning to make their way toward the open sea, and away from Roskilde, I turn aside. I'm ready to begin what must be done, Svein at my side, his mouth, for once, firmly shut.

I wish Harthacnut well. I want him to be successful in England. But that's not what concerns me. My homeland is Denmark, and it's Denmark that needs to win free from King Magnus. I know that. I just need my son to realise the same.

# CHAPTER 22

*AD 1040*

"King Harthacnut is proclaimed King of England."

The words of the messenger ring with triumph around the hall, to be greeted with acclaim. Svein startles beside me, and I caution him with my eyes. This isn't news to either of us. I knew of King Harald of England's death, but only after Harthacnut had already left for Flanders to retrieve his mother. I'm relieved that the need for war in England was averted, even though I pity King Harald, and of course, Lady Ælfgifu. Both of her sons are now dead when they had barely had time to be men. She must be entirely inconsolable.

I would not wish such a loss on any woman. Although I consider, I've not shown the same kindness to Lady Emma and the loss of Lord Alfred. But then, I doubt Alfred would have considered Emma anything more than the woman who birthed him.

"Bring mead and ale. We'll toast our king, king of England and Denmark." The few men and women who remain within the hall at Roskilde, cheer, and then cheer even louder when the servants appear with jugs containing mead and ale. There are few to hear of Harthacnut's victory. Most are either with him or off, tending to their estates. The royal court is a small thing with Harthacnut absent. Although I grow it, and so does

Svein.

"To Harthacnut, King of Denmark, and England," while the words I speak are the correct ones, there's much less emphasis on England. Yet, I drink deeply of the wine, and Svein does the same, the hall an echo of laughter and good cheer as voices spike and fall, the promise of riches to be gained in England keeping the Danish happy, a reminder of when my father was declared king of England running through my mind.

"My Lady Estrid," the servant who bows and then hands me a tightly rolled vellum sheet is one of my most trusted men. He may look as though he spends his days tending to my needs in the hall, but in actual fact, it's rare for him to be here. He's only just returned from his most recent commission.

"My thanks, Halfdan," he does not indicate as to what it is he hands to me, and I almost wish he was less discrete. But if he were, I would not need him.

Svein eyes me over the lip of his ale.

"What news?" the words are innocuous enough, but they mask so much more. Perhaps I shouldn't have allowed Svein into my secrets. Perhaps.

"I can't tell you while it remains unread."

His grunt assures me he'll be silent, as I unravel the vellum.

The words surprise me less than they should.

"Tell me, Lady Mother," but I shake my head, instead concentrating on my wine, and trying not to allow my hand to shake. I would have been better to keep my hand hidden in the layers of my dresses.

"I thought we were to have no secrets?"

"Ah, but you only apply that sentiment when you wish to discover my secrets. You have no problem keeping your own."

"I can't imagine that I know anything that you do not," the frustration in Svein's voice, almost makes me smile. Almost.

And then I relent. Better to tell him something rather than nothing.

"It's merely news of how King Harald met his death. It doesn't make for pleasant reading. It seems he was assassinated and bled to death in his own hall." I keep from my son the rest of the information, but it makes me restless. While the men and women of the royal court drink and toast the success of Harthacnut, I'm forced to my feet.

"I'll pray for Harthacnut's victory and the soul of poor King Harald." A sly smirk on Svein's face and I know he'll be doing no such thing.

"I'll keep order here," he promises me, but I know he'll be the worst of the lot. He has the excesses of my father and can bring all men and women to his cause, but he is, unfortunately, unskilled in keeping them by his side.

Frida is quick to join me, peeling away from her place beside the hearth. Outside, it's almost dark, the wind blowing shrilly so that as the door to the grand hall is opened, I'm forced to cower into the cloak she hands to me.

"To the church," I instruct her, and that more than anything, makes Frida hurry her steps.

"Tell me," Frida demands to know when we're through the doors, the priest and his monks, busy with their service in God's name.

I would have her read the missive, but it's too dark, and her eyesight is not as good as mine.

"There's a child."

"A child?"

"Yes, King Harald had a son."

"Your brother's grandson?" The wonder in Frida's voice reflects how I feel. "What does it matter, if no one knows of him, and Harald never claimed him?"

The words still my rapidly beating heart, restore me to the here and now.

"You're right. It makes no difference, other than the child is coming here, fearful of Harthacnut killing the rival to his claim if he should ever be discovered."

"It's right that you should protect your brother's grandson, not just from Harthacnut, but also from Lady Emma, but you don't have to acknowledge the child as a member of your family."

"No, I don't. It would be better if I didn't."

"It would, yes, for everyone."

I take to my knees all the same, beneath the shimmering mass of the thirty candles that light the inner reaches of the church. I allow the words of the priest and the responses of the monk to drown out all reason, all retribution for what I must do, and only as the final word of the service drains away to nothing more than the breathing of the monks and the priest, do I turn to Frida.

"We'll find a pleasant home for the mother and her child. I'll not allow Cnut's grandson to be raised in poverty, or in need of anything. It seems that King Harald wasn't a gentle husband. His death might have been less an assassination, and more the righteous rage of a woman tested beyond her limits to survive. I task you with ensuring the proper care is provided for the child. I must keep as far distant as possible, and yet, there must also be guards to ensure Harthacnut doesn't attack the boy."

Frida rises fluidly from the ground, her hand making the sign of the cross on her chest before she turns to me.

"You honour me with such responsibility. I'll see all is done as it should be."

"Then you have my thanks, and I'll reward you handsomely. No one is to know of this. It's Earl Leofric who sends word, or rather, his son has asked me to intervene. Other than us five, and of course, the child's mother and grandmother, it must be a secret. Nothing can imperil Svein's kingship, nothing. It's too close now. I just know that it is."

She reaches out to grip my arm, the movement both to reassure and to assure.

"I'll do this, for the House of Gorm and the future of Denmark. Your son will rule, and after him, his son, and so on. The line of King Swein will not be broken, even if it descends through the female line."

I lay my hand over hers, squeeze tightly. She's been the one person I've always been able to trust. She's been a greater support than my own family. And then I stride to the candles left burning by the priest.

I hold the vellum to the flame, watching it crumble before me.

Just another secret.

All in the name of my son's kingship.

# CHAPTER 23

## AD 1040

"*L*ady Estrid Sweinsdottir. Dearest sister."
I would sooner the letter had come from my son, but of course, he doesn't feel the need to gloat quite as much as Lady Emma.

"*I demand to know what you have told my son about me? He is cold and distant and holds me responsible for Harald's kingship. He's so wrathful. He's had Harald's body disturbed from its burial and up-ended into the River Thames. While I approve of treating the usurper in such a way, it speaks to me of a disturbed mind. He's not at all the man I believed him to be. Send me word, immediately, of what has befallen him since I last saw him. Your loving sister, Lady Emma, Dowager Queen, written at Winchester.*"

"Hah," I bark as I place the parchment before me. I read between her words, and determine that Harthacnut is not only cold toward his mother; he's keen to be entirely free from her. She was to help him gain the support of the English nobility, but of course, there was no need, not when there was no one else who could be named king after Harald's death.

The young child has arrived in Denmark, unfortunately with his grandmother in toe, so Frida informs me. But the family have been well-housed, not near Roskilde, but instead close to Viborg, on a small royal estate, on Jutland. It's better if we're distant. Then I need never see Lady Ælfgifu again. Frida said she would have been concerned for Lady Ælfgifu, but she dotes on her grandson. I know what it is to be a grandmother. I'm quietly pleased for her. I hope she accepts her obscurity with equanimity. I know that I wouldn't.

I glance up and meet Svein's eyes.

"Lady Emma," I shrug, and he winces, as though feeling my pain.

"And what of Harthacnut?"

"She's filled with criticism of him, and of me, for raising him all wrong and filling his head with stories about her that have made him hate her. I think she managed that all on her own, personally.

"So, nothing of importance then?"

"Only that Harthacnut had King Harald's body disinterred and flung into the Thames."

"Sounds rational."

"Completely," I agree, wondering what it is that Svein wants.

He's changed in his years away from Denmark, and yet I still see the child peering at me from his moustached face.

"There's to be another child," he shrugs, and I feel my eyes roll at the news.

"Will you marry this woman?"

"No, there's no need. She's content, and I'll acknowledge the child, as I do the others."

"Will you ever marry?"

Svein chuckles darkly. "Why would I? The women are keen to be in my bed without such a contract. They see me as Harthacnut's regent, nothing more. They probably dream of a better husband, in good time."

"Then congratulations, and I look forward to welcoming your new child."

"Excellent," and Svein lopes from my presence. I despair of him, and yet I also understand why he doesn't want to marry. If I'd been born a man, perhaps I'd never have married either.

The thought brings a smile to my face. I can just imagine what my father and brothers would have thought of that.

**"Lady Estrid Sweinsdottir. Dearest aunt."**

I've not heard from my niece, Astrid, in Norway, for some time. I'd expected exulting letters because of Magnus' triumph, and her silence has been more ominous because of the lack of them.

*"I'm pleased that this alliance has been struck between Harthacnut and Magnus. I'm sure that Magnus will enjoy ruling England, just as much as Harthacnut does, now that he's finally claimed it. Perhaps, when Magnus is the king of England, I'll even ask him for the properties that your traitor husband once held."*

*"Certainly, I'll ensure he ousts both Earl Eilifr and Earl Godwine from power. No family should be allowed to hold so much in their hands. Ensure your sons are aware that King Magnus will not think of them as family, and as such, they'll be entitled to nothing. I'll not demand that he gives them anything, even if you beg me to do so. They'll know what it's like to lose their country, just as you will."*

*"Your niece, Lady Astrid Olofsdottir, Mother of the King of Norway."*

"The bitch," I could scream with frustration at her letter, but I know I'm as much to blame as Harthacnut. I told him to do whatever must be done if he wanted to go to England. If we'd only known that King Harald would die so young, then none of it would have been necessary.

And in all honesty, perhaps I should be pleased that Lady Astrid is so bitter. It means that she's unable to stop herself from warning me of the future. Not that I expected anything other than that from her.

**"Dearest sister, Lady Emma."**

It almost costs me too much just to write those words. She's never been dear to me, and I would never count her as my sister.

"I'm dismayed by your allegations against me. I've told Harthac-nut only the truth. If he's made his own decisions about his years living in Denmark, it's not my fault. You have been almost entirely absent from his adult life, and I'll not even mention what happened in England following my brother's death. I suggest you look to yourself before you blame others."

"Your son has been forced to fight for his inheritance, and not just against one foe."

"You do not mention my son. I would be pleased to hear how he's received amongst the king's nobility. And tell me, is Earl Godwine beloved by my son? You make no mention of him, which I find strange."

"When you next write, I'll be pleased to see an apology."

"Your dearest sister, Lady Estrid Sweinsdottir, written at Roskilde."

**"Lady Estrid, dearest Aunt, from your nephew, Anund Jakob, king of the Svear."**

"Please ensure Harthacnut is aware that I congratulate him on becoming King of England. But, I must caution him. The alliance he made with King Magnus was not done well. My sister will push Magnus should anything happen to Harthacnut, to claim not only Denmark, but also England, and perhaps even my kingdom as well. My sister's ambitions are truly without end. I would wish the blasted child had not survived."

"I've made some attempt to determine what happened to King Edmund's children, if a rival to King Magnus is needed for England. It shouldn't concern me, but it does. I know they still live, but they have not lived under my control for many years. I'll not allow my sister to fulfil all of her ambitions."

"I would also ask after your son, Svein. He's a fine young man. Should he ever have the need, he would be welcome to return to my kingdom. I would support him if he should ever need it. Your loving nephew, Anund Jakob, king of the Svear."

"Well that's just wonderful," I say aloud, although there's no one to hear. It seems my nephew regrets his actions in throwing his support behind King Magnus and his allies. It's all far too late, and yet, I also detect that his offer to Svein is genuine. It's just possible that it might be needed, in the future. After all, I know that Harthacnut will die, and soon. Then, it seems, I'll have to contend with King Magnus. It's not what I wanted. I want Svein to rule, and perhaps he just might, with the aid of King Anund Jakob.

**"Lady Mother, from your beloved son, Beorn, in England."**

Of course, I've had no reply from Lady Emma since I wrote to her. I hope that Beorn will provide more details.

"I find England to be little different to Denmark, as you said. Certainly, the nobility is a cantankerous lot. King Harthacnut rules with an iron fist, perhaps not the best approach, but he'll not be cautioned. When would he ever be, I hear you say?"

"I'm sure you heard of what he did to King Harald's body. I was there. It was a despicable scene, and yet, I had no choice but to play my part. The body was stinking. I've heard rumours that Earl Leofric ensured the body was retrieved from the Thames and suitably reburied. I hope there's truth in those rumours, although Harthacnut is cool towards the man."

"Lady Emma and Harthacnut are much estranged. She tries too hard and irritates Harthacnut. He has all but banished her to her property in Winchester."

"I've yet to be given any great reward, but I will inform you that Harthacnut plans to summon Lord Edward from Normandy, and have it known that he's his heir, should he die. It's a sensible solution, and yet likely to cause further friction between Harthacnut and his mother. I truly find her intolerable."

"Earl Godwine has attempted to make me his ally. Honestly, mother, you would not believe the size of his family. There are so many sons, and the earl is greedy for enough positions to provide for them all. He's tried to make his peace with Harthacnut, but Harthacnut will not accept it readily, not when he blames him for the death of Lord Alfred. Harthacnut has no problem humiliating *any of his earls."*

*"I'm sure that by now the Danish ships must have returned to Denmark. The king demanded a huge geld, and when people could not pay it, he sent tax collectors to take anything of value from the poor people. I understand they've had two years of famine and many have nothing. Harthacnut is a harsh ruler. Even though two of his reeves were killed by the men and women of Worcester, although I am led to believe it might actually have been an act of war by the Welsh, his demands for the geld continue to grow."*

*"Earl Leofric is the only man who will speak against Harthacnut. He's a brave and principled man, as you said. There is much unease, and I don't know how any of it will end. I feel I may have been hasty in coming to England. But I can't return, not now."*

*"Have my brother write to me. I should like to know how he fares, and just how many children he now claims as his own. Randy bastard."*

*"Your affectionate son, Beorn, written at Winchester."*

I chuckle as I read the end of the letter.

"What is it?" Svein lifts his head from where he polishes his sword, and I arch an eyebrow.

"Write to your brother," is all the reply I give him, and Svein huffs with faked annoyance.

"But you know I don't like to write."

"I know you like to do very little but make war, make love, and drink," I criticise, but Svein merely laughs.

"What else is there for me to do? Denmark is at peace, and I can do nothing unless Harthacnut gives me instructions. If I tried to do anything else, he'd only berate me."

"Perhaps," I condescend to agree. "Or perhaps not. Harthacnut intends to have Lord Edward brought to England, as his heir."

"Then, Harthacnut means to break the accord with King Magnus."

"Perhaps, or perhaps England was never a part of it. Maybe, Lady Astrid is mistaken."

"I doubt it. It seems that Harthacnut means to reward his half-brother, even as he desecrates the burial site of one of his other half-brothers. I should like to know how he justifies it all to himself."

"Why would he bother to justify it? He's proud enough to believe no one will question him. But all the same, if Harthacnut is making plans for the future of England, then perhaps we should begin the same for Denmark. It's not right that King Magnus should rule here after Harthacnut's death."

"Do you mean to start plotting?" Svein asks, but his eyes are alight with the promise of rebellion.

"Do you believe I ever stopped?" I demand of him, and his chuckle is all the answer I need.

# CHAPTER 24

*AD1042*

I wake sweating, my hair damp down my back, my legs tangled in the sheets and furs. It takes all of my will power not to shriek, as my heart thuds painfully in my chest.

I knew this moment would come, but there's a distinct difference between knowing and experiencing it.

Hastily, I grab my cloak and leave the comfort of my bed, on soft feet.

The door creaks noisily, but no one comes to see if I'm well. Why would they? This is far from the first time that I've been forced from my bed by dreams. Even Frida leaves me alone now.

It's far from dark, as I make my way along the shadowed, rather than the darkened corridor to the main hall, where the embers of the fire add a glow that isn't needed.

I make my way to the chair on the dais, that's mine, treading carefully so as not to wake those unfortunate enough not to have access to a bed for the night. There aren't many of them, not in the height of summer. The hall is barely inhabited. I'm there. Frida is there. Some of my son's warriors are here. So too are his two young sons and their mothers, as well as his latest woman, but other than that, there are only servants and they all sleep.

Settled in my chair, I reach for the waiting jug of cool water, placed there for such occurrences. My servants know me well. It almost makes me smile; only my thoughts rush back to what I've seen.

Harthacnut is dead. I know it, even though the news will not reach Denmark for days, if not weeks. Unlike when Cnut died, as winter had gripped the land, the journey will be quickly accomplished because it's the summer. I'll not have to keep my secret for long.

In his brief two years in England, no, not even two years, I've been the recipient of increasingly terse messages from him, some almost frantic. Harthacnut knew, of course, he knew, that he'd not enjoy even as many years as his father. It saddens me and angers me. My brother should have loved his son more. But he saw him only as a piece on the tafl board, and he's paid for his callousness by losing his life, and then being quickly joined by all three of his sons. My brother was a thoughtless man, although many will not ascribe such a word to him.

They're too caught up in the glory of what he achieved, never once thinking that it was unsustainable. No man can be king of more than one country. My father learned that lesson, and Cnut, rather than taking the lesson to heart, strove merely to outdo him. He dreamed of an empire, and he made one, but it was unsustainable.

I sip from my ivory-carved beaker, left for me because it's strong and sturdy when I feel weak and distressed. Not for me a fine piece of glassware. No, I'd break it and then I would be angered by such a loss, on top of the one I've seen while I slept.

I consider how, even after all these years, my servants don't know the secret of my late-night excursions. I wonder why no one has ever lined up the momentous events that have befallen the House of Gorm and realised that my wakefulness is related. I suppose I should be pleased.

My eyes fasten on the rings that adorn my fingers. They tell of my wealth and birthright, and yet they give me no means to claim the kingdom of Denmark. Would I, as Swein Forkbeard's daughter, wish to do so? Would I, as King Gorm's granddaughter, want to do so?

I can't say, not with any honesty. Certainly, I would rule better than my brothers, my nephew and my son will. Perhaps I can say then. Maybe I'm arrogant enough to think that I could hold Denmark whole against her enemies and ensure she prospered. Only, that's never been my position.

I sigh again, drink more cool water, try and banish the taste of ash from my mouth.

I think back, to that true dream that showed so much of the future to me. Over time, I've deciphered those who claimed those eyes. I've made my peace with those I've loved and lost, and those I've loathed and been forced to live with side by side.

Not that the death of Harthacnut paves the way for Svein to rule. Far from it. And in fact, now is the time when the future becomes the most unclear to me. With the deaths of my father, brothers and nephews, I now face something entirely different, or rather, someone altogether different.

Magnus of Norway. He's a powerful youth, with the support of my royal niece behind him, even if he's half bastard-born. Not that it excludes him from ruling in the northern lands, far from it.

But Magnus has wily men and women behind him, and of course, there's the matter of the agreement forged between Magnus and Harthacnut which brought Harthacnut the peace he needed to go to England, five years late. I consider what Magnus will do with Svein? I have half a thought that Svein is already his puppet. Svein has never been patient, and he's not oblivious to the fact that when Harthacnut dies, Magnus fully intends to claim Denmark as his kingdom.

I would move to make Svein king in his own name, but I know I can't do so yet. Now is the time for patience, for biding my time, for calling on the alliances I've long been fermenting.

And of course, I have time before everyone knows of Harthacnut's death, but how should I make the best use of it? For all the years of planning, and knowing, suddenly, I'm unsure, and that sits ill with me.

Standing, I swirl my cloak tightly around me and head toward the main door. In times of uncertainty, I've always sought assistance from elsewhere, and today will be no different.

"What do you want, Lady Mother?" Svein's tone is curt, and I tut, shocked by his rudeness.

"Come, we must speak. It's urgent."

"What can be so damn urgent?"

"Read then, if you'll not allow me to explain."

**"Beloved mother, from your affectionate son, Beorn, in Winchester."**

*"With a heavy heart, I write to inform you of the death of Harthacnut. I should like to say that his death was easy, but it was not. I believe he suffered greatly in his final days. No warrior should be forced to ensure such an end."*

"He's dead?" Svein doesn't even read to the end of the letter, and I'm unsurprised.

"Yes, your cousin is dead."

"So what of Denmark?" Only he's reading the letter once more, and I hold my tongue. I know what the letter says. Svein isn't.

"Lord Edward has been declared king of England, as per Harthacnut's wishes," Beorn continues. "Harthacnut didn't speak of what should happen in Denmark. I've ensured that King Magnus is not made aware of what's happened. That's for you to arrange, Lady Mother, if you wish. I'm aware that if Harthacnut died, then the accord with Magnus means than he should become king of Denmark as well. But that doesn't seem correct. Surely, Svein should rule in Denmark? After all, he has been doing so since Harthacnut travelled to England."

"Please choose carefully, and inform me of your plans. I wouldn't wish to look uninformed. I'll remain in England, for the time being. King Edward and I have struck up an unlikely friendship. No doubt, Cnut would be horrified, but I find Edward to be honourable and loyal."

"I believe that Earl Godwine will not contact King Magnus, but he might do so, just to spite us all. Do what you must. Your loving son, Beorn Estridsson."

"What will we do?" Svein's gaze almost sears me with its heat.

"I believe we must inform King Magnus or face an invasion once more."

"Do you not think me capable of defeating him?"

"I do, yes, but the details of the accord are well known. Harthacnut named him as his successor."

"Damn fool," my son complains, his face undergoing so many changes, I hardly know what he thinks.

"Denmark should be mine."

"I agree," I seek to calm him. "I'm in full agreement. But, King Magnus will not see it that way."

"Then what should I do?"

"I believe you should go to Magnus. Inform him of his new position. He'll reward you, richly, for being the one to tell him, even more so because your claim is just as valid as his. He'll know you as one of his most loyal supporters. While that's happening, we'll determine a way to steal Denmark from him."

"So, you want me to tell him he's the king, and then determine how to take it from him. Surely, it would be better if I just became the king?"

"You don't have the support to do that. Not yet. Let me assure you on that matter. You've been gone from Denmark too often. Yes, you've ruled well in the name of Harthacnut, but you still need more for the nobility to accept you as king."

"I have the ship-army that Harthacnut dispersed when he became king of England." It seems that Svein is far from convinced by my suggestion.

"Do you, though? Or are the majority of those ship-men halfway to the land of the Rus in the hope of spoils, and the other half, perhaps on the way to Ireland? I don't believe there are even a quarter of those ships remaining. But, tell me if I'm wrong." Svein's silence tells me all I need to know.

"Go to King Magnus. Tell him he's now king, and welcome to Denmark, but ensure he makes you a jarl in return. From that, much more can be accomplished."

Svein's unhappiness is evident in the sharp angles of his jaw and cheeks, but he grunts his agreement.

"I'll do what you say, Lady Mother. You've always been wiser than I have in such matters."

His words sound like a compliment, but they're not. But, if he means to criticise me, I'll take it. There's much he still needs to learn.

I worry about my son, and the future of Denmark until he stomps back into my presence at Roskilde. Of course, the death of Harthacnut is well known. It's been impossible to keep it a secret, and I didn't actually see the point of doing so. I think it would be better if the nobility felt uneasy.

They're used to serving Harthacnut, and Svein and now they'll have a new master. The potential for unrest doesn't require my involvement. Just as happened with Cnut in Norway, new kings tend to overreach themselves and make mistakes with those they trust.

"Well, Lady Mother, I come from King Magnus. He's made me one of his jarls, of Jutland."

"So you're jarl of Denmark then?" The news excites me, even while Svein looks mutinous, as he bursts into the hall.

"Yes, I'm now jarl of a kingdom I should rule as king. I thank you for your sage advice." I would snap words at him, but I've another matter for him to consider.

"My nephew has a proposition for you?"

"Who? King Anund Jakob?"

"The very one, yes."

"And what is it that he wants?"

"He wants to diminish his sister's influence in the region. He wants you to marry his daughter?"

"His daughter? But surely she's too closely related to me? The church would never approve."

"Some would say that others would say that the relationship is tenuous, and we can work with that. She would be your half-cousin's daughter."

"But I don't wish to marry, Lady Mother, I've made that clear. There are too many women to enjoy as it is."

"Not even if it brings you even more support from King Anund Jakob? I would think carefully about it before you dismiss it." I speak softly, hoping to entice him with such an image of the future

"Surely, you wouldn't approve of such a match?"

"It needn't be forever. You already have sons aplenty, from your more casual relationships. This will merely be about reinforcing your connection with King Anund Jakob. He's prepared to support you. What he wants is the knowledge that his sister will no longer be able to laud her vast influence over him. They've grown bitter towards one another. I'm hardly surprised, and we can exploit that."

"Then, yes, I'll do what you ask. But there will be repercussions."

"Aren't there always, where you're concerned, dear son?"

His silence is telling.

"There is to be war." Svein has been in the land of the Svear, wedding and bedding his wife. He was correct. There have been numerous complaints about the union, but Gytha is with child, and Svein is assured of his bond with King Anund Jakob, even if he never returns to the land of the Svear again.

"War with who?" I'm surprised to see him. I'd assumed he'd remain with his wife for a little longer.

"King Magnus has recalled me and summoned the ship-army. The Wends mean to attack Jutland, and as its jarl, I must defend it."

"Why are they attacking Jutland?"

"Because they believe it to be weak, now that King Magnus rules Denmark, and he spends so much of his time in Norway."

"So, you'll fight?"

"I'll fight, yes. And hopefully, I'll win a great victory and the gratitude of the nobility of Jutland."

I laugh at his tone. Svein's ambitions are impossible to ignore.

"Then, I suggest, you make war well, and win so resoundingly, that none can even imagine another being their king."

Svein jumps to his feet, a kiss to my cheek, and then he's striding from the hall.

He's filled with firm resolve. Perhaps, this will be his moment of glory. Certainly, few are content with King Magnus. He's his own worst enemy. I don't believe he should have summoned Svein back to fight on his behalf. But what do I know? I am merely Svein's mother and a woman of little influence and even less experience. I laugh softly to myself. I'll pray for Svein's victory. Surely, this will be his moment?

*"Lady Mother."* The letter I'm handed is held together by sheer luck and nothing else. I can see that it's been badly damaged, no doubt by the terrible weather.

I'm not expecting a letter, I'm expecting Svein, and a slither of unease makes my fingers fumble as I uncurl the letter.

*"I won a great victory over the Wends, just as I promised, and the men of Jutland proclaimed me as king of Denmark, but King Magnus is not content to accept that. His retaliation has been bloody and quick. I've taken refuge with my wife and her family. My son has been born. He's a delight. I'll return as soon as I'm able. Care for my country in my absence. Your loving son, Svein Estridsson."*

I crush the parchment tightly in my hand. This is not what I wanted to read, not at all.

I was sure Svein would triumph.

**"Dearest Beorn."**

*"I write with the news that your brother has been forced to flee*

to the land of the Svear. He was proclaimed king of Denmark by the Thing, but King Magnus will not accept it and has driven him from Denmark. Tell me, how are affairs in England? Does King Edward rule well? I remember meeting him so many years ago, in Normandy."

"Has King Edward mastered Earl Godwine? I would hope he has. I'm perplexed by just how long that man has survived in England. I had hoped for him to fail, many, many years ago. I know he's your uncle, but I would again advise you to keep your distance from him."

"Will you marry and remain in England?"

"Your loving mother, Lady Estrid Sweinsdottir."

**"Beloved Mother, Lady Estrid Sweinsdottir."**

"I'm dismayed to hear of all that has befallen Svein. He should be king, not Magnus, but I believe many fear Magnus. His ship-army has quite a reputation."

"I can only inform you that the king much loves Earl Godwine and his sons. Of course, he also means to marry Lady Edith, their daughter. I don't believe you will ever get your wish. Would it not be better to see Earl Godwine as an ally? Perhaps? He's influential with the king, far more than I am, to date. I hope the king will gift me with a decent earldom, but it hasn't happened yet. I would return to Denmark, but of course, it is no longer ruled by my family. I will remain in England. For now. Your loving son, Beorn Estridsson."

**"Dearest son, Lord Beorn."**

"I beg you not to see Earl Godwine as your ally. He has always had ambitions that were too lofty for such a family. Do not encourage him further."

"It's a pity that King Edward has been forced to marry the daughter. It would have been better for him to have taken a bride from elsewhere. I can only foresee the potential for problems now. Remind King Edward of our past meeting. It may be that he's forgotten. He is also not aware that I spoke to Cnut about him and his siblings when I was in England. I begged my brother to leave his wife's children alone, and he did as I requested. That might aid you in gaining an earldom."

"You don't mention Lady Emma. Am I to assume that she's still little regarded by her son? I've heard nothing from Svein, but King Magnus has made his intentions clear. I will remain in Denmark. I will keep Roskilde for when Svein is king here."

"Your loving mother, Lady Estrid Sweinsdottir."

**"Beloved mother, Lady Estrid Sweinsdottir."**

"King Edward has made me an earl. The land is rich," and I'm also in command of the lithesmen, the hired crews of the king's fleet. I didn't even need to remind him of your meeting with him in Normandy. He remembered, anyway. I believe I'll marry. I should like to have a child, but perhaps not as many sons as Svein. Is it true that he now acknowledges five sons? He's been a very busy boy."

"Your loving son, Earl Beorn Estridsson."

**"Dearest son, Earl Beorn."**

"I'm overjoyed at your success. The king must value you highly. It is beyond time, but I shall not chastise, now that you're an earl. I wish I could see your estates, but I fear, I never left Winchester when I lived in England, and would not know one place from another."

"If you'll allow me, I would advise you not to make a marriage alliance with Earl Godwine and his family. I wouldn't like to see you swallowed up by them. What is this I hear of your friendship with your half-brother Asbjorn? Is it true? I would be surprised to hear that it was, but I imagine you need some allies in England, and your half-brother might well be one of them. I wouldn't be angry if that were the case, although you should be wary. I know Lady Gytha raised the boy. She's even more ambitious than her husband."

"Your brother has regained Skåne with the aid of his allies. I'm hopeful that he'll soon take back all of Denmark. King Magnus is not to be trusted, and neither is his foster-mother. I can hardly believe that she's my niece. Such ambitions are unseemly from a woman who didn't even birth the man."

*"Your loving mother, Lady Estrid Sweinsdottir."*

**"Lady Mother."**

*"Greetings from Uppakra, Skåne. I write to inform you that while I'm in possession of Skåne, King Magnus is not making it easy for me to return to Roskilde. I will persevere, be assured."*

*"I need more allies. Do you believe that King Edward might be one of them? Or, and I know you despise the man, would Earl Godwine assist me? After all, I am his nephew, even if I would sooner not be. Perhaps it's time to admit the relationship as it might well do me some good. I will write to Beorn. I understand he's now an earl. About bloody time."*

*"Your loving son, Lord Svein Estridsson."*

**"Dearest son, greetings from Roskilde."**

*"I forbid you to approach Earl Godwine. The man's daughter is already married to the king. That must be enough. He surely expects his grandson to inherit the kingdom. It is beyond imaginable. I don't believe that your uncle would ever have countenanced such as this for that family."*

*"I suggest you try Count Baldwin, in Flanders. He seems amenable to all comers and assisted Lady Emma when she was banished from England. A pity she returned."*

*"You might also consider approaching Emperor Henry. He's the father of your cousin's daughter. He won't appreciate having King Magnus as his neighbour. Write to me and assure me that you'll not approach Earl Godwine. If you must, King Edward may consent to assist you, but I'm not at all convinced."*

*"Your loving mother, Lady Estrid Sweinsdottir."*

**"Beloved Mother, Lady Estrid Sweinsdottir."**

*"I write to you with news of terrible problems for Earl Godwine's son, Swegn. It will amuse you, although no one will laugh about it in the presence of the king. He's only gone and abducted a prioress and taken her to his bed. Such a scandal. His father is so angry, and the king, well, the king will take heed of no advice from Earl Godwine. After all, as the king says, if he can't control his son, how*

can he hope to control a country? I will tell you more when I know more."

"Your loving son, Earl Beorn Estridsson."

**"Dearest son. Lord Beorn."**

"You're correct, it did amuse me to hear of Earl Godwine's problems, although I wish it had been Godwine himself who'd fallen foul of the king, and not one of his children. A ship arrived from England not long after your letter, and those disembarking could speak of little else. I hope the king will punish Swegn Godwinesson, but I somehow doubt it. Earl Godwine has a well-oiled tongue and is rarely refused. But, do tell me more, when you know."

"I hear almost daily from your brother. I hope he'll soon return to Roskilde. Support for his kingship grows. No one wants King Magnus to rule over them, not anymore."

'Your loving mother, Lady Estrid Sweinsdottir."

**"Lady Estrid Sweinsdottir, beloved mother."**

"The scandal surrounding Earl Swegn continues to grow. The king has banished him and split his land-holdings between myself and his brother, Harold. I find Harold to be far more amenable than his brother. Swegn acts with even less regard for his heritage than my brother. Perhaps it's something about the name. I hardly know. But, I'm pleased to have been rewarded for my loyalty."

"Your affectionate son, Earl Beorn Estridsson."

A pity, I think that Earl Godwine was not more directly involved in the scandal. I am pleased for Beorn, although there is much to occupy my mind in Denmark for Svein has returned to Roskilde.

"Lady Mother," his flamboyant bow, before his children dashed into his arms, brought tears of joy to my usually stringent expression.

"Is it over?" I ask later, when we're alone, drinking wine and relaxing in one another's company.

"I hope so, but I imagine not. King Magnus is bloody persistent. I've heard from my cousin, Earl Swegn Godwinesson. He begs for my assistance."

I smirk then. "Don't give it to him. Or, if you decide to, it must be on the provision that he pledges his loyalty to you, and not to his father."

"Ah, I see you're more than aware of matters in England."

"Beorn keeps me appraised. I confess I enjoy hearing of Earl Godwine's misfortunes. After all these years, it somehow felt inevitable that he'd achieve his greatest wish, but perhaps not. Beorn has certainly made no mention that Queen Edith is with child."

"Yet Beorn is an ally of Harold Godwinesson."

"Yes, but I forgive Beorn. He needed someone other than the king to be his ally."

"What of Earl Leofric and his son?"

"Oh, I believe they're not unfriendly towards him. Earl Swegn's lands bordered Earl Leofric's, so they're now neighbours. But enough of England. What of King Magnus?"

"It's up to him now. Let's see how desperately he wants to retain Denmark, and let's hope, that it's not that desperately. I've had enough of war, for the time being. I should like to spend time with my children before they are so old that I can do them little good, other than accept them as my sons and daughters."

# CHAPTER 25

## AD1043

"You must leave Denmark with me?" I don't recognise my son. His face is a welter of bruises, and a linen is tied around his left arm, the smell of blood unmistakable.

"What has happened to you?" I'm on my feet, already seeking to summon hot water to bathe his wounds, but he shakes his head, dismissing the loitering servant.

"There's no time, Lady Mother. You must leave here. Take only what you need. Your life is worth more than your jewels and your rich dresses."

I startle. What is he saying to me?

"I can't leave here. Denmark is my home."

"Denmark is lost to us, come, hurry. King Magnus will be here soon, and he'll desire revenge for my actions."

Still, I refuse to move.

"This is my home; this is where I live." I almost screech the words. I vowed never to leave Denmark again.

"Over ten thousand warriors lie dead, Lady Mother. Magnus has his great victory. Denmark is no longer mine to claim."

I shake my head. This is wrong, very wrong.

"No, no, you'll be King of Denmark,"

"I'll not be King of Denmark today, or anytime soon and we must leave here, or he will have you executed for treason, for supporting me."

"No." I stand firm, meet my son's frantic eyes.

"You must go, as you said. You must leave here. I'll remain. I'll stay here and ensure the men and women of Denmark don't forget who is the rightful king here."

"No," my son's voice is almost a howl of rage, so much conveyed in just one word.

"Yes, my son. Yes. You know, as I do that I must stay. I have powerful allies, men and women who'll protect your children and me even as they support bloody Magnus."

King Magnus takes too much upon himself. I wish I could detest him, but I'm in awe of all that he's accomplished in such a short space of time. I know that my brother would have admired his tenacity even as he decried his successes that came at the expense of his own.

"Frida," I call her to me, her eyes aflame with the image of my son, and I decide not to notice how stiff her movements are becoming. We're not getting old. I'll not allow it. "Gather my most portable treasures, those that can be easily carried. I'd not have Svein leave Denmark without the means to maintain himself and his supporters."

Immediately, she's gone from my side, while Svein's mouth opens and then snaps closed. He knows better than to argue. For once, he shows his wisdom.

I think he'll say more, but he surprises me by remaining silent and instead allowing me to administer to his bleeding cuts. They snake along his right arm, and they're jagged but not too deep.

He winces as I apply hot water to the cuts, a servant bringing me honey to add to the binding. I feel the tremors running through Svein's body. I want to ask him more, to tell me of the battle, but I honour him by staying silent. If he can stop his thoughts from taking form, then I can do the same.

I've sent warriors to watch the roadway to the quayside, to ensure that Svein is not trapped here by King Magnus' forces, and yet time runs too fast and too slow. Every action I take is purposefully protracted and yet also too quick. I'm shaking and also still. I find it hard to process what's happening. I had every hope that Svein would have his success, but it seems it is too soon.

Frida returns, two saddlebags bulging against the catches, and yet tightly and firmly closed.

I take them from her, wincing at the weight, considering what I've just given away.

"I'll send more, if I can," I assure Svein, as I hand them to him. He meets my eyes, and I see his shame and his resolve.

"You'll win this," I assure him. "You *will* become king."

"I wish I could claim such certainty for myself," he mutters.

"Then take mine with you. Take mine, and be reassured, you'll become King of Denmark. It's not Magnus' to rule."

"It is for now," he corrects, and I could slap him.

"It is for now, perhaps. But the Danish will not take kindly to a Norwegian bastard trying to tell them what to do. Keep yourself safe, and I'll see you again. And it will be soon."

"And I would have your word that you'll abide by the same rules."

"I'll be safe. I'm protected. Lady Astrid once assured me that she would allow me to continue to live in Denmark. That won't have changed."

"If you're threatened, and can't come to me, then go to Beorn, in England. He has the ear of the king."

"I will, if it becomes imperative," I acknowledge, although both of us know that I'll not leave Denmark.

"Thank you," he speaks, a rough kiss on my cheek, and then he's striding from the room.

Frida rushes to me, her lined face filled with worry.

"Are you sure about this?" she demands to know.

"No, but it's the right thing to do." My words are far from reassuring.

### "Beloved mother, Lady Estrid Sweinsdottir."

"I have a letter from Svein, asking me to intervene with the

*English king and send ships to aid him against King Magnus. I'm
amazed by such a request. Did you advise it? I can't see it."*

*"I'll speak with the king, but I'm afraid, I don't believe Edward
will be amenable, even though Svein is my brother, and it would
ensure a strong alliance between the two countries. Caution my
brother to find allies elsewhere. Perhaps from Flanders. Certainly,
Count Baldwin might intervene if he knows that King Edward has
refused. The two men are not allies, not at all. But what has happened? I thought Svein had returned to Denmark? Has there been
such a great reverse?"*

*"Your loving son, Earl Beorn Estridsson."*

"My Lord King," I execute what I hope is a perfect courtesy,
willing my knees not to turn traitor on me. I've not yet even
looked at the king, keen to show my subservience, rather than
my defiance.

I can feel my heart beating too quickly at my breast, and yet
I made the decision to remain in Denmark, and specifically in
Roskilde, to protect my family's interests. I can't wish that I'd
acted otherwise. Not now.

"Lady Estrid," the youth, for that's all he is, speaks clearly,
his Danish impeccable. But he doesn't bid me rise, and so I
remain, head low, knees beginning to tremble. If he wants to
make this a test of wills, then I'm not truly sure who'll win.
Both of us are aware of the eyes that scour us. Both of us must
gain the upper hand.

"Please rise," his voice reaches me just as I think I might
tumble to the floor, and it takes too much of my self-control
to rise, and stand before him. Only then do I allow myself to
gaze at Denmark's usurper king.

The man before me sits inside the ceremonial chair that
was once my father's and both of my brothers. I startle, even
though I'd known this would be the way. It's for a conquering king to fill the spaces of the vacant kings. And Magnus is
definitely a conquering king even as he cites his accord with
Harthacnut as his justification for being here, in Roskilde.

It's impossible to tell his height from where he lounges in the royal chair, but I can see his intelligent eyes, his light blond hair, so typical of the Norwegians. I see the weight in gold, silver and gems that adorn him, and yet I can see no trace of the warrior build that must have allowed him to claim so many victories against both Harthacnut and Svein. It's almost disappointing to see him in the flesh.

I consider what he sees as he gazes upon me. Does he see my son etched into the lines of my face? Or does he merely see the arrogance that has for so long been the shield I've hidden behind?

"I've summoned you before me so that I may know the truth that lies in your heart. Do you mean to support my kingship, or deny it, as your traitorous son does?"

It seems Magnus is not one to court those before he demands their loyalty. An interesting tactic to employ.

"My son is in England, My Lord King. He's a most loyal and loved supporter of King Edward of England. I don't believe that he even considers Denmark his home anymore." The words bring an ache to my throat despite the truth of them.

"I do not speak of Lord Beorn, but rather of Svein Estridsson. He's the son I know to be a traitor."

I consider looking perplexed, or perhaps saying both much and nothing.

"My loyalty is to my homeland of Denmark," the words ring from my mouth, while Magnus watches, his one hand overlaying the other, twirling the ring that sits so prominently on his middle finger. It's a ruby, of monstrous size. I could not hazard a guess as to its true worth.

"That doesn't answer my question."

Such forth-righteous surprises me.

"I've been forced to leave Denmark three times, all of them on the pretence of a happy marriage and a prominent position elsewhere. In all three cases, I was denied all of those promises. Denmark is my home. I'm loyal to those who rule her."

My clarity of thought surprises me.

"Then you'll disown your son, and disinherit him from your House of Gorm?"

"It's not my place to do such as that. I'm not the ruler of the House of Gorm."

Confusion settles over Magnus' face, his lower lip jutting above the beard that marks his chin, his eyes roaming over those who stand and listen to this meeting. He's come as an emperor, as my brother once did, although he has no claim to that title. And never will.

"Then, as a mother, you must disown him."

"You wish me to disown Svein?" I ask the question to give me time to think. I can't disown Svein, not before the king. I have a network of allies who are willing to declare their support for Svein when the time is right. Should I disown him, that network will fall apart, and Svein will never take the place of his grandfather, uncle and cousin. But, neither do I wish to fall foul of the king.

"If you disown him, then he'll no longer be a member of the House of Gorm."

"Surely, it will merely serve to make me no longer a member of the House of Gorm? Svein, as the oldest living male survivor claims his inheritance. I can't remove it from him."

"Then you refuse to follow your king's orders?"

"On the contrary, my king asks me to do something that I can't do. I'm not refusing him. I'm merely unable to comply with the request."

I can see the unease on the faces of those who stand beside their king. Surely, one of them must have realised that I was being asked to do the impossible. Surely, one of them must have warned their king?

I don't know who these men are, but I can guess, all the same. One of them must be Einarr Thambarkelfir. He brought Magnus back to Norway when Lord Swein died.

But Magnus is well beyond the age when he needs someone to rule for him. He doesn't need these men to tell him how to rule now. If that is what they do.

I eye Einarr. I've heard his name many times over the years. He's dressed in just as much splendour as the king, his cloak fastened with brooches of gold and emerald, his fingers ablaze with golds, silvers and flickering gems.

And where I consider, is Lady Astrid? My niece assured me I'd be safe in Denmark. She told me that she would command her king to allow me to remain in Denmark? Has she retracted her statement?

Magnus' fingers drum on the arm of the wooden chair, dragging my attention back to what his position means. He's king here. My son is not. One day that will not be the case, but for now, it is. Should I accept it with more eloquence? I hardly think I should.

"The decision is simple, you can disinherit your son, or you can travel to England, to find shelter with your other son, not that I can promise you that England will stay free from my influence. My claim to the kingdom there is as legal as the claim to Denmark. I simply follow my predecessor, as is only right, and proper. King Harthacnut imperilled his brother by bequeathing him the kingdom."

I feel the heat of the gazes of those in that hall which both judge me and expect me to be able to find some means of accommodating both my king and my son. But there's little choice for me, not now.

I've sworn to remain in Denmark, to safeguard my son's future. I can't abandon Denmark for England. I refuse to go to a place that carries such unhappy memories for me, and worse, it's where Lady Emma still lives, and of course, Lady Gytha Úlfrsdottir.

"Then, My Lord King, I disinherit my son. May it be known throughout Denmark that Svein Estridsson is no longer a member of the House of Gorm." I speak clearly, ensuring my words reach the farthest reaches of the crowded hall. It helps that I have no intention of keeping that oath. It helps that few in the hall expect me to keep it.

By forcing the issue, Magnus has revealed his weakness and

his fear.

Svein might not have been successful in his attempts to hold Denmark, to date, but there's time yet.

The quiver of a smile ripples over Magnus' face.

"And now, Lady Estrid, it's time to determine the lands and estates that you hold as the daughter, aunt or sister of the King of Denmark, for they're no longer yours to enjoy."

I nod. This, I had been expecting, and now it's my turn to smile.

"Then it pleases me to assure you that my landholdings are entirely mine. Here," and I beckon Frida with her priceless wooden chest of legal parchments forward, "I have brought my proof. Nothing that I own should be in the hands of the Danish king. Nothing."

I manage to hide my delight at the look of shock that crosses Magnus' face. Did he truly think I'd leave myself so vulnerable, that my father wouldn't ensure that my land could never be taken from me, that my brother, and nephew and even my useless husband, didn't do the same?

But Magnus hasn't finished.

"The parchments will be examined. In detail." His voice sounds severe, although it wobbles a little.

"And you'll find nothing remiss, I assure you. And, of course, these are not the only copies. I have others, witnessed by the archbishop and other holy men. They'll attest to the legality of my landholdings."

Einarr bends to whisper something in Magnus' ear. I'm curious as to what he'll advise the king, only Magnus waves him away, a brief flurry of fury covering his face.

"Then, be welcome to our feast this evening. It will be filled with tales of my battle glory, against my weaker enemies."

It seems that Magnus may be a worthier opponent than I first thought.

"I look forward to hearing of the battles you have fought, and the men you've killed, and of course, of your Uncle. Is he here?"

I'm keen to meet Harald Hardrada. Svein assures me he's a warrior of great renown, even more so than Magnus.

"My Uncle remains in Borre," Magnus states, his voice clear, even if he no longer meets my eyes. "He rules in my name, in my absence."

The words hang heavily in the air, as though spoken to summon Harald. But, sadly, he doesn't materialise, and I'm dismissed with a flick of the king's fingers and move to find myself a seat where I can be both seen and observe the others who've been brought before the king.

I think of all that's been said, and all that's been threatened, and for a moment, I consider the wisdom of my wishes. Perhaps Magnus would be the better king for Denmark. Certainly, he has the confidence to rule the unruly Danes. But no, it's not his competence that will make Denmark great once more, but rather Svein, and his heritage. I must remember that.

Curious eyes seek me out, later, when the feast is in full flow. I know some of them well, and I know what they're thinking. I'm least familiar with those who look at me with unfeigned amazement. Do they truly believe I've changed my allegiance so easily? They're fools, and yet it's better that I've convinced them. If they believe, then so too will King Magnus.

Better for all of us. And certainly, for my son.

For a moment, I consider whether or not I should encourage the king to dabble in English affairs? I've no love for the country, and it's been such a distraction to the two previous kings, surely, it could be so again?

While I eat and drink, toasting King Magnus, somehow without giving away my real emotions, my mind is busy, considering and thinking about England. Would I dare? What of King Edward, the youth I met all those years ago, or even Beorn, my son, now raised high in Edward's estimation although Harthacnut kept him almost as a pauper.

And then King Magnus has me summoned to his side, perhaps a show of honour, but more than likely, a means of trying to enforce his will over me.

"I should like to talk to you in a more intimate setting," he states after I've curtsied once more, and been allowed to sit beside him.

"My Lord King," I bow my head, showing my pleasure at his words, and yet allowing time to compose myself. My ideas about England are still a little wild; they run counter to everything I've ever wanted for Denmark. And yet? The allure is a real and genuine one.

"I would ask you about these rumours that King Harald Cnutsson had a male child." The words startle me so much, I'm pleased I hold nothing in my hands. The child is my secret. I didn't believe that anyone knew of it.

I dredge a small chuckle from deep inside me.

"King Harald was never even married, My Lord King."

"Ah, but that's not what I've heard?" I'm unsure what to do, or what to say. I wanted to draw him into a discussion about a possible invasion of England. My mind is still filled with that conversation, not this one.

"And from who have you heard such? I would know if there is a grandchild for my brother. I would welcome meeting him, as I would his young granddaughter, being raised by her father in the Holy Roman Empire."

King Magnus has turned aside, searching for his wine glass, and I'm grateful for the small respite from his interrogation.

"The news flusters you?" His comment is perceptive but hardly needs to be said.

"I've spent over a decade mourning my brother. I don't know what happened to his first wife after her son's death, and my own sons are far from Denmark. I would welcome such an addition to my depleted family."

"You might, My Lady, but I would not." Magnus' voice echoes with menace, and I'm surprised he would ask the question if the news disturbed him so much.

"I would think it little more than a rumour, no doubt a rumour began by a desperate woman who wishes to be given wealth to raise her son. Perhaps, she's heard of my oldest son's fondness for women and siring bastards, and hopes Harald was a similar sort of man."

Still, the furrow on Magnus' face doesn't lift, and I fear I might be making the situation worse, not better, as he sits rigidly before me, and I hear a hiss from someone behind me.

"A man and woman need not be married to have a child together. It is not, alas, the child's fault, and need not be termed a bastard if the father acknowledges the child."

I'm not a stupid woman, and I quickly comprehend what unsettles the king. Wherever his bastard child is, I can't imagine that he or she is left wanting for anything. And after all, Magnus is a bastard himself.

"My Lord King, I would not give undue credence to this story about King Harald Cnutsson. I'm sure that we would have long known of any child."

"Perhaps," Magnus acknowledges, his eyes sweeping the attendees of the feast before him. "But such rumours can prove harmful, especially when the House of Gorm already has your son as a rallying cry."

"Ah, but my son is far from Denmark now. I imagine you must know of his whereabouts, although I don't. Svein has been absent from Denmark for many of the last few years. He's even been imprisoned before now by the Archbishop of Hamburg-Bremen."

A grunt of agreement is all the reply I receive, and I take a chance and reach for my wine, because my throat is dry, my tongue feeling too large for my mouth. It's been some years since I've employed all of my tact and political guile. It seems I'm woefully unused to it.

"Then we'll talk of England. Your father, he tried to invade for many years."

It's no act for me to purse my lips, reflecting my unhappiness at his actions.

"King Swein was determined to claim England for himself. He had a long-running feud both with the King of England, Æthelred and with the ealdorman, Leofwine, who once prevented him from killing Olaf Tryggvason in the Shetlands, many, many years ago."

"And, in the end, how was he successful?"

"King Cnut told me that Swein simply wore the English down. He tore at their resolve to stay loyal to Æthelred. He conquered first one area, and then another, he turned loyal men against the king with dire threats, and in the end, the English had no choice but to proclaim him as king, even though it proved to be short-lived, in the end."

Magnus nods, as though he knows the story well, and yet still wants me to tell it to him again. I don't like to dwell on my father's failure. The passage of years hasn't stopped me from being angry that King Swein abandoned me to a far distant husband and land, and then bloody died.

"And your brother? King Cnut."

"King Cnut had the support of the Jomsvikings, and Thorkell the Tall. He was a careful strategist."

"Well, I can't call on the Jomsvikings. Not now their stronghold has once more been destroyed." I can't tell whether this cheers Magnus or not. Does he regret his actions? It's impossible to know.

"And of course, King Æthelred didn't live for long after he'd been restored to his kingdom."

"No, he didn't." I feel as though I'm expected to answer, even though there's little more to be said. I was not with Cnut when he invaded England. The stories of that time have always been filled with brutality and pure happenstance.

"On what basis did your father and brother claim England?"

"As conquerors."

I allow that word to hang in the air. I'll not give King Magnus the easy answer that he desires. If he wants England, he must conqueror her, and if he decides to do that, he'll leave Denmark open for my son to reclaim. Perhaps that's what must be done.

**"Dearest son, Earl Beorn."**

"It is desperate in Denmark. King Magnus has won a great victory, and Svein has been forced to flee once more to the land of the Svear. Do what you can to encourage King Edward to support your brother. I fear that King Magnus has too many warriors and will simply overwhelm the Danish. I intend to petition Flanders and the Holy Roman Emperor on behalf of your brother, but I fear they'll not send assistance."

"I will remain, as always, at the family seat, in Roskilde. Do not worry about me. I will be safe. After all, what use am I to anyone?"

"Your loving mother, Lady Estrid Sweinsdottir."

**"Beloved mother, Lady Estrid Sweinsdottir, from your affectionate son, Earl Beorn."**

"The king is immovable. It doesn't help Svein's cause that Earl Godwine has determined to petition on his behalf. Damn the man. He thinks to assist, but of course, he does precisely the opposite."

"Earl Leofric is adamant that England not become involved in Danish affairs, not when problems are brewing between the Emperor and Flanders, and King Edward's loyalty must be to his ally, the Emperor. I can send my brother a handful of loyal Danes and money, but nothing else. I fear it will not be enough. Keep me informed of matters in Denmark."

"Your loving son, Earl Beorn Estridsson."

**"Dearest son, Earl Beorn."**

"Damn Earl Godwine. I imagine he does it to spite me, nothing more. He must know the king's true mind; after all, his daughter is queen. I'm aware of problems between the Emperor and Flanders, but it doesn't concern me, not when Magnus is so firmly entrenched in Denmark. I must hope that your brother manages to overcome Magnus. I do not wish to be ruled by a man who means me nothing but ill."

"My niece once assured me that King Magnus would protect me, because of her relationship to me, but I fear that's no longer the case. I'm fearful that I might be forced to leave, travel to Skåne to where Svein once more shelters. King Anund Jakob guarantees I'll be welcome in the land of the Svear, but it is not my home."

"Your distraught mother, Lady Estrid Sweinsdottir."

**"Beloved mother, Lady Estrid Sweinsdottir."**

"I've received some men and money from my brother. It's not enough, but his support honours me. We were not always the best of brothers."

"If he were king of England, I'm sure that King Magnus would have been routed years before. I intend to return to Denmark shortly, but I will not give you the details. Not because I distrust you, but because I don't want King Magnus to intercept our correspondence and find out my intentions. Pray for my success. This can't go on for much longer."

"Your dearest son, Lord Svein Estridsson."

# QUEEN

# CHAPTER 26

## *AD1047*

I eye my son, my lips downcast at the sight of him.

His brown eyes gaze at me, his chin raised in defiance.

"Sit," I command, and for a long moment I think he'll refuse my offer. When he sits, he may as well bend his tail between his legs as the hounds do when deferential to their pack leader.

I raise my hand, dismiss those attendants hovering close by, all apart from Frida. After all this time, she deserves to witness this.

Svein reaches out to pour himself wine, and I shake my head when he moves to fill a shimmering glass goblet for me as well. I don't need to reinforce myself for this meeting.

I toy with the words I need to say, running them through my mind, my tongue moving inside my mouth as though I give voice in the cool air that hangs between us.

He swigs the rich wine, a slight wince as though finding the taste less than agreeable, but he's already reaching for more.

My oldest son.

Both a trial and a triumph.

The silence grows between us, and still, the words seem beyond me.

Svein slugs yet more wine, refilling his glass, no other sense that he's growing frustrated with the extended delay. He's come to Roskilde, as I commanded him. He's left the relative safety of Skåne. He must wonder why I would force him to such an act.

"King Magnus is dead," the words finally take flight, and with them, my son transforms before my eyes.

I watch, almost dazed, as his shoulders straighten, his face becomes taut, and his clothes seem to suddenly fit a man chosen to be king. I keep the wry smile of joy to myself.

"Is it well known?"

"Not yet, no." I'm impressed he doesn't even ask how. I would tell him, but perhaps it doesn't matter, not anymore.

Svein makes to stand, and then pauses, his eyes seeming to scour me with more force than beach-blown sand on a windy day.

"What of Beorn?"

"What of Beorn?" I retort.

"What will he do?"

"He's an ally of King Edward of England," I state, refusing to rise to the bait that he offers, refusing to voice the words he longs to hear.

He sucks his lips, his tongue sticking through them.

"You'll support me?' he demands to know. I wrinkle my forehead at him, shocked he would ask such a thing after all I've done for him, and yet far from surprised.

"There was only ever one kingdom on offer," I speak slowly, as though to a child who doesn't truly understand the situation they suddenly find themselves in. "Your brother has always understood, even if you haven't."

The pent-up breath that Svein unleashes almost has me changing my mind.

"I'll be the uncontested king of the Danes," he offers, meeting my eyes squarely.

"You'll be king of the Danes. There's no one else with even half a claim," I confirm with conviction, almost wishing I could reach out and embrace him. But that's never been our way.

We've weathered the storms, and now his triumph, and my triumph, is almost upon us.

The seven words once more affect a change on my son. With that statement, he has become more than the man I've always hoped he'd become. He's more than his traitorous bastard of a father. He's his grandfather, and I smile to see it, for all I've never made my peace with King Swein, dead for three decades now.

The hint of a smile touches cheeks that I know are unused to the action. The strain shows, and yet his hands are nimble, drumming over the wooden tabletop, no doubt keen to be about his duty.

"The treasury must be seized," Svein urges.

"I already hold it," I confirm. My plans are far advanced, even if they've been delayed by five years.

"The huscarls?"

"Are loyal to me and you and your children," I hastily add.

"I'll take wine now," I confirm, and he hastens to fill my goblet with the ruby mixture, standing to do so.

"From now on, I serve only you," my son bows his head low as the soft words reach my ears. It should have been this way for many years, but when did children ever listen to their parents, and more, when did they ever believe them?

"I accept your oath." I place my hand on the back of his head, and the movement startles both of us.

"Know that I give it freely," Svein states, and I incline my head to him, appreciating the statement more than he can ever know.

"You'll rule Denmark with me. You'll be her queen." His words startle me.

"You're married." But he's already shaking his head.

"Not anymore. The archbishop has separated us. And anyway, I would not have made Gytha queen of Denmark. It has always been your birthright." Svein's clear vision of the future astounds me.

He smiles, his lips curving gently.

"You would deny yourself? You would deny me?" But I'm shaking my head.

"I know what you endured when your father died. I know that your mother had too little influence, Lady Gunnhild even less, even though she was the mother of the king, in fact, two of them. I'll not allow that to happen to you."

I open my mouth once more, determined on telling my son he can make no such promise, but he's suddenly standing beside me, not in front of me.

"See. The two of us, together. From now on, it'll not be your father's legacy that people remember, or even that of your brother's, or my cousin. It'll be your dynasty."

I reach out, gripping his hand tightly, swept up in his vision of the future. And he laughs.

"My father was a traitor, and my brother has gone to England. You're my family. Your loyalty is beyond question. You've been steadfast, honourable, determined to fight for Denmark and her people. If you'd been born a man you would have been Denmark's greatest ruler. I'll give you what is now in my power to gift you, a place as Denmark's queen."

I find I like the title too well, and I nod slowly, accepting Svein's request.

After all, he's the king. How can I refuse him?

# EPILOGUE

## AD 1050

I'm smiling, watching my grandson as he toddles around on the floor, eager to reach his wooden toy sword.

It seems as though centuries and not just decades have passed since I watched my sons do the same. How times have changed?

I smile at my youngest grandson, pulling my cloak tightly around my legs, aware of a draft caused by a door opening and closing, but dismissing it. It will be a servant, or one of Svein's men and will not concern me.

I rest my hands on my lap, allowing the warmth of the fire to wash over me, the promise of a doze, appealing.

The sounds of a child at play are soothing; especially when I know, I'm not responsible for him. Svein. He's a good father to all of his children. He's almost fair to their mothers as well. Certainly, I've heard few complaints, despite the number of children he acknowledges with different women.

"Lady Mother," a hand on my shoulder, and I find myself staring into Svein's face. He looks pinched, his lips tight, and immediately, I seek out his child. But he's asleep as well, face down on a fur rug, his legs tight beneath him, bottom raised in the air. I envy him such a position. I couldn't do the same, not anymore.

"What is it?" My mind is fogged by sleep. Surely, I've only

just closed my eyes?

"I have news from England." I nod. I can't imagine it's anything too important. And yet, Svein wakes me from my sleep. He comes to me himself.

"Has something happened to King Edward?" Who will be king if Edward dies? Surely, there's not about to be another war over who rules a kingdom?

"No, no, King Edward is well. It's not Edward." And his voice trails away, as he settles on a chair between my seat and the fire, his eyes looking anywhere but directly at me.

"Then what is it?" The first faint stirrings of dread are beginning to grow inside me, my mouth dry, my hands clasped tightly, one to another.

"Tell me?" I demand when Svein looks as though he'll do anything but speak.

"It's Beorn."

"What about Beorn?"

Svein's tight swallow, his throat prominent as he finally looks directly at me, warns me that the news will be dire.

"He's been murdered."

I shake my head, close my eyes, look once more at my son. I'm trying to determine what his words truly mean. I'm trying not to see every facet of Beorn's life flash before my eyes.

"Who has murdered my son?" I demand to know, but I'm not sure I need ask, I imagine I already know, and all traces of sleep leave me, and I'm suddenly too alert, almost praying that Svein does not speak again.

"Swegn Godwinesson."

I feel tears begin to slither down my face, my lips trembling, my breath almost too ragged, my heart thumping so loudly in my chest, I imagine that Svein can hear it.

"The bastard," I exclaim, standing abruptly, a forgotten beaker in my lap crashing to the floor, to roll noisily toward the sleeping child.

Svein reaches for it, and picks it up, without even looking at it.

"It was two months ago."

"Two months?" I screech, clamping my hand over my mouth, aware that the child still sleeps. "Why have we not heard before now?" News from England has never taken so long to reach Denmark. Not even in the darkest times of winter, when the storms out at sea can rage for days, if not weeks.

Svein holds his hands to either side and in his face, I can see the grief of this new betrayal.

"I, I have no answer to that."

"We must seek restitution. We must seek our revenge."

"It's all done," and Svein's voice is soft, as though he doesn't wish to tell me the truth of what's happened.

"What's all done?"

"Beorn's body has been interred beside our Uncle's, in the Old Minster. King Edward has exacted full recompense from Swegn Godwinesson."

"For who?" I hiss, knowing only too well that it's a matter for Edward to decide, not me.

"All those lost years," Svein sounds broken, and that surprises me. I would have expected remorse for his dead brother, but not for the arguments that marked their relationship.

I nod, words beyond me.

I can't process that my son is dead. I struggle for clarity, for acceptance, but it's not there.

"Bastard," the single word carries so much emotion, it almost breaks me.

Unbidden, an image of that long-ago true-dream comes into my mind. I'd always thought I understood what it was trying to tell me, but suddenly I'm unsure.

The woman, I've long believed was Lady Emma was not her at all, but rather Lady Gytha Úlfrsdottir.

"I must pray," I announce, already moving away from Svein. His next words stop me.

"King Edward has invited you to Winchester. He's extended the invitation to both of us."

"England?" I'm shaking my head, but suddenly Svein is before me, his hands on my shoulders. I peer upwards, into his eyes, noting how tall he is, as I peer into eyes that have lived many lives before.

"I would ask you to go," he says, the words beguiling, for all he speaks between choked gasps of grief. "I can't, but you, Lady Mother, can, and one of us needs to be there, to ensure all is done correctly. I have only the words of King Edward. I trust him, but he's not as strong as he should be. We both know how ambitious Earl Godwine is."

"I can't face them," and Svein knows of whom I speak.

"You must, for Beorn." And hearing his name spoken out loud is too much for me.

"I need to pray," I state, slipping from Svein's grasp, keen to find some solace alone.

"I'll escort you," he offers. But I shake my head.

"I need to do this alone. Please." Unwillingly, he accepts my words, and I stride from his presence, head high, desperate to be alone, trying to ignore my trembling legs.

I encouraged Beorn to travel to England. I thought his future lay there. But I couldn't have been more wrong, and now I must mourn my son.

My knees are cold from the slabs beneath them, and yet I don't rise. I can't. Not yet. Perhaps I never will.

Beneath me, lies the body of my brother. He was once the king of both England and Denmark, and Skåne and with more than half a hold on Norway as well. And while I sorrow for him, his death is old, and I've long reconciled myself to it, just as I have so many of my youthful companions.

No, the cause of my anguish is for something far more immediate, something I might never become resigned to, something I could not believe would ever come to pass.

I could scream with fury for what has happened to him. I could howl into the wind, raging outside as though a mirror of my pain, and I would still be heard above it because my grief is so intense, and my anger impossible to dampen.

I know some wait to greet me, respectful silence and compassion, keeping them at bay, and even now, I don't believe I can face them. Well, perhaps I can face the new king, thank him for his honourable burial of my dead son.

My hands press into the cold grey slabs, the weight of the magnificent church pressing around me, as it veers into the sky overhead. This is the Old Minster in Winchester, and I've not been here for nearly three decades. I never imagined returning to it. I hoped I was done with England and her rival claimants to the throne. These men, well boys, really, all cursed with who their mother was, or who their father.

I think of my son, of all he should have been, and all he has been, and of those who have cut his life short. It's they who should be dead. It's they who took his life merely because the king granted him lands that the other coveted. There was treason and betrayal at work.

Should I blame the king for this? Even now, he accompanies me in my prayers, on his knees, his soft words reaching my ears over the thrumming of my blood through my ears.

He's respectful. He's sorrowful. He's the best of all of them. I would wish he were my brother's son, after all.

I wish I'd never allowed my son to leave my side, to journey to England, and to become embroiled in what is little more than the continuation of over thirty years of aggravation and ambition.

Yet, I can't delay the inevitable forever. I'm a guest in this country, although my sons were born here, and my brother was once its king. But as a guest, I must confront people I'd hoped never to see again, not while I drew breath.

Rising, more smoothly than I have in years, my knees stronger than my resolve, I make the sign of the holy cross on my chest, hearing the sound of other prayers ending. Then, I turn and finally meet the gaze of those gathered here to mourn with me, or rather, to look at me, a name from across the sea. There are many here that I've never met before, even if we claim to be members of the same family.

I allow myself to examine King Edward. I never met his father, but if I deduct the elements of his face that I know belong to his mother, I can determine that Æthelred was once a handsome man, even if he'd been beaten down by the resolve of my brother and father.

"My Lord King," of course, he's not my king, but I've been a courtier for decades. I know the correct forms of address.

"Lady Estrid," his voice is soft, and also persuasive, even in just those two words. His eyes are rimmed with sorrow. Here, at least, is someone who genuinely mourns for my son. A stranger friendship I couldn't have imagined, although it had seemed to work. For a time, at least.

"I'm sorry for your loss. Your son was one of my firmest allies, as eccentric as people always thought it."

He reaches out, as though he'll embrace me, but then seems to reconsider. All the same, I accept the action and feel his strength surround me. It's bizarre to be embraced by a virtual stranger, a man I met when he was little more than a child, but he was my son's ally and friend. That's all that matters.

His smell is manly, the scent of incense appearing to linger in his clothes. Edward is also taller than me, and that surprises, although it probably shouldn't. Most men are taller than me. I allow my eyes to close, taking the comfort as it's offered.

Edward lingers, holding me, prepared to do so until I no longer need his support. If I were weaker, I would stay there forever, comforted by the one person who might perhaps understand.

But no, I've others to confront, the lines between friend and enemy impossible to know, and so I step back, find a tight smile for my lined face, and finally meet the eyes of people I wish I'd never known.

Earl Godwine is my brother by marriage, Queen Dowager Emma, my sister by marriage. I would sooner lay claim to neither of them. How different my life would have been without them? How different would my sons' lives have been?

And yet, Earl Godwine is old and wasted. I struggle to find even the resemblance of the ambitious man he once was, in the hunched figure that greets me. His thick black beard and moustache are fragmentary and even where visible, grey, almost white. His long hair is all gone, the top of his head shining under the light of the hundreds of candles, the only part of him that seems oiled, as he used to take such pride in doing when he was younger.

His clothes speak of wealth and prosperity, his billowing paunch of too much excess, and I can't imagine he's been as gaunt as he once was, for upwards of at least a decade. This man is a ruin of who he was. Yet, I can't deny my gaze is drawn to the rings that glitter on his stubby fingers, or the silver and gold thread that runs through his deep blue cloak, clasped tightly with a broach that would pay for horse and equipment for upwards of ten warriors. Damn the bastard.

I don't meet his eyes. I couldn't tolerate the self-satisfied gloat that I know will be there. Instead, I examine the woman at his side.

Lady Gytha Úlfrsdottir. In the tilt of her wobbling chin, I can see my dead husband. He was a traitorous fool. She is no better. Yet her many, many years of child-bearing have turned her slight figure into a vast excess. She wears her loyalty to her husband in layers and layers, and not even her bulbous cloak can quite mask the ruin of her body. They're as bad as one another.

What have they both done to accomplish what they see is their triumph?

Lady Gytha's eyes are downcast, and her hands clasped tightly together. It seems she, at least, carries the guilt of her family's betrayal. As well she should.

As much as I wish to rage at both of them, my family, and yet most assuredly, not my family, it's to the Dowager Queen that my eyes are drawn.

I wasn't sure if she would be here, and equally, I'm unsurprised to see that she is. I know that her relationship with the king, her son, is beyond problematic.

She's dressed as dramatically as I remember from my time in England. She's the woman who was twice a queen, both to Æthelred and then to my brother. I want to hate her, but of them all, I'm surprised to find compassion in those eyes. She knows what it is to lose a child. She knows what it is to lose more than one.

I hold her cool blue eyes, determining how to respond to her. I want to know why she did so little to intervene. I want to know why it's my son who's dead and not the sons of Earl Godwine, or her own, but to ask would be to speak treason, for her son, the king, is the only one who yet lives.

But I hold my tongue, consider whether her sorrow is real or not. When she opens her mouth to speak, I shake my head. It's still too raw, too new, especially here, where my son lies cold and unresponsive beneath the worn slabs of the church floor. I don't wish to hear anyone speak.

In the dazzling lights of the hundreds of candles that have been lit to honour my arrival at the burial place of my son, I lift my chin. I meet the eyes of the men and women of my past, Lady Emma, Earl Godwine, Lady Gytha, and for a moment, consider stalking from the church.

But no, I've travelled for many days to reach Winchester from my home in Denmark. I have more mourning to do. Instead of leaving, I turn once more, settle myself to the floor, tucking my cloak tightly around my knees, and bow my head.

My youngest son is gone. I've spent a lifetime waiting for Svein to become king of Denmark. I've spent my adult years, waiting to share in his triumph, but in doing so, I've sacrificed Beorn to the ambitions of his father's family, and it sours everything.

I'm known as the queen of Denmark, as my son commands, but Beorn will be forgotten about, just as my brother, Harald, is hardly recalled at all. It hardly seems a fair price to pay. Yet, the exchange is already complete, and I have no choice but to accept it.

I think of Svein, and his sons, and the far distant future. I must hold to that because if I don't, I'll never rise from my knees again.

My family. United by blood and marriage. Divided by seas. Torn apart by ambition.

But my son's family will rise from the ashes of all that my father created. It's my name which will be remembered in Denmark, not my father's, for my son is Svein Estridsson, King of Denmark, and he has fathered a dynasty that will endure for centuries to come.

# GENEALOGICAL
# TABLES

Lady Estrid's Family Tree

The family of Ulfr, Eilifr and Gytha

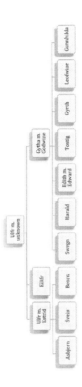

The family of King Æthelred of England

The marriages and children of Lady Emma of Normandy

# HISTORICAL NOTES

Sadly, no letters written by Lady Estrid survive, but letters written by others, most notably King Cnut himself, gave me the idea of carrying on correspondence between Estrid and her family members. After all, how else were people to keep in touch across such vast distances? (Cnut famously wrote 2 letters to the English, one in AD1020, and one in AD1027, when he was absent from the country. These have survived). Messengers were also in use, and there is a list of messengers employed by the ruling family of Normandy which is incredibly interesting, and can be found in Norman Rule in Normandy by Mark Hagger. The use of both options allowed me to keep a narrative going, as if a conversation, even though it covered such vast distances.

Lady Estrid is an elusive character in English language nonfiction books of the era. I have struggled to find 'her.' Consult any book of the period, and turn to the back, and you'll find Estrid mentioned either in relation to who her father was, her brother, or her son, and often, who her husbands were. She doesn't really seem to merit a great deal more mention.

It's unknown whether she did indeed marry three times, or just the two, the confusion surrounding whether she married, or didn't marry, Duke Richard or Duke Robert (Richard's son) of Normandy, impossible to disentangle (as is the date of when it actually occurred). There are also arguments about what order she made these marriages, and whether she was Cnut's half-sister or full sister.

As such, we don't even know for sure who her mother was,

although Sigrid the Haughty is usually taken to be the correct identification, even though King Swein married on a handful of occasions. It has been suggested that the first 'two' marriages, Lady Estrid made, may have been symbolic. Perhaps she even remained in Denmark even when married to her Rus prince and her Duke of Normandy. Only her marriage to Úlfr can definitely be said to have taken place, because of the birth of her sons, but even the date of the marriage is subject to interpretation.

As to the number of sons she had, much of what I've read suggests she had the two sons, Svein and Beorn, with the mention of Asbjorn only occasionally cropping up, along with the suggestion that he was Úlfr's son, not hers. It does seem as though Asbjorn and Beorn were allies in England.

What is fascinating is the inter-connectiveness of the Scandinavian ruling dynasties at this time. If Sigrid was Estrid's mother than she was first wife to the king of Sweden and then the king of Denmark, with some even saying that Olaf Tryvaggason (the king of Norway from 995-1000) also wanted to marry her. Alternatively, if her mother was the same as King Cnut's then she was related directly to the ruling Polish family.

Estrid's greatest success seems to have been as the mother of King Svein. He ruled Denmark for many years and Estrid was greatly honoured as his mother. Yet, she must also have had her own life aside from that of her son's, and this book has been an attempt to highlight all the, better known, people she would have encountered in her long life. She was the daughter of a king, the sister of two (but actually three if Olof Skotskonung was her step-brother), one who claimed both Denmark, England, Norway and parts of Sweden. She was also the Aunt of two further kings, Harthacnut and Harald Harefoot, and in time, the mother of yet another, as well as the grandmother of another three Danish kings. Her family laid claim to Denmark, England, Norway and Sweden.

Equally, she was, if Sigrid was her mother, the half-sister

of the King of Sweden, Olof Skotskonung, and the aunt of his sons, Anund Jakob, and Emund, who ruled from AD1050. She was also the aunt of Astrid, who married Oláfr Haraldsson, King of Norway, who was the father of King Magnus of Norway. Even if Astrid was not Magnus' birth mother, she still supported Magnus, as did Anund Jakob, until Anund switched his allegiance to Svein Estridsson. And this is all without taking account of her other niece, who married into the ruling house of the Rus.

I would have liked to have found more of what Estrid accomplished just for herself, and confess, I did draw on my experiences of what the English queens might have been up to at this time – Lady Elfrida, Queen Emma and Queen Edith, were all involved in the running of England's nunneries – not an insignificant role as it would have involved having a say in how they controlled the wealth of the establishments.

The inter-connectiveness of England, Denmark and Norway (and also Normandy) throughout the eleventh century centres on the simple fact that they were all 'northmen.' It's important to remember this and to try and move beyond the idea that they were different countries, as we would understand them today.

The historical narratives of events in Denmark, Norway and Sweden are as complicated to understand as those in Early England. There's no chronicle to offer a year by year accounting of what was happening, and although there's a rich source of potential information contained in the complex saga material, it can be problematic, and just as in Early England, it's necessary to factor in problems of transmission as the dates for the written sagas are so many years after the events they purport to record. Personal opinion will play a large factor into how historians and more casual readers interpret the saga material.

I have quoted two skalds in the book – the translations come from the essential source book for the period 'English Historical Documents Vol 1' by Dorothy Whitelock. Both skalds are said to have composed directly for Cnut, although transmission to the present day is, of course, subject to the usual problems.

In previous books, I have sited the Danish royal family at Ribe, Jelling and Hedeby. I understand that this was incorrect, as these sites were variously abandoned throughout the tenth century, with the establishment of the House of Gorm. The royal site of Roskilde was founded in the mid tenth century, by Harald Bluetooth (Swein Forkbeard's father). The reason for this might well have been to do with the adoption of Christianity and a desire to distance himself from the previously pagan sites. I am indebted to the following Open Access resource for this information. "Rulership in 1st to 14th century Scandinavia. Royal graves and sites at Avaldsnes and beyond," which is available here; https://www.degruyter.com/view/title/510392?language=en

I have been largely unsuccessful in finding Lady Estrid's sisters, other than Gytha, who was married to Jarl Eirikr and mother of Jarl Hakon. For that reason, they are largely absent from the narrative, although I have given them all Danish husbands.

The scene when Svein states his mother will be known as queen is entirely fictitious. I am unsure how she was named as queen, although it is evident that she was, as she was known as Queen Estrid even though she was not a queen consort. It's also significant that Svein names his dynasty after his mother, not his treasonous father.

Throughout this book, I have attempted to reconcile English sources, with Danish sources, and also with my series of books – The Earls of Mercia. This has, I hope, been successful, although there may be some slight deviations, for which I must apologise. It has been a thankless task (and not one I would ever recommend to anyone else.)

As ever, all mistakes in this book are my own.

# CAST OF CHARACTERS

## *Denmark*

**King Swein of Denmark**, (AD987-1013) **and England** (AD1013 only)

> m.1 **Gunnhild**
>> 1)**Gunnhild**
>> 2)**Santslave**
>> 3)**Thyra**
>> 4)**Harald**, King of Denmark (AD1013-1018)
>> 5)**Gytha**
>>> m. **Jarl Eirikr**
>>>> 1)**Jarl Hakon** (c.AD980/90-AD1030)
>> 6)**Cnut**, King of England (AD1016-1035), King of Denmark (AD1018-1035)
>>> m.1 **Ælfgifu** of Northampton
>>>> 1)**Swein Ælfgifusson/Cnutsson,** King of Norway (AD1030-1034)
>>>> 2)**Harald Harefoot**, King of England (AD1035-1040)
>>>
>>> m.2 **Emma of Normandy**, previously married to King Æthelred of England, with whom she was mother to **Edward**, **Alfred** and **Goda**
>>>> 1)**Harthacnut**, King of Denmark (AD1035-1040), King of England (AD1040-1042)
>>>> 2)**Gunnhild**, married to the son (Henry) of the

Holy Roman Emperor (Conrad) (in AD1035). She was forced to change her name to Cunigunda. She had one daughter named Beatrix before her death, from malaria in AD1038.

      m.2 **Sigrid the Haughty** – previously married to **King Erik of Sweden**. She was already the mother of **Olof Skotskonung** and **Emund**, both Kings of Sweden in time.

        1)**Estrid Sweinsdottir**

        m.1 **Ilja**, a prince of the Rus

        m.2 **Richard**, Duke of Normandy

        m.3 **Earl Úlfr of Orkney** – he already had a son called Asbjorn

            1)Svein Estridsson

            2)Beorn Estridsson

## The Svear Royal Family

**King Erik of Sweden**
**m.1 Sigrid Storråda, the Haughty**
    1) **Olof Skotskonung**
    m. **Estrid**
        1)**Astrid, married to Olaf Haraldsson of Norway**
            1)**Wulfhild**
        2)**Anund Jakob**
            m. **Gunnhildr Sveinsdottir**
            1)**Lady Gytha**
            m.**King Svein of Denmark**
            1)Swein Sveinsson
        3)**Ingegerd**,
            m. to **Yaroslav the Wise**, of the Rus in AD1019
    2) **Emund**

## The Norwegian Royal Family

**Olaf Haraldsson, King of Norway dies AD1030**

m.1 **Astrid Olofsdottir**, daughter of Olof Skotskonung of Sweden
    **1)Wulfhild**
m. 2 **Alfhild**, an English concubine
    **1)Magnus**, King of Norway (AD1035-1047), King of Denmark (AD1042-1047)
        **1)**a son with a concubine

## The English Royal Family

**King Æthelred II** (AD978-1013, 1013-1016)
    m.1 **Lady Ælfgifu (daughter of the ealdorman of Northumbria)**
        **1) Athelstan**
      **2) Edmund, King of England**, AD1016
        **m. Ealdgyth**
        **1) Edward**
        **2) Edmund**
      **3) Eadwig** (and many others not mentioned)
    m.2 **Emma of Normandy**
    1) **Edward**, King of England (AD1042-1066)
    m. Edith, daughter of Earl Godwine and Lady Gytha Úlfrsdottir
    2) **Alfred**, dies AD1037
    3) **Goda**
    m.1 **Drogo, Count of the Vexin**
    1) **Walter, Count of the Vexin**
    2) **Ralph**
    3) **Fulk**
    m.2 **Eustace of Bolougne**

## English Earls and Danish Jarls

**Jarl Thorkell**, Jomsviking, and Earl of East Anglia in England
    **1)Harald** – his son
**Jarl Eirikr** of Hlaðir in Norway, and then Northumbria in Eng-

land,

    **m. to Gytha Sweinsdottir,** Swein Forkbeard's daughter

    **1) Jarl Hakon,** jarl of Hlaðir after his father's death

**Jarl Úlfr** of Orkney

    **m. Estrid Sweinsdottir**

    **1) Svein Estridsson**

    **2) Beorn Estridsson**

    **m.? unknown**

    **1) Asbjorn Úlfrsson**

**Eilifr,** brother of Úlfr and Gytha, earl of Gloucestershire in England

**Earl Leofric of Mercia**

    **m. Lady Ælfgifu**

        **1)**   **Ælfgar,** later earl of East Anglia and Mercia

**Earl Godwine of Wessex**

    **m. Gytha,** sister of Jarl Úlfr and Eilifr

    **1) Swegn Godwinesson**

    **2) Harold Godwinesson**

    **3) Edith**

        **m. King Edward of England, AD 1045**

    **4) other children**

**Earl Siward of Northumbria** **Other noble families**

**Count Baldwin of Flanders**

**Emperor Conrad of the Holy Roman Empire**

**Emperor Henry** (son of Emperor Conrad)

    **m. 1 Gunnhild/Cunigunda,** daughter of King Cnut and Lady Emma

    **1) Beatrix**

# MEET THE AUTHOR

I'm an author of fantasy (viking age/dragon themed) and historical fiction (Early English, Vikings and the British Isles as a whole before the Norman Conquest), born in the old Mercian kingdom at some point since AD1066. I write A LOT. You've been warned! Find me at mjporterauthor.com and @coloursofunison on twitter. I have a newsletter, which can be joined via my website.

Books by M J Porter (in chronological order)

Gods and Kings Series (seventh century Britain)
Pagan Warrior
Pagan King
Warrior King

The Ninth Century
The Last King
The Last Warrior
The Last Horse

The Last Enemy

<u>The Tenth Century</u>
The Lady of Mercia's Daughter
A Conspiracy of Kings (the sequel to The Lady of Mercia's Daughter)
Kingmaker
The King's Daughter

<u>Chronicles of the English (tenth century Britain)</u>
Brunanburh
Of Kings and Half-Kings
The Second English King

<u>The Mercian Brexit (can be read as a prequel to The First Queen of England)</u>

<u>The First Queen of England (The story of Lady Elfrida) (tenth century England)</u>
The First Queen of England Part 2
The First Queen of England Part 3

<u>The King's Mother (The continuing story of Lady Elfrida)</u>
The Queen Dowager
Once A Queen

<u>The Earls of Mercia</u>

The Earl of Mercia's Father
The Danish King's Enemy
Swein: The Danish King (side story)
Northman Part 1
Northman Part 2
Cnut: The Conqueror (full length side story)
Wulfstan: An Anglo-Saxon Thegn (side story)
The King's Earl
The Earl of Mercia
The English Earl
The Earl's King
Viking King
The English King (coming soon)

Lady Estrid (a novel of eleventh century Denmark)

**Fantasy**

<u>The Dragon of Unison</u>
Hidden Dragon
Dragon Gone
Dragon Alone
Dragon Ally
Dragon Lost
Dragon Bond

Throne of Ash (coming soon)

<u>As JE Porter</u>
The Innkeeper

Printed in Great Britain
by Amazon